Dunya:
The do or
die

Dean Hamid

DEDICATION

To Bushwick-Hylan Projects, Brooklyn New York.
Headquarters: My Home.

Dunya: The Do Or Die

Editor: Lashonda Johnson/Ghostwriter Inc LLC

CHAPTER ONE

Summertime 1985, New York City

A Baby Heat Wave...

'*Damn, this muthafucka' ain't saying shit! Nothing, and, it's hot as a muthafucka,*' Rasheed thought as he wiped the bead of sweat pouring down his forehead.

Flushing Avenue was a mystery to most people from Brooklyn. All they really knew were the old factories, abandoned buildings, dead-end streets, some going places that no one ever dared travel down. Old trolley car tracks, and sewer holes, holes that seemed to be made exclusively for rats...both rodent and the humankind. From what Rasheed knew about Flushing Avenue, it ran from one end of Brooklyn to the other. Fort Green and the Manhattan Bridge was on one point, and Bushwick Projects, his piece of the world, was the point where it ended as far as he was concerned, with Marcy Projects right in between. At least, that's the route the Flushing Avenue, number fifty-seven bus would travel.

Otherwise, it was the perfect place for criminal activity. A perfect spot, and a perfect place to start. Inside a raggedy old building on Flushing Avenue.

"Damn, it muthafucka, I ain't gonna say it no more! Where the hell is the money?" Born's stocky, five-eleven, linebacker frame towered over the now frightened Colombian as he rambled off in Spanish. Incensing Born, it only made him more pissed by the minute. "Look, I'ma squeeze this fuckin' trigger, then, you're a dead man..." He cocked his head to the side. stepped back and listened to the passing sound of the bus go by. The last one on the late hour schedule: 3:45 AM. It was getting later and later. "Okay, since you on that don't understand no English shit. I guess what the fuck I'm going to say next won't matter?" He bent over and whispered into his ear, "I'm going to kill your wife and kids. One by one...starting at..." He turned and walked over to the four figures duct-taped in the corner of the old, dilapidated, abandoned warehouse and said, "Hmmm, let's see..." He stopped by one. "...this youngin' looks like she's, let say...uh..." The tiny frame of the young girl cringed as Born approached her.

4

Dunya: The Do Or Die

As she closed her eyes tight, it still didn't stop the tears as they ran heavy down her cheeks. The Columbian hollered, chewing away at the remnants of the duct-tape that covered his mouth. The broken English he spoke made everything he said sound like a bunch of babble, until, "Okay...okay, just, don't touch my family...pleeaassse!"

Born stroked the side of the young girls face with the muzzle of the .44 Caliber Magnum Revolver and smiled. "Damn, English got better real fuckin' quick, huh?" He shook his bald head as he stared at the hung-head silhouette of the man known as Carlos Miguel Bustes.

Big boy cocaine dealer who supplied Brooklyn by the way of Bushwick Avenue, from Williamsburg, and as far as East New York and was looking to spread his cream a lot thicker to Bedford Stuyvesant one whole third of Brooklyn.

Born had watched this muthafucka as he grew fat...greedy. He waited a long ass time for this day. "So, what's up...and remember! Tell me where it all is...the money...cocaine...dugeel and...the weed!"

Rasheed, Born's right-hand man for the job, reached over and ripped the duct-tape off Carlos' mouth, ignoring the fact that damn near half his mustache went right along with it. "Talk, muthafucka!" he hollered. "Talk!"

"Aiieey!" Carlos screamed at the pain, then spit back. "Cocksuckas, you neva' get away...neva!" he yelled.

"Oh, hell no!" Born yelled back, then turned around to what appeared to be the oldest female hostage he had Carlos' wife. She was drop-dead gorgeous, her flowing black hair moved like silk as it tried to conceal the healthy full set of titties hanging out where her shirt had been torn opened earlier. When Born wanted to play the rape card, Rasheed wasn't having none of that. He didn't play those games. Born's eyes narrowed to a slit as his near charcoal skin appeared to disappear into the shadows as he pointed the gun to her head. Glancing over at Carlos, he squeezed the trigger. The flash from the muzzle lit up the sneer that came across his face.

Her body dropped to the ground and wiggled, squirting blood in Carlos' direction. Her beauty was splattered viciously against the wall. It was brutal but necessary. Not missing a beat, he moved on, to the next victim and raised his gun. Ready to pull the trigger.

"Okay...okay, I'll tell you where it is!" Carlos screamed as he watched in terror.

Born pulled the trigger anyway. "Too late..." The body fell on top of the other like a domino.

The same movements, the same blood squirting. The only difference was that this was the eldest daughter. He stepped over the bodies to the other two.

"Please…please, no more! I'll tell you where everything is, just please…don't…" he whimpered like a baby without a pacifier.

Born stared at him with no pity and said, "You see, Carlos, that was all your fault. Do you think I'm fuckin' playing now? Give my man over there the numbers to the safe. Oh yeah, don't look too surprised, we knew you had a safe. Then, you can take care of the business. And after that, you can bury these two. Then take your broke ass back to Columbia"

"Stop it…okay…okay!"

Rasheed leaned over towards Carlos and started taking numbers. There were already other partners in crime in place. All Rasheed had to do was run out to the payphone and make the call. "Be right back, Carlos. I hope this shit is right." He glanced over at Born meticulously cleaning the blood off the barrel of the .44. "For your sake."

Rasheed came running back about fifteen minutes later and said, "It's straight!"

"How much?" Born snapped.

"Bout two whole suitcases full of money. Plus, they found some drugs…hell 'bout ten keys."

"There's got to be more money!" Born spun around towards Carlos and said, "That's just front money, right?" He looked back over at Rasheed and explained, "Look…ten keys, then, only two suitcases of money to push it? Rasheed…the projects alone can suck up that shit in less than a week!" He turned his attention back towards the hostages, this time picking out the youngest.

He threw her face down in front of Carlos. She looked up at her father. The betrayal in his eyes spoke volumes to her. "Just tell him the truth, Papi!" she cried out.

"You tryin' to fuck me, Carlos?" Born screamed at him. "I know your moves! It's a stash house…so, where's the fuckin' stash?"

Carlos trembled as Rasheed held the sawed-off shotgun to his head. Carlos looked up at him, his eyes begging him to shoot and get it over with. But Rasheed backed up and spat. "Not gonna be that easy…"

"You want to fuck me, Carlos!" Born fumed. "We'll just see who gets fucked!" He put the freshly polished barrel to the little girl's head, and it was then that Carlos shouted, "They didn't look in the basement!"

6

"In the basement?" Born looked over at Rasheed, whose job had been to map the place out, which he said he did thoroughly, and said, "There was no basement, right...Rasheed?"

"Yes, a basement!" Carlos blurted out. "There's a trap door! I'll tell you...even some of Felix's money is down there!"

Rasheed stood his lean figure of six feet plus upright, rubbing his goatee, in thought, trying to figure out how he missed the basement...and, even a trap door.

Born had his foot fixed on the little girls back. She squirmed trying to get free but Born paid it no mind. All he could think of was Felix. Carlos' partner, the real loot. They'd hit the motherlode. He was next on their list anyway. Might as well catch him slippin', too.

Rasheed had gone back out and this time when he came back, his eyes were as big as quarters. He gasped in between his words, until he finally found his breath, "Man...they found...all the shit, Born!"

"Rasheed, damn-it man, calm the fuck down and..."

"Room full of money." he blurted out. "Piles of dope-shit, we need way more fuckin' bags!"

Born stepped off the little girls back and walked over towards Carlos. The little girl scurried back over towards the corner wall. "See, was that hard?" Carlos shook his head. "But there is one thing..."

Born turned away from him and looked down towards the floor. "It's a shame, but you're all gonna die. I'm gonna end up killing the rest of your daughters anyway. On G-P, you understand. right?"

Carlos screamed so loud, the echo shook all the windows adjacent from them, causing dust to stir about in the moon's light. "Felix knows where more money is, get him!"

"I know...I know!" Born reached into his pants pocket. and pulled out some fresh, shiny .44 cal. hollow-point bullets. He started reloading his gun. "But...witnesses, my face...names, it's not good."

"Nooo, you fuckin' nigger! You promised me, you, black bastard!" Born turned on his heels, looked him square in the eyes and said, "Yeah...a nigger, but I won't be one of those niggers you'll be selling that poison to, now...will I, huh?" He rushed over, jammed the .44 into Carlos' mouth, and squeezed the trigger, twice. Making a hole in the back of his head larger than a baseball. Then, he turned and looked over at the now terrified hostages he had by the wall and wiped off the gun. He paused, and for the first time spoke softly, "If you close your eyes…you won't see it coming…peace."

****

One sure thing about the projects in New York, if nothing else, the elevators stayed broke. Weekdays weren't really bad, but on the weekends; unless you lived on any floor below six, you were shit outta luck. Walking up the steps was definitely in order. Derek another partner in crime lived on the sixteenth floor, but when the elevators were down, he hung out at another partner's apartment named Ice.

They all grew up together. Bushwick-Hylan Projects, or the Wick, as it was called. 849 Flushing Avenue-Headquarters. The tall, twenty-story brick building towered on a hill overlooking the rest of the vast project. Most called this side of the squared cornered projects-the front. Everything, whether coincidental or incidental was set up that way. Bus stops, the elevated trains-J-M, the big park. Just about everything. This was their home and their life.

Rasheed and Born ran through the front door of the elevator barely making it on time before the doors shut behind them. Surprised to see them working, Born, bent over wheezing from the run.

"Might want to leave those cigarettes alone," Rasheed joked.

The elevator started slowing to a halt, Born, whispered under his breath, "I wish I could." When arriving on the 16th floor, Born, got off first. He stared out off the balcony toward the skyline in Manhattan, saying, "The city, that's where we need to be!"

"One day…one day. Maybe, after a few more jobs…maybe," Rasheed answered.

He knocked on the door at the far end of the hallway, apartment D. Not much movement was heard from inside except loud screeching of a kitchen chair on the tile.

"Who is it?" a voice barked from the other side.

"Rasheed and Born."

They moved away from the peephole as the heavy locks clicked off one by one, echoing down the hallway, then the big steel project door opened up.

"What's up?" Ice answered back as he swung open the door moving his wide body to the side letting them both in, staring into the hall all the way to the stairs and elevator.

8

Once he felt the coast was clear, he slid the .38 he had in his hand back into his waistband and fell back. Derek was sitting at a table in the kitchen with a sawed-off shotgun posted on the wall behind him; counting money. Lots of it.

"Hey, what's up Rasheed...Born?"

"See you got your hands full, Derek...that's good," Born said as he smiled at the stacks of money scattered on the table in piles.

"Yeah, ...it's cool. We made it out safe. No one saw shit... figured I'd start counting the take. Been at it since early this morning, right after we came in."

"Cool," Rasheed said as he stepped towards the table and picked up a band of hundreds. "'Bout how much?"

Derek leaned back, his gap-tooth smile showing, as he turned towards them both. "Look to be little over two hundred grand...maybe three, so far."

"Damn, that ain't bad. Where's the other shit...the dope?" Rasheed asked scanning the floors.

"Backroom, go head, check it out. Devone's in there now."

A slight grin came across his face when he heard the name. Devone was the final member of their crew. The one who set up the work and made the calls. She was actually the one in charge. She was also the one who pulled them together.

"Damn!" Rasheed said as he opened the door.

"I hope that was for me." Devone purred as she turned towards him. "The thing is trying to get rid of it all."

Rasheed and Born stepped back awestruck as they scanned the room looking wall to wall at two piles of silver packed bundles. Off to the right was a filled black plastic bag.

"What's that?" Born asked.

Devone stepped over it and opened it up. She pointed inside. "Look, small baggies full of small crystalline rocks." She plucked at the small baggie with her pinky finger and said, "This is that new product. I first heard about it in California. They were cooking it up like this...rock form." She walked over to Rasheed, smiling ear to ear as she looked him up and down, then back down towards the bulge in between his legs. "I heard it does wonders...for your nature."

Rasheed chuckled, and said, "Then, I know it's not the drug for me, I'm straight."

"Maybe, but a little help wouldn't..."

9

Dean Hamid

"Hey!" Born interjected, stepping between them. He snatched the baggie out of Rasheed's hand and turned towards Devone. "How do we get rid of this shit!"

Devone stepped back and leaned against the door, crossing her arm, pouting at Born. "You just can't stand..."

"What?" Born asked.

"Nothing...just nothing, Born." Rasheed started to say something.

"Hey, uh...sorry about the basement..." Born abruptly cut off, still pissed about the trap door thing.

He figured he'd speak to him later, privately. Ignoring him he held the clear plastic bag up in his hand, stared at the crystalline rocks, and said, "That's the new shit, right?"

"It's called crack," Ice said, stepping between Devone, picking up a bag looking it over.

"I can't believe this bullshit makes so much money," Born said holding the bag up to the light. "Quick, too, hell, more than heroin." He glanced over at them. "I dunno fellas, but I think this shit is gonna take over New York...watch!"

Rasheed rolled a bag around in his hand and frowned before tossing it back in the corner with the rest. Wiping off his hands he stepped towards the window and stared out into the streets.

"You a'ight?" Devone asked.

"C'mere, check this out." Rasheed half-assed smiled, then waved Born over too. "Look down there, towards Humboldt Street. You see?" he said as he pointed towards an alley running past the Post Office on the other side of the projects near the parking lot.

"What about it? Ain't nuthin' but a bunch of crackheads...whores selling pussy." Born threw up his hands and smirked. "Like, what the hell that got to do with me?"

Rasheed continued to stare, then ever so slightly turned towards him, and said, "You right, it is gonna take over New York." He sighed. "But, one thing, tho..."

"What's that, Rasheed?" Born of all people knew Rasheed to be moody, and unpredictable. So, he played along, getting closer to the window anyway, looking out.

Rasheed suddenly grabbed him by the neck and slammed his face up against the window. Blood splattered from his nose. "One of them crackheads...is my sister!"

10

Ice tackled him up against the wall and yelled at him. "Rasheed don't take that shit out on us!"

"We ain't making her do that shit, and we damn sure ain't the ones out there buying no pussy either!" Devone screamed at him. "Now, get off it!" Rasheed shook his head snapping out of it, then looked over at Born. He knew he'd spazzed, just that damn quick. The blood trickled out of Born's nose. His hand quivering, inching closely towards his waist where his gun was. Devone caught on to it and turned her attention towards him.

She treaded lightly so as not to upset the tension any more than it had been. "Born...sweetie...you a'ight?"

He waved her away and straightened himself up. Glancing over at Rasheed he said, "I'm a'ight...but. we need to muthafuckin' talk."

Dragging their feet, and asses back towards the kitchen, Derek stood up and folded his arms. Talking shit, "What the fuck? Y'all muthafuckas buggin! You know the people next door can hear."

"Derek shut the fuck up!" Born said as he held a towel up to his nose.

"Ain't no one buggin'. It's just Rasheed...on some of his bullshit, again." Turning towards him he finally pointed the finger. "You know good and damn well you shoulda known about that fuckin' basement! You had the floor plans!"

"I'll take the blame for that. I should have gone over them myself," Devone butted in, "But, Born, hell, you ain't no better. You didn't have to kill no one last night."

"For real," Ice cut in. "You ain't gonna do nuthin' but bring heat on us...a lot of it. You understand?"

"I fucked that up," Rasheed said, still feeling some sort of way about the basement. "I made a mistake. Won't happen again."

"It can't, Rasheed," Born mumbled under his breath.

"I said it won't, trust me."

"A'ight enuf said on that. Now, what's up, Born?" Devone turned her attention towards him again. "Killing them like that? You executed them!"

"Fuck them!" Born spat pure venom from his heart. "I did them a favor! You see, Carlos was already a dead man, right?" He looked at them all, waiting for someone to say something. Waiting for an objection he knew would never come. "Holding out on, Felix, are you kidding me?" He pointed at the stacks of money on the floor and table, as they grudgingly shook their heads in agreement. "So, keeping them alive, with Carlos and the money...I mean, hell, that's why they were here in this country any

11

muthafuckin' way. Devone, Felix woulda tortured them just trying to find out who we were. I did them a favor." He stared over at Derek. "Trust me, I know."

Tears began welling up in the big man's eyes from anger that was built up inside of him. Ice walked over and put his hand gently on his shoulder and said, "Look, Born, I love you like a brother, but, don't let this thing get too personal." Steering him into the kitchen towards Derek, he added. "You've always been on point, no doubt. But we've got to be careful. One more job..." He turned towards Devone for confirmation. "...just one more, and we'll all be straight!" Derek cheesed at the homeboy's portrait being painted in front of him.

Devone still frowned and said, "A'ight, we finished with that now, but Born...rape?"

Throwing up his hand, with gestures trying to mount a defense didn't work, so he started copping deuces. "Just bullshittin'. Damn, Rasheed, why'd you tell her about that shit anyway?"

Of course, Devone was pissed being female, she definitely wasn't into rape, but there was other business at hand. "Tighten up, Born!" She sat at the table with Derek continuing to count money, while the rest of them went into the living room.

They kicked their feet up, talking about the heist, and all the bullshit that went along with it.

Finally, Derek peeped his head up from the books, and said, "Okay, five-way split." At that point, it was finished.

Devone looked around at them all. "Yeah, five-way split. Cool?"

It was at that point, that if anyone had beef or an issue, to speak up. After a pause that made everyone feel really uneasy.

Born leaned forward and broke the ice, "I think we should use the money to go after Felix, the big man." He looked over towards Devone and asked. "That cool with you?"

Derek sunk down into his chair, smiling at the thought. It was time. He rubbed his hand along the scar embedded deep across his cheek and stared over at Rasheed. His mind drifted back when that mark became a part of him forever.

"You remember?" Devone asked as she latched on to where he stared, snapping him out of his thoughts long enough to answer.

"Yeah...do or die!"

Devone's cunning had pumped them all up. She knew Rasheed would act up. She crossed her arms and leaned back overlooking the table set up with large amounts of paper and pondered on the intrigue. She thought real carefully about the path they were going. Either success, or to their doom, but, one way or another, they'd all go down together. She figured one thing was for sure, they might as well get it over with.

CHAPTER TWO

"I promise...I promise!" Rasheed yelled out as he fought with the pillow that covered his face. His body was immersed in sweat-eyes wet from tears.

"Rasheed, you alright?" Mya asked as she slowly leaned over him. She grabbed a towel from the bathroom and wiped the drenching sweat off his chest and forehead. "It's okay, baby. You were having another one at those nightmares." She thought he was done with them because he hadn't had one in a while.

Rasheed's eyes blinked rapidly trying to get hold of his senses. He ever so gently stroked his girlfriend's face and said. "Yeah, baby...a nightmare." Relieved, he laid back and delicately pulled her close to him, then kissed her. "Only, this one never seems to end."

Mya's brown, slanted eyes welled up with tears. "End...am I the cause..." Mya stroked her long brown hair.

"Of course, not," he assured her, kissing her again.

This time way more passionately as he pulled her closer to him. She held on tight as he tenderly twisted her over onto her stomach.

"I love you, Rasheed." Escape from her lips before she slow grinded her ample round ass into his thighs.

He uttered softly, "I...love you...also!"

She reached back and guided his hand to the entrance of her now moist vagina. She laid her head on the soft, goose feather filled pillow. He moaned, pushing his swollen muscle inside of her as her eyes rolled back into her head. He started his movement slow, with deliberate motions. Steady, aiming to please as she begged for more. The ecstatic pleasure excited and stimulated her until...

"Damn, it won't stay...hard!" Rasheed bitterly dropping his head and slid out of her in failure, his dick was limp.

Mya turned around trying to calm him. "It's alright, baby. I know it's been difficult for you...it's alright." Sensing his frustration, she wrapped her arms around him, pulled him back down tenderly on to the bed and stroked his back. Rasheed buried his head deep into the softness of her shoulder. Tears rolling down from his eyes, saying, "It's gonna get better, Mya. It will. It will..."

"Shhh, baby. It's alright, it's alright," she continued to say, soothing him.

She laid there for a while holding him in silence. Deep in thought. Loving this man so dearly. She knew there was no one else. No other woman. Her only competition it seemed was his time. His obsessions, and mostly the nightmares he struggled with. She loved him much more powerfully than her own physical needs would let on. But his fixations seemed to cling closer to him than her, and she grew tired of it. Her body longed for him, more, and more.

As Mya lay sleep, Rasheed awoke, silently crept out of the bed and eased his way towards a window overlooking Atlantic Avenue. Brooklyn's busiest expressway. He stretched, then propped his leg up on the windowsill. Watching cars zoom by in blurred colors, thinking about the next target. Felix. In a couple of more weeks…it's was a go.

Right now, he had on his hands, other than setting up for the job and finding all the right equipment. He figured now would be a good time to see his mother and his brother, Mustapha.

Rasheed motioned to the cab driver to let him out on the corner of Flushing Avenue and Broadway. He figured he'd walk over to the projects, take in the view. As the taxi maneuvered its way in front of Woodhull Hospital his mind raced back to Mya the night before. He wanted so much to build a life with her, but there was something that just kept telling him something wasn't right. Right with her, right with him. Right with the whole damn situation and Devone pushing up on him wasn't helping matters, any.

He gave the driver two crisp twenty-dollar bills. He was feeling more generous than usual considering he only came a good fifteen minutes away, max. But he had money, after the score the other night, and the plans to hit Felix now being a go. He was feeling himself, maybe, his time had come. Money and lots of it was on the way. He footed down Flushing Avenue towards Humboldt Street. Waving at a couple of people he recognized, then stopped briefly at a Bodega. He glanced over at the Colombians that stood look-out for the in-house drug operation taking place. He still couldn't figure for the life of him what was the point of all the ice machines. He smirked; he'd see them soon enough.

He thought about how much Bushwick Projects had changed. Drugs, mainly crack cocaine had come into the picture, shaking the place upside down. He shook his head clear of any and all old memories and walked towards the front of the building. 811 Flushing Avenue where his mother lived, faced the handball court, overlooking the swimming pool. From it you could see the whole half of the projects: 24th Humboldt Street, 869 Flushing Avenue, and 849 Flushing Avenue the building he grew up in.

His mother opted sometime after Rasheed's father was killed, to move into 811 from 849. She didn't feel comfortable being around the memories his father's death brought, but she didn't want to go too far. The family had been situated in the projects long enough already. Even though she was only across from the park. That was enough of a change of scenery for her.

A friend of his father, Iman Malik, now Councilman, Malik Shabazz had been coming to see her, helping to make the transition from wife to widower smoother. Eventually, he started spending more time there lately. Mustapha didn't like that, or him, but Rasheed didn't mind him. He was no threat, but he wasn't real comfortable with a role, he felt he was trying to fill. His father's, his other siblings, Shaheeda his sister, Rasheed couldn't reach her anymore, which hurt him deeply. Latif-his younger brother stayed with his grandmother uptown in Harlem.

"What's up, Rasheed?"

"What's up, Mustapha?"

"Asalaam Alaikum, my brother!" He heartily replied as he marched towards him; hands outstretched in front of the building.

"Alaikum salaam, ain't, expect to see you. What brings you to Bushwick?"

They embraced and sat down on the benches lined up in front of the building. Rasheed started telling him, "I just came to see, Ma, wanted to drop off a couple of dollars. Knamean?"

"I hear you. That's what's up. So, what's been up with you?"

"Nothing much, working hard...maintaining." Rasheed didn't put his business out to no one.

No one outside his circle of Ice, Born, Derek and Devone knew what he did. Even Mya didn't have a clue, she thought he hustled. Rasheed felt if nothing was said, no one could snitch, or even unknowingly give them up. He also knew that by mentioning anything to his family, their lives would be in grave danger.

Most of the time, Rasheed would only come to see his peoples. But there were instances, more frequently with Devone. He'd slip in and out through the back of the building and make a beeline into Bed Stuy. He knew what his family was into already, and what they were doing from word of mouth, mostly Devone's.

"So, Mustapha...you still selling weed or what?"

That threw Mustapha all the way to the left, wondering how the hell he knew that. "Damn." He started fidgeting with his hands. "Just getting by...a couple of dollars." What else did he know, he wondered.

Picking up on his agitation, Rasheed pressed on. "You know, you need to stop selling that poison..."

"Poison? Naw, weed ain't no poison. It's a mellow type of head..."

"Guess, you'd know, huh?" Rasheed smirked.

Mustapha got up from off the bench, bent over Rasheed and whispered in his ear, "You come here to start this bullshit...or see family?"

Rasheed stood up, too. At least a half a foot over his brother, and bigger made Mustapha back up some. But Rasheed knew from experience that a scrap with his brother was a handful, so he submitted and said under his breath. "To see...family." He sat back down. He damn sure didn't need the headache, he thought to himself.

Mustapha embraced his brother. "I'm glad." He meant that because he damn sure didn't need the headache either.

They strolled up to the front of the building quietly, until Rasheed broke the silence. "So, what's up with, Ma? Give me a heads up."

"Ma, she's a'ight, doin' her thing. You know she stopped working?"

Rasheed had heard something to that effect from Devone. "Naw...for real."

"Yeah, back been bothering her lately. I mean, I give her money, and the rents paid. So, she's cool." He leaned over a railing in front of the building. A frown etched across his face. "I ain't no freeloader, Rasheed!" he spat.

Rasheed rubbed his back; he knew he was feeling some sort of way. "I know, Mustapha. You did the right thing by staying here with her. I mean, the way everything went down with Dad..."

"Damn, right I did the right thing," Mustapha said as he locked eyes on him. "I only stayed because I was supposed to stay, look after y'all young asses."

"And you did good..."

"You don't think I wanted to leave, too? You don't think I wanted to go uptown? Or even one of those good ass schools downtown, Brooklyn? Hell yeah, but I stayed...kept my promise..." The last statement was mumbled silently under his breath.

"Hey, look Mustapha, maybe I better go." Seeing the hurt all up in his brother's eyes, and where it was going, he turned towards the doorway.

17

Dean Hamid

A poorly dressed older junkie damn near ran him overcoming out the building. He breezed over to where Mustapha was pulling some wrinkled money out his pocket.

Mustapha directed him to the side, waved at Rasheed and said, "Hold up bruh. This will only take a minute."

Mustapha took the money and pulled out what appeared to be to Rasheed a baggie full of vials. The tops colored like the ones he had seen from the night before. Mustapha served the man with two and shooed him away.

The scraggly dressed man walked over to where Rasheed was and stopped. "Yo, what up man?"

Startled, Rasheed looked the man up and down. He didn't recognize him and instinctively got defensive. Backing up he asked, "I know you...do you know me?" He reached into his pants pocket feeling for the butt end of the .25 he was carrying.

Ole boy snatched his skull cap from off his head. "It's me, Jeff 849. We grew up together...remember?" He put the skull cap back on and walked off into the building examining the vials in his hand. He didn't pay Rasheed anymore mind.

Rasheed just stood there numb not believing his eyes. Jeff had been one of those smart-type brothers in school. Got good grades, played all types of sports.

"*Damn, what the fuck happened to him, is it that bad?*" he thought out loud.

"Yeah, man that's Jeff," Mustapha said as he walked up on him. "He got hooked on that dope shit. But hey, he's one of my best customers. That's the way it is!" He started laughing.

Rasheed backed up and spit. "That's the way it is? Hell naw, that's not the way it's supposed to be! And, when you started selling crack, anyway?" Rasheed said pointing to the swell in his pocket.

"Hold up..." Mustapha threw his hands up. "...don't come over here with that old Nation of Islam righteous shit! I need to eat, too! Listen here, son, when you do come over here and drop off some money. It goes where? I damn sure don't know, and I don't give a fuck! It doesn't go in my stomach that's for damn sure!"

Rasheed frowned and was just about to crank it up, but then... "Yoyo, Mustapha!" This interrupted his train of thought.

Someone had called from the handball courts. They both turned and from out the shadows, Rasheed could make out a man, and woman. The man looked vaguely familiar. It was. Randy. Another goddamned Brainiac from back in the day. The female caught his eye, too. He squinted to get a

18

better look, but she turned her face away slightly. It was too late, though. He'd already got the peek he needed and hollered out. "Oh, hell no, Shaheeda!"

He stomped down the walkway towards the handball court heated. "What the hell you doing?"

Mustapha ran up behind him and pulled on his arm. "Yo', bruh, let it go! Ain't nothing you can do, she's grown. She made her choice!"

Rasheed jerked his brother's hand away. "I know you just didn't say, what I thought you said?" He shook his head in disgust. "That's your sister…blood…family!" He stared fiercely at him, then walked back towards the building. "We'll talk about this shit later," he said coldly as he glared at Shaheeda who tried in vain to shy away from his eyesight.

Evidently, Rasheed didn't know it all. He didn't have a clue that Mustapha was selling drugs. Most likely for Felix, that hurt. But, what else did he not know? That changed the game big time.

Mustapha waited for his brother to go inside the building before he headed to where his sister and Randy were. "Damn, Shaheeda!" he said as he climbed through a cut-out hole in the fence, the makeshift entrance of the handball court. "C'mon now, you know better than that!"

Shaheeda stared inquisitively into her brother's face. "What? Hell, he knows what's happening. You think he doesn't? I mean his friend, Derek sees me all the time, and I serve his ass like any other trick!" She grabbed Mustapha by the arm and pulled at him. "He knows…people talk." She guided him off to the side away from Randy. "I'm afraid of him, Mustapha. Of what he might do. You know, he hasn't said a word to me in months. All he does is give this…look."

Mustapha jerked his arm away from her, looking her up and down. "Look at what you're doing to him…us, it hurts!"

"Well, if it hurts that much! Why do you still use me?" she screamed back at him.

Mustapha's body jolted, he shot back, "I never put a gun to your head and made you use drugs! I tried to warn your dumb ass! I tried to help you when you got caught up into that…" his voice stopped abruptly.

"Go on, say it!" Shaheeda clasped her hands over her eyes attempting to stop the already flowing trail of tears running down her cheeks. "No, never mind, just shut up…shut up!" she cried out.

19

Randy stepped in between them with a snide remark, "Hey...hey! I know y'all got some old family shit going on here, but, Mustapha...I need a hit."

Mustapha sucked his teeth and turned towards the backside of the court well out of view and reached into his pocket.

Randy tried peeping over his shoulder. "Yo...Shaheeda said you'd be able to hook me up. I'll give her something!"

Mustapha spun around and grabbed him by his collar. "Don't you ever, ask me to hook you up because of my sister! Now, where's your money?"

Randy tried wiggling out of his hold, but his weak crack infested body had no wins. It was to no avail, so he just frowned up and sneered. "Oh, yeah, well, maybe Felix might think differently!" Hearing the name Felix, Mustapha loosened his hold and let him go. "Yeah, thought so. Just give me my damn dope!"

He took out four vials and gave them to him. He glanced over at his sister, reached back into his pocket and pulled out two more. "She better get it, too!"

Randy shoved the dope into his pocket, turned to walk away, then stopped. "Oh, yeah, she'll get it alright." He grabbed his crotch and laughed. "Every drop, trust me." He called out to Shaheeda, "C'mon girl, let's go!"

She walked off behind him. Her face turned downward, then she peeped up at her brother and mouthed the words, "I'm sorry!"

"Didn't I say, let's go!" Randy doubled back and roughly grabbed her arm, shoving her in front of him. He looked over at Mustapha again. "Oh, yeah, tell your brother Rasheed, Asalaam Alaikum! That's what it is, right Shaheeda? Asalaam Alaikum!" He doubled over in hysterics, clowning.

All Mustapha could do at that moment was stand there. Fuming. Wishing that this was all just one bad dream. He turned around and walked back towards the building reaching deep down into his pockets. He pulled out all the cash he'd made earlier and started counting. Fistful of ones, and fives, tens, twenties, fifties and even some Benjamins.

'Yeah, one bad dream, except, all this money,' he thought to himself.

* * * *

Rasheed bounced up the steps to the floor where his mother stayed: 2G and hesitated in front of the door before he knocked. It'd been a good minute since he last came to see her. They'd had a couple of words pertaining to the running of the household then. But regardless of how old he gets he was still her child. Rasheed knew she was dead right, but he couldn't get past the whole picture, and the reality of Shaheeda being hooked on drugs. Now, Mustapha was pushing it. She, nor he couldn't do a damn thing about it. He knocked lightly.

A faint, "I'm coming." was heard coming from the other side of the door.

He stood up straight, even though every inch of his body wanted to walk away. To hell with this...*run*, but it was his mother. Like Mustapha had said, family.

"Rasheed!" she said pulling him through the door, hugging him. "Asalaam Alaikum!"

He beamed all teeth and the memories he had. The bad thoughts, all melted away. He was her little boy again, and that was something he could never escape. Nor, would he want to, so he embraced her back.

"Wa Alaikum Asalaam!"

They held onto each other for what seemed to be not long enough. As though letting go would lead to the realities of their circumstances.

"It's so good to see you, I wasn't expecting you! Come on in baby."

"Yeah, Ma, sorry I didn't call." It had been a couple of weeks since the falling out. He knew for a fact she wouldn't be expecting him, but he had to see her. So, he came up with an excuse of sorts. "I was in the neighborhood and I wanted to stop by...drop something off."

"Wha...drop something off?" Waseema started feeding in on her temperament.

Still thin-skinned due to her being let go from the job, she wondered if this was a gift...or charity. She bit her tongue, keeping quiet, knowing it would only run him off. She missed him, so she put her best face forward, took him by the hand and strolled into the living room and sat down.

Rasheed followed her like a puppy. He examined the room and noticed the changes. New furniture, curtains and then when he turned, he saw opposite the couch a new floor model television. "You doing alright, I see," he stated. "New TV, furniture...cool."

Waseema wriggled around trying to get comfortable on the couch they sat on. She was getting a little older, and as she moved, her once graceful swag produced subtle sounds of aging. "Ouch, my body, or at least my back ain't what it used to be."

"You need a pillow?"

"No, no, I'm alright. This couch has pretty good cushions. That's why

21

Malik bought it…"

"Malik…bought it!"

"Uh, yeah, baby…Malik."

Rasheed slid away from her some. "Malik, why is Malik buying furniture for your place, Ma?"

She leaned up grabbing one of the throw pillows and maneuvered it behind her back, then pulled some of her long silky hair out of her still youthful face. "Now, hold up. I love you son, but there's one thing you're not…that's my father. Do you seriously want me to continue with this?"

Knowing where it would lead from past experiences with her persuaded Rasheed to concede, so he reached over and hugged her instead. "No, ma'am, I didn't come here for that." He reached into his jacket pocket and pulled out a nice wad of money wrapped with a rubber band and handed it to her. "At least, not now." He started to get up assuming he was going to get put out, but she reached over and stopped him.

"Rasheed, baby, you don't have to give me this," she said.

"Please Ma, take it."

She stared at the money, then him. She knew that denying it would hurt him more than her own bruised pride. So, she thanked him, she would do with it like she did all the other money he had dropped off for her in the past. Put it in the bank under the presumed name she used. She also didn't want to give him the impression that she needed any of it.

"Ma." Rasheed pulled closer to his mother and clasped her hands. Rubbing them like he used to do when he was little. "What's going on with, Shaheeda? I thought she was going to rehab or something?"

She watched the sorrow on his concerned face as he spoke his sister's name. Her own concern was all she could offer as she caressed his face. "I've tried everything I can do, I set her up for an appointment. She didn't go, I tried to take her myself, and she wouldn't stay…" She paused momentarily to reflect on all the moments she intervened for her daughter. "Hell, the only thing I can think of to do now, is to force her."

"Yeah," Rasheed said as he looked off. "We could do that." She was talking his language now.

She could see the viciousness in his eyes when she said that, and it snapped her back into the moment. Wondering briefly where it came from? Where did he pick it up? She'd heard about his moments of impulsiveness but never experienced it firsthand. She thought, sure he was a little hotheaded. Passionate even, but violent, she couldn't fathom the thought.

"She's grown, Rasheed. I mean don't get me wrong, I love her. But, I ain't trying to do no time in prison behind her choices. And, you better not either! She knows better…was raised better!"

"That's what I'm saying. But what happened? I never would have thought, Shaheeda…drugs…selling herself."

The more he spoke of her sister, the more, irate she got until she couldn't hold it anymore. "She chose that life, the worldly life! The Dunya and that's her reward for her choice!" She kissed her son's hands and continued. "Your father always spoke out against drugs. He spoke…" She shook her head and stared into the floor watching the tears from her eyes splash onto the carpet. "Even when they killed him for it. He was a strong man…" Her voice weakened as it trailed off.

"Ma, who's they?" he asked.

She sat back now, it stung, she was pissed and saying what was on her mind. "Niggers…snitches…all one and the same!" She leaned into him with a hushed paranoid type voice and went on. "You have to be careful, Rasheed. Don't let this life of the Dunya suck you in…don't."

He gazed deep into the wisdom of his mother's *seen-it-all eyes*, illuminating out of her soft, yet strong black woman's voice, "I won't, Ma," he said.

They both sat back peacefully, listening to some refreshing silence until he broke the ice and asked her. "Any more information about, Dad?"

"Funny you asked," she answered. "I just got a call yesterday from a Detective about the case."

"Really, what'd he say?" Rasheed asked teetering on the edge of the sofa all in her mouth.

She got up and listlessly walked towards the window like she didn't have a care in the world. She separated the crushed velour curtain she had lavishly covering the window and opened them. The emerald green velvet ferns she had hanging viewed the park-like sentries.

She then said, "Well, he asked about your father's involvement in politics at that time. Didn't know too much about that, except for his community activism and that's what Khalid was about. The marches and all that." She turned back towards him playing with the leaves of the long hanging plant. "I thought it was strange, though. Thought he might have been talking more about, Malik, but he was sure it was your father."

Rasheed leaned back on the sofa soaking up what his mother was narrating and let out a silent, "Hmmmm."

23

"But…" she continued. "Khalid was killed in Manhattan and this cop…Detective, called from the Eighty-first precinct. Ain't that in Bed Stuy?"

Rasheed stood up and walked over to where a picture of his father was framed and hung up. "Yeah…damn sure is."

"Rasheed! You know better than to curse in front of me."

"Sorry about that, Ma, but yeah that's Bed-Stuy. Somewhere past Roosevelt Projects." He moved closer over to her and asked, "Why would they call? The only connection I see is the Mosque, and it wasn't even up and running yet, right?"

"Well, not exactly. Your father had already been looking at a place. That's how he met, Malik. In a basement study group somewhere on Madison Street, off Sumner Avenue, I believe. He'd just gotten out of prison."

He got closer and put his hand on his mother's shoulder and caressed it. "Did you say something to, Malik?" He was probing now, looking for more. His thug instincts kicked in. What did she know? '*C'mon Ma*,' he thought as his mind raced.

"Yeah, I did, he said he'd take care of it. You know he's a City Councilman now."

"I heard," he said dryly. He couldn't help but see all the posters that had been put up during the elections. "Take care of it, he said…I see." Just then, Waseema's eyes flared as she shouted out the window. "Look at that…your damn sister!"

"Calm down, Ma." He stroked her back trying to calm her, but she started trembling in anger, blinking excessively. "Rasheed…" She stared briefly off for a moment. Then, just that quickly, she thought back to earlier when she wondered where he got his temper from. Now, she knew, apples don't fall too far from the tree. "It's just your sister, I mean, I just want to…"

He closed the curtains back and guided his mother towards the kitchen, changing directions. "Hey, check it. Why don't you show me your new kitchen set? Yeah, Ma, I peeped it out, c'mon now."

She giggled gently. "Rasheed, I don't know what I'd do without you. But, yeah baby, your mama's getting brand new up in here." She walked around the kitchen totally forgetting, at least for now, what she saw on the outside a while ago.

Shaheeda getting into the car with a John. She paraded around the kitchen introducing Rasheed to her world and how she could change the focus when nothing else seemed to make sense to her anymore. Rasheed knew what it was. It was the same focus he'd had at times. Confusion, anger, and love. All too familiar emotions for both of them.

* * * *

Devone watched from the window as Rasheed walked up to the building. Closely watching as he and Mustapha conversed. She leaned up against the window with her hands down her pants playing with herself. Rasheed made her wet... hot...bothered. She wanted him that bad, but then, Mya. She hated that bitch. She couldn't see what Rasheed saw with her poor ragged ass.

Devone put together this team based on the people her mother had dealt with when she was little. Hustlers, some honest, but for the most, dishonest. She realized by watching, and observing them, that the drug pushers were eating off this neighborhood easily.

'So, why not eat off them?' she thought.

Her first recruit was her brother, Derek who she knew would do anything she asked. She asked for Rasheed, and she got him. Sometimes she didn't know what to expect from him, headstrong, at times unpredictable, but that's what she liked in him. It turned her on.

Her hand rubbed up and down her crotch as she stared. Moaning lightly, she leaned with one hand posted on the windowsill trying to maintain her balance as she lifted her leg higher getting it all in. Her index finger slowly rubbing her clit. Faster, harder, the more she looked at Rasheed's tall, light, cocoa tanned skin, and soft kinked hair. She got horny as all hell. Yesterday she wanted him bad, too, and could have had him, but that damn Born fucked up a wet dream, easy.

Her eyes rolled as her nerve endings tingled. Gasping, she rubbed faster. The way Rasheed moved, she rubbed harder. The way Rasheed walked, she rubbed faster. The cream frothed on her pubic hair and she was ready to release. She couldn't take it anymore it was too hot, so she snatched down her pants. Standing there, butt-ass naked in the window. Rasheed walked towards the building, and his swag, his tight ass. She screamed out and bit her lip. Blood squirted inside her mouth as cum ran down her legs. Her hand was soaked and wet, she took a deep breath, and exhaled. She heard a key, then turned towards the door. It had to be Derek.

He called out. "Devone!"

She grabbed a towel and started cleaning herself dry, but it was too much. Rushing towards the door she shut it. "I'm in here getting dressed."

He stayed in the living room and she could hear him plop down into a chair saying, "Can't seem to find anyone. Thought I'd look at vans today for the next job."

Then it dawned on her. "Right, hey, why don't you check, Rasheed?"

"He's probably at the house with his old lady."

"No, thought I saw him going to his mother's house, eight-eleven?"

Eight-eleven, you sure?"

"Think so...hmmm, Mya's home, alone." Derek sat for a while plotting. Maybe he'd go by and say hello. He snatched his keys and hollered out. "I'll catch you later!"

Devone listened as the door closed. She came out of the room and eased into the bathroom running some water for a shower. The mischievous grin on her face spoke volumes. She knew her brother had a thing for Mya. Unhealthy as it was, but she needed her out of the picture, and she had to manipulate the setting for that to happen.

She stepped into the shower and let the warm water soothe her body as her hand continued to stroke her pussy. She just couldn't get enough of it...or Rasheed. Even, if it all was in her mind.

Dunya: The Do Or Die

CHAPTER THREE

Malik had just finished his twilight prayer when he heard knocking at the door.

"Who is it?" he asked.

"Rasheed!"

He put away his prayer rug and quickly opened the door. "Asalaam Alaikum, my brother!" He put out his hands to embrace him, but Rasheed pushed right past.

"Walikum," he replied.

Malik felt the chill as he brushed by. "What brings you to this neck of the woods?" he asked as jovially as he could without seeming too inquisitive.

Rasheed ran the tips of his fingers across the finished, cherry-wood, grained desk set up towards the rear of the spacious office and said, "Need to talk."

Malik stepped around him and pulled up a chair for him to sit. "Sure. What's on your mind?"

Rasheed waited for him to sit before he abruptly pulled the chair around in front of him and sat down. "Look, I'ma get straight to it. My mother told me you were going to handle some...uh, let's say business."

"*Business*? I really don't know what..."

"Police...business. Know what I mean now?" Rasheed's eyes narrowed in on him like a hawk to its prey.

Malik leaned back, real easy, sensing his demeanor and fell into it to see exactly where he was going with this. "Oh, yeah, your mother told me a Detective called looking for some sort of information, but I handled it."

"*Handled it*...handled what?" Rasheed questioned.

He folded his arms and leaned on the desk trying to come up with the right words to tell him that it was none of his business and couldn't. "Uh, nothing much...just..."

Rasheed jumped up out of his seat and said. "We can play this shit out any way you want, but I guarantee, I will get the information I'm looking for!" He balled up his hands into a fist. "One way or another."

"Hold up now!" Malik said putting up his hands in defense. "Sit down, no need for that. It's me, brother Malik!"

"Yeah, whatever," Rasheed mumbled under his breath and sat back down. "Brother, huh? Whatever happened to Councilman?"

"He said something to do with a tape they found the night Khalid was killed."

"A tape?" Rasheed leaned back in the chair, still tense. "Why did this come up now?"

"Well, I really don't know. I didn't know what he was talking about, so I told him to leave it alone…"

Rasheed jerked back like he was violently grabbed by the shoulders, almost falling out of his chair, and hollered. "You told him what! Are you crazy? That's evidence!"

Malik stood up, his tolerance had been pushed to the limit, he was fed up. "Khalid's dead, ain't nuthin' gonna bring him back…nuthin!" he spat. "Why would you want your mama to go through that shit again anyway?"

"Go through the shit…again? I should kick your ass!" He was the length of the desk away from Malik as he raised both fists up high and crashed down on it's top. "Somebody murdered my father, I want…no…we want to know who did it, understand!"

Malik shuddered at the sound of the earsplitting crash, then backed up against the wall behind him. "It…it…was a long time. Let it go, Rasheed. Allah will—"

"No, not Allah! Me, I'ma find out what happened if it's the last thing I do. You hear? And…" He slung the chair he sat on to the side and it broke into pieces as it hit the wall. "I better not find out you tried to hide something or hinder anything!"

"Hinder? Naw, what are you talking about?" Malik shouted back.

He turned towards the door and said, "Another thing, if you ever step to my moms. You better do it right. If I find out you creeping…" he grabbed on to the shiny brass doorknob that mirrored the anger on his face and twisted it. "I'ma beat you down myself for disrespecting her…and my father! You hear?"

The reverberating of the door slamming in Malik's ears caused him to snap out of the trance he'd fallen into…*Rasheed's.*

'He's crazy,' he thought to himself.

Pulling himself together long enough to sit down, he slowly reached into a desk drawer. The first thing he eyeballed was the .38 snub nose, but right next to it was a small liquor flask. He went for the flask but stared intently at the gun. His hands shook nervously as he did. He reached for the phone, too.

29

"Yeah," he said as he took a swig, and dialed some numbers. "I hear you; I hear you loud…and clear."

* * * *

Mya caught hell lugging the bags of groceries that she carried in her arm up the steps to her and Rasheed's apartment. She'd walked over to DeKalb Avenue earlier to pick up some groceries, and when she finally made it back, she was exhausted. She'd learned early on to be there early in the morning when the trucks came for the freshest picks of greens, fruits, and the likes after watching her mother, Earlene do it for years.

Earlene was the go-to for dinners, cakes, pies, and gossip in Bushwick. She also ran numbers out of her apartment which was usually frequented by the maintenance men, bus drivers, and even the occasional Housing Cop. Mya was the only girl of three children she had. Her other siblings were: Martin, who was known as Black, and Kenneth, known as Flip. The boys were always into fights, and they robbed plenty of people coming in and out of their mother's apartment. They stayed in and out of trouble. She knew like everyone else that something was bound to happen to them, so she wasn't too surprised when they were both found killed. Victims of their own bad behaviors. Earlene didn't last too much longer after. Was it because of actual heartbreak from her sons, or just bad health stemming from a four pack-a-day cigarette habit? One could only speculate.

Finding herself alone, everything happened quickly for her afterward. She tried to pick up the ball and run with dinners, and cakes to make some money, but with fast food spots on the rise, she didn't have no wins. Also, she didn't have the reputation her mother had, and the same applied to the numbers game when she tried her hand at that. Being that OTB and Lotto were on the horizon there just wasn't any real need anymore, and the neighborhood bankers wouldn't front her any money to operate.

Word got out to the rent office, and soon after she lost her apartment because she couldn't pick up her mother's lease, so she stayed from friend house to friend house. From Earlene's friend's houses to Earlene's friend's house. From there, to molestation, rape, and abuse. Waseema came in from work one night and found her cold, shaking, and crying hysterically on the steps. She bought her in, fed her, clothed her, and treated her with decency.

That's how and when she met Rasheed. Soon after they would become real close. Close enough so that one day when Waseema came home early, she found them having sex. Not one to raise hell, but bags were packed: Mya's, and Rasheed's.

Dunya: The Do Or Die

It wasn't like she was kicking them out. She'd seen it coming. Both had fallen for each other, and besides, they needed their own privacy, and, she needed hers. They were grown, and she knew Rasheed would do the right thing by her, handle his business, like his father.

Rasheed loved her, and he like most young men his age went through the same rhetoric, get married, have children, move out of the city and buy a house. Mya knew he hustled he didn't have a normal 9-5. She didn't know what, and she didn't care to know. The money was frequent and always on time. The bills were paid. The one thing she did know was that when she needed his loving lately, he just wasn't there for her. What most men took from her, she couldn't give to the one man she truly loved.

"Hey, Mya! Need some help?" Derek had been in front of the building posted up for a while spying her as she fumbled with her keys. She didn't have a clue how long he'd been watching, plotting, studying her. She peeped her head up and her eyes got stuck on his shiny blue Cadillac. The spoked wheels and carriage top got her attention, and Derek caught on to it.

'Got her,' he thought briefly about Rasheed, and he just knew he'd be held up for a minute. "Hold up, girl, I got that." 'Here's my chance,' he thought as he bounced up the steps.

"I'm alright, Derek," she said as she dropped her keys again.

Derek reached down and snatched them up, and said to her, "What's up?" Then he looked up at the windows to the apartment they were all closed. He asked, "Where's Rasheed?"

"Uh…" she stammered nervously. "He had to go somewhere. Pick up some things," she lied. She didn't know where he was. He'd left much earlier before her.

Derek knew all this, he played on it. "Oh, yeah…I see…" Turning around he wanted to make sure no one was watching. "Hey look, uh, I could help you with those bags at least upstairs to the door. Cool?"

Mya had known Derek and Devone from the projects growing up. Their mother would frequent Earlene's and pick up men who'd come through looking for a quick fuck, then turn around and give Earlene a cut from the money she tricked. Their mama would leave them in the backroom to play with Mya while she went to her apartment to handle the business.

"I don't know, I mean…Rasheed."

"It's just up the steps won't be long." One day Derek had raped her while they were left alone, Devone didn't say a word.

"Okay…just up the steps." She was still scared of him to the point that when she found out he and Rasheed were friends; she didn't say a word to Rasheed as long as Derek no longer continued to molest her. But these days, he started to get bold.

He picked up her bags as she opened the front door. "Go ahead, I got this," he said as she strolled up the flight of stairs leading to the apartment. He kept his eyes fixed on her thick, round, luscious ass that seemed to dance in front of his eyes. Her skirt eased up with every twist and turn as she moved.

"Okay, here we go. You can just put them down. I'll get it from here," she said as he put the bags down.

Just as she turned to stick the key into the door, he pushed up on her. "What's up Mya?"

She felt the stiffness of his dick pressed against her ass and she liked it. She didn't know why he would want to try her, but she got wet between her legs, as he fondled her.

She moaned softly. "Derek…no. You can't…"

"Like old times, huh? I mean, you feel this hard ass dick, right? Rasheed ain't gotta know shit," he whispered in her ear.

"You won't tell?" she asked as she pressed her hand hard against the door, and the other on the doorknob bracing herself.

"Hell naw, I ain't saying shit. Have I yet?" He put his hand between her legs and rubbed her pussy. Kissing the crack of her neck as he did.

She twisted the doorknob and the door opened. She knew it was wrong, and she hated herself for it, but all she wanted was some comfort in the way of sex.

'This one time,' she thought.

She needed it, and Derek had it for her. Derek had always wanted her again and planned for this moment a long time. She fell for Rasheed and not him and he resented that. His sister knew it was much too long for a grudge that one day may prove to be fatal, but he didn't care. He just wanted what he thought was his, right now.

* * * *

Mustapha was up early this morning considering that he'd been up most of the night outside. It was the first of the month. A good day for selling drugs. Two days max with cash money before other items were brought to him for tradeoffs. TVs, VCRs, jewelry, clothing, whatever a dope fiend could steal, tote, or otherwise conceal. All was fair game for a hit. He liked it when the first fell on a weekday it meant more cash and the banks were all open. Checks were cashed and there was no holding on to a piece of paper with obscure numbers marked in hopes that maybe the dope fiend was still smoking, and, hadn't run to the police to report a check stolen, then stop payment on it.

Mustapha sat back on the bench in front of the building watching the employed go to their respective jobs. Though he'd smile and speak out of respect, he could still feel the cold contempt that they had for him. A drug dealer, the problem and not the solution. He snarled back at them with that same look of sneer and mockery. Go on to the master.

"Psst...psst, Mustapha. Yo!" He was pulled out of his thoughts by his name being called coming from the side of the building.

He turned and spotted a bent over, wide-eyed, suit and tie wearing, briefcase toting man waving his hands for him to come over to him.

Who the hell is this?' he thought. More so because his curiosity for this strange site caught the better of him.

The man looked back and forth as if someone were searching for him. Trying to get him, like he was hiding from himself. "Hey, I need something...a hit."

Mustapha got up and cautiously walked over to him. Had him peeping around and shit. Paranoia had begun to take hold of him, too. But, as he got closer, he recognized him. "What the hell! What the fuck is up with you, man?"

"Hey, what's up, Mustapha?" His lips were white and his mouth dry, and hands dirty. "I need a little something before I go to work. You got it?" He smelled.

"I thought you went to rehab. What happened?"

"Fuck that shit! Them people don't know what they're talking about. I ain't no damn drug addict. That's crazy, I can stop whenever I want to!"

"I can't tell," Mustapha said. "What you want?"

He reached into his pocket pulling out some crinkled money. "I got seventeen dollars and..." he reached again. "...some change. Bout fiftyeight cents." He smiled like it was a lottery ticket, and he just paid his way into paradise. "We good? I'll pay you the rest when I get paid. You know I'm good for it. Got this job lined up..."

"Shut the fuck up! Your dumb ass is about to lose that job!" Mustapha stepped back looking him up and down, then screamed at him. "Look at yourself!"

He stood back and momentarily checked himself out. Reality seemed to kick in, if just for a minute, but then he frowned and looked at the money in his hands. "What you gonna do! I can go somewhere else." Mustapha just sighed. "Here." He pulled out three vials from his pocket. "Just go to work...rehab...somewhere, just go." He took the dope, stuffed it in his pocket and turned to go Mustapha hollered. "Mark!"

"Yeah...what?" He turned around, ready to haul ass.

"My money!" Mustapha reminded.

"Oh, yeah, sorry about that. Hey, uh, look...I might be able to see you later. Once I do this, I know where I can get some more..."

"Man, get the hell out of here, okay!" Mustapha turned and walked off grumbling under his breath.

Mark called back out to him, "Mustapha!"

He glanced over his shoulder. "What now?"

"You ain't seen, Randy?"

"Naw."

"How 'bout that girl he be with all the time. Where she at? I wouldn't mind getting up with her. Hear she suck a real good..."

At that moment, Mustapha turned all the way around facing him. His fists were balled up. "Yeah, I heard that also. Haven't seen Randy or that girl either."

His eyes widened after realizing he'd struck a nerve, then he bolted off. Mustapha's eyes followed him as he headed up towards Humboldt Street where his sister prostituted herself. He thought to himself as he watched. He's just another trick that's all. He sat back down on the bench continuing to check out people as they went to work.

'Yeah...slaves,' he thought but so was he.

"Damn!" he shouted, as he banged his hand on the bench. "Somethings got to change!" He stood up, and with his head down he walked into the building and took the stairs upstairs to the crib.

Mustapha walked into the apartment as quietly as he could manage, cutting through the kitchen. His routine; opening the refrigerator; looking in the oven-baked, there was chicken?

'Strange,' he thought, more than the usual, then baked potatoes, broccoli. "Naw, I know this ain't for me."

"Good morning, baby!" Waseema peeped her head into the kitchen. "Go ahead and eat the rest of that food before it goes bad."

"Ma, not again. I thought we discussed this whole situation."

She shot her head back into the kitchen. "What...excuse me, Mustapha. I was under the impression that this was my place!" She walked her little petite ass up on him and with her index finger waving it in his face. "If you got a problem. New York has more than its fair share of apartments," she snapped.

Mustapha leaned back on the sink. "Yeah, ...it's all good."

He held his head down biting his lip. Thinking about the fact that he knew it wasn't that he wasn't able to find his own place or pay the rent. He wanted a place of his own, but he was bound by an oath made years gone by.

What he swore was that he would never be too far from his mother since his father was killed. He swore he'd be the man of the house. The protector, the vigilant one. He swore, but many days had gone by wishing he'd never. Nothing seemed to turn out right since. Rasheed left, Shaheeda was in and out. Mostly out, Latif went uptown to stay with his grandmother. It just wasn't the vision he saw when he made the oath to the memory of his old man.

Waseema moved over closer to him and softly held his hand. "Mustapha, I'm sorry. I didn't mean that you're my son. You're always gonna be my, baby, but...your mama needs someone."

He yanked his hand away from her. "Yeah, whatever. Family ain't good enough if daddy was alive..."

"Your father is not alive! He's dead Mustapha...dead!"

He brushed past her to the stove and turned the eye, igniting a flame underneath the stewed broccoli and chuckled under his breath. "Yeah ma, you're right...dead."

Waseema let out a heavy sigh and moved sluggishly past him going in the direction of her room, then stopped. "Uh, when you get time, I'd appreciate if you go into your room for a minute."

Mustapha could only stare at his mother as she stood by the entrance of the foyer. Her hair was down, she had on a robe, and he could see she had nothing underneath. She still had a youthful figure. Four grown kids and she held the swagger of a woman in her late twenties.

"Yeah, I know the routine already," he said dryly and as sarcastically as he could. He sneered as he walked past her to his room pausing when he came to her door. He knocked three times and said, "I-am-going-to-thebathroom...okay?" Silence came from the other side, but as he listened closer, he could hear some movement and even the scuffling of feet. He turned towards his mother. "Damn, he ain't even man enough…"

"Mustapha!" she yelled out. Then softly and silently said, "Please…it's hard enough."

Mustapha walked into the bathroom and closed the door. He pulled the cover flap down from the toilet seat and sat. He could hear the stirring around outside of the door and the squeaking of her room door as it opened. A zipper being hastily zipped, and then hopping on one foot because a shoe hadn't been put on yet, or at least, all the way. Then the killer, the silence, a kiss…perhaps, a hug?

The steel metal front door slammed shut from being caught in the cross draft from off the balcony. It startled him and he jumped a little. He could hear his mother's slippers as they dragged heavily across the floor making her way back to the bedroom. Her door closed, then locked. As he held his head close to the door, he could still hear the soft murmurings and mumbling. Then, a hush, some crying and a cleansing sob.

'*Same routine,*' Mustapha thought as he held his head down between his legs, he cried also.

Waseema woke Mustapha up sometime in around 2:00 p.m. She was on her way to a job prospect and she needed to get there as quick as possible. Mustapha was sprawled out on the couch, she smiled watching his bright brown eyes adjust to the sunlight peering into the apartment from in between the curtains. Normally, she'd be riding him hard about going to sleep on the sofa but took exception this time. The morning had been a rough one for them both.

"C'mon, Mustapha, get up. I gotta go, I need you to walk with me to the GG train on Flushing Avenue up near Marcy Avenue."

"Damn," he grumbled. "I thought you took the J train into the city?"

"Normally, but I'm running late."

He groggily raised up from the couch, yawned, then pushed his long dark dreads away from his face. "Alright, just let me wash my face and brush my teeth."

"You need to do something, you look rough!" Waseema joked, kidding around with him. Trying to lighten things up. Mustapha smiled and rushed her, wrapping his big muscular arms around her with his lips poked out. "Yeah, but I'm your baby, you love me."

"Boy!" She giggled. "If you don't get off me"

He made his way into the bathroom and she continued getting herself together. Combing through her thick, long silky hair as she thought about her potential employment. Cash money under the table. The job would

36

keep dollars in the house along with Mustapha's hustle money and keep the rent office out her business. She tucked away money in another account she had for the day when she planned on making a move South. Her daddy's family left them some land and a house somewhere around Charleston, South Carolina. The plan was to leave the city for good.

Baaam! Baaam! Baaam!

"Mustapha...Mustapha!"

"Who the hell is beating on my door like that, Mustapha?"

"Ma'am?" he called from the bathroom.

"Someone's beating on the door...hard and calling your name!"

"Alright...alright, I got it."

"That better not be one of those people coming to my door for..." She dug through the closet searching for her baseball bat.

Mustapha rushed the door. "I said, I'll take care of it, Ma!"

Mustapha also knew it had better not be someone looking for a sale. He told everybody not to ever come to his apartment looking for anything. Dope, money, trying to sell shit...nothing. "Who is it!" he barked as he looked through the peephole.

"Roots." Mustapha opened the door to a well-dressed young man out of breath. "Yo mon, gots ta come." Roots was a native Jamaican who struggled with the English, especially once he was worked up.

"What the hell..." Waseema tried pushing past him with her bat but he stopped her. "Excuse me, Ma, I said I got this!" He held her back by the kitchen as she pouted with her hands still clutching the bat.

"Mon...some..." He took a deep breath. "Man, just beat up ya sista, mon. Come now, quick mon!" He finally spit it out.

Waseema put her hand up to her mouth, dropped the bat and stared at Mustapha. "Mustapha, go, I'll call the police!" She rushed for the phone and picked it up.

Roots pushed through and stopped her. "No!" He turned towards Mustapha. "Dem der crack house, Felix's place mon! No can call the man!"

"Damn!" he said punching the palm of his hand.

Roots was right, he couldn't bring no heat like that. There'd be too many questions, he couldn't answer. Dealing with Felix there was bound to be questions.

"You talking about the one where, Randy, hangs out!" He'd have to handle this on his own and sort through the mess later.

"Mon, I tink Randy is the one who beat her."

Dean Hamid

Mustapha ran into his room, finished putting on his clothes, and pulled up his mattress. His mind darted around in all different directions.

"To hell with, Felix. Randy, gotta pay for this." He pulled out a shiny snub-nosed .38 out of a sock just as his mother walked in. "No Mustapha, no!"

He pushed his mother gently to the side and said, "Ma, it's got to be." He started for the door. She ran to the phone again saying. "I'm gonna make a call, my friend, he'll..."

Mustapha turned abruptly. and hollered, "He'll what! He couldn't even speak to me this morning like a man. This ain't his problem!" He jetted out the door down the hall to the steps with Roots right on his heels.

Waseema was right behind them at the door yelling out. "Be careful Mustapha!"

"Call Rasheed!" he yelled back before disappearing down the steps.

She rushed inside to the phone and looked through her phone book sitting on the counter. "Okay, calm down. Here it is, 7-8-6-3-8-1...Rasheed, please be home."

Mustapha ran out the building first and Roots was right behind him, but he detoured and rushed towards his car. "Mon, me hafa park me car, wait-tup!"

Mustapha pointed towards Humboldt Street and said. "Over there, right!"

Roots stopped, then looked at his car parked by the fire hydrant and frowned. Considering all that was going on he knew he had to go right then, but his ride was too dirty.

"Give me a minute." He opened his trunk, reached under the spare tire, grabbed a .357 Magnum and stuffed it in his waist under his shirt. He was ready to slam the trunk and haul ass but paused then reached into the underside of the carpet and grabbed a box full of shells. '*Yeah,*' he thought. '*Gonna need these.*'

Mustapha waved him on. "C'mon Roots...c'mon!"

Still not wanting to keep his car there and possibly get towed, he spotted a crackhead by the park and called him over. "Yo...c'mere!" He ran over to him. "You see tis' car man?" He nodded his head. "Well..." Roots pulled up his shirt a little and flashed the gun. "Park it in a good spot mon. Up on the hill, and don' fuck with anyting. Ya, hear mon?" The dope fiend nervously took the keys, then Roots tossed him a sack he had in his pocket. About a whole cookie of cooked crystal coke. "Take tis...it's yours." Roots took off running behind Mustapha hoping he was doing the right thing.

38

He didn't really care about going to bat with Mustapha. That was his man, no biggie. It was the whole thing about leaving behind his brand-new Beamer, and about a half-ounce of dope with a crackhead. He had to smile at the irony.

Mustapha jumped the fence by the parking lot that was on the other side of 811, going towards Humboldt Street. He looked both ways for traffic that was normally heavy this time of the day. He ran towards the building Felix owned; a six-story walk-up across the street from the Post Office. He shot through the front door and started pushing his way through some dope fiends who had gathered.

He yelled out, "Shaheeda! Where you at?"

Someone stepped forward from the crowd. Someone who recognized Mustapha and said, "Shaheeda's upstairs, don't look too good. And Randy...he just left out of here running."

"Where, upstairs?"

"Up on two, the second apartment," he said as he pointed up the stairs to where another small crowd gathered at the door. "Where those people are?" Mustapha didn't wait to hear the rest. He bounced up the steps two at a time hollering. "Where she at!" As he stepped through the crowd into the apartment. "Aw...hell!"

Shaheeda laid sprawled out in the middle of the floor. A pool of blood had already started to puddle around her body. Her face was bruised, black and blue. He eased towards her and asked, "Is...is...she still...alive?"

A small hunched over older Spanish woman who was already bent over her said, "Yes, but barely."

"What happened?"

"She's been beaten and stabbed. Her back is cut up real bad and she's losing a lot of blood. You need to get her to a hospital...fast!"

Mustapha was in shock, he was stuck and couldn't move, or react. By that time Roots made his way through the crowd. "Mustapha!" He shook him. "Look here mon, I got tis! Trust, mon." He looked down at Shaheeda's body. "I heard Randy ran towards dem der factories on Bushwick Avenue, behind eight-six-nine mon."

Mustapha was still dazed as he rubbed blood from off his shirt, muttering to himself, "Eight-six-nine...factories."

Roots slapped him, hard. "Mon, sorry but..." He raised up again.

This time Mustapha grabbed his arm. "Factories…yeah, I got it." The tears that welled up in his eyes had turned to intense rage and anger as he answered him. "Roots, I trust you. Take care of her, tell my moms…"

"Yo man, just go! Get dat blood-clot, I got tis!" He grabbed Mustapha and pulled him close. "Here, take tis ting." The .357 and the bullets. "Ya might need them mon."

CHAPTER FOUR

The Detective was from precinct 81 over on Ralph Avenue in BedStuy. Rasheed figured he'd pay them a visit. The cab he took dropped him right across the street from it. He got out and looked around at all the squad cars parked in front, then it amused him why it was so easy for his people to do crime. All the police were here.

He'd never been in any real trouble, he had a clean record, which worked well for him because he also had good credit. His being able to rent the vehicles needed and get equipment for some of the jobs they did didn't cause a red flag and that was a plus. Still. he never trusted the police. Considering all that went on in the city, he had good reason. Being young and black in the eighties made him a mark. He politely smiled at some of the officers as he made his way to the front desk. If it wasn't for his goatee and kufi he wore, he could have easily just been another cop.

He opened the front door to the precinct house and caught eye contact with an arrow that pointed towards a big overweight black man occupying the space marked, *Desk Sergeant*. He had a good idea from the television cop shows that this should be his first stop.

"Young man, what can I do for you?" he asked.

"I'm looking for a Detective." He looked at the name on the card that was left with his mother. "Detective Michael Giovanni." He held it out in front of him.

"Okay, Mickey, right over there," he said pointing to a door marked *HOMICIDE*, then glanced at his watch saying. "He should be in."

"Is it okay…"

"Sure, go right in…" He leaned over the desk. His eyes darted in and around his jacket looking for suspicious bulges. "You not carrying nothing…"

Rasheed quickly opened his jacket. "No, sir." He threw his hands up. His shirt was tucked in his pants. He knew the routine, but still, with a smirk, he thought to himself that he didn't need a weapon to take him on. Just a donut.

"I see you wearing one of those beanies. What you call it? You, uh, Jewish or something?"

"No sir, Muslim. Would you feel comfortable with me taking it off?"

"Naw," he said as he shooed him in. He was bored already. "You look like a good kid, go on in." The Sergeant smiled and leaned back in his already overburdened chair eyeballing Rasheed as he walked towards the door. He shook his head thinking he'd seen a lot in his time, and he liked the way Rasheed carried himself, especially for a black man.

Rasheed opened the door to a small office space with four different desks filled with papers piled up high in front of the faces that sat behind them.

He asked, "Uh, excuse me, Detective Giovanni?" Three detectives, all white, looked over at the desk tucked in the far end of the office and pointed. A black Kangol cap was all he could see as he tried peeping around the stack of paper.

"Give me a sec." came from behind them.

Then, he stood up, a short, stocky, mock-neck, black leather jacket wearing, light-skinned, black man waved him over and asked.

"What can I do for you, brother?" He threw that out there figuring it to be an ice breaker. Then, he raised his hand to give him some dap, but instead, Rasheed held out the card. "My moms told me you've been by her apartment to see her." He left him hanging.

"And who's your, moms?" Giovanni used the opportunity to reach for the card.

"Waseema Muhammad, Bushwick Projects…eight-one-one flushing…"

"Oh yeah!" He pointed him towards the chair by the desk. "Have a seat. So, what can I do for you?"

"Well, sir, from what my moms tell me. You have information concerning my old man's murder, Khalid Muhammad."

The detective fumbled through some papers on his desk and said, "Matter of fact, I do." He leaned back in an old, faded leather swivel chair and read the incident report he'd picked up. "Your father's case was closed, hmmm, about ten years ago." He took off his Kangol and scratched what was left of his balding hair and continued, "But it was reopened."

Rasheed leaned towards him, peeping at the papers in his hand and asked. "Re-opened, why?"

"Well, it seems that some guy was arrested a couple of months ago and said he had information about it or something."

"Who was the guy?"

He flipped through some more papers on his desk, it amazed Rasheed that he knew his way around the clutter so well. "Ali...Ali Abdullah. Ring a bell?"

"Ali, no don't ring a bell."

The detective leaned forward. "Well son, tell you this much. Your, uh, moms...sure knew the name."

Rasheed squinted his eyes looking off from him and muttered. "I see."

Giovanna glanced into his face trying to get a bead on what he was thinking. "So, you think she may have lied or something?"

Rasheed quickly snapped out of his trance, caught himself, as well as Giovanni, staring, and asked him, "Is that all you have?"

Giovanni stood up, reached into his desk and gave him another card. This one had a different number on it, a home number. "Look here, you might want to talk to your mother again. See if she knows a little more than what she's letting on, or even remember. It's been what...ten years?" Rasheed took the card out of his hand. and stood also. "This is my home number, call me. What's your name again?"

"Rasheed Muhammad, I'll call you if something comes up."

"Cool." He took the chance on the dap again. Rasheed ignored it again, instead, he said, "Oh, yeah...the tape?"

"Yeah, yeah, the tape. Sorry about that, apparently a tape was found at the scene. It was filed away with the evidence." He walked with Rasheed towards the door. "Strange though, it was never entered on record. Anyway, I sent it to the lab to be analyzed. It was pretty old, but I should hear something back, soon."

"Alright, I'd like to be notified as soon as it gets back. Here's my number also." Rasheed wrote it down and handed it to him. "Remember, as soon as you get..."

Giovanni patted him on the back. "As soon as I get it, I promise. We'll get to the bottom of it. See what really happened, okay."

Rasheed thought about what he'd just said. What really was supposed to have happened? Did he know more than what he was telling him?

The door swung open barely missing him. It was the Desk Sergeant from earlier. "Hey, Captain wants every available man over on Flushing Avenue by the Bushwick Projects. Now!" "What's up, Sarg?" Giovanni asked.

"Don't know for sure. Gunfire...riot maybe. You know how them niggas act..." He peeped around and saw Rasheed and stopped the direction his tongue was going in and switched up. "Yeah...crack house, a girl got beat up real bad." He sulked as he walked out the door. "Yep...same old thing!"

Giovanni went over to his desk telling Rasheed, "Hey look, I'll call you as soon as I hear something." Then rushed by him and momentarily stopped to see if the other detectives were getting up. They weren't, he sucked his teeth and grumbled under his breath about something dealing with their incompetence, then hurried off to the area where the other cops had gathered.

Rasheed walked by slowly on his way out trying to eavesdrop. Mostly a lot of talk about a crowd gathering. Getting some riot gear, hoses, dogs. The young, mostly all-white rookie cops in uniform seemed to be the most eager. All worked up in a frenzy. He listened to the scenario that was painted by the Captain to make the projects seem like a hell hole, but what startled him back into his own reality was when the victim's name was mentioned.

"Oh shit, my sister, Shaheeda!"

Giovanni overheard him and looked his way as he turned to rush out the door. "Rasheed, hold up!" he yelled.

Rasheed stopped long enough for him to catch up with him and told him, "What's up? Gotta go!" He looked the detective square in his eyes. He could see some sincerity radiating from them. He had that wanting to save the world look. Good cop on the beat, like some sort of TV show or movie.

"Talk to me. What's going on?"

Rasheed wasn't buying it; he was still police. "It's all good." He pulled his arm from him and turned away.

Detective Giovanni stood at the doorway of the precinct house rubbing his head. "Hmmm." Then he turned back around and ran toward the squad cars on their way to Bushwick Projects.

* * * *

43

Mustapha hopped the fence of the parking lot; squirreled in between the parked cars and jumped the fence on the other side. Straight to Bushwick Avenue. He had a run ahead of him. In all, a good quarter mile of the projects. From one side to the other, an all-out sprint.

Born and Ice sat on the benches in front of 849 drinking a beer, Born pointed. "Ain't that Mustapha running through the grass?"

Ice looked. "Damn sure is!"

"Wonder what the hell is going on? Where the hell is, he running to?"

"He's hauling ass!" Ice stood up and looked behind him. "And, I don't see no one behind him."

"Me neither, hold up!" Born pointed towards the backside of the parking lot on Humboldt Street. "Look at all those Police cars."

Ice walked over to the fence squinting to get a better look. "Yeah, ain't Felix's spot over there?"

"Bet that's where they're going."

Ice turned his attention back to Mustapha who was already across the other side of the big grass. "Mustapha!" Mustapha slowed for a minute, waved his hand, acknowledging them and kept going. "Damn, he's probably in some trouble."

Born got up to go to the building. "I'ma go call, Rasheed."

"Yeah, do that," Ice said. "I'ma run over and see what's up. Look like there's an ambulance going that way, too."

"I'll meet you over there."

Born sprinted to the building while Ice started down the hill toward 811. By the time he made it there, a crowd had already gathered in front of the building. He pushed through making his way to the front and saw Waseema running out the building putting on her coat.

He hollered out to her, "Waseema, what's up!"

He caught her attention and she stopped rushing over to him. "Ice, something's happened to, Shaheeda. They're taking her to Woodhull Hospital now!"

"Shaheeda? I just seen Mustapha…"

Grabbing his hands, she started pleading with him. "Ice please, try to stop him. I think he might do something crazy."

His eyes widened, then he asked. "Did you call, Rasheed?"

She turned from him and started heading towards the street, doubletiming her way to the hospital. She yelled back at him. "I tried to call, but he wasn't home!"

Ice turned from her and focused his attention on the chaos in and around the building. "Damn, Rasheed, where the hell are you?" He was hearing talk about how the police was going to come in the project, start hosing everyone down and sic dogs on them. They were ready for them though with pipes in hand. Chains and bats were strewn along the grass. Waiting, Ice balled up his fists in the midst of it all. He was about to get sucked into the madness himself, but a hand touched him on the shoulder. It was Rasheed.

"Something about my sister, Riot...something?"

Born ran up on them. "I just tried calling you!"

Ice motioned to the both of them to the back of 811, and instinctively they took off running. They reached Felix's building just in time to see the police finish taping around the front. A small crowd still buzzed; Rasheed pushed his way through trying to catch the attention of a uniformed cop. "Officer...officer!"

"Yeah, buddy, what's up?"

"I believe my sister, Shaheeda..."

"Hey Sarge! This man says he's the vic's brother!" He waved another cop over. A big burly, red-faced, white Sergeant came over giving Rasheed the once over. Then, he stepped up in his face. "Son..."

"I'm not your son. My name is, Rasheed Muhammad, Sir."

The young uniformed cop that was with him got up in Rasheed's face. "Hey boy, don't get smart!"

Rasheed didn't flinch as he moved within breathing distance of his face. "I said, my name is Rasheed Muhammad. Not boy...yours...or no one else's! You understand?"

The Sergeant stepped in between both of them and prodded the young hot-headed officer away. "Sorry about that Mr. Muhammad." He lifted the tape for him to come under. "It seems like your sister was the victim of a pretty brutal assault."

"Is she alright?"

"Far as we know, she's lost a lot of blood and was rushed to the hospital. That's where she should be now."

"But...but, what happened?"

"Yeah, cracker! What the hell happened?" Born hissed.

The Sergeant frowned, Rasheed figured since Sarge had pulled his bulldog back, he'd do the same. Besides, he needed to know as much information as possible. "Born, I got this. Now. Sergeant, what happened, sir?"

Dean Hamid

The Sergeant directed his eyes back to Rasheed only after doing a visual over Born. "From what I'm getting so far. A drug deal gone bad sort of thing. Possibly, someone, she knew beat and stabbed her multiple times. So far, no signs of any sexual assault, but like I said so far."

"Okay, where's the guy who did this?"

"Witnesses say he ran out the building. Don't know where yet. We're still trying to get a description."

The same old woman who helped administer first aid to Shaheeda crept over toward Rasheed and whispered in his ear, "Randy…Randy did it. Your brother went after him." She walked off as stealthily as she appeared.

"Mustapha." Rasheed rasped roughly from the corner of his mouth.

The Sergeant still stared at the woman suspiciously trying to keep a visual as she disappeared into the crowd. He made an attempt to call her. "Hey lady wait a minute! You know something?" It was no use, so he turned back to Rasheed. "What did she tell you?"

Rasheed stepped back under the tape into the crowd and said, "Nothing, nothing sir." He leaned over toward Born and Ice. "You seen, Mustapha?"

Born pointed toward the projects. "We saw him running towards Bushwick Avenue!"

"I knew it was something!" Ice punched into his hand. He remembered something. "That's where Felix's spot was, remember!" Born and Rasheed were clueless.

"That's where we…" Ice peeped over at the Sergeant. He was all in his mouth and whispered to them. "Let's get the hell out of her." He pointed them towards an opening.

Rasheed was just about to walk the other way to the hospital when Ice stopped him. "Hold up, hear me out. The first spot we hit back in the day. You and Born need to go over there to make sure everything is cool. I'll go to the hospital."

"That old warehouse? What the hell…"

"Born, just listen across the street from it there's an apartment building."

"Damn sure is, our first hit! Right off Bushwick Avenue!"

"That was one of Felix's spots, too. That's probably where Randy ran off to. To probably stay low until the heat cools. More than likely that's where Mustapha was headed. He might need some he-ha."

"You right, Ice." Rasheed dapped him up. "Alright, let's make it happen. Tell moms I'll see her later."

Born led the way sprinting in the same direction as Mustapha through the projects. The Sergeant that Rasheed spoke to was called over to an inconspicuously unmarked car with two male occupants inside. The darktinted windows were rolled down and a detective's badge was flashed…Giovanni's.

"Hey, Sarge! What was that young man's problem?"

"Hell…" He put his hands on his waist and said, "He was the vic's brother. Strange though, he didn't seem too worried about her."

"What do you mean?"

"Well, it seems like all he wanted to know was who did it? His friends were kinda shady, too. Especially that big black one he called Boon or something. His breath smelled like alcohol bet he got some warrants. The other one, the tall one let's stick with him."

Giovanni asked, "What was he talking about?"

"He acted…" The Sergeant leaned into the window. "Real proper, like he was better than anyone else. Rasheed Muhammad." He laughed. "Some sort of Moslem or something."

"Excuse me, Sergeant," Giovanni interrupted. "Do you see something funny? Maybe I'm funny or something…what?"

He straightened up. "No sir, it was just different. That's all." He looked back over toward the officers who'd gathered in front of the building. Someone waved him over and he was glad. He needed to get from under the fire he'd lit for himself. "Uh, Detective I gotta go. Is that all?"

"Yeah, Sergeant, that's all." The window rolled back up and the car burned rubber heading towards Woodhull Hospital.

* * * *

Mustapha stood across the street from the old, decayed building 1010 Lorimer Street. The broke down tenement had once been a home for happy, healthy families, mostly Dutch who'd come to America seeking opportunity and a better life. Out of breath, he bent over for a breather and moved unsteadily toward the front door, peeping inside. A light was on, blue flame and smoke blew into its murkiness. He ascertained from the sizzle that it could only be crackheads. Catching his eyesight, they drifted further away from him into the rat-hole of a building. Mustapha felt the side of his pants. His belt carried the .38, as he pulled it, loose shells jingled in his pocket for the .357 he hauled in his jacket.

47

Dean Hamid

It was too much of an arsenal but in the heat of the moment he just got caught up with Roots and took off running. He thought to himself as he felt for it that if the police were to run up in the building. He definitely would be through gambling, but if he needed to use them, he would. He tipped quietly through the lobby and then heard the door shut behind him. He ducked quickly underneath the backside of the stairway. He pulled his .38 up, he could hear footsteps getting closer.

"Yeah, Randy," he sneered.

Then as they got closer, he jumped out with his gun raised in the perpetrator's face. He pulled back, it wasn't Randy, it was Devone.

"Damn girl, I almost shot you!" he said as he put his .38 back into his waist. "What you doing here?"

Devone also put up something, a straight-edge razor. She had it up to his throat. "I almost got you, too."

Mustapha swallowed hard when he saw the light reflect off the steel. "What the hell you doing here anyway?"

"I saw you running this way after, Randy. Thought you might need some backup."

Mustapha nodded; he knew Devone was thorough. "Thanks, you seen Rasheed?"

"Naw, but, I'm sure between Ice and Born they're on it."

He turned and looked up the steps. "I think he's up there."

Randy had just cleared the 5th floor heading to the roof. The building had a few families left. Mostly gutter apartments used as drug dens. He figured he'd seek refuge in one of them. Wait for the sun to go down, then call Felix for help. He pushed the door open. and it creaked, loudly. Devone and Mustapha heard the whine of the door up the stairway. They looked fixedly toward the roof entrance, and some sun had just peeped through, then none. A door had just been opened. They headed up the stairs to the roof, cautiously stalking up the steps. Scanning each floor. Realizing Randy could be anywhere in this darkness, Devone knew it could just as well be crackheads, but it could also be a trap.

Randy backed up near an air vent on the gravel-covered asphalt. The *chug-chug-chug* of the gravel as his foot hit the ground pricked his ear. So, he tiptoed and proceeded as silently as he could. Crouching down, he jumped slightly as he heard the squeals of a rat running nearby. Mustapha and Devone slowly crept up the stairs towards the 4th floor. Hearing something Mustapha pointed his gun in the direction. His eyes penetrated the darkness as he slowly eased his way over. Then, he lowered his weapon. Sex, oral sex was being performed on a man in a business suit who'd strayed way too far

48

outside his realm. He jumped, and she didn't miss a beat. She fanned Mustapha away. Mustapha noticed she was young. She was sucking slowly, hungry to satisfy an urge: her addiction, and the crack. It was ugly.

Mustapha turned and motioned to Devone. "Hey, uh stay here, look out for the cops."

"No." She started to walk past him.

He grabbed her arm. "Devone, please, I got this. It's my beef."

Devone stared at him for a minute. He was focused, and it was his business. She conceded. "Okay, I'll be downstairs. Holler if you need me!" She hugged him and went back downstairs to the lobby.

Mustapha nodded, he waited till she was downstairs, then turned, continuing his mission. Randy peeped over the edge of the building. There was no fire escape. It had been rusted out a long time ago and fell over. There were no other buildings besides this one except for a diner that had been shut down for years now. All he could see was the shiny tin rooftop. A good five-story drop. He thought about tying sheets together, then dropping down safely on top. He let out a deep sigh. That was only on TV, with his luck the sheets would rip, or tear. He cringed at the thought as he looked down at the sharp pieces of metal that were twisted upwards from wear and age of the remnants of the collapsed fire escape.

Mustapha, with his .38 still out to his side, and with the other hand clutching the handrail, slowly moved up the steps. He heard some movement at the far end of the hall. His eyes focused near a corner wall.

'*Over there,*' he thought! '*No, just some children playing cards out of place with the present reality.*' A reality that was to them so very real. Mustapha lowered his gun a little as they laughed at him, oblivious to their danger.

Randy sighted a pipe coming out the roof. He pulled at it, but it wouldn't budge. Still very much attached to the object on the other side below. He bent and twisted it until the metal weakened under his grasp. It finally broke free, now, he had a weapon. He moved back into the shadows and a hiding place that would be his temporary shelter. Mustapha's eyes were still fixed on the door marked: *ROOF*. He noticed it was unlocked and half-opened. He figured he'd check the roof then make his way back down. He and Devone would do a thorough search of each apartment for Randy's hiding spot. He eased up as he approached, wiping sweat from his brow. Holding the gun tightly in both hands. His palms were sweaty as his heart raced rapidly with every step taken.

Dean Hamid

Randy cowered down as he watched the door open, it was Mustapha. He stilled his breathing as best he could as he thought, *'I've got to kill him, or he's gonna kill me.'* His mind raced over and over. He saw the muzzle of the gun as it showed itself coming through the door.

Mustapha peeped cautiously through the doorway. Looking down at the gravel, careful not to make any undue noise as his weight carried with every footfall.

Randy held on tight to the pipe in his hand. He thought about springing out. Surprising him with a blow to the back of his head, at least, that was the plan.

Mustapha's eyes twitched nervously as he heard the movement behind him. He played dumb to set up a trap as he moved out of the door, step by step. Listening for the sounds that would get him closer to Randy.

'It's time,' Randy thought. *'Now or never.'* He swung, missing Mustapha's head as he ducked. The force sent him sprawling to the ground hard.

Mustapha stood over him with the gun pointed at his chest. "I got you now!"

"I didn't mean to do that! No…no, it wasn't me!" Randy pleaded. "C'mon, Mustapha." He started to stand very slowly.

Mustapha kept the gun aimed at him. "You beat my sister…stabbed her! You gonna pay for that!" He moved closer to Randy as he eased back closer to the ledge of the building.

Backing closer, and closer as Mustapha kept a bead on him while he still held onto the pipe in his hand. "You don't want to do this. Look, we can hook up, get some dope…some money. I can pay off your sister's hospital bills. Work the money off…" He lunged, but this time he caught Mustapha on the arm. "I got you!" he hollered out.

Mustapha staggered as his mind went black from the pain. He squeezed the trigger of the .38…nothing. He squeezed again…nothing. No bullets, he never loaded his gun. He remembered he still had the .357, he threw the .38 at him. Randy ducked it and charged at him. Mustapha took the full force of Randy's weight in the stomach. He fell backward, his arm was still sore from the blow earlier. He swung wildly, and blindly with blows that landed hard on Randy's back and head. He cried out from his pain.

Mustapha wrestled out from under him, kicking him in the chest. Then, he pulled the .357 from his jacket pocket. He didn't know if this one was loaded or not, and he didn't want to take any more chances, so he glanced at the barrel. That was just enough time for Randy to kick at him. Knocking the gun out of his hands. He dived for it and Mustapha caught his ankle. Randy shoved the back of his foot into Mustapha's face as he felt the butt of the gun in his hands. He swung again, throwing Randy offbalance enough so that he stumbled toward the ledge. Randy had the gun now, but his balance was altered, and he stumbled. It dropped out of his hands towards the ledge near the edge of the roof.

He dove for it and slipped off the gravel under his footing careening headfirst over the ledge. Mustapha got up as Randy's hand caught the edge of the rooftop. He dangled, and his legs kicked as he looked down at the five-story drop. He thought maybe he could jump on top of the roof of the diner, but his fear answered him back, no.

"Mustapha...Mustapha, help me!" he cried out. Still, his eyes gazed at the gun he reckoned was at least an arm's length away. His twisted mind conjured up a plan.

Mustapha was positioned over him with his arms outstretched telling him. "Why should I help you? I should let you fall."

"No, Mustapha, you ain't like that! We can work it out! Please just don't let me fall!"

Mustapha leaned lower to grab his hand. He had a plan also. "Oh, yeah, we gonna work this out!" Mustapha figured he would report this fiasco to Felix who would reward him with a come up. Lieutenant, or something, he could have control and call some shots.

Randy grinned as he reached up for Mustapha's hand. "I didn't mean to hurt her. That bitch, she should have..." He stopped knowing that his thoughts had just become verbal.

Mustapha's eyes grimaced when he heard. "*Bitch*...a dog? *My sister*...you think my sister's a dog?"

"No, that's not what I meant!"

Mustapha held his hand as he continued to kick. His other arm dangled. He literally held Randy's life in his hands, and he knew it. He yelled at him in rage. "I'm gonna kick your ass!"

"Let's make a deal!" Randy screamed out. Still trying to grasp onto the edge of the roof where the gun laid. He'd have to make a choice. The gun, or the hand that reached at him to help. That was his plan. He jerked at the gun and missed causing him to wriggle loose from Mustapha's grip as he swung for it. He made the wrong choice; it was a bad plan.

Mustapha kept his eyes on Randy as he fell backward onto the roof of the diner. The twisted rusted metal ripped at his flesh as his head was cut clean off from his body. What was left of him was impaled on the steel picket fence that surrounded the diner. A fence someone had put up years gone by for decoration. Hoping to pull in more customers.

Without batting an eye, Mustapha uttered a prayer that his grandmother taught him years ago when his father was killed. "To God, we belong and to Him, we return."

Devone stood at the door watching. Rasheed had just come up behind him. They stared at each other for a short while in silence, then Rasheed extended his hand to his. "C'mon, bruh, let's get out of here." There was nothing else to be said.

Mustapha staggered lightly, then glanced back over the ledge. "Yeah, let's get the hell out of here."

CHAPTER FIVE

Detective Giovanni checked his watch it was 2:23 pm. He'd called the hospital and was informed that Shaheeda was going into emergency surgery. So, after he got a bite to eat, he figured he'd go by to see her and see if he could get some answers. Randy's body was discovered by NYPD after an anonymous tip reported kids playing with a decapitated head in the street. The Coroner's Office had to literally scrape the rest of his body off the diner's roof. His structure may have stayed intact had it not been for the crack cocaine that ravaged his drug-infested body.

Detective Giovanni got out of the squad car in the hospital parking lot and stretched new life into his jaded body. "Okay, Giovanni, let's do this." He sighed as he walked up the rampway towards the newly constructed hospital.

Woodhull Hospital was supposed to be the solution to the problem, but Woodhull by itself couldn't contain the problems of crack cocaine to the impoverished district. King's County Hospital across town was too far and just as stained. Shootings, overdoses, stabbings, all came along with the unwelcomed scourge, but all in all, it was what it was.

Detective Giovanni walked through the double sliding doors and made a beeline toward the front desk: INFORMATION. He was all too familiar with the hospital, and too many homicides and robberies to count. He flashed his badge and said, "I'm looking for Shaheeda Muhammad."

"Sure." The pretty, voluptuous clerk looked through her files. "Alright." She fingered her way through the stash of folders in front of her.

"She's in ICU, just got out of surgery."

Giovanni slipped into the elevator, once the elevator doors closed, he pressed three. The elevator door opened one more on the third floor: *INTENSIVE CARE UNIT*. Giovanni stepped out into the sterile atmosphere. The odor of surgery and the hospital made him depressed.

'*Damn, I'm so tired of this,*' he thought.

He moved sluggishly toward the nurse's station and a heavy-set nurse approached him. "Sir, can I help you?"

Giovanni half-smiled thinking of the girl downstairs. Figuring, with his luck, that'll probably be the play he needed. She snapped her fingers in front of his face abruptly interrupting his thought. "Sir, I don't have time. Are you looking for someone or not?" She looked him up and down. "Or, maybe you're lost?" Picking up the phone she kept her eyes peeled on him. "Maybe, security can help you find your way out?"

Giovanni reached into his jacket, and she cringed. Staring in fear as his hand started pulling back. "No need." He pulled out his badge.

The nurse quickly put down the phone, but still scrutinized the badge in front of her. "Sorry, officer, we just get so many strays, in here. Homeless people, people trying to steal. We just can't tell."

He put away his shield and replied, as best he could without snapping, "Well, maybe if you ask and not assume, that might help. Shaheeda Muhammad, please. What room?"

Her face turned red from the remark. She asked as she looked on her desk for the chart. "Are you family?"

"No, police business."

"Figures." She mumbled under her breath as she reached behind her grabbing Shaheeda's medical chart. "Here it is, young crackhead girl…room fifty-eight. Straight down the hall."

Giovanni shook his head and mean-mugged her. A prejudiced nurse in a predominately black hospital.

'*Real progress,*' he thought.

He walked down the hall to the room and spotted two well-dressed young black men standing by the door in suits. They both turned toward him, one of them, a rather stern-faced young man, looked to be in his early twenties stepped in front of him. "Can I help you, sir?"

"I'm, Detective Giovanni."

"And…" the other responded rather slyly. He was slim, probably just out of his teens, and rather cocky as he stepped up in Giovanni's face.

53

"What can we do for you?"

Giovanni noticed they both had bowties and stood very upright. An alarm went on in his head, but he wasn't quite getting it, so he stayed formal in his approach.

"Well, for starters. You can both get out of the way." It didn't work, but least it was the best he could do.

The youngest one sort of smiled and looked him up and down. "With all due respect, you haven't shown us an I.D. badge. We ain't got no idea who you are. You just look like another nig…"

Giovanni reached into his jacket and pulled out his badge, shoving it into his face. "Is this good enough?"

The other one looked at it and said, "Yeah, sure. Now, like we said before. What can we do for you, Officer?" Giovanni tried to step in between them and was not with resistance. "Sir, please, don't force our hand."

He stepped back and said, "Who the hell are you?"

"We were requested by the family," The stern-faced one said. "Fruit of Islam security."

"Security, for what?" Giovanni's face was twisted. "Damn, the hell with the police, huh."

"Well, sir, you said it."

"Alright, that's enough…" He hollered as he moved closer to them. A commanding voice came from inside the room. "Let the man in!" Giovanni recognized it. "He's okay brothers." Waseema came to the door.

The two young men stood at attention like soldiers and backed off. "Yes, sister."

She grabbed Giovanni by the hand and led him into the room. "It's okay," she said as she closed the door. She then turned back toward Giovanni. "Thank you for your patience. They mean no harm. They're just friends of the family. I was once a member of the Nation of Islam."

He continued his eye contact on the two men as the door closed. "Yeah, heard of them back in the day. Malcolm…right?"

Waseema escorted him over to a chair near the bed where Shaheeda laid. "Yes, Brother Malcolm. My mother sent them she didn't know what else to do. There's been a whole lot of police here asking questions. It's much too much for me, scary at times."

Giovanni pulled a chair over for her. "I'll take care of that." He sat next to her and in a whisper asked. "How is she?"

Waseema held Shaheeda's still hand and rubbed it. "The doctors say she'll be alright. Her jaw has been broken pretty bad and she lost a lot of blood from the stab wounds."

Giovanni leaned in toward her and asked, "Is she in a coma?" "No, just out of surgery." Waseema sighed lightly.

Giovanni reached into his pocket and pulled out a napkin he'd got from a restaurant he'd been to earlier and passed it to her. She dabbed at her now moist eyes.

"By now," he said. "I'm sure you've heard about her attacker, Randy Taylor?"

"Yeah, I have. The police said he was found dead. It's crazy you know. This crack...the neighborhood, it's real bad-real bad."

Giovanni reached out and held her hand. "Look, it'll be alright, just be strong."

Waseema smiled back at him. "I will, I will!"

They sat back while looking watching Shaheeda and listening to the beep of the heart monitor attached to her chest. He found himself dozing off after the respectful stillness between them. He'd felt comfortable with her. Much had been going on in his own life. He struggled to find peace as he grappled with the job. Maybe, some serenity could be discovered, but there were so many undue issues his profession accumulated. The glass ceiling, he wrestled with for one, and two, the Lieutenant badge he longed for. So much was going on, that when he had a chance to sit and be still. His body just relaxed and went with it. These times were few and far in between.

"You okay, Detective?" Waseema asked after hearing light snoring coming from him.

"Oh...uh, yes." He straightened up in the chair. "Sorry about that," he said as he wiped the drool that ran from his mouth. "Please excuse me, it's just been so busy."

Waseema smiled again, then said, "Don't worry, I understand. You have a wife?"

"Uh, no ma'am." He wriggled in the chair uncomfortably at the question. "Too many demands...time...hours and all."

"You know, Detective jobs come and go, but life...one chance. Enjoy it, at least while you have the chance."

Giovanni nodded his acknowledgment. "Thank you, maybe I will...one day."

He moved up in his chair to get a better look at Shaheeda. "I have to ask a couple of questions, Ms. Muhammad."

"Sure, ask."

"Well, we questioned a few people at the scene where your daughter was assaulted. We heard that your son, Mustapha, I believe his name is…"

"Yes, Mustapha…Mustapha Muhammad, my oldest."

"Uh, yes, it was told that he was seen running away from the scene or something to that effect."

Waseema turned towards him and said, "Well, uh, Detective." She rubbed at her hands, she knew those questions would come, so she prepared for it. Giovanni sensed her body language and had a good idea her answers would be rehearsed. "Mustapha was with me. He was coming to get me, then I sent him to a payphone to call his Grandmother."

Giovanni got up and calmly walked to the window looking out over the vast rooftops of Bedford-Stuyvesant, listening to her as she staged her story. "Hmmm, someone, or at least your mother can confirm this, right?"

"Yes, of course." Waseema had spoken with her mother earlier; the plan was already set in motion. A phone call had been made from a phone booth across the street from the projects just in case of verification. Mustapha's alibi would be her mother and so on. "Would you like to call her, Detective?" On top of it all, her mother had a real good lawyer.

"No, that won't be necessary, yet…" He turned towards her; his keen eyes focused in on her. "You do live in eight-one-one Flushing Avenue, right?"

"Yes."

"Okay, thought so." He walked back over towards the chair he was sitting in and sat down. "Strange though, it was said, Mustapha, your oldest son, was seen running toward Bushwick Avenue. But not into the building where you live like you said. You did say he came to get you, right?"

She felt that it shot through her like a shotgun, and the air came out of her. "Well…maybe someone…must have been mistaken." She became evasive, her left leg developed a nervous twitch.

It was a dead giveaway. Giovanni crossed his legs and leaned back from her. He could easily interrogate her right now. He could probably break her it wouldn't take much. She was fragile, but as he stared into her, he could see she was also emotionally unstable. Too many issues going on. She was backed into a corner and at any given time she'd collapse. He leaned back instead, and thought, later. She's already given me enough. He watched as she turned her body away from his gaze.

Giovanni patted her shoulder as he got up walking towards the window. "We'll talk later, you've got your hands full, right now." She turned toward him.

"Sure, if you want to talk to my mother…" "Later."

He was giving her an out.

As he leaned against the windowsill of the wide, metallic window he thought about how they were brought together by the cold case that was thrown on his desk. He'd gotten no further with that than he was before. Now. he had a fresh case involving the same family, that was strange. He glanced over at her, remembering the conversation he had with her son. Rasheed.

"Your son came to see me, you know?"

"Really." She sighed. *'No telling what he told him,'* she thought. Hopefully he didn't get too hot-headed or explosive.

"He's a good young man, smart, intelligent. You should be proud of him."

She got up out of her chair and walked over to him. "Yeah, he's a good son. What did you talk about, anyway?"

"Mainly, the case, trying to fill in some holes that's all." He faced her. "Ali, that's the puzzle."

She started reflecting. "All I remember is, Khalid, helped him get a job at the place where he was killed."

"The papers say he was questioned but released."

"That's all I know, too. Maybe, Malik might know more."

"Hmmm, Councilman Malik."

"Remember, we spoke about him."

"We did, it's not that, though. Your husband's case was always a cold case, but this whole thing with Ali stems from the Feds. Hmmm, wonder what…"

"You know what, Ali was introduced to Khalid by Malik."

"Malik Shabazz, City councilman, District eighteen…blah, blah, blah? There's a whole lot going on with him." Giovanni leaned back against the side of the window and crossed his arms. "You get it now? That's why the case was reopened in the first place. Somehow or another he's tied in, Ms. Waseema."

"And?"

"And…that's where it goes cold." He snapped his fingers, rushed over to his seat and grabbed his coat. "I've got to get back to the office and dig

57

up some stuff. I'll get back with you, soon. Then, we can sit down and discuss it some more. Okay?"

"Sure." Waseema turned toward Shaheeda and said, "Hold on Detective, I'll be leaving with you."

Giovanni grabbed her coat and help her with it. "I'll give you a ride."

"That's alright, Detective, thanks anyway. I'll walk, got some things on my mind." *Like Mustapha,*' she thought. She'd have to let him know what was going on. She reached over, kissed Shaheeda on the forehead and whispered in her ear. "Bye-bye, baby, be back later."

They walked out the door together, Giovanni glanced over at the two men that stood there earlier and asked. "They still here?"

"Till Shaheeda gets discharged."

"Just them?"

"There are others...they take turns."

"Uh, really, that's alright," Giovanni said as he waved at them. One of them acknowledged him saying, "Asalaam Alaikum, Officer." Giovanni looked at Waseema speechless. "Uh..."

She smiled at him and said, "Just say Wa Alaikum Asalaam."

"Wa Alaikum Asalaam?"

Waseema chuckled along with the two men as they headed towards the elevator. They were unaware of the presence that lurked in the shadows and watched as they passed by. Rasheed crept into the room undetected, let through by his childhood friends from the Nation of Islam.

"Okay, Rasheed, the coast is clear."

"Thanks, Brother Rob X." He walked over to his sister and shook his head in disgust. "Damn, sis, I should have been there for you." He grabbed a chair and pulled it close to the bed where she laid. The barely audible sound of the heart monitor hypnotized his thoughts for a moment, easing out of his trance, he held her hands and sobbed quietly. "I'm sorry, I'm sorry..."

Shaheeda suddenly awoke, dazed and swinging her arms wildly.

"Whoa!" Rasheed said as he held onto her. "It's me, Rasheed!"

"Randy's going to get me! Rasheed...help me! Help me!"

"Calm down, sis! It's over, you're okay now."

She groaned in pain, her broken jaw was swollen and the wires that held it in place ached as she regained full consciousness. "Where am I?" she asked as she stared up at the devices surrounding her.

"The hospital, Woodhull. Randy beat you up, pretty bad."

"I remember him hitting me...chasing me."

"Why sis...why?" Rasheed struggled with his anger trying to suppress it.

She tried raising up, but the pain held her down as she struggled to speak. "He said, Felix wanted to see him about something, but he didn't want to go. I knew he'd messed up some money. He said if I didn't work it off for him and do what he wanted he'd kill me!" she said. The bitterness spewed out of her mouth.

Rasheed got up and walked into the bathroom getting a towel. "Here you go, don't worry," he said as he wiped her eyes. "Everything's gonna be alright. You'll see."

"Rasheed."

"Yes."

"You look just like daddy." She managed a smile as she stared into Rasheed's deep brown eyes.

He kissed her softly on the cheek and said, "Get some rest, I'll be right here," he assured. He tasted a salty tear as it fell from his eye.

She squeezed his right hand tight and said, "I know you will! I know you will..." Her voice trailed off as she slipped back into restfulness.

Rasheed raised his head swiftly after hearing the commotion coming from outside the door. He wiped his face and slipped into the bathroom then slid the .38 he carried in his waist belt underneath the sink.

"I'm a friend of the family!" The voice shouted as he put his ear against the door.

"Yes ma'am, but there's no one here to confirm that. You might have to come back later. Ma'am. when someone..."

"No, I want to go in now! It's visiting hours so if you just step aside! Who the hell are you, anyway, the police?"

Rasheed recognized the voice and sass, it had to be Mya. "Let her in!" he called out.

Her eyes glittered as she burst through the door into the arms of her man. "Hey, baby, you ain't gotta be so mean." He chuckled as he looked over her shoulder and winked. "I got this, she's cool."

"Rasheed, I didn't know you were here," she said as she reached up and kissed him tenderly on the lips.

"Whoa, c'mon now, sweetheart. The bed is already occupied. I mean, I just left you this morning. What's all this for?"

"Does there have to be a reason, Rasheed!" she said frowning. Ready to go at him she put her hand on her hip. "Who are those guys at the door, anyway!"

Rasheed continued laughing as she turned around to let him take off the full-length shearling coat she wore. "Friends," he said. "Friends of the family."

"Yeah...okay, friends," she smirked as she cut and batted her eyes. Cuddling closer to him, she asked, "How's your sister?" Leaning into the bed she reached over and stroked her hair. "This doesn't make no kinda sense."

"Yeah, but she's alright, pretty broke up, but she'll pull through."

"I hope so." She motioned toward Rasheed and whispered. "You think she's finished with that..." She cut her eyes back toward Shaheeda. "Crack?"

Rasheed leaned back against the window and pulled her soft, curvaceous body closer to him. "I hope so, I really do," he replied bitterly. His mouth told on him as his mind replayed the scenario with Mustapha and Randy on the rooftop. From what his sister had just told him. He knew he'd have to find Felix and make him pay like Mustapha had done to Randy.

Mya looked into his face and read his mind. Rasheed thought she didn't know what had happened. She knew for sure that Rasheed would kick down the doors of hell trying to find out what actually happened. She herself didn't want to know.

She changed the subject to a more pleasant one. "Rasheed, baby, I was wondering if we could go downtown after we leave here? Get something to eat...Juniors or something?" Mya stroked the back of his neck, playing with the curly locks of his hair. He purred he loved the way she handled him.

"Baby, not tonight," he said.

"Rasheed...please."

"Baby..." He pulled her face gently toward him and kissed her. "I gotta get up with, Devone, and them."

"Devone!"

"C'mon, Mya, you know I'm about this money."

"Well, what about me, Rasheed? You barely spend time with me, I need you."

"Baby, I need you, too." He kissed her again. "I need you to be strong and...patient." He kissed her earlobe. "Trust me."

She cooed under his touch and her body responded by grinding her soft firm hips into his crotch. "Rasheed, I'm trying baby, I'm trying."

"Trust me, Mya, it's all gonna work out."

"You promise?"

Rasheed kissed her lips softly again, ran his tongue in her mouth and wrestled gently with hers. "Mya, I love you!" He hugged her and walked toward the chair where his coat lay then put it on. "Another time, okay."

Mya strutted towards Shaheeda's bed and pouted. "Alright, I love you, too!"

Rasheed glanced over his shoulder as he rushed outside the door. "Tomorrow, I promise! See you later on."

'*Please baby, I need you so bad*,' she thought as the door closed slowly behind him. As she rubbed the palms of her hand nervously, she thought about Derek. The sex, the lust they shared for each other. Would he tell? She bit her lip and grimaced slightly at the pain as a little blood poured through the bite. "Don't let Derek get what belongs to you, Rasheed. Please help me," she said softly under her breath as tears flowed gently down the sides of her face. "I'm not that strong." She jumped slightly as she felt a hand grab hers and squeeze.

It was Shaheeda. "It's gonna be alright, Mya...it will," she said then closed her eyes and dozed back off.

Mya smiled as she wiped away her tears. "Yes, Shaheeda, I hope so."

Rasheed stepped out of the entrance of the hospital lobby. The wind blew chills through his bones. He reached down into his pocket and pulled out a pair of soft leather gloves and stretched his hands into them. He thought about the conversation he'd had with Detective Giovanni. He needed to find answers. But where? Malik had to know more than what he was letting on. He'd definitely have to talk to him again, soon.

He waited for the bus to pull by as he jogged across the traffic-laden street in front of Woolworth and headed swiftly toward Bushwick projects. He was gonna find Felix. This time, before the heist, he knew Mustapha knew where to start.

****

"Hell no!" Another hole was punched in a wall along with several others. A door hung off its hinge. The victim of someone's anger, someone's wrath, and someone's fury. "What the hell is going on!"

A small, wiry Latino man cowered in a corner by a window in fear. His life hung in the balance. Questions had to be answered quick. He had no answers, just the reality that, one: his main runner, Randy was dead. Two: his boss' associate, Carlos had been killed along with his family and three: he might be next.

Rasheed and them had hit four of Felix's dope spots already. Thousands were taken, a very significant amount of his new product crack cocaine was stolen, and Felix didn't have a clue who was doing it. He put men on top of buildings. In the streets. They stood watch at his spots; snitches were employed. Bushes shook, but no one. Now, he raged over losing more money, drugs, and manpower. He didn't have the notion that this was just the beginning.

He stalked over to the man cowered in the corner and said, "You said you had this under control!" He punched the wall next to his head. His huge, fat-bellied, bald-head, massive demeanor hovered over the scared man. "I've lost a lot of money! You need to find me some answers." He grabbed the man by the throat and picked him up off the floor. "Now!"

He wriggled under the grip around his neck, gagging for air. Not daring to swing on Felix and said, "I...I...don't...know!"

"What the hell you mean, you don't know? Find out!" Felix hollered as he loosened his grip and let him fall to the floor. "Look, Juan, if you don't find out who's robbing my spots..." He reached behind his back and pulled out a shiny, steel 9mm, then shoved it in his mouth. "...I will kill you! You understand?"

Juan nodded, Felix walked back over to his desk and sat. He swung his chair around with his back away from him and said, "Find out what happened over on Bushwick Avenue, too."

Juan was still shaking as he straightened his clothes. "Felix...we might have an idea who killed, Randy."

Felix turned toward him and asked, "Why do you say that?" Juan eased over cautiously toward the desk. "You have one minute before I blow a hole in your..." Felix cocked his gun.

Wasting no time Juan babbled. "That bitch...she had a brother that worked for us! I heard he might have been the one who killed, Randy!"

"Bitch..." This threw him to the left. He'd seen Shaheeda from time to time, and he'd wanted to get his claws into her, but he never figured anyone else knew. "What the hell are you talking about?" He stood up. "I'm tired of your stories, I'ma kill you now...hold still." He pointed the gun to his head.

Juan held up his hands pleading. "His name is, Mustapha! I can find him...prove it! He may also know something about the robberies! Please, Felix, don't kill me..."

Felix stared down the barrel and said, "Either, you find him, or I will kill you." He walked toward him his breathing told how bad his body labored with every inch from the weight he carried. "Your family..." He put the gun back up to his head. "...and everyone that knows your family!"

"Y...y...yes, Felix."

He turned abruptly and walked back to his desk. "Ten thousand dollars."

"What?"

"Ten thousand dollars cash for the man who brings me...this, Mustapha." He sat down, then opened the top drawer of his desk and set the gun inside it. He leaned over and opened another drawer with stacks of money, bundled in thousands, he pulled out ten. "Ten thousand dollars, here this should open some doors." He turned his attention back to Juan and said, "If not...I kill you." He laughed.

Juan picked up the bundles of money and drifted towards the door as Felix's laughter echoed in his head. Moving cautiously, he noticed the wetness between his legs, but he didn't care. It was the last thing on his mind, he was alive. He exited quickly out the door.

"Okay, Felix, okay," he said as he closed the door.

Felix stood and watched. He glimpsed over his desk at the floor where Juan stood. "What the fuck...Juan!"

He peeped his head back inside and answered. "Yes, Felix!"

"Clean that up!" He pointed to the spot on his floor. "What the hell! You pissed on my fuckin' floor! Clean it up, now!"

Quickly Juan dropped to his knees with the handkerchief he had in his pocket and started scrubbing. After all, it was the last of his worries.

CHAPTER SIX

Ali paced the floor of the old, tiny holding cell at Central Booking. His mind raced over and over to the night Khalid was murdered. Piecing together every little detail he could think of. He knew he missed something, but he couldn't quite put his finger on it. He thought back to the first time they'd met. It was at a Mosque, uptown in Harlem. Both were ex-cons recruited from prison by Malik into Islam. He thought of Khalid as a straight-up brother. He even got him the job as the janitor in the building in the first place, not too much longer after he'd gotten the gig there himself.

Khalid wanted to work construction at the mall that was being built downtown. What was being called Albee Square, but he remembered Khalid bitching about not knowing the right people. They both thought about the shipyards over in Fort Greene in Brooklyn, but the only catch was they needed to carry a firearm, and they had felonies. New York State wasn't having it. So, when Action Security offered him the gig over on 28th Street, Khalid jumped on it.

It was a nice gig, sit down, sign 'em in and locked doors until morning. The instructions were real easy. They'd both been there for at least six months and got to know the building well. The comings and goings. The people were mostly European, friendly and considered safe. He shook his head thinking about the robbery and how he really wasn't down with it at first. But Frank kept pushing, telling him he could have all the cash. He just wanted some old papers. He didn't know what the papers were all about, but they were important enough to Frank. Hell, all he wanted was money. Enough to pay off some old gambling debts and possibly start some fresh ones.

Khalid would check the cat he relieved all the time. He was a lightskinned, red dude from uptown named Dave. There were too many times to count when he'd come in and he'd be in the lobby, eyes wide open, shirt unbuttoned and high on dog food-heroin. Yet, he was always complaining. He was probably the one who told him Frank was still in the building anyway. Probably said he was doing film work upstairs in graphics, that was Frank's alibi.

Ali peeped out the window that day and saw the little white girl that came into the building. The boss's daughter, that's probably how Dave kept his job. Hell, she got just as high as he did. He also saw them both rush

64

back outside. She and Dave, about fifteen minutes later were heading towards the Village. She needed a fix and Dave was possibly her connect.

More than likely Khalid went through his routine. He walked into the back room, a little makeshift locker room. A large utility closet shared space with the electrical room, with some tossed around furniture and a little paint on the walls. Action Security may have been safe, but they damn sure didn't ask for anything.

It was just about 9:45 once Khalid reached the fifth floor. He knew because it was normal when he made his rounds. He'd step off the elevator and spot checked the doors. Making sure they were locked and kept it moving. This time it was different, he turned on his flashlight and looked around. Dave more than likely did tell him Frank was up there.

He heard him when he came through the double, glass-doors. By the time he got around to let Frank know what was up, Khalid was already up on them.

His flashlight was raised high, his fists balled up and yelling. "Freeze!"

Ali knew that wasn't a good sign, but he wasn't expecting to see him anyway, then he saw Frank on his knees in front of a safe with papers scattered about. The only other thing that was vivid in his mind was when he hollered, "Ali, that you?"

At that point, all he could do was shove the cash he had in his hands in his pockets. He motioned for Frank to get up, they were busted. The safe was still open and Frank still ruffled through the papers, trying to conceal what he had.

Khalid bellowed loudly, saying, "What the hell is going on?" He couldn't believe it.

Ali pleaded with him, "It's not what you think."

Frank stood his dumb ass up and tried to so-call, smooth over the situation by pulling out a folded stack of bills wrapped with a rubber band out of his jacket and tried handing it to him. Khalid pushed it away. He already knew the ball was in his court. Ali told him to take it. He knew he needed the bread, as well as he did. The janitor job he had didn't pay nowhere near the type of bread he had in his pockets right then. He loved Khalid like a brother, but he wasn't trying to hear none at that righteous rhetoric Khalid pushed on him.

Khalid was no snitch, he was straight-up street. He would look the other way if he could, but it was also his job. A job that paid the bills and took care of his family. Ali remembered seeing him contemplating the maybes. Maybe, there was another way. Maybe, he could profit it from it. Khalid had come up with a plan. He told them not to close the safe. He'd keep the door unlocked. He explained that he would finish his rounds because he knew he'd have to probably explain things to the Police. A robbery, so, he needed everything to be as simple as possible. Ali recalled checking the clock on the wall, it was already 10:30 pm. All they would have to do is get their stories straight, then Khalid would wait for them to leave. Call the police and report a robbery.

Frank was perched by the door as Khalid came to let them out. Ali remembered because he was still stuffing money in his pockets. He didn't know exactly what that company did, but they had a lot of cash in their safe. Frank pulled out the envelope. A big-boy bulge and handed it to Khalid.

He thumbed through it, as Frank asked, "Will that hold ya?"

Khalid looked down at it, then at him and said under his breath, "Yeah, but. this is between us, right?"

Frank looked both ways as he exited the door, then looked back over his shoulder at us and said, "Just us." He disappeared into the streets with the small, hand-held briefcase tucked under his arm and a sly cheese-eating grin on his face.

That was when Khalid said to Ali, "You need to dip."

Ali tried to talk to him, but Khalid wasn't trying to hear nothing. He'd put him in a bad situation, he told him, "If I ever hear you say anything about what happened tonight to anybody. Even your own mother, I'll kill you." Ali knew he meant it.

Ali always kept up his end of that, even now. But it wasn't over yet. Ali walked over to his bunk, sat down and grabbed the side of the steel bed letting out a wail. "Damn, why? I should have just…left!"

That night he made it about a block away, he couldn't shake the fact that he'd fucked up that bad. His friendship with Khalid was important, he didn't want them to end like that. He felt at the bulges of money in his pocket. No, not like this. He was going to give Khalid half, make him take it, so he turned back around.

On his way back he noticed a tall, white man, maybe around six-three or so at the door. He was ominous looking wearing a dark trench coat making him look somewhat sinister in appearance. Ali quickly dipped into a doorway, but he was close enough to hear the man as he spoke through the door. He'd asked to have a word with Khalid. Ali didn't understand his dialect, Spanish maybe, and his curiosity pricked his ears more as Khalid unlocked the door and opened it. He told him the building was closed for the night.

The man pushed up against the door and said, "I'm looking for a Mr. Frank Hammond."

That threw him, Frank? He just knew Frank didn't send no one to the building at Khalid. Why? Maybe, the money, to rob him? Damn, was Frank that petty? Maybe this dude had something to do with Frank and what he took out of the safe? Khalid told him he'd left already, so it didn't matter. The man turned and walked off towards 7th Avenue as the winds coming off 8th Avenue swayed his trench coat around his body. Then, he disappeared out of view.

Years later, Ali remembered wondering what that whole exchange was about. He stood there debating what he should do. He knew the night would be about over for Khalid anyway. A few more rounds and it was a wrap. Maybe, he should come back then. They could get some coffee on 23rd Street and see what they could do then. It didn't seem long to him as he thought about what to do, but it must have been. He didn't even notice the two figures that stood at the door. His mind had drifted that quick. This time closer and Khalid started opening it. He could hear the keys jingle as he searched for the right one. That sound was what brought him back to his senses. He peeped out from his hideout checking them out. One wore a tattered old Army jacket. The other one was the same guy that came there earlier. This time they pushed through the door. Ali couldn't let it go down like that. Whatever it was, he had to help, so he went to the door and peeped in. Waiting to make his move.

One of them, the man in the Army jacket had a ski mask over his face, then Ali could see the sawed-off shotgun in his hands pointing at Khalid. If he busted in, he would be shot. He needed to be cool, he pushed up against the door to see if it was open, it was locked.

"Damn," Ali cursed as he thought back and shook his head. His mind throbbed in pain at the memories forever embedded in his mind.

He put his ear up against the door, he could hear them asking Khalid, where something was. The man in the trench coat approached the door and Ali ducked. He looked out the window then said, "The coast is clear!"

Khalid had done his fair share of dirt back in the day, so he knew better than to buck. "Yo' man, the money is in the back!" he told them.

"What?" The man in the Army jacket questioned. "Money?" He rushed up on Khalid. "The briefcase where is that!"

Dean Hamid

The trench coat wearing man stepped away from the door closer to Khalid and told him to hit, while the other stomped into the back room. Even from the outside, Ali could hear him tearing the place apart. When he finally came back out, he had the envelope that held the money Frank had given Khalid in his hand.

"This all you got!" he yelled at him.

Khalid told him to take it, while the one in the trench coat barked at him to keep looking. Khalid yelled out that was all he had, and he was slapped upside the head. The chair fell over that he was sitting in, and he slammed hard to the ground. The raggedy piece of chair broke into pieces. That's when he jumped to his feet and lunged at the one wearing the Army jacket. He dodged him and threw himself down on top of him after a brief struggle. The man with the trench coat charged at them but stumbled. The shotgun fell out his hand and hit the floor. Army jacket dude jumped at it, grabbed it and spun toward Khalid.

"Okay, that's enough!" he yelled looking over at the trench coat wearing man getting up off the ground. "You said it would be here! The papers where are they?"

Khalid yelled out again, "What fucking papers! I told you that's all I got!"

A fist came swinging out of nowhere catching Khalid's jaw. A sickening thud and blood spit out of his mouth. They positioned him up against the wall, then drug him into the back room. Ali pushed up against the door feverishly trying to pry it open. It was useless. He could hear them questioning Khalid, but he kept telling them he didn't know what they were looking for. Then, it changed up.

Khalid started pleading, "No, let's talk…don't do this!" His pleas seemed to fall on deaf ears.

Ali looked around for a pipe, brick something to smash the lock and break open the door. He ran to a dumpster and searched through it. Nothing. He looked around and saw a pipe. He picked it up, rushed back to the door, and he could hear Khalid screaming.

"Who are you! Who sent you here! This got something to with Frank…Ali!" Khalid yelled.

That was enough for Ali to hear. He had to help his friend. He picked up the pipe and backed up a little from the door to jam it through, then bend open the lock. He wanted so bad to yell inside and let Khalid know he was coming. To hold on, he slammed at the lock and tried jimmying it.

Then he heard one of them say. "You really don't know do you?"

Khalid hollered, "Damn, you, don't do this!"

Ali backed up and charged the door, hitting it, at the same time he heard a gun discharge muffling the noise he made at the door, but before that, he knew he had heard Khalid cry out. Sorrowful. A word he never ever forgot. It would haunt him to his grave. "Dunya!"

Ali panicked and backed away from the door as they came running at it. The lock wouldn't work for them, so Ali thought he had them trapped in the building. Then the door was kicked open and they charged out. The trench coat wearing man glanced around and saw the pipe on the ground. He looked around and zeroed in on the orifice where Ali was. He started walking his way, but the Army jacket-wearing dude charged and grabbed him by the arm.

"Let's get the fuck outta here!" He turned and they ran out of sight up 27th Street.

Ali rushed into the building, but it was too late. Khalid had blood pouring out of his chest. A big burn marked the spot where the shotgun blast tore up his chest. He kneeled and propped up his head.

"Khalid...Khalid!" He started crying but it was short-lived.

A police siren wailed in the background. He had to go; he didn't want to catch the charge on this. There were too many questions to be asked and not enough answers. Maybe, later he'd let the police know what had happened, but not now. He was sure the cat in the trench coat had seen him. He had to go. He glanced over and saw the money that Khalid had on the ground and picked it up. He could give this to Waseema. So, he picked it up, looked back over at him, then slipped out the door into the night. That was the last he ever saw of Khalid.

'It seemed like a good plan,' Ali thought.

Get in, bust open a safe, grab some money and some papers, and they'd be out in about two hours, tops. That was the plan Frank had sold him on. They never expected one thing to happen. Khalid wasn't supposed to come into the office. Something he never did, he made rounds sure, but going into an office, definitely wasn't expecting that.

Thinking back, he knew things were strange. So, he tried looking up Frank for some answers. He was told that he was killed. He looked into it and damn sure enough. A victim of an apparent execution. His body was found on the Jersey side of the East River. Things must not have panned out the way he'd expected. Ali was alone now, looking at murder, Khalid's.

The police investigated the scene, asked questions and all that. He laid low and went about the business of what he normally did. Clean building,

69

so they left him alone. The office that was robbed moved out of the building. He helped them. The Moors Institute of Science. He didn't know what they did, but it somehow involved a lot of real-estate contracts and deeds. Mostly around the Brooklyn area, from what Ali spied: Bed-Stuy and Bushwick. But he didn't care, they paid him cash-off the books. Soon after that, along with the money he had from the robbery, plus Khalid's money he never gave to Waseena. He quit, thinking maybe they didn't have anything, but he didn't trust that theory much. Paranoia had set in, so, he caught a flight to California. Trying to get lost. He was doing well until an old gambling debt came back to bite him in the ass. He never would have thought someone would have recognized him. Threats were made. He'd have to handle the situation the only way he knew how to run. He got caught up in another killing instead. He fucked around and got arrested.

Once the Feds spotted his name in the system he was immediately extradited back to New York. They said it had something to do with Khalid's murder. They hammered him, pressed him, and he came up with something. A slight slip of the tongue that somehow became relevant.

He told them he remembered when Khalid let him out that night that there was a tape recorder on his desk. No big deal so he thought. Then, all hell broke loose when they played it. A name was called. An important one judging by the way they reacted. He questioned them about the tape, but they never told him jack. He never did find out about the papers Frank grabbed either. If he would have asked that one question, then they'd know he was directly involved with the robbery, anyway.

Khalid's murder was never really high profile considering the locale and brutality of it. Especially in a city like New York where reporters climbed over each other like roaches vying for a hot topic. It passed by quickly. Still, he needed a good lawyer for the body he had in Cali. He tried calling Malik. He wasn't large then like he is now, but he was always connected. He knew how to deal with people. But Malik didn't return his calls, so here he was sitting on Rikers-C-95, for what seemed to be forever.

He was confused and didn't know where to turn. He reached into his jumper and pulled out a business card. He knew he had to trust someone. When this guy came to talk to him about the case they seemed to click. Ali told him he knew Khalid's family personally. That he was a friend. He got up and walked to the C.O.'s desk, but there was no one there. He walked to the door and saw him outside in the sally port. He slowly read off the name: Giovanni, Mickey Giovanni, New York City Police Department, Detective.

He exhaled deeply, then banged on the steel door getting the C.O.'s attention. He yelled out, "Yo', I need to make a call. Now!"

Dunya: The Do Or Die

CHAPTER SEVEN

Felix pondered on the day's mayhem as he cruised up Bushwick avenue towards the Brooklyn-Queens Expressway. His drive into the suburbs would be long, so he reached into his glove compartment and pulled out a Cohiba. He pushed in the lighter then waited for the silent click, lit up the Cuban blunt and took a deep drag. Cracking the window, a bit he pulled onto the expressway. Traffic was normally chaotic, but today it seemed rather mellow. He leaned back and blew out the smoke, looking forward to a relaxing ride.

He thought about the reward he'd put up for Mustapha, wondering if he knew anything about the chain of robberies on his spots. "Have I met this guy before? How the hell do I have people that close working for me, and don't know who the hell they are…" The car phone rang, he put the cigar in the ashtray, picked up the receiver and said, "Hello."

"Felix!" His wife, Maria was on the other end. "I'm going shopping with my cousin I won't be in until later."

"Shopping for what? You just went shopping!" His wife Maria had the hunger of a lioness when it came to spending money. Money that Felix saw less and less of. He barked back into the phone and asked, "Your cousin…who?"

Maria had plenty of cousins, millions it seemed like to Felix. All illegals from Columbia. She was like Mother Theresa of illegals. Importing them to the States like they were bananas. Felix had more of his fair share of socalled cousins that worked for him, too. They spoke little or no English. They had no job skills, but they knew how to kill. When it came to the authorities, they knew how to be loyal. Most of the women were used as mules or sold into prostitution.

"Rachel just came in…"

"Rachel?"

"My cousin on my mother's side."

"Damn, how many cousins on your mother's side do you have? Hell, what about your father!"

"To hell with you, Felix! I'm going to take them…"

"Them! How many are there this time?"

Silence came through the receiver for a brief second. "You make fun of me and my family." Her voice gave way to compassion as she responded.

"Are you not well off? How dare you!"

Felix gripped the wheel of the car as he banged his fist against the side door. "Okay, okay, just don't spend too much money. Understand!"

"You talk to me like that? I'm not one of your workers. I'm your wife! Remember, it was my father that set you up here!"

Felix frowned. "Yeah, you hold that over me all the time."

"Well, maybe, you need to be reminded...all the time. Bye!" She abruptly hung the phone up.

Felix slammed the receiver down as he pressed the gas pedal and roared off towards the Belt-Parkway exit. Felix cursed his commitment to her because it was also a commitment to the South American Los Andres Cartel, but he had no choice. A gun was literally put to his head. He started out in Columbia as a hired hand in the fields overseeing the workers who picked the precious coca leaf. He would see the petite, demure Maria when she'd come in from school. His lust got the best of him, he hid inside her bedroom on a late-night, pounced up and raped her. He threatened her, told her to keep it a secret, and tried to intimidate her, but she got pregnant. He was busted. She had no choice but to reveal to her father who it was.

He tried to run he knew he was a dead man. A field hand accused of raping a drug lord's daughter. But strangely enough, Maria begged for his life. She miscarried the child and her father wanted to cover the shame of his daughter. He sent her away, that's what she wanted. A way out of Columbia, from under father's thumb. Felix was set-up, he was Maria's flunky for life. Her father didn't kill him, instead he told him, Maria would be his pardon from a speedy execution planned for him. As long as he took care of Maria in the States, and handled Los Andres' interest.

Maria's father ended up giving Felix a small tract of New York to do business in, Brooklyn; Bushwick. He warned him that if he screwed it up, he would disappear forever. A threat he took seriously having seen many who worked for his now father-in-law get lost, chopped into pieces and families killed, brutally.

Carlos was Maria's cousin, the direct contact to the Los Andres cartel in New York, but now he was probably dead. Probably murdered along with his family. The money was gone, the dope was gone. Felix knew he'd better come up with some answers quick before the Cartel sent someone to find out what was up. So far, the money he sent them was his own. They didn't notice anything yet, and he would make sure the bodies of Carlos and his family would not show up. At least until he found out what happened.

Dean Hamid

He thought maybe he could orchestrate a car accident. A house fire, or something, if needed. He couldn't let them know he wasn't handling business. His time, money and options were running out.

Felix picked up the phone and dialed. "Juan!"

"Yes, boss!"

"Did you find this, Mustapha, yet?"

Juan's voice quivered in fear as he held the receiver to his ear and said, "I haven't…yet."

Felix had just left him no longer than an hour ago, and already he was growing impatient. "Go find him…now!" he yelled and slammed down the receiver.

Juan's ears rang at the sound of the phone's violent crash. He called out to his cronies, "Diego, Manuel, get the car ready now!" He had to find Mustapha's ass quick, and as Malcolm X had once said, By, any means necessary! Or it was his ass.

****

Waseema finally made it back to her apartment and opened the door. She didn't hear a sound, so she thought she was alone until Mustapha peeped his head from around the kitchen.

"Ma…that you?"

She looked cautiously out toward the hallway and came all the way in, putting both locks on the door. "Yeah, it's me."

Easing out from his concealed shadow in the kitchen he rushed her, hugging her tight. "This whole thing is crazy." His voice cracked as tears started running down his face.

She held her son closely and gently rubbed his back saying to him. "It's gonna be alright, don't worry."

Mustapha picked his head up off his mother's shoulder, looked in her trusting eyes and answered, "Yeah, ma." He walked towards the kitchen table and picked up some napkins, wiping his eyes, then asked her, "How's Shaheeda?" He didn't know what had happened since Rasheed and Devone escorted him back to the projects.

"Doctor said she'll be alright she got a broken jaw."

"He beat her up pretty bad, huh?"

Waseema walked towards the window, pulled back the curtain and said, "Pretty bad." She stared out over the park. "Mustapha…she needs to get off that stuff."

Holding his head down, he blasted himself for the problem. Felt like he didn't do enough to stop her. His conscience scolded him, but he didn't flinch as he thought about Randy and what happened earlier. "What else do we know?" he asked.

Waseema turned towards him saying, "Well, there's another rehab that Malik looked into. When she gets out, I'ma send her there."

"Another rehab, is she that bad?"

"What, bad? Mustapha, your sister sold her body for drugs. Got beat up by a crackhead…in a drug house. A man is dead! Yeah, it's that bad."

It was only going to get worse. Randy was dead and he knew eventually Felix would ask questions and send people looking for him. He cupped his hands to his face, pulled them through the long soft locks of his hair and sighed. "Then, that's what we need to do."

Waseema walked toward the sofa straightening out the soft throw pillows she'd arranged earlier and said, "You should think about your life, too."

"What?" He didn't need no speech after all he'd been through today.

"Mustapha…" She sat down and leaned on the pillows. "Stop selling drugs."

"But ma, we still need the money…"

"No, we really don't. I always wanted to say something, but I'd turn my head instead. Figured things weren't that bad. But as I look out over the projects, things have changed. Mustapha, I don't want you to be a part of it, no more…period!" She got back up, walked toward her bedroom and said, "Later, we're going to go see her. Be ready."

He hung his head as his mother shut the door behind her and said, "Yes ma'am." Then he walked over to the couch and sat down. He thought about how right she was. They really didn't need the money anymore, for a long time now. They had enough money to at least move. He needed to talk to Rasheed and ask him about the money their mother had put up.

A tinking sound came from the window interrupting his thoughts. Again, the same sound, "Mustapha…Mustapha." It was Diego, one of Felix's henchmen.

He ran over and looked out. "What's up? You know better than to come over here!"

"Sorry, bro, but Juan wants to talk to you."

"'Bout what?"

Diego stood underneath the window in the grass looking up at him and said, "Don't know, he just sent me to get you."

Mustapha glanced toward the street and spotted Juan's car. A burgundy four-door Cadillac Brougham. The same car he'd picked out for him the day they drove out to Queens during better times. Biting his lip, he thought about their conversation. About how Juan told him then pointblank, about his loyalty to Felix. How he would die for him, or even kill and how he should be the same way.

Now, he watched as the back window rolled down showing a glimpse of a hand slowly, methodically pulling off sunglasses from the face that stared back at him with steely black eyes: Juan's. He also spotted another man sitting right next to him, and another one he didn't recognize in the front seat who pointed his way. He knew who he was, the snitch. Mustapha knew immediately what it was.

He called down to Diego, "Hold up!" It was time to dip.

"No, no...now." Diego also read his look and knew what it was.

Waseema came into the room and asked, "Mustapha, who's that?"

Mustapha eased his way from the window and said, "It's the guys I did business with." He knew he had to somewhat get out and divert them away from his mother, just in case things got violent, with Juan, he knew it could.

Waseema rushed over to him and pleaded, "Mustapha, don't go out there, please." She held onto his arm. "Please!"

"Ma, I'm just going out there to break it off..."

"Mustapha, come down!" Diego yelled back up at the window.

Mustapha stepped back towards the window again and yelled back. "Yeah, yeah...coming!" He peeped over towards the car and it was now empty. Turning away he looked and saw Diego running toward the front of the building reaching inside his coat.

"Damn!" Mustapha spat as he rushed to the front door and put his ear up against it. Sure enough, he could hear noises in the hallway, and a gun being cocked. "They're gonna try me!"

Waseema ran to the door and tried to pry it open. "Who the hell do they think they are!"

Mustapha grabbed her. "No ma, they got guns! They're gonna try and kill me!" She backed away, visibly shaken. "No Mustapha...no!"

He grabbed her hand and they rushed into the backroom. Mustapha rummaged through the closet and pulled out a sawed-off, twelve gage shotgun, then reached for the box of shells down near the baseboard. "Ma..." he paused, listening for any sounds at the door. "Get in your room." She stood still. "Now, ma...now!"

She was fixed in a trance and state of shock. "Mustapha, maybe we should call the police?" She started walking toward the phone. Just then, a hard bam came from the door. "Mustapha!"

He grabbed his mother, pushed her gently against the wall and looked towards the back room, thinking out loud, "I'ma have to..."

"Mustapha...Mustapha!" they yelled out again. "Come out before we come in!"

He hustled his mother toward the window and looked out. It faced Flushing Avenue, there was a lot of people traffic going back and forth to the train. He stared hard at the ground below and thought two stories, she can make it, she can, she's got to. He turned toward her and said, "Ma, you gots to jump."

Waseema's eyes dilated as she looked toward the window, then back at him like he was crazy. "Jump, what..."

He shook her. "Ma, you got to jump, it's the only way."

"But baby, what about you?"

"I'll hold them off. Then, I'm right behind you, I promise."

"Mustapha, please." He moved her away then kicked out the bottom frame of the window. He grabbed a blanket from the bed and started padding the bottom of the window frame so that she could crawl out unscathed. "C'mon, Ma, now!"

The banging on the door had gotten louder. They had kicked enough of it to bend the frame so that the next move would be on the one Waseema dreaded. Mustapha ran to the edge of the hall and looked around. "Damn, they gonna shoot at the lock!" He loaded the shotgun and pumped it, then aimed at the door.

Bodoom! Bodoom!

The shots hit the doorpost and they scattered. It bought him enough time to see about his mother. She was already climbing out the window when he came in.

She hollered at him, "Baby please, don't stay in here...come on!"

He helped her out the window and started telling her. "I will, I just need to get some things."

She held onto the frame and eased her legs down. Her feet dangled as a small crowd gathered below. Two men stood in the grass beneath her ready to catch her. To break her fall. She looked up at Mustapha, then let go, and at that time the front door was kicked open.

Blaaam!

"Come, now, Mustapha!" It was Juan. "Felix wants you alive, we won't kill you…yet," he said under his breath. He fired two shots down the hall that ricocheted around the bathroom walls. "C'mon, nigga, before I change my mind!"

Mustapha loaded four more shells in the chamber, gripped the gun to his chest and held his head down. He could hear his mother calling him in the background from a distance. He picked his head back up and gazed at the entrance into the hall, then shook his head as his mind raced trying to make sense of it all. Things were happening so quickly. He thought maybe it was his time. He rushed out the room pointing the shotgun down the hall and fired. *Bodoom! Bodoom! Bodoom! Bodoom!*

The smoke cleared; two shells hit Diego. His arm hung limply to his side. Juan fired back. *Click! Click!* His .38 Revolver ran out of bullets.

"Damn!" he cried out in frustration.

Manuel, another one of Felix's honchos grabbed Juan and started pulling him back toward the door. "Juan the police will be here soon!" Diego limped behind them his blood squirted all over the walls as he moved.

Juan fought with Manuel and said, "I don't care about no cops. I have to get him!"

Mustapha had moved up on them swiftly and leveled the shotgun. "You better leave…" Then pumped it. "…while you can!"

Juan cursed him. "I gave you a chance, you bastard! Felix will hear about this!"

Mustapha stepped closer to Juan, pointed the shotgun to his head and said, "Tell, Felix, he can kiss my black ass!" He was about to squeeze the trigger when Waseema called out. "Mustapha, the police coming!" He looked Juan square in his eyes. "This ain't over!" Then he ran to the backroom.

Juan screamed at him, "Yeah, nigga, it ain't! Ten thousand dollars will see to that!"

Mustapha glanced back as he heard ten thousand. He now knew that was the price on his head. It was a good piece of change. Every jack boy in Bushwick as far as East New York would come looking for him. Scrambling into the closet he pulled out a leather satchel bag and opened it. It was money owed to Felix that he skimmed off bogus deals he'd made. He picked it up along with the rest of the shotgun shells and rushed towards the window. He let out a sigh of relief as he saw his mother on the ground unhurt. He stuffed the shotgun shells inside the bag along with the money and tossed it outside, then crawled out the window.

Juan had managed to wriggle out the grip of his men and rushed toward the backroom. Mustapha watched as he pulled out a long dagger and charged toward him swinging. "Nigga!"

Mustapha let go and Juan cursed him as he fell to the ground, got up and watched as he and his mother took off running into the crowd.

"Mustapha, you're a dead man...dead!" he yelled at the top of his lungs.

****

Felix was still upset he needed to go somewhere and relax. He glanced over his shoulder as he cut in front of the vehicle in front of him. The car's horn honked loudly, he grinned and mumbled, "Fuck you."

He pulled off the exit at 216th Street on Hillside Avenue in Queens. The gas station on the top at the hill coming off the rampway was the sight he looked for. It was the stop he needed to make to get guns and condoms. The plan he devised was set in motion, his relaxation would come in the way of sex. Felix pulled the big-body Benz back into traffic onto hillside Avenue toward Queens Village and turned left on 218th Street. Two blocks down he pulled into a small powder-blue, two-story brick home with a garage set off in the back. Grabbing his bag, he headed towards the back of the house, nervously looking over his shoulder as he crept. A small Latino woman opened the backdoor, then peeped behind him as she let him in.

"Ah, Sonia, good to see you," he said.

She rolled her large, long eye lashed eyes, held out her hand to him and asked rather coldly, "You have money?"

He stammered toward her in an attempt to hug her saying, "C'mon, it's me, Felix."

She dodged his embrace and instead responded, "So what!"

His eyes twisted downward as he angrily reached into his pocket and said, "You, stupid little whore, of course, I have your fucking money! Who the hell do you think I am?"

She tapped her foot impatiently. It only incensed him, he grabbed her by the arm. She tried to wriggle free, but his weight had her trapped like a mouse under the pressure of a boa constrictor.

"Bitch, don't you ever disrespect me like that!" he threatened.

"I've had a bad day, no money-and Maria..."

79

"My wife…what?" He tossed her small body against the refrigerator, questioning her. "What about, Maria?"

Struggling to her feet, she said, "She came by looking around. She left about two hours ago." She walked over to a small dining table and sat, grabbing a cup of warm coffee, telling him, "I think she knows something." Felix towered over her. "You didn't say anything to her, did you?" "No, of course not!" She put the drink up to her lips and took a sip. "But you'd better be careful, that's all."

"Did she take any money?"

"She said she could pay the bills herself," Sonia said as she looked up at him. "I couldn't do anything…"

"Of course, of course."

She composed herself, got up and walked past him. She didn't say a word as Felix rubbed her ass as she walked by him to a closed door and knocked. "Helena, you ready? It's Felix."

The drool had already started coming out his mouth as he handed Sonia some money. "Here, take this and don't bother me. Go!"

She scrambled down a flight of steps to the basement mumbling under her breath. "Fat pig."

He paused as he walked in, thinking about what Sonia had just said about Maria. Normally, she didn't come to Queens without letting him know. What was she looking for? Maybe, he thought she was trying to catch him doing something. Or, just being nosy. Who knows? But he knew she was up to something. He opened the door to a somewhat, youthfullooking, blonde Latino woman standing by a small futon pushed into the corner of the room.

She looked up at him nervously and said, "I'm here."

Felix reached into the brown paper bag he'd got from the convenience store, pulled out a few condoms, tossed them beside her and said, "You know what to do."

His relaxation for the day would be this girl, an immigrant from Columbia. One of Maria's, so-called cousins, bought and sold, but this one exclusively to him. He paid Sonia good money and she rewarded him with her daughter. The fat, greasy slob he was, was okay with the arrangement. He'd been down this road with several different illegals and this was his pedigree. He was a dog, he moved toward the girl. She didn't try to move as he groped her. He walked over to the curtains, pulled them closed and laughed, saying, "Come now!"

The young girl named Helena turned toward the bed. He watched attentively as she bent over, playing with himself, continuing as she sat on the side of the bed and started to undress.

The dark blue Sedan outside was running idle, letting the cool air conditioning, which was turned on high inside, blow. The windows were closed except for a slit on the driver's side, heavy thick blue cigarette smoke blew through. Maria tapped her finely manicured nails on the steering wheel as she eyeballed the curtains to the windows upstairs in the house close shut. She wasn't with any cousins. She'd been sitting there now for at least a pack of Marlboro cigarettes waiting. She watched Felix pull up and go in, she'd seen what she had been waiting so long for.

"That fat ass muthafucka! After all, we did for him. They should kill him!" she said as she put out the butt of the last cigarette she had, "But no, I've got just the thing for him!" She smirked as she pulled out of the alleyway across from the house, he'd gone in. She slowly drove by as Sonia peeped out the back door. Rolling down the passenger side window she tossed out a small waist bag then pulled off.

Sonia looked both ways before she stepped outside to pick up the bag. She was the one who'd called Maria and told her the deal with Felix, but the information wasn't free. It never is! She scurried back inside and closed the door quietly so she wouldn't bring any attention to herself. She silently zipped open the bag and thumbed through the money that was in it.

"It's all here," she said as she glanced up the stairs for a second, then turned her attention back to the cash and smiled a sinister grin saying to herself, "He'll pay…one way or another!"

CHAPTER EIGHT

"So, Devone, did you get the truck?" Born asked as he took a swig from a half-pint bottle of Bacardi rum, then reached over Ice for the CocaCola he had sitting in front of him.

Devone pushed it away and mean-mugged him, "Buy your own damn soda, at least." She leaned back in her chair and shook her head slightly. "We couldn't get a truck, but we got a van."

They'd gotten together for a meeting making sure all their ducks were in order for the next job. They didn't plan out their last couple of jobs and something always seemed to go wrong. Devone thought it would be good to have these meetings and eliminate or possibly even add to the equation if needed. Rasheed had picked up Born before he could get missing, and Ice was already there. Derek was a no-show.

"A van?" Born said as he stuffed the paper-bagged bottle back into his pocket.

"Yeah, a van," Devone said as she reached for some papers sitting off on the table by the easy chair, she lounged in. "Uh, let's see…yeah, we pick it up on the day of the job."

"Cool." Rasheed looked over the papers passed to him and asked Devone, "It can't be traced, right?"

"Uh-uh…no." She glanced over at Ice and motioned for him to continue.

Ice leaned his heavy, stocky body forward. He was the quietest of the group and the most diligent. A trait he most likely developed from his stint in the Army. His knowledge of weapons, planning, and precision had been a plus for them, and he didn't have any heavy baggage. No one knew a hell of a lot about him. He just seemed to be one of those cats that popped out of nowhere. Devone had told them a story once about how she'd met him at a club over on DeKalb Avenue, a place called The Cellars. But, no one really believed that.

"I personally went to the car dealer like you said," Ice resumed. "You know, over on Atlantic Avenue down near Nostrand…"

"Yeah, yeah, yeah…and?" Born interrupted him, he never trusted him. He didn't trust mostly anyone except Rasheed anyway.

"I went to the Italian dude like you said and he shuffled me around to the back. Where they had all types of rides. Four-door getaways, souped-up Chevy's and more specifically for stick-ups, hits, and getaways. It's a Mafiaowned spot."

Rasheed stood off by the window watching police cars frantically scramble down Bushwick Avenue, bringing him back briefly to earlier in the day. Paying it no real mind he walked over towards the sofa and sat on the armrest.

Devone flipped. "What the hell!"

"What?"

"That sofa cost me a couple of grand, easy. At least sit in it!" She smirked, she'd been watching Rasheed anyway, half-ass paying Ice any mind. She couldn't keep her eyes off him.

Rasheed shook his head, then laughed. "A couple of grand on a chair!" He scooted Born over and sat down after mumbling "*ghetto ass*," under his breath. Devone threw a pillow at him.

"Anyway," Ice butted in. "I gave this dude…"

Born cut him off again. "Who is this, dude? He got a name or what?"

Ice was growing tired of the interruptions and now Born was trying to dis him, too. Ice was half Italian, a red, light-skinned, almost white looking dude, and he always seemed to be the target for Born's personal racist remarks.

But he played him off. "I'm getting to it," he said. He was just like his name suggested, cool.

"Well, c'mon, we ain't got all day!" Born wasn't as cool, but itching to get drunk, and raise a little hell, somewhere.

"Vito, that's his name. I paid him about eight grand, and put those plates on from down South, then left."

"Tell them about the paint job, too," Devone said.

"Oh, yeah, the paint shop over on Flatbush Avenue. It's gonna be painted…"

Born interrupted him again. "With the type of paint that washes off, right?" He looked over toward Devone paying Ice no mind.

"Yeah, Born! He told the Jamaican dude what we wanted. Paid the money…"

"Look, Born, if you want to check everything out yourself, feel free." Ice got up and sneered, his patience was growing thin. "Cause obviously you don't trust me."

"Naw, it ain't that, Ice. Don't catch feelings, just don't need no fuckups…anymore."

Ice leaned against the wall and calmed down. He was starting to understand now. Though some of it was personal, this wasn't. Born had put in some serious work lately, especially on the last job. The drinking was getting to him, and he didn't know how to deal with it, or he just wouldn't.

Ice himself was trained for stress. He lived for that shit but Born wasn't built like that. He had to deal with being on the front lines the best way he knew how.

"Born, I told him, I'd be there to get it in another week or so. It'll be ready, keys on the floor under the seat and all that. That's my word." He stared in his eyes looking for a response, anything but the light in Born's eyes had left a while ago.

This would be his last job. His coldness would soon turn to callousness, and his lack of feelings could result in more deaths. Something they couldn't afford.

"Sounds cool, Ice," he said, then reached for his bottle. Rasheed leaned in and snatched it away. "Hey, give me back my shit!" Born protested as he reached for it.

"You had enough, Born." Rasheed started getting up from the sofa and Born snatched at it again, but Rasheed quickly pulled back and he missed, then he rushed down the hall to the bathroom.

Rasheed shouted from the bathroom, "Born, I'm not gonna watch you drink it." He poured the drink down the toilet saying, "Besides, you're starting to smell like this shit!"

Ice glanced over at Devone, he knew it was bad, but not at this level. Born ran down the hall behind him, but it was too late. Rasheed flushed the toilet. He wasn't trying to disrespect him, and he knew it.

"Damn, Rasheed, you didn't have to throw it away." He had his fair share of trouble already behind drinking. At times he would see him shake. His hands trembled, D-T's had started to set in. Then, he'd have bottles stashed all over the place. They all just had to accept the fact that Born was an alcoholic. He was functional for now, but neither one of them wanted to face up to it, not yet. It was way too close to the job and he was needed as much as he was deadly.

Devone was growing impatient of the foolishness and called out to them. "C'mon, hurry up! We still need to go over a couple more things!"

"A'ight, coming. You got a trash bag back here?"

"Look in the bedroom by the dresser."

Rasheed stepped into the bedroom looking around the floor, then spotted it. He moved towards the small plastic bin and noticed that Devone had spent big money on the expensive furniture in there. A cherry wood dresser with huge mirrors. Big fluorescent globe lights running along the top. 'Nice,' he thought as he ran his hand along the trim admiring the soft luxurious leather. A small piece of wrinkled paper caught his hand and fell to the floor. He picked it up and unfolded it. It read: Mya: 5-3-8-2-4-6-3.

Why was his number with Mya's name on her dresser?

He stepped out of the room coming down the hall with the paper in his hand and asked, "Devone, what you doing with this?"

Devone's eyes glared wide open when she saw it. She thought Derek had thrown it away, apparently not. She remembered vividly when she gave it to him before he dipped over to Rasheed's place. She exhaled deeply she really didn't need this to be happening now. She had to come up with something, a good lie and deal with it later.

"Rasheed, baby, you snoopin' around or something?" she purred softly.

Born got up and leaned against the door by the kitchen. He waited to see how Devone would explain herself. He kind of knew something wasn't right but couldn't put a finger on it. Devone knew Rasheed's number by heart. Why would she have it written down on a piece of scratch paper with Mya's name on it, folded? It didn't seem right. Then breaking the tensed mood, all their attention was directed toward the door. They heard keys, then it opened, it was Derek.

"Somebody better have a good answer, for real," Born smirked, as he looked Derek's way. The liquor only adding to his sarcastic rancor.

All eyes were on him as Derek entered, instinctively, he scanned the room. When he got to Devone his eyes locked. Hers led him straight to the number in Rasheed's hand. Her expression told him something was up, and he knew immediately it had something to do with the number he'd forgotten to get rid of earlier. '*Did Rasheed know something about his dealings with Mya?*' he thought. He went with his gut, okay, Rasheed didn't seem too pissed. So, he didn't know much about that, he couldn't have. '*Probably asking about the number,*' he thought. He stepped in between them and nudged him back a bit, then abruptly snatched the paper out of his hand. '*Damn.*' His theatrics had better be good to pull it off, and hopefully his hunch.

"This is from earlier. When your sister got beat up, Rasheed!" he lied.

Rasheed stared, his eyes narrowed like a hawk, as he watched him.

Derek knew he'd better be on point. He raised the paper up and started waving it around. "Trying to find you! Had to get with someone...Mya...someone!"

"I meant to get it back from him, but after all that went on," Devone added.

Dean Hamid

The tension was a little thick, a close call, but Devone had her out. "Yeah, Derek was supposed to call for your moms when she went to the hospital."

Rasheed went for it, with all that had gone on, it seemed legitimate enough, and Derek co-signed it. Still, he was going to ask Mya if someone had called the apartment. She might not fair too well under pressure, and Derek knew that. He knew he'd have to touch base with her asap.

"Yeah, no problem, sorry about that," he said.

Derek reached out his hand toward him as he tried to secure the Oscar for his performance. "That's alright. Hell, I would have done the same thing," he said as he glanced Devone's way, then sat. "So, what are we talking about now?"

Born watched Derek closely. He could see the beads of sweat pop-up around his forehead, and he knew something wasn't right, right then. He knew it had something to do with Mya. He remembered her from back in the day and based on what he knew about her. He didn't trust her either, but she was Rasheed's, old lady. Not his headache.

He moved back over towards the couch where Rasheed sat and eased past Devone. He studied her hard, so hard his thoughts could almost be read.

'I know you know something I know you do,' was all he could think of.

Devone mean mugged him, grabbed the rest of her Coke and drank it down, giving him that fuck you nigga look.

The whole scenario had moved Ice, too. He remembered talking to a couple of people he knew from Fulton Street near Brevort Projects that mentioned to him they saw Derek and his new Cadillac cruising their way, around Rasheed's place. He blew it off, thought maybe he was just going to see Rasheed, but come to think about it. Rasheed was always in Bushwick, or somewhere else at the time. After the heist, he was going to approach him about that, maybe even after this meeting. He didn't trust Derek, or even Devone much anyway. Things weren't right with those two.

"Alright, people where are we?" Derek asked as he sat up in the chair. It was his way of changing the subject and hopefully the tension. Derek was a skilled manipulator, along with his sister Devone they always seemed to know what to say and do to control them. "Rasheed the guns. What we got?"

"So far, Tech 9's, three shotguns, pump sawed. Couple boxes of shells, hollow points and, uh...oh yeah, four Revolvers, Snub Nose .38's. Two machetes..."

"Machetes?" Ice asked. "What the hell we need machetes for?" Rasheed leaned up and looked over at Ice, then Born and laughed. Born answered, when he did, he stared Derek right in the eyes. "In case we need to chop a muthafucka up that's why." He turned towards Devone too, and maliciously grinned at her. She could feel the chill. In all her years she'd never met anyone person as crazy as him and hoped to never meet another.

"You're crazy," she said.

Derek popped up. "Hell, yeah he's crazy!" His mind raced back to the day he met him. Born's hand trembled for yet another drink.

"What y'all looking at!" Born barked as he felt all eyes on him. He was getting uncomfortable and he tried to hide the shakes. At one time he was able to control them, but recently along with the cold sweats, he battled at night. His health seemed to go downhill rapidly.

Derek zoomed in for the kill. "Born, Born, Born, I remember when you were about that life back in the day. You and your brothers." He bent over and got closer in his face. "The biggest stick-up boys in Brooklyn!" Then, he stood up scoffing him. What did they call y'all again? Oh, yeah, the Mack boys. Yeah. that's what it was right, Rasheed."

Rasheed shook his head. He didn't like Derek sneering at Born. He didn't deserve that. Not after all the work, he'd put in. "Yo', Derek, chill the fuck out with that."

"No, I mean, everyone was afraid of them, right...remember?"

Rasheed ignored him. Born got up from his seat and strolled rather casually toward the window. He leaned, staring out over Bed-Stuy, watching the elevated J train roar going up Broadway. "You know Derek don't get it twisted."

"What!" Derek fell back in his chair and started snickering. "I mean, you was the man, right, Devone? They had the money. Hell, y'all pushed up on my sister." He snickered again. He was going for the throat now. A move that could go either good or bad. "But, look at your ass now!" He banged his fist on the arm of the chair and hollered out, "You depend on us! You's a has-been, Born. A fucking drunk, so, don't try putting that tim shit down on us! You hear!"

Born shook his head and turned ever so slightly getting a head-on Derek and said, "You right but you got one thing wrong..."

It happened unexpectedly, in an instant he was already up on Derek and had the barrel of his pistol dug deep into his temple. Devone jumped up and went for her gun, but Rasheed stepped in the way.

"He started it," Rasheed said.

Derek's eyes grew wide as his bottom lip quivered. Born pulled the trigger back and said, "I ain't slow, and I don't have a problem blowing your fucking brains out."

Devone didn't say a word as she inched closer to her gun. Derek had played the wrong card and put his foot in his mouth. She hoped Born didn't take him seriously but, she was wrong. The chamber clicked as the hammer fell, and Derek jerked. Nothing, the gun was empty. Born pulled up off him and laughed. A sound that sounded like years of phlegm from the alcohol built up in his throat.

"Look at you now, but you was never built like that, anyway." He flashed the bullets he took out of the gun and shoved them in his pocket. "Or are you? Bring it…" He gestured for him to get up.

Derek was hot, but so was Devone. She eased in, her gun was already in her hand, looked at Born and said, "Don't you ever…ever, do that shit again." He looked down at the .45 in her hands, she said, "Mine is loaded and cocked."

"Man, I oughta…suppose it was loaded. If I had my piece on me?" Derek was hot, but he remained seated.

Rasheed and Ice laughed. They'd seen Born cuff the bullets, but Devone stared at Rasheed and mugged him. Born walked over to the closet to get his coat and said, "I'm out of here, fuck this."

"Yeah, okay…run!" Derek yelled still shook. "I should try your…"

Devone glanced over at him and said, "If I were you, I'd let it go."

"Yeah, Derek, let it go," Born snarled.

"I can handle mine!" Derek shouted, "I ain't no sucka!"

They both screamed at each other, but it was cut off unexpectedly by a hard knocking on the door. Devone went to answer it, glaring at Rasheed as she walked by. "Alright, alright, I'm coming." She looked around at everyone to make sure they were straight.

Ice had the tendency to carry his piece, too. A .357 Magnum stuffed in his pants. She opened the door and a little boy stood in front of her. His kinky hair had small beads of sweat along the nape of his head. His small beady eyes were wide as hell as he huffed trying to catch his breath.

"Is…is, Mr. Born h-here?" he asked.

Devone glanced over at Born and beckoned the little boy in. "Catch your breath, I'll get you some water," she told to him.

Born rushed him. "What's up, Tyree, what's wrong?"

The little boy looked up only after wolfing down the glass of water Devone handed him. "Mr. Born…" he still gasped trying to catch his breath.

"What?" Born questioned as he guided the little boy to a chair by the kitchen table. "Did you run up the steps?"

Rasheed and Ice had surrounded him also and Rasheed asked, "Who this Born? Damn, he looks like Pinky. This her son?"

"Yeah," Ice said as he leaned back against the kitchen sink. "She strung out on dope. Probably ain't been home…"

"Damn, everybody on dope!" Rasheed blurted as he banged the top of the kitchen table and the little boy jumped.

Born frowned at him as he tried calming him down.

"Something's happened over at eight-one-one. A shoot-out! Some people tried to kill that dude, Mustapha, and his mother!" Tyree spat.

Rasheed damn near fell back over a chair. "Mustapha…eight-one-one? Oh, shit!" He ran to the backroom window that faced 811 and looked out the window. "Ma!"

Born was right behind him. "Look at all those cops!"

Ice grabbed his coat and yelled out. "Let's go!"

Rasheed was halfway out the door, he hollered over at Devone. "Later, gotta see what's up!"

Devone waved him on as Ice, Born and the little boy all piled out the door. Derek doubled back over to the dining room table where the number Rasheed had found earlier, laid. He picked it up and thought, *'Damn, gotta handle this.'*

Born yelled from down the hall, "Derek, c'mon!"

Derek ripped the number up and flushed it down the toilet, then ran to his dresser snatching up his keys. The phone rang, he rushed over to the phone and was about to pick it up; then noticed the caller I.D. It was Mya.

"Derek…Derek!" Born called out again.

"I'm coming!" he yelled back as he contemplated picking up the phone.

It rang again, he was just about to pick it up when he heard Born come back into the apartment. He had peeped the caller I.D. on the wall phone in the kitchen coming in. "You, uh gonna answer it or what?"

Devone rushed behind him. She hoped Born didn't recognize the number, and said, "Don't worry about it, it's probably nobody…just bills." She rushed the both of them out the door and locked it.

Born was first as they headed for the stairway then stopped and blocked the entrance. "I know the type of muthafucka you are, I really don't hold it against you."

"Yeah, alright c'mon, let's go." Derek tried to brush past him. Born held him. "But uh, just don't write a check yo' ass can't cash…"

"What" Derek sounded confused.

"You know…for your bills, remember?" He looked up the hall at the apartment. "That's what."

Derek finally pushed past, then looked at him. "I hear you."

"Good," Born replied. "Loud and clear I hope."

****

"Here you go, Detective," the young red-headed rookie cop said to Giovanni just before he sat down in front of all the folders he had stacked on his desk. "Need anything else, just call."

"Sure thing," Giovanni said as he looked up from the desk. Looking him up and down he asked, "Hey, uh, are you any relation to, Bobby Ravanel?"

The young rookie officer stood up straight and beamed proudly. "Yes, sir, I'm his son."

Giovanni stood also, reached for his hand and shook it. "Your father was a good man."

On that note the young man looked down, sad, and said, "Yes…he was." He turned and walked out of the office as Giovanni just stared.

Detective Bobby Ravanel was killed ten years ago in the line of duty. He'd responded to the scene of a botched-up Bodega robbery and was shot dead. He didn't even have a chance to use his weapon. Giovanni had just joined the force and Ravanel was one of the only few white officers that embraced him. Taught him the ropes, so he wouldn't get his ass killed, he would say.

'*Yeah, a good man,*' he thought as he sat back down and picked through the folders Bobby's son had just bought in. '*Okay,*' he thought. '*Let's see.*' "The building had two entrances. The killer came through the front. The door looked like it was pried open. The back door was unlocked and halfopen. It was late, the streets would have been empty at that time of the night. He or she wouldn't have been seen. But, why would the door be pried open? Maybe, Khalid wasn't there? Wonder if he would have opened the door. Did he know who it was? Cause hell he could have run out the back door. The building manager never reported any theft of any kind.

Nothing was taken, or was it?" He leafed through some folders and came across one that was marked conspicuously: Warehouses-The Moors Institute of Science.

He'd asked the young man to research some names for him. Locations, and he'd done well. He went through all the names of the tenants in the building at that time. He dug through some logs that were given to the police, then. The ins and outs of the building and noticed there were shipments made frequently, but not there. To addresses in Brooklyn, Flushing Avenue the Bushwick area near the projects. But someone there signed for the deliveries. He pondered on it and remembered the area. The buildings were abandoned, but still, it rang bells. It was staring him right in the face, but he couldn't figure it out.

He sat back in his chair on its hind legs and kicked his heels up on his desk trying to recall, then it hit him. The break-ins, a couple of drug busts over there. The word on the street was that that was where the big dope man Carlos kept his stash. All the locations were all on Flushing Avenue. But it didn't mean anything, it could be a coincidence. There were lots of factories over there. He reached over and picked up the phone. "Hey Sarge, send in that new cop…red headed." "Bobby's boy?" he asked.

"Yeah, Bobby's boy."

"Ricky! Okay, hold on."

He needed some research done quick and the young rookie cop had already proven he was the man for the job.

He rushed through the door asking, "Sir, something wrong?"

Giovanni smiled, the kid was nervous, just like he used to be. "Naw, everything's cool. I need you to do some more research for me."

"Yes, sir, no problem."

"Dig up any break-ins or any activity from Flushing Avenue factories dating back…hmmm, let's say ten years, to start. Homicides also, we might get lucky. Bring them all to me. Look here kid, it might take a day or so, then we…"

"We…sir?"

"Yeah, we…we need to dig through them, okay."

"What exactly are we looking for, sir?"

"Well, let's just get the facts first." He turned to leave, but Giovanni stopped him and added. "One more thing."

Ricky held on to the knob of the door tightly as he turned. Still nervous. "What's that, sir?"

"Kill the sir bit, Detective Giovanni is good enough."

"Yes, sir…Detective Giovanni." He turned back around again, this time all teeth. He stopped once again, but this time he reached into his shirt pocket and said. "Oh, yeah, Sarge told me to give you this."

Giovanni took the yellow scratch pad filled with numbers and the different times he'd been called. "Damn, tell Sarge thanks."

The note read: Central Booking: 5-6-3-8-1-1-7; 9:30 a.m. call from Inmate Ali. Next line: 9:59 a.m., 10:18 am, 11:19 am, 1:28 p.m., 3:10 p.m., 4:18 p.m. He checked his watch, it was already 5:05 p.m.

He picked up his phone, dialed and barked into it, "Hey, Central Booking, it's Detective Giovanni. I need to talk to the Captain on duty. Now!"

Dunya: The Do Or Die

CHAPTER NINE

Rasheed had just made it through the hole in the fence surrounding the handball court in front of 811 when he spotted his mother surrounded by a bunch of cops.

"Move back!" he hollered rushing toward her.

They charged at him, and one yelled, "Hey fella! Who the hell are you!"

"Just back the fuck off her..." He inadvertently reached into his jacket.

At the same time, they all reached for their guns. "Alright, just stay where you are!"

He froze, with his hand still in his pocket, standing motionless.

Waseema stepped in front of him with her arm outstretched, yelling, "Officers, this is my son!"

The cops still didn't stand down. Evidently misinformed, they continued questioning. "Wasn't your son the one involved in the shootout?" They slowly stepped toward Rasheed, inching closer and closer.

Ice reached into his coat for his gun and was ready to blaze if he had to. But Devone pulled up next to him and held his hand. Checking out the setting and peeping out the other cops as they rushed toward him.

She said, "Rasheed, just be cool."

Rasheed slowly looked around and the situation dawned on him. One sudden move and he was dead. "Whoa...hold up..." he said, as he cautiously, and very slowly put his free hand up in the air. "Okay, I'm going to pull my other hand out...slowly."

The officers kept their aim on him. Then, Giovanni appeared pushing his way through the crowd and ran up next to them.

His hand was on his gun also. "What's going on here?" he asked.

"Sir, he ran up on us out of nowhere as we tried questioning the victim. Then he grabbed for something in his jacket."

Giovanni walked carefully over to where Waseema stood, in front of Rasheed. "Okay, just hold on, I know these people." He focused his attention on Waseema. "I really don't know what's going on here but, right now, I need you to step away from your son."

But instead, she pulled Rasheed closer and said, "Hell no! Y'all won't kill my son! I know how y'all kill these young boys around here. Then say it was an accident. Hell no!"

"Ms. Waseema…" Giovanni drew near to her cautiously, watching as the other officers enclosed them. Hoping no one's finger twitched or anyone got a little too anxious and pleaded with her. "We really don't know what he was reaching for, c'mon now. I got this trust me."

She slowly started backing away, but only after Rasheed prompted her to.

"Ma, it's okay," he said, slowly pulling his hand out of his jacket, along with a black bandana. "I was just reaching for this. Saw her crying, that's all."

Two officers rushed him. "Hands up over your head. Now!" Then wrestled him to the ground and started searching him. "He's clean!"

Ice and Devone slowly backed away from the crowd, not wanting to be next. Very aware that it definitely wouldn't have gone quite as well for them. They were both strapped.

Giovanni reached down and extended his hand to Rasheed, but Waseema pushed it away saying, "That's alright! Don't help now, he's still breathing!"

Giovanni started apologizing, "Rasheed, I'm sorry about that. We didn't know. I mean damn, after-all there was a shoot-out."

Born moved in instead and helped him up. Waseema was still being questioned by the cops until Giovanni stepped in between them.

"I got this, officers." He moved her over toward the building after receiving high-browed frowns, and silent murmurs from the other cops that were standing around. He asked, "What happened? All we know is that there was gunplay. They said your apartment looks like hell. Blood…bullets… shotgun blasts, a little war zone."

She looked over at Rasheed and he asked her the same question. "Yeah, Ma. What happened?"

She glanced up at him, then Giovanni and said, "I can only tell you both, what I've been telling them. I really don't know much except for what, Mustapha told me."

"Alright then."

They all went to the benches and sat, then Derek signaled to Rasheed that Born and him were going upstairs to look around.

Rasheed nodded and then looked at his mother and said, "I'm listening."

Rasheed stood up from the bench after hearing the details of the shooting, at least what his mother had explained so far, and cursed Felix. "Damn you!"

Giovanni peered out into the crowd that had gathered and asked, "Where's Mustapha, now? Is he alright?"

Waseema hunched her shoulders. "I don't know, he left before you all got here. He didn't get shot or anything that I do know…" Pausing for a second, she asked, "Can I go now? I'm tired." Long worry lines across her face showed signs of weariness. It had been a long stressful day for her.

"Okay, just hold on for a sec."

Giovanni walked over to where his superiors had gathered and pointed Waseema's way, they shook their heads slightly. He came back over to them and said, "My bosses say you can leave. Someone will be assigned to your case, might even be me. Hell, no one will probably want it anyway too much work. And oh, don't go back into the apartment until fingerprints and ballistics finish up, okay. And, don't worry," Giovanni continued saying as he looked up at the windows to her apartment. "They should be through before nightfall, but not sure if they'll let you stay. It'll more than likely be taped off."

"Ma, you can come to my place, you know that."

"I know Rasheed, but I still don't want to leave the place open like that."

Ravanel walked over to where they stood and waved Giovanni over. "Excuse me." Giovanni got closer. "You might want to take a look at this." He held up a small plastic bag that held some vials of crack cocaine.

"Where'd you got that?" Giovanni asked.

"It was found underneath the window that was busted out."

Waseema peeped over and saw it. She knew that was probably the bag that Mustapha tossed out of the window. She definitely knew now that she would have to go back into the apartment and look through his room, especially the closet.

Rasheed nudged her, and whispered, "I told him about that shit." He'd seen it too.

"Okay, bag it up and take it in. I'll file the report," Giovanni said to him.

The officer looked over at Rasheed and Waseemaa suspiciously and asked, "You want me to check the place out… sir?"

Giovanni knew to do that would turn up even more perhaps and knowing Waseema's present situation he didn't want it done at least until he dug up more information first. He'd have to come back later for that. "No, I'll need a warrant first."

Ravanel turned towards the building and thought, '*Warrant*?' He had probable cause. He could just as well do it himself. He glanced over towards the gold badges that were assembled near the street. He knew they would have his back.

Giovanni stepped in front of him and said sternly, "Didn't I say I got this, officer?"

"Uh…yes, sir."

"I, don't have to tell you how to play by the rules, do I?" Giovanni had a good idea what the officer wanted to do. It was textbook, but he needed time. Maybe, he should bring the officer in on what he knew. *'If he was built anything like his old man, I would,'* he thought. He turned his attention back to Waseema and Rasheed.

"What was up with all that?" Rasheed snapped. "My mom and brother don't do no drugs!" He glanced over at his mother, all she could do was hold her head down and sigh. She knew more than what she was letting on. He quickly silenced himself, saying under his breath. "Now what?"

"Well, to be honest, it don't look good…at all. You better believe they'll be searching for your brother. They'll have questions…plenty of them."

Waseema sighed again saying, "Why now…all this?"

Rasheed pulled her closer to him, comforting her. "I don't know, Ma, I really don't know."

But, strangely enough, he did, unbeknownst to him. It was all about what that had done to Carlos.

Giovanni glanced over his shoulder at the crisp white shirts getting into their vehicles and said to them, "I've got to go. There'll most likely be a briefing and I need to be there. Anyone need a ride anywhere?" "Nah, we good," Rasheed said to him.

"Okay then." Giovanni reached for Waseema's hand and shook it gently. "Ms. Waseema, I'll talk to you later."

Looking up at him she smiled. "Okay."

"By the way, how's your daughter doing?"

"Damn, Shaheeda, I forgot. I was supposed to go see her!"

"Calm down, Ma! I'll get you there, but you really need to get some rest."

"That's a wise suggestion," Giovanni added. "She should be alright. Those fellas still there, right?"

"Yeah, they were there when I left…" Rasheed stopped himself.

"Oh, okay, Rasheed. I didn't know you were there. I was looking for you." Giovanni turned and started to walk off.

"Damn!" He realized he'd slipped, he asked his mother, "Now, he's gone. Where's Mustapha?"

"Baby, he went uptown, he had to leave. They said they were going to kill him. So, I sent him to Harlem. To my mother's."

Rasheed kissed her on the forehead and said, "You did the right thing. But a contract?"

"He said something about a Felix person. Who is he, Rasheed? Why is he after, Mustapha?"

"Got to ask him that, Ma."

Ice and Devone walked over. Devone asked, "You alright?"

"I'm alright, Sweetie." She looked at Ice who asked the same thing and nodded yes.

Ice started telling Rasheed, "Devone spoke to a cop friend she knows, she said they should be wrapping things up in a few."

"I'll go with you upstairs and we can get some things together. Born and Derek are up there too, they can help," Devone added.

"I can ride over to a hardware store real quick and find something to cover the window up in the backroom.

"Housing should come and fix it in the morning," Devone said.

"Thanks, y'all." Waseema hugged Devone and looked up at Ice. "You're a good man." She stood up fixing her blouse then started running her hands through her long silky hair in an alluring way.

This prompted Devone to ask herself, "*Where the hell did that come from?*"

Ice stared at her as she moved forcing himself to turn away from the femme fetale that stood before him, all up in his face. "Rasheed, I gotta go," he said backing up. "I'll be back in a little while."

Devone squinted her eyes at that. '*So that was the guy,*' she thought. '*All this time Ice was that dude.*' She stood and glanced over at Rasheed, checking him out as well. It was a good time to talk and expose her devious plan. She had to let him know how she felt, and what Mya was doing with her brother. "Rasheed, you ready to go upstairs?"

Rasheed paid her no mind as he watched his mother checking out Ice. He questioned why she was staring so hard. "*What's going on with that?*" he asked himself.

Ice was no slouch, he had swagger, and his well-built, lofty figure of sixtwo, two-hundred and fifteen pounds was well taken care of. He was still fixated when Born called him from off the terrace interrupting his thoughts and motioned for them to come upstairs. Devone wrapped her jacket around Waseema and they pushed their way through the crowd that had gathered.

Dunya: The Do Or Die

****

Another hour had gone by as Ali stretched out on the hard, cold slab intending to be a bunk. Years old decay had reduced it to a huge chipped up concrete block. He tossed around impatiently as he thought about his impending conversation with Detective Giovanni. He sprang to his feet, something had just registered and hit him hard. He rushed over to the cell door only to be met by a C.O. turning the key and opening the steel door. He was bringing in a rough looking, bearded, handcuffed man looking to be in his late fifties.

"C.O., what's up with my visit!" Ali shouted.

"Get back!" he shouted as he took out a handcuff key to take off the belly chains and leg irons the man had on.

Ali complied he didn't need any trouble he was too close now. Any cause for alarm or incident would mean a couple of days in the tank on lockdown. He damn sure couldn't afford that. He'd miss his visit it was now or never. He had to delay his trip to Rikers Island by means of information. Maybe, they might even give him a bond being that he was going to snitch.

"If you hear anything…" he said quietly.

The C.O. pointed him back to the concrete slab and said to the other man he'd just brought in, "You'll be here for a while until your lawyer comes." The man hunched his shoulders in response. The C.O. turned his attention to Ali. "He should be on his way soon. Something happened at his precinct. He did call, though. He said he'll be on his way once he got free."

Ali knew from the way the C.O. expressed that he was being straight. There was no need to harass him any further. "Alright, just let me know when he gets here."

"Trust me, I got you," the C.O. said as he closed the cell door and locked it.

Hearing the thrusting of the lock closing the door, he let out a long groan and stress set in. The long lines across his forehead had grown. If it wasn't for his already bald head, his hairline would have receded long ago. He turned toward the man who was with him in the cell and asked, "What you in for?" He figured maybe if he started a conversation it might pass the time.

He looked over at him and answered, "Murder."

"Yeah." Ali nodded. "Me too."

Dean Hamid

The hell with hearing the details. Most worth their weight wouldn't let you know anyway. He stepped toward the small steel-encased cell door window and stared down the tier in no apparent thought. Suddenly, he was caught off balance by an arm around his neck. Before he knew, he was slammed to the bare floor and was being dragged to the far end of the cell. No chance to yell before he was met by a kick to his jaw. As he reeled back in pain, he glimpsed up seeing the man charging at him. He tried to duck underneath him, but it was no use. He caught all the weight in his chest and blood spat out his mouth as he made an attempt to crawl toward the door to holler out for a C.O. He was taken totally off guard and didn't have time to defend himself.

The short stocky prisoner grabbed him by the ankles yelling, "Where the hell do you think you're going? Take it like a man!"

Ali looked up in the face of his attacker trying to shield the blows being thrown at him and yelled, "Who the fuck are you? Why are you doing this?"

The beating stopped only because he was being pinned down by him. He said to Ali, "I was sent to take care of you."

"Take care of...what!"

He raised up some and said, "You really don't know do you?" He grabbed him by the collar, picked up his bruised body and tossed him against the wall.

Ali couldn't believe the strength he had. He was just a little over five foot, but thick as hell. He knew he had to fight back. At least long enough for the C.O. to come back. He made a feeble attempt at taking a stance. He clutched his hand to his rib cage. It hurt like all hell. Something had to be broken, and his arm was no better.

Still, he balanced himself and said, "Alright muthafucka, we going down with a fight."

He cracked his knuckles and said, "Sure whatever, but you asked for it!"

"Yeah, yeah, yeah, whatever! Who sent you?" Ali hollered.

"You mean to tell me you kill a man and don't remember?"

"What...when?"

"California!"

Ali's eyes damn near popped out his head when he heard him. His head seemed to literally explode thinking to himself. No, not now! "Who sent you?"

"Vito, now, that's all you need to know!"

'Damn, how the hell did Vito manage to catch up to me? After all the time that has passed,' he thought. He'd put miles between them. "Look, maybe we can

work something out?" Ali tried stalling. "I got this deal going on," he pleaded.

"You think you can buy your way out of this?" He rushed Ali and they both fell hard to the floor. He thrust his hand on his neck constricting his breathing and said, "You won't get out of this."

Ali struggled under the weight, squirming, trying to get free, but every move he made only made it worse. The load on his throat and air passage only made it hard for him to breath, and he gagged. He had him, he thought, '*Why doesn't he get it over with? Choke me out, if that's what he wants to do*'. "I can pay the money I owe I promise." Ali gasped in between breaths.

The stranger looked down at him with a slight grin. His teeth were cracked and jagged, and spit in his face. "You remember the man you killed?"

He remembered. "He was trying to kill me!" he yelled back.

"No, he just wanted to kick your ass! Put the tim down. Vito had already given you a warning. Hell, he knew you would take forever to pay him, anyway. He just sent a man over to put the tim down, that's all!"

Ali could see in his eyes that this was personal. His mind flashed back to that morning as he made his way out to go to the racetrack and play the horses before he made it to work. This young kid, he thought might have been a delivery boy or something, knocked at the door. He told him he hadn't ordered anything. He didn't see a pizza, a bag of groceries or anything. He figured maybe he was at the wrong door.

Never would have suspected a thing until he suddenly busted through the door wrestling him to the ground. Then, he pulled a gun. Ali thought it was a stick-up, so instinctively he responded by grabbing at the gun. Trying to pry it out the boy's hands. He damn sure wasn't going to shoot him, but he sure as hell didn't want to get shot either. Once he got it, he'd hold it up long enough to haul ass. Then toss it, that was the plan.

He didn't want any trouble, the Feds were already searching for him, for what, he didn't know. So, he scrambled to his feet and pointed the gun back at him. He never would have thought he'd lunge, and the gun went off. Ali stepped back and all he could see was blood squirting out of a dark hole in the boy's chest. His body was hurled against the wall. Ali jetted for the door, not looking back. It was too late for the kid now. His eyes had already rolled back in his head. He was gone!

He damn sure couldn't afford the police messing with him. He'd have to leave town indefinitely. He'd meet up with Vito to give him the forty racks he owed him later, or at least an excuse.

Another lie. "I didn't know who he was!" Ali screamed.

The man suddenly pulled out a knife from underneath his shirt. It wasn't a shank, but a double-edged stiletto and said, "He was my son!"

"Shit..." Ali mumbled under his breath. That's what he didn't need. Maybe, if he could just wrestle from up under him, then rush the door and holler for the C.O. He looked over at it, it was as if he read his mind.

He was punched square on the jaw for even thinking about it. "No muthafucka, it won't be that easy!"

The door finally opened, and the C.O. popped his head in. "Everything alright?" The sarcasm spat from his tongue as he stared over at the man that was on top of Ali with a knife in his hand.

Ali screamed out, "Hell no, it ain't alright! Help me!" He figured the C.O. would bust in and help. Wrestle the man to the ground, but he just shook his head, backed up and shut the door closed behind him.

"What the fuck?" Ali couldn't believe it.

The man raised the knife up and sheared at Ali. "This is a contract hit. Vito knows a lot of people...a whole lot of people." He sliced him across the face as Ali grimaced in pain. "You son of a bitch. You didn't even call the police." He sliced him again. "We found his freakin' body rotting in a stinking hotel after three days." This time he plunged it into his throat. "You left him to die...my son! You left him to die...you bastard!"

All Ali could hope for was Detective Giovanni coming through the door. He didn't want to die, not like this. His mind started to go black as the half-crazed man stabbed at his chest over and over. He couldn't even feel it anymore. Maybe, it was better like this. Maybe, this was his destiny after all. As he laid there, his mind started to dim. He couldn't stop thinking about what it was he wanted to tell Giovanni. That the papers belonged to a couple of warehouses. Deeds, they looked like. Titles to properties in Brooklyn. The names on them he didn't recognize, but he knew the locations though. Flushing Avenue, down near Bushwick Projects.

Frank had turned his back for a minute while searching the safe and he got nosy and picked up some of the papers that were scattered about. Assuming them to be bonds. Figured he'd steal one, or two. That's when he noticed the different names. Then, Frank unexpectedly turned and caught him reading them. He snatched them out of his hands, reached into the safe, grabbed a stack and shoved it at him.

The hell with it, Ali figured, especially once he flipped through the money Frank had thrown at him. Frank then gathered up the rest of the papers. Stuffed them into a small brown legal briefcase, and it was then that Khalid had come in, catching them.

'*But it was too late for him,*' Ali thought as he laid there feeling the blood ooze from his body. Painful, but he somehow twisted his head toward the man who was responsible for his now imminent demise. He was huddled in the corner, mumbling, murmuring to himself.

He was crying in pain at the remembrance of his deceased son. He knew avenging his death would never bring him back. He dealt with that issue inwardly, mentally. He never should have let the boy in on the business anyway; gambling, extortion, loan sharking. He wasn't ready and he told him. All he had to do was cook the books. He was smart like that. He didn't want him to be a thug like him.

Vito had flatly told him no when he asked him, but the young boy begged more and more until he finally gave in. So, he gave him this small job, in and out. A couple of threats, that was all. But the boy took it to the next level, sneaking his father's Revolver out of the house. Thinking he'd really put it down and make the old man proud. Possibly get a couple of dollars, but it didn't work out that way. It didn't work out that way at all. Now, his only son was dead, and he wasn't coming back regardless of all the blood that now pooled up on the floor. He cried out bitterly.

Now, here it was, the hole in Ali's throat made it difficult for him to breath. He started choking and spitting up blood. When he realized he was no longer breathing, the darkness had overcome him, and, it was over with.

****

Detective Giovanni arrived at Central Booking shortly after 7:00 pm. He was tired, it had been a busy day. The incidents in Bushwick and the reports that followed had worn him out, but he still had to chase down this lead. He hollered out to Ravanel that he had to make a run. As he entered the busy hub he ran into an old buddy of his, Mike Davis. He and Mike put in work at the 83rd Precinct back when they were rookies coming out of the Academy before Mike moved on to the Feds.

"Hey, what's up, Mike-Mike!" He embraced him asking him about his wife and kids.

Mike told him he was divorced, and the kids were doing well. He just caught hell keeping them in line. Giovanni chuckled he couldn't believe he had two boys grown enough for high school already. Had it been that long? He felt old just thinking about it. He asked him why he was at Central Booking.

"Don't you work Homicide at the nine-o, Mickey?"

"I'm just sniffing out a lead. One of the inmates here might have some information I could use. On an old cold case that may be relevant. What about you?" At that moment Giovanni looked around and noticed the buzz, he'd walked into. He never did take notice to the ambulance outside in front, parked directly next to a coroner's van. Cops were all over the place. He pointed to a uniformed C.O. in cuffs over by the elevators and asked the Captain at the control desk. "What the hell happened here?"

"All hell broke loose, C.O. snuck in a hitman to take a cat out. He would have gotten away with it, too. But dude, the perp flipped out and did himself in when he tried to sneak him out. A bloody mess upstairs." Giovanni shook his head and said, "Crazy, I'm here to see Ali Abdullah."

The Captain shot him a look, then pointed towards the coroner's van. "Right there...he's the bloody one."

"What the hell?"

Mike walked up right behind and asked, "Everything alright? And, what's the deal with that guy?" he said as he turned towards the cuffed officer.

"Like I said, someone snuck the guy in. He was the one that got caught. If you ask me, there's a whole lot more inside situation to it."

Giovanni looked over at the C.O. in cuffs, then back to the Captain. "Hey, the one that was killed was the guy I came to talk to. You mind if I ask him a few questions?"

He looked around, especially towards Deputy Warden. "One or two Detective make it quick, alright."

"No problem." Giovanni eased closer to the C.O. and asked, "Who sent you? That's all I want to know. No details or nothing."

The C.O. looked at Giovanni, then the Captain. "Hell, it don't matter now one way or another. It's over for me."

"Hey, Mike, watch my back." Mike nodded but got a little closer to them, ear hustling.

"Vito, that's who."

"Vito...Vito?" Giovanni rubbed at his chin thinking out loud.

"West Coast," the C.O. said.

Mike pointed a finger at him and snapped, "Damn, Vito, from Cali?"
"Yeah, that's him."

Giovanni shot an eye over at Mike, he figured something. A couple of C.O.s came over and started whisking the handcuffed C.O. away once the white-shirted Deputy peeped over and saw them. Mike and Giovanni eased back over toward the Captain.

He said, "That's all I can do Detective. They'd have my badge if they found out I did that much."

Giovanni dapped him and said, "'Preciate it, that was good enough." Then, he turned to Mike, "Vito, huh?"

"You remember, Vito from back in the day? Big fat dude from Spanish Harlem. Ran dope for the Los Andres Cartel out of Columbia. It was a big bust remember a whole trailer full of cocaine."

"Okay, now I remember! We pulled doubles watching the damn thing. Yeah okay, I remember now. But wasn't that a Fed case?"

"That it was, and that it still is. That's why I'm here. Your boy was being held for the Feds. Somebody on the inside had to let someone know that he was here. Even you wasn't supposed to know anything."

Giovanni walked over to one of the plastic body bags and unzipped it. "Is this him, Ali?"

"Naw, that's the guy who did him in. Another West Coast flunky. Petty loan shark...extortion, the name's Peter Cote. An immigrant from Columbia works directly for, Vito."

Giovanni zipped the bag back and walked towards the other, then unzipped that one. "That's your guy," Mike said. "Wonder what his ties were to, Vito?"

Giovanni zipped it back and said, "Okay, Vito...Victor Reyes Ortiz...he's the Cartel's chief extortioner and loan shark man. He hauled ass to California from New York years ago. But still, it don't add up."

Mike noticed some dark suit and tie wearing men walk through the door flashing badges and said, "The Feds, Mickey. I gotta go, take care, and keep in touch."

Giovanni embraced him again. "I will, Mike...I will."

He made his way through the now crowded lobby, then out a side entrance. On the way to his car, he tried piecing together the puzzle that Ali started. What the hell did this have to do with Khalid's death? What the hell did he have to tell me? He got in the car, cranked it up and thought to himself, *It's got to have something to do with whatever was stolen that night. It's got to!*

CHAPTER TEN

Malik was headed out the door when he heard the ringing. He turned back around toward his office and rushed over to the phone.

"Ah, Malik, my friend." It was Felix.

"Felix, what's up now?"

"I need to talk."

"About what?"

"I think you know what."

Malik took a deep breath and pulled out the chair from his desk before turning toward the window and closing the blinds, not noticing the big-bodied Mercedes Benz parked inconspicuously across the street and sat down.

"Okay, Felix, talk."

"Malik...Malik, you act like you have a...uh, what do you call it? A problem...yeah, a problem with me calling?"

"C'mon, Felix, you know what time it is. What do you want?"

"Wait a minute, I would not be calling you if we did not have a business arrangement..."

Malik banged his fist on the desk and said, "Listen, Felix, and listen well. We are not partners, of any kind, and I really don't like calling..."

"No, shut up!" Felix's patience had run thin and Malik was treading heavily on it. "You listen the fuck up you black bastard! I said I want to talk to you. I want to talk to you, right fuckin' now! Who the hell do you think you're fuckin' with?"

Malik sensed the anger, and already disturbed by his tone of voice asked, "Okay, okay, where at?" He obeyed and fell right in line. Felix was way too deep in his pockets for him to buck. At least not yet, if ever.

"I just saw you close your blinds. So, you know I'm watching you. Don't try anything stupid. Come outside, I'll be waiting in the car."

He got up, walked over to the window and peeped through the blinds looking over on Gates Avenue, he spotted the parked Benz. "Yeah, yeah, I'll be out in a few."

"No, Malik, I said now!"

The phone went dead in his ear. He hung it up on his end and sat staring blank-faced at the wall. Thoughts running through his head like crazy. Asking himself over and over again, how'd he get this deep? What the hell do I do? I need to get out of this, now. His reflection was interrupted abruptly by the honking of a horn from outside, Felix's. He reached into his desk drawer, he stared at the loaded gun and took it out. Checking the safety, he slid it into his briefcase. He was on his way out the door, then he turned back and gazed into his office.

He stared at pictures hung on the wall. Friends…family…many lives changed as a result of his involvement. His chair on the City Council. He was moving closer and closer to a Mayoral bid. He glanced again. Khalid, homeboy. He'd wished over and over that Khalid would have stuck to the plan and trusted him. Things would have been different. Now, he had to come face to face with the realities that Felix could expose, on a regular basis.

"I'm coming…I'm coming." He sighed as the horn blared. He shut the door silently behind him.

Felix pulled in front of the old Met food store that was now converted into makeshift office space properties. He waited patiently for Malik to come outside. Looking around in paranoia, he never did like being in BedStuy. He complained about there being too many cocolos. The Spanish lexeme for niggers. The window was halfway down as he barked at him coming out the door.

"C'mon, hurry the hell up!"

Malik ignored him best he could, taking the time to acknowledge and smiling politely at his neighbors who passed by. "Okay, Felix, here I am," he said as he got in and slid over from Felix with his back up against the door. Felix stomped the gas pedal and sped off down Lewis Avenue.

"Next time I tell you I'm waiting for you, hurry up! You know I hate this place. Fucking cocolos all over."

"Felix, what is it you want?"

He looked at Malik shaking his head at him and said, "You know, you live in this dream world, but you're just as dirty as me. If not more, you despise me, don't you?"

The Benz pulled up in front of a bodega, and Spanish music blasted loudly in the background. "Now, this is much better." He cut the engine and angled his wide bellied girth facing Malik. The struggle made him breathe hard. "I need to pick up some things from…"

"Things…what things?"

"Look muthafucka." Felix slammed his fist hard on the console between the seats, rattling the frame, and hollered, "I'm tired of playing these fuckin' games! What thing? You little bitch! The fucking money, and my fuckin' dope!" He snarled and got closer in Malik's face. "That's what things."

Malik continued to maintain his cool. He knew how volatile and explosive he could be. He pulled the briefcase closer to him. "Felix, I only do what I do for you." He motioned calmly. "Like a lease."

That only made Felix more pissed. His eyes grew wide as he stared at him. His lips trembled as he grinned slyly looking him up and down. "Okay." Gradually, he reached underneath his huge ass, pulled out a shiny. nickel-plated, .9mm and pointed it at Malik's head. He froze, not even trying to blink an eye, Felix said, "You want to play, I see. Okay, then let's play." He pulled back the hammer. "Yeah, let's play."

Malik stared off from him, not wanting to excite him. He knew any sudden moves would be his last. Then, on top of that, he was the one with the concealed weapon. Felix's paid lawyers would chew it up in court. Claim self-defense all day long and spit a murder charge straight out. He carefully turned his head back toward him.

"Look, Felix, calm down."

"No, no, you want to play and uh…by the way. I know you have a gun in your briefcase. Thinking about killing me, eh?"

"No, of course not, I always carry it…for protection."

"From me?"

"That's not what I meant, Felix. Now, come on, put the gun down before…"

Felix leaned into him and pushed the gun hard into his temple. "The next time you want to play games, it will be your last. You hear boy?"

"Yeah, man, I hear you," his voice quivered.

Felix finally lowered the gun and laughed in his face. "You should have seen your face. You looked like a fuckin' monkey!" Malik stared at the floor as he humiliated him, thinking to himself about how he put himself in this position. "Okay, I need you to be at the building we just let…"

"You talking about my office?"

"Yeah, yeah, right. You're fucking office, whatever." Felix stuffed the gun buck underneath himself and said, "The place share, the dope, and money is my stash house. That better, you need to leave the book loading dock open. So, I can move some more money, and uh...let's say, about a quarter ton..."

"What, a quarter two of dope. You're bringing in some drugs!"

Felix looked out the window perplexed, then back at him like he was crazy. "You niggers like this shit! Look out the window, look!" He pointed to buildings where crackheads and junkies moved in and out copping dope. "This is all you fucking people want!"

Malik stared until he couldn't bear it any longer. From what he was seeing, he was right. This is what they seem to want. Dropping his head in shame, the only thing he could manage to come from his lips was, "What time?"

"Good." Felix smiled. "I'll call you, just be there." Malik started to get out of the car, he stopped him. "No, I'll drop you back off. I'm not finished with you, yet."

"I've got to go, Felix, I'll be there alright."

"That's too far to walk. C'mon, I'll drop you off." He reached slowly underneath his seat toward the concealed intimidation from earlier and said, "Okay."

Definitely not wanting to pursue that situation and incense him anymore today, he asked, "What's up then?"

Felix cranked the car up and pulled a U-turn in the middle of the twoway traffic amidst curses and name-calling, all aimed at him. "Fuck them," he said, giving them all the finger.

Turning up Sunner Avenue he gunned it toward Gates Avenue and circled the whole length of the block. "I want to buy this whole fucking block," he said as he beamed coasting the car to a halt.

"A whole block!" Malik stared at him in utter disbelief. It almost seemed comical, and if the tim hadn't been put down on him earlier he would have laughed at him. "Are you crazy?"

"No, not crazy." He reached into the middle console, pulled out a brown manila envelope and shoved it toward him. "It's business, it's always about business."

He opened it asking, "What the hell is this?" He pulled out a couple of sheets of the contract he had in his hand and read briefly through it as Felix ogled at the prostitutes who strolled Broadway.

"One hand washes the other."

"Wait a minute!" Malik yelled as he continued reading the paperwork he was given. "This is made out already..."

"Right, all you have to do is sign them."

"No way." He threw them on the console. "This'll make it seem like I'm responsible." He shook his head at the thought. "Hell no. What are you kidding me?"

"No, I'm not kidding you!" Felix turned toward him. "You wanted us to take this Ali guy out for you, right? Did you think it would cost you nothing?" Felix pointed his finger to his face. "Let me tell you something, and you listen good. The Los Andres Cartel put you in this…" He grabbed at his tie. "…situation, a fucking City Councilman. But, you're just a crook in a suit hiding behind a desk, that's all. It's strange how you forget that you brought us into this neighborhood!"

"Hold up now, I never meant to."

"Fuck what you meant! It is what it is, you created this shit!" He pointed to the squalor around him. "We made all the moves you wanted us to do. We killed those you wanted to be killed. We didn't always agree, but we did it anyway. We put you in office so you could set up the warehouses you stole from your other so-called Muslim brothers that you set up. What was the name you told us?"

"The Moors."

"Yeah, them, and we paid you good. But you see my friend, it's still not over. There's more work to be done."

Malik looked over at him gritting his teeth and said, "It's got to stop."

Felix leaned back, watching the pain rack up in Malik's face.

"Look, let's be real. We've been together for a while. Now I understand you don't like me, but we both have this big brother lurking over our shoulder…the Cartel. We both have to jump through hoops to please them, whether we like it or not. So, let's just jump through this hoop and get it over with, okay?"

Malik bit down hard on his lip. He knew he was right. As much as he detected the man across from him, he had indeed said a mouthful. It is what it is. "You need to take out the guy I told…"

"We got that covered."

"Okay, we can't make the same mistakes we made years ago. Hell, I'm still paying for them. These papers have to be secured a whole lot better."

"You're right, we never did find out what happened to them the last time," Felix smirked. "You should have killed that Ali guy then. I knew he would be trouble."

"Yeah, well, you wanted to trust the white boy…Frank. You see what happened with that." Malik opened his briefcase and slid the envelope inside. "It can't happen again I'll sign these and have them ready once I look over them. I probably need to make some calls. So, I can sell this whole thing to the other council members, then dress it up."

Felix cranked up the car. "Okay, cocolo, now we're talking. Now, get the fuck out of my car. I need to find a guy, too. You know a guy from the projects in Bushwick named, uh…oh yeah, Mustapha?"

'Damn,' Malik thought. 'What the hell is going on now. Why is he looking for, Mustapha?' "Nah, name don't ring a bell. Why?" he answered.

Felix revved up the gas listening to the roar of the engine, then casually peeped over at Malik. He knew he was lying, and said, "I'm going to kill him."

He had to get in touch with Waseema and find out what happened. He didn't want to appear suspicious to Felix any more than he was, so he shrugged it off. "Nope don't know him, but check this out, Felix."

"What?"

"Stop calling me cocolo…you understand."

Malik got out of the car and stared at the Benz as it sped up Quincy Street. 'Felix has to be stopped,' he thought as he walked off. He couldn't let him get away with it. He knew he had to tell on him eventually. Pull someone in to stop him because, at this stage of the game he couldn't, he'd already sold out.

The apartment was torn up from the floor up with plaster chips all over the place. Waseema's brand new furniture had bullet holes from shotgun blasts, causing shreds of cushion, burnt and singed to litter the floor. The front door locks were busted up and blood was splattered over the walls. Waseema sobbed quietly to herself seeing the carnage. Devone comforted her the best she could, but she wasn't into it because her mind and eyes were fixed on Rasheed.

Waseema excused herself to go into Mustapha's room. She knew she needed to search the closet and underneath his mattress. She knew he hid money in the frame of the bed. But first, she had to b-line straight to her room and get some personal belongings. The biggest being her bank book. If they saw all the money she had put up, there would definitely be questions. Considering she had two others in false names. It would be a bad day.

"Excuse me, Devone, I need to go to the room. Get some things…"

"Sure okay, I'll be right here." Devone watched as she stepped into the room. She turned her attention toward Rasheed in the kitchen and stepped toward him. "Uh, Rasheed, can I do anything for you?"

Dean Hamid

Rasheed's mind was on Felix, on revenge. They rolled on his brother with his moms in the house. A straight violation. He turned toward Devone. There was no need to disrespect her, she only meant well. "Nah, I'm cool. Thanks."

Devone eased up closer to him and reached for his hand. He didn't resist, his mood was somber. "Look, if you need us to roll. You know we can make that happen."

"No, we need to stick with the plan. We gonna need the money anyway to really hit him hard."

She rubbed his hand. "Rasheed, you're so tense. What's going on with you?"

"What do you mean?"

"I mean, I'm not trying to be nosy, but you and Mya."

He sighed. "Does it show..."

"Yes." She moved in on him and started rubbing his back. "If things ain't right, baby. You might want to look elsewhere."

Rasheed smiled. "Elsewhere, huh...that easy?" He looked down at Devone's shapely figure. She was definitely a dime piece. Any man in his right man would go to hell and back for her. But for what it was worth, he had Mya. "I appreciate it but..."

"But what, Rasheed? Look, you deserve a good woman." She rubbed his chest and got closer. Licking her lips sensuously she added. "We know each other, I mean we can travel. Do nice things. You deserve that."

Rasheed was definitely ready to bite. Things were pretty rough lately between him and Mya. He looked into her brown, chinky eyes, and luscious lips. "But what happens with, Mya, huh?"

One thing Devone admired about him, he was loyal. He'd be a good man for the right woman, and right now she felt she was that woman. "I can take care of you." She reached up and rubbed his face. She was about to pull him closer and said, "You can stay with me tonight." Her hand reached for his crouch and she hit jackpot. His dick was hard as a rock, she caressed it. He looked at her and drew closer.

"Damn, Rasheed. What the hell was your brother shooting a cannon?" It was Born. "Big ass holes in the wall by the door. And, who's blood is this anyway?"

Devone rolled her eyes and sighed. "Damn." She kissed him on his earlobe and purred in his ears. He pushed her back gently, smiled and said, "We'll talk about it later."

112

He walked over to Born, pissed off. Devone shot Born the eye when he looked back at her. He turned his attention back to Rasheed, but only after he stared back at Devone a little harder.

He thought to himself. *'I bet she's in on the bullshit, too.'*

Waseema came back into the room with a bag. "Devone, help me with this, sweetheart."

"Yes, ma'am."

On their way to the door, she looked back one more time at the apartment as they closed the door. Born put the yellow police tape backup and Rasheed was already across the hall dividing out a few dollars to the neighbors to keep watch. Waseema stepped down the stairs with Devone, she reached over and grabbed her by the hand.

"I thank you. You're always there for me. Don't know where Mya is."

Devone smiled then cut her eyes over at Rasheed. "Anytime."

As far as she was concerned, she was in. Now she just had to get rid of that damn Mya, and if everything worked out. That wouldn't be too much longer now.

****

Malik didn't stray too far in anticipation of Felix's phone call. Hanging outside the building, he spoke to people briefly as they stopped by. He also opened the window to the office with the phone ringer turned up high so he could hear it when it rang. He thought about all the good he'd done in the area since opening shop in the seventies. The neighborhood, in turn, showed their love by respecting the building and surrounding community. A somewhat safe haven in the middle of the chaos that surrounded it. He threw occasional block parties and sponsored charity events, never asking for a dime. The money he'd use for these affairs came strictly from the cash Felix gave him for the storage of the dope.

He felt guilty at first but figured if he used the money for good it would somehow justify everything. So, no matter how many events. block parties, neighborhood watches, whatever he wanted to call it. He still sat waiting for a call from a man who hated everything he stood for. A man whose primary aim was to bring more drugs into the area. But for him, more drugs, more ill-gotten venues, made more money for his own personal political aspirations, and ways for him to shine.

"What's up, Malik?"

113

Ice had pulled up in front, Malik didn't notice he was still in thought. Ice had been there a while before he realized it. He finally answered. "Hey, my brother."

Ice got out of the car and dapped him. "I saw you out here coolin'. Drinking a little iced tea. That is iced tea, right?"

"You know I don't drink," he lied. Malik looked behind him at the car and said, "Even though sometimes I'm tempted nice ride."

"It is." Ice wiped a spot of dust from the hood of the shined-up Caddy. "Just got it." Ice returned the favor, he lied, too.

"Doing good for yourself I see. Where you coming from anyway? You's a good little way from the projects."

"Have to make a run to the hardware store to pick up a couple of rolls of duct-tape."

"Why, you plan on tying someone up?" He snickered.

Ice leaned back against the car and said, "Damn, you don't know, do you?"

"Know what?" Malik shook his head.

"Then, you need to call, Waseema."

Malik picked up his drink and rushed towards Ice. "What happened...is she alright?"

"Yeah, she's alright, but there was a shootout..."

"Hold up!" He almost dropped his drink. "A shoot-out!"

"In her apartment! Mustapha had to go into hiding and all that. Some guys rolled up on him."

"Who?" Malik leaned back on the car at the same time Ice did. Felix came to mind. '*That's probably why he asked about Mustapha,*' he thought.

"Some of Felix's people, I think. Said there's a contract on his head at least, that's what I got so far."

"Felix's boys, huh? A contract on Mustapha?" That he didn't know.

"Rasheed's over there with her now." Ice opened the door to get into the car and said, "You need to call..."

Malik stuck his head in the window and said back to him, "Definitely, thanks for letting me know."

Just then, someone called out Derek's name, a female. "Derek, baby! Hey, sweetie!"

Malik poked his head up, it was Mya. He looked back into the car at Ice and mouthed, "What the hell?"

"Mya had recognized the car and crossed the street in hopes of seeing Derek, or so she thought. Sticking her head in the passenger side window she seductively said, "Hey, Derek, baby…" she was cut short swiftly as Ice cut his eyes at her.

"What the hell is up with you!" he roared.

Realizing now that it wasn't Derek, but Ice and that she'd fucked up. Her eyes damn near rolled out her head. She wanted to scream, and Malik staring dead in her face didn't make matters any better. "Uh…uh…" she stammered trying to think of something to clean up the mess she made.

Ice always had an idea that something was up, and all this confirmed it. But still, he couldn't let her drift out there like that. He and Rasheed were still cool. He'd deal with her stupidity later.

"Damn, girl, I thought I told you to stop playing like that." He glanced over at Malik. "Someone may take it serious."

Catching his attempt at a cover-up, she slyly played along with it. "I know…I know, Malik we were just messing around…" "Inside joke," Ice chimed in.

Malik wasn't buying it, he stepped back a little way from the car and said, "Yeah, sure. Uh, excuse me, Mya. Ice, can I have a word with you…in private?"

Ice scowled at Mya, who flippantly got into the car with him. He briefly caught a glimpse of the tight-fitting jeans she had on as she stretched out her thick. shapely legs.

"Sure Malik…uh, what's up?" he asked as he got up and walked to the front of the building where Malik waited with his arms folded.

"Ice, what the hell is up? Derek messin' around with Rasheed's old lady?"

"No, they just friends." He couldn't cover up what he didn't know for a fact, so he had no choice but to come clean. "Okay, look, Malik. I really don't know what the hell is happening. I can only assume."

"Assume! Hell, she damn near dived into the car…that you said was yours, by the way."

"Alright, you got that, but like I said, I really don't know. I was gonna confront him about it when I got more facts, but…"

"But?" Malik cut him short. "I guess this is all the facts you needed then, huh?" He pointed towards the car and said, "Either you tell him, or I'll do it for you."

"Hold the fuck up, Malik!" Ice stepped back a little and poked his finger in his chest. "Don't even try to put the tim down. Hell, this ain't even my business."

"You stupid or what? Damn, I thought you were smarter than this?"

Ice's patience was pushed as he glanced back at the car at Mya, then said, "Check this out, Malik. I'll take care of it myself. You hear me?" He turned and started to walk away.

Malik sucked his teeth. "I hope so like you said someone might take it serious." He walked into the building smirking.

Ice turned back around, grabbed him by the arm and spun him. "Look, I'm tired of being nice with your ass. Let's call it what it is so we don't got no misunderstanding!"

Malik pushed him back and said, "Back up!" He peeped around to his office and thought about the briefcase on his desk, his gun. That was his next move, to hell with Ice.

"I know you're in on the game with, Felix. I also know you hold his stash. So, how about we call it even and just mind your muthafuckin' business? Cool!" Ice was selling wolf tickets with that content. He threw out the rumor he'd heard from around the projects.

Stunned by what he was hearing come out of his mouth, he wondered, *'Damn, who else knows Felix's dope is here?'* He was backed up against the wall. He felt the ups that Ice had put on him. "No…not cool," he replied. "There's three things I'm certain of, right now. One…" He turned and started walking towards his office, mildly enough to not cause alarm. Ice followed him. "You're right, I need to mind my own business." He opened the office door, strolled over to his desk, around to his chair, and pulled it out. "Two…" He sat calmly and pulled the briefcase in front of him. "If you ever threaten me again…" He popped it open and eyed the gun. "I'll kill you, and three…" Ice was defenseless, he knew by the way Malik acted that he was strapped. He inched closer toward the window just in case he had to make a quick move.

Malik watched him like a hawk, but he'd made his point, clear. So, he got up and walked over to him with his hands open, showing Ice he wasn't a threat. He brushed past, opened the blinds slightly and pointed to Mya. She was totally oblivious to what was developing. "You need to cut her ass loose before Rasheed thinks it's you, and not Derek. You know where that'll go." He turned and looked him in the eye, then walked over to the door and opened it. "Straighten it out that's all I gotta say."

Ice at first wanted to attempt at a rebuttal, but he had no wins. Malik was right, he had to straighten this out before their next move. It was no time to lose focus, especially for Rasheed. He definitely had to touch base with Devone to let her know what was up, too.

He turned back to Malik's office to try to find out some more. "Check this out..."

Malik knew he'd already said too much. "Go, just remember those three things. Especially the last one, and, oh yeah, tell Waseema I'll see her in a little while."

"I'll do that," he said as he stared off into the car at Mya. He had to put the straightening on it and right now was as good a time as any. "Nah, I won't forget, the, uh, second thing, but you better call Waseema yourself. I'm not going back to Bushwick just yet."

Malik shook his head. "You're on your own." Then said under his breath, "Mya, you, dumb bitch."

Ice got in the car and cranked it up. "I gotta make a stop before I drop you off." He pulled into traffic and asked, "You going home, right?"

"Sure," she answered back, but inwardly she needed to try to clean up what he knew about her and Derek if anything. "Ice, uh, we need to talk."

"'Bout what, Mya? Ain't really shit to say, right now."

"You're not going to say anything to, Rasheed, are you?"

Ice shook his head at her candor and looked her way. "You fucked up! You know that. What do you think?"

"Ice, it's not what you think, pullover, let's talk." She pointed to a lot off Dekalb Avenue.

He pulled in and then frowned. "What's up, Mya? Why you fucking around with, Derek, anyway? I mean, Rasheed treats you good, right?"

She had to do something she couldn't let Rasheed know. It would kill him, or he would kill her. "Maybe, we can work something out." She eased closer to him and started rubbing his chest.

That threw him. "What the fuck? No way!" He pushed her away and started to crank up the car.

That's when she reached for his crotch. Manipulating her fingers around his dick. It hardened as she rubbed it against his thigh. He was already half-assed worked up sneaking peeps at her full, round titties exposed by a deep cleavage. Ice put up a feeble attempt to stop her. But, when she unzipped his zipper and pulled out his rock-hard dick, he surrendered. She opened her mouth and gulped down his dick, deep throating the head, while slowly sucking. She only came off it one time.

She asked, "Can we keep all this to ourselves?"

His dick pulsated as he reached over and caressed the back of her head. His answer was no surprise. "Yeah…o…kay!" He was seduced, dangling in the twisted web she'd spun called deception. He fell for the bait.

Malik peeped his head out from the building. Looking around to make sure Ice wouldn't double back on him looking for trouble. He thought about what he'd told him about Bushwick. He really needed to call, but the phone rang first. Double timing it back to the office, he eased over to it.

'*Must be Felix*,' he thought, but it was way too early. Slowly, he picked up the receiver and answered it, "Hello."

"Hey, Malik, it's me Waseema."

Blowing the air out of his mouth he said, "Good to hear from you! I just heard about what happened, I was on my way over."

"I sure could have used you here, it was crazy!" She started explaining the details.

Malik stopped her. "You can tell me everything when I get there."

"Okay, Rasheed is here, too. Say's he needs to talk to you."

'*Damn*,' he thought. '*Can it get any worse?*' "Tell him, I'm on my way over."

"I will, we're waiting for Ice to come back. He went looking for a hardware store to get…"

"Yeah, I know cardboard and tape."

"How did you know, you saw him? Well, whatever, I'll talk to you when you get here."

Malik hung up the phone and walked over to the double-glazed window overlooking Sumner Avenue and smirked. "Yeah, Rasheed, I got something to talk to you about, too."

Dunya: The Do Or Die

CHAPTER ELEVEN

Mustapha sat on the front stoop of the three-story brownstone leaning back watching cars go by; Mercedes Benzes, Jaguars, Cadillacs, and the occasional limo. He still couldn't believe all this wealth was legally situated in Harlem. His grandmother's brownstone sat midway on 152nd Street between Saint Nicholas and Amsterdam Avenue in the Sugar Hill section of Harlem.

Juanita Jones was a native of Harlem, born and raised on the Eastside; *Spanish Harlem* as it was called. Her family had strong ties to racketeering and banking for the various illegal number activities. Their reputation for fairness exceeded their presence and they had respect, but they also demanded it from all. But, as she peeped through the curtains from her bedroom window on the third floor, her long streaked gray hair dangling, she was now just a concerned grandmother.

"Mustapha!" she yelled downstairs. "Why don't you go meet your brother at the Riverside Church? I think he had a basketball practice or something."

Mustapha looked up at her and said, "No problem." He got up, exited the house and walked toward Amsterdam Avenue making a left heading downtown. Realizing how long the blocks were in Harlem, he'd wished he'd asked for the car.

He posted up in front of a Chinese restaurant just across from the gym on 145th Street, picking through three egg rolls he'd bought. Shortly after a group of boys came running out of the gym across from him. He squinted trying to get a bead on his younger brother and although it had been a while since he'd last seen him, he could always tell. By his walk and his six-footthree height. Mustapha couldn't help but notice how much Latif resembled his father.

Mustapha threw the half-eaten egg roll in the trash and started walking towards the group of adolescent boys as they bolted out of the gym. Their practice had just finished and the group of twenty or so ran out. All of them seemed to look the same; tall, skinny and clumsy. As Mustapha spotted his brother, he also caught a glimpse of a dark blue, four-door Ford Sedan pulling across from the crowd and stopping. He smiled when he spotted him, but still kept an eye on the inconspicuous vehicle.

Latif spotted his older brother and waved at him. "Mustapha!" Latif came running toward Mustapha beaming his pleasure.

Suddenly, the car pulled up, heading toward them. At first, Mustapha thought it was just following the flow of traffic as it pulled away from the curb, but it slowed down as it approached. He kept his eye on it and his brother as Latif moved closer toward him. Sensing danger and the paranoia he felt causing his heart to race, he thought it may have been one of Felix's cronies and they might open fire on him at any time. He slowly backed away. He turned instead, looking for an obstacle to duck and take cover behind if any shots were indeed fired, but he knew one thing for sure. He'd have to take the threat away from the boys.

Latif didn't understand his brother's caution, and stopped, then turned toward the vehicle as the car coasted and stopped in front of him. The front door opened and out stepped a short, stocky young man not much older than himself. Mustapha reached into his waistband and pulled out the .45 he carried with him. Another young man, the driver, also got out and walked toward Latif.

Mustapha was dumbfounded but somewhat relieved. He didn't see a threat, yet. So, he tucked away the gun and called out to Latif as he walked up on him. "Latif what's up!"

Latif turned his way. "What's happening, bruh! What are you doing up here?"

"We'll talk later, grandma sent me here to meet you. Everything cool?" he asked as he locked eyes on the two young men. The driver slowly starting to lurk menacingly behind him.

"Yeah, man everything's cool," Latif answered as he stuck his hand out to the young man in front of him, who slowly reached into his pocket. "He's my brother." He spoke out, but that didn't stop him though. He walked up on Mustapha with his hand dug deep into his pocket, suggesting he was strapped while the other stood behind him.

"Look, I don't want no trouble. Let's go, Latif!" Mustapha said as he slowly backed from in between them.

Latif started moving toward his brother when the short, stocky young man stopped him, then turned towards Mustapha and said, "Who the hell do you think you are?"

All Mustapha could do was shake his head and sigh. His long dreads swept across his face as he glanced towards them. "Look, man, I just came here to meet my brother, cool?"

The stocky one took Mustapha's humility for weakness. "Me and your brother got business, cool?"

Latif stepped in front of him. "Nah, you got it fucked up. Told you we ain't got no business."

That was all Mustapha needed to hear.

"Alright, that's enough." He pulled out the .45 from his jacket, put it upside the now wide-eyed boy's head and whispered in his ear, "Leave us alone." He cocked back the trigger. "Back off and leave. Now!" The other boy quickly crept back toward the driver's side of the car. Mustapha didn't know who else or what else was in the vehicle. "Stop, right where you are!" he ordered.

"Mister, I don't want no beef..." the boy stammered.

Mustapha still held the gun to the boy's head as he lowered down some and peeped into the car. It was empty. He scanned around and saw book bags and asked, "What's in the bags?"

"Books!" the boy with the gun to his head spat. "Just books."

Latif butted in. "They want me to sell dope, but I don't want to."

The boy frowned. "My cousin will find out what you said!"

Mustapha put the gun down and spun him around. "You tell your cousin my brother doesn't want to sell drugs for you or anybody. You hear me!" He pushed the boy towards the door. The other one had already gotten in and cranked the car up.

"C'mon, Papi, let it go!"

He turned towards his friend and yelled back, "Fuck you! I'll let you know when to let it go!" He turned back toward Mustapha and Latif. "I'll see you both again."

Mustapha pointed the gun and the car sped off. He stuck the gun back into his jacket as he noticed that a small crowd had gathered. "We gotta go!"

Latif grabbed him by the arm. "C'mon, I know a shortcut to get away from this crowd."

"Cool, let's go."

They walked up the long sprawling hills off Riverside Drive in silence. Enjoying the moment until Latif broke the stillness. "They wanted me to sell drugs for them. I kept telling them no."

"That's good, Latif, that's good."

"I mean, I know what it brings...trouble. Besides..." He took the basketball out that he'd stuffed in his bag. "...I'm nice with this."

Mustapha laughed. "What! Me and Rasheed brought you up on that."

He swung at the ball. "We gave you that when you didn't want milk!" Latif laughed. "It's a good thing, too." He glanced up towards the Polo Grounds. "Check it, before we go in. You still play right?"

Mustapha finally stole the ball out of his hands and started dribbling. "You ain't said nothing slick." Then he pulled out the .45 he had in his pocket and started looking around. "Hold up, I gotta stash this."

"No problem, I got a spot for that."

"Safe?"

"Safe."

"Alright then, let's go."

Latif kicked back in his room pouring over his books while Mustapha laid out in a full-bodied, ivory tub, gazing around at the pastel panels that were hung on the wall; brass fixtures and tiny stained glass, in awe of the brownstone that his grandmother lived in. From the basement walk-in, she utilized as a bakery, and the lower level beneath it enjoyed as a wine cellar, all the way up to the guest room where he stayed on the top floor amidst a sprawling spiral staircase. It was immaculately done. The whole second floor belongs to her and although she never let anyone else in, Mustapha was free to browse through, glimpsing some of the pleasantries she had set up for herself. One: a huge library in the foyer with lighting not only from the huge six-foot windows but also from a glittering chandelier with a sweeping staircase attached.

Latif's room or space as she called it, had its own bath, study, and bedroom. It was situated directly above hers. Latif was pretty decent in school. Not exactly a genius but he held his own. He played basketball and was clumsier as he was graceful at times, but for the most part, scholastics was his thing. Having seen enough ball stars at the Rucker Park tournaments to know, here today, gone tomorrow. He figured it would be good to have some sort of education, then maybe, a little ball on the side, if any. He had it all figured out the best he could. Knowing he was blessed to have been sent up to Harlem with his grandmother, it still made him feel guilty at times for seemingly deserting his siblings.

So, this was his way of making things right. Just like his mother said when he left Brooklyn. "Take advantage of it all, Latif. Your father would have wanted that." Every day he would remember just that.

He almost didn't hear his grandmother as she entered the room and said, "Latif, we need to talk."

He turned and she held his gym bag from earlier in her hand. "What's wrong, Grandma?" he asked, then reached for the bag and chuckled. "Oh yeah, I should have put my dirty socks in the laundry bin. Sorry 'bout that..."

She jerked it back. "No, Latif, your socks are okay." She reached in a pulled out the .45 from the bag. "But this isn't."

Latif grimaced. '*Damn,*' he thought, he'd forgotten all about it.

"Now, who's is it?" she questioned. "Better not be yours...or is it?"

He remembered putting his brother's gun back in the bag after they'd returned to his stash spot to retrieve it once they left the park. One thing's for sure, their grandmother didn't play the gun thing or drugs. None of it, but he wasn't about to tell either. She literally would kick Mustapha out of the house.

He stuttered, collecting his thoughts. "Uh...well..." "It belongs to me," Mustapha said walking through the door.

She turned and glared at him, then said, "Latif, leave the room. Mustapha and I need to talk."

"But, Grandma, it wasn't his fault," Latif pleaded.

"Now!"

He picked up his books and turned to leave the room. Walking solemnly past Mustapha he whispered, "Sorry, but I ain't no snitch."

Mustapha patted him on the back. "It's okay. But always remember, some things you don't always own up to. Especially, the wrong things. Got it?" Latif hung his head down and nodded as he slowly closed the door shut.

She pointed Mustapha towards a seat. "Sit down, please." She sat across from him and pulled up an ashtray. Lighting up a cigarette, she leaned back in the chair and puffed a few times before she said, "You know I'm not pleased with this at all. When I told you to come stay with me, I didn't mean for you to bring this." She held up the gun. He reached for it, but she pulled it back.

"Sorry, Grandma, but things are pretty rough out here for me, they just tried to kill me...and Ma."

"I understand, but you're safe here. You're my grandson, not no thug. At least while you're in my home."

"Yes ma'am," Mustapha said as he humbly looked down at the floor.

"But..." She reached over and picked up his head. "Don't pull, Latif, into it. I worked too hard to give him a life!" She leaned back in her seat again and took one last drag of her cigarette before she outed it, then said, "A life I wish I could have given you all."

"Why didn't you take all of us in. Why?" Years of resentment spewed out with that one question. A tear even rolled down his face as his mouth quivered. "Why did we have to stay in Bushwick...a ghetto?"

She eased up in her chair closer to him and pushed aside her long grey curls from her face. "I prayed...every day about what to do." She kissed his forehead. "But I didn't get no answers. So, I did, what I thought was best."

"Best...for who?"

"Look, Mustapha, you were the oldest. You had to stay with your mother. Especially once she made the decision to stay in Brooklyn. So, someone had to watch over her. Then, Shaheeda had to care for all of you...she's the girl. And Rasheed, well he was just too headstrong for me at the time. Just like his daddy and his grandfather. Somehow, he was needed to keep everything in order and balanced." She sighed. "I'm sorry."

Mustapha leaned in towards her and kissed her. "That's alright. It almost seemed to work out like that. I think I understand."

She stroked his long dreadlocks and said, "Almost, we'll get it together, as a family." She started to get up.

He pulled her by the hand and asked, "Grandma, what kind of man was, Granddaddy? What did he do? How did y'all get so much respect up here?"

"Whoa-whoa." She picked the gun up off the small stand and said. "I tell you what, get cleaned up for dinner, and I'll tell you about your Grandfather then." She pointed the gun towards the floor, snatched back the chamber with her other hand and a slug spit out. "Maybe even more." Pushing the notch, the clip fell into her waiting hand and she put the weapon back onto the table and stuffed the clip and bullet back into the bag. "You probably didn't know there was one in the chamber." She shook her head and sighed. "Tsk, tsk...youth is wasted on the young."

The door closed behind her as Mustapha sat there soaking in what was said and what had just taken place and said to himself, "I know my grandmother just didn't handle that .45?"

****

Malik was locking up the door when he heard the sound. He turned and looked. Nothing, shrugging it off he bent over to pick up his briefcase when he heard a voice, "Shhhh, don't make a move." A blunt object was pushed into his back. hard and cold. "If you do…I'll put a hole in you so big…" It was a .44 Magnum.

Dropping the briefcase, he stood motionless, thinking maybe this was a stickup. Maybe, someone had been watching him and thought he was an easy mark. Maybe, it was someone that hadn't known of his reputation and status. Maybe, someone new to the neighborhood, after all. Deviants were moving into the now crumbling community quite frequently these days. He thought about it, but he was too closeup on the door. Maybe, if he could just turn around…another pistol was put up to his head. That thought was out of the question now. Maybe, he'd just better cooperate.

"Don't make any sudden moves!" the voice instructed.

Who the hell would try him? Malik? City council member? No respect! He shook his head, racking his brain. He knew all the gangs, homeboys, gangsters, hell even the stickup kids themselves. Who!

"Okay, Malik, open the door back up…slowly."

"Huh?" That voice was someone he knew, or who knew him.

"That's it nice and slow," he responded.

He put the key back in and turned the knob. The door seemed to pop open and he was roughly shoved through. Falling to the floor he thought of spinning around, making a power move. He was a black belt, second degree. All he would have to do is make a sweeping leg kick. Throw his man off balance and-good, there were no lights on. He'd make his move quick, that was the plan now.

But the lights were switched on instead, and a voice said, "Yeah, I know you know that karate shit. You think I was gonna fall for that?" It was Juan.

The shadow that stood behind him moved closer, breathing hard, hulking and stink. It was Felix. Juan stepped aside and he said, "Ah Malik, I told you I would be back. I see you didn't expect me." He leaned forward and extended his hand. "How the hell are you?"

Malik paused, then swatted his hand away. "Fuck you!" He started to turn when Felix swung his hand back and slapped him. All he saw next were stars. He staggered back against the wall falling to the ground thinking, '*Where the hell did, he get that much strength?*'

"I told your black ass I wasn't too damn happy with you not wanting to help me." He moved closer toward him again and slapped him. "After all we've been through together." Then, he kicked him in the stomach.

"Ugghhhh…chill!" Malik shouted.

Felix handed his gun to Juan and turned and whistled outside the door to the awaiting vehicle, and a lone figure got out. Looking both ways he moved cautiously across the street. His long strides moved him as swiftly and stealthily as a panther. Coming through the door he peeped back out the door and slammed it. Locking the bolt shut.

"I want you to say hi to a friend of ours." Malik held his hand to his now bleeding mouth, wiping away blood from a busted lip and sighed. "Hell."

"Yeah." Felix laughed. "I thought you would recognize him."

The man slowly stepped forward and said, "We meet again?" He stomped on Malik's hand. "And, it's too bad for you, too."

He motioned to Juan, who reached down and held out Malik's arm, then the other. He drop-kicked it and a soft thud was produced the moment his arm was broken. He cringed on the floor in agony. screaming out, "Go to h-h-hell!"

Felix sighed. "Well, you have to take the hard way out, I see." He backed up and looked over at Malik rolled up like a ball in the corner spitting blood out of his mouth. Holding his bent arm. "Beat him until he talks!" he hollered out.

Malik could only close his eyes as the shadow of the tall, dark figure of a demon, not a man, stood over him. He knew it was going down. Knowing this man from years gone by, it was definitely going to be brutal. He prayed and asked for mercy and forgiveness from Allah, as a tear rolled from the corners of his eyes.

After the thorough ass-kicking put on Malik. Felix stood over the now crumbled-up hull of a body; blood splattered all over the walls and floors, looking to be at least a pint, talking cash shit. Malik groaned as he laid there. Felix smiled and motioned the two administrators of the brutal beating over and said, "Looks like he'll make it."

Juan kneeled and pushed his head up. "Boss, he's still breathin'."

"At least straighten up his nose so he can breathe. I need him to live."

"Okay, Boss." He reached out toward Malik's face and in a crude attempt straightened his nose. Malik shouted as blood squirted out his nostrils. "There ya go, that should be good."

Felix turned his head and rubbed his ears. "He screamed like a bitch. You'd think he'd be used to it by now."

Malik opened his eye, the one that wasn't swollen shut, and made an attempt to pick himself up. "F-F-Felix…" his voice was scratchy as he spoke. "F-F-Felix."

Juan called out. "Hey boss, he's callin' your name."

Felix bent over and said, "Good, maybe he has something better to say."

Malik reached out and lunged at him, grabbing him by the collar. "I have the p-papers...to...the...p-p-property."

"What! Tell me where they are!"

The still-unidentified figure stood by the side wiping down the tools he'd just used: brass knuckles, and a steel-encased rubber bar, and asked, "What's he talking about, Felix? What property?"

Felix hadn't discussed this business with him at all. "That's just about dropping off the drugs..."

"No, Felix!" Malik shouted. "It's about the other papers! The ones you stole..."

Felix turned. "You bastard...after all these years?"

The man stepped over to him and said, "Papers...stolen, huh? Maybe, I should question him about these papers?"

"No!" Felix said as he turned away from him. "Your job is done! This is between me and him now."

"You...and him, I see. Well, maybe the Cartel may want to know about your business...between you and him." His dark beady eyes narrowed as he continued, "You're not hiding anything from us, are you, Felix?"

Felix averted his eyes away from the stare and looked towards the floor escaping his glare. He damn sure as hell couldn't let the Cartel know he was holding back, now or even then. "Of course not. Why would I do that?"

Malik was still half-dazed but still managed to catch most of what was said. "T-T-The papers...are...upstairs. Take me!"

"Well, Felix, what are you going to do? Take him?" The man asked as he towered over him. "Or, do I?"

"No! Juan, get him up and let's get him to his office. Now!" he ordered. He knew he had to be careful. The Cartel couldn't know anything about it or the next ass whippin' would be his. If he was lucky. "Okay, okay, we go now and see what he's talking about."

"Good Felix, good."

They picked up Malik's broken body and took him up a flight of stairs leading to his office, a trail of blood ensued, but Malik, though in agony, had conjured up a plan. Possibly he realized his last plea. "T-T-Take me to the desk." Juan dragged him over to the desk and propped him up in his chair. "F-Felix...you mean to tell me, you never...told the Cartel..."

"Shut up, nigga! Just give me the papers!"

The unidentified man belonging to the Los Andres Cartel now stood directly behind Felix, sensing something was amiss. He put his hand on his gun and said, "Felix, let him talk. It seems like he has something to say, perhaps."

"Hell no, he's just babbling!" He rushed the desk and banged down on top of it saying. "Give me the papers!" Then he motioned Juan over and reached for his gun. "Or else!"

Malik grinned, teeth cracked, some missing; he knew he had him now. "Felix…" he coughed, blood was starting to fill his lungs and he spit up all over the desk. "You are a f-f-fool…" He reached into the drawer where he kept his flask, his papers, and his gun. He didn't have much time. He had to be precise, just right. It was his last chance. He lunged. "Fuck you, Felix! Go to hell!"

Pulling out his gun he pointed it at Felix who was bending over in front of him and aimed. Felix made a half-assed attempt to move out of the way of his sights, but he was too slow and too fat. Malik squeezed the trigger. The man that was part of the Cartel ducked to the side out the way and pulled his own gun. Juan, well, Juan decided at that time how loyal he was going to be to Felix. He jumped in front of him. The reflexes of a faithful bodyguard. The bullet was fired, and Juan was caught dead in the chest and his body fell to the floor like a busted rag doll.

Felix finally reached for his gun, but Malik just didn't have the strength to fire off another round. Felix pulled the .38 he had from the black leather holster strapped around his waist and said, "You, black bastard…you tried to kill me!"

Malik jerked back, at the same time his mind flashed back to the days when he and Khalid had decided to start a business and be independent men outside of the system. He remembered how they were befriended by a then, young, aggressive Colombian looking to make a start in the lucrative drug trade, Felix. He remembered how he'd approached him and Khalid with a plan to flood Brooklyn with drugs and use them as a front to launder money back and forth to the Los Andres Cartel without them knowing, by saying they were up fraudulent community programs.

To Malik, the plan sounded good. He would have a seat bought specifically by the Cartel on the City Council to make moves and sway the majority of the votes his way. Buy property and change long-standing existing commercial and residential zoning. Literally, allowing trucks of cocaine in and out of the community undetected, legitimately. On top of that, they would collect money unbeknownst to the Cartel, by skimming. But to Khalid, it was way too risky.

He was much too cautious to make a bold move like that. He'd already been given too many chances. He wanted something better and the Cartel wasn't offering it, and Felix didn't put him in on his side deal with Malik. So, he became a problem. Malik remembered how the plan was set in motion to get rid of Khalid. Put the tim down. He remembered vividly. He also remembered what he'd said to him that night as he took off his ski mask. The argument that followed, and his last words. Then, he shot him. How clearly, he remembered all his life. It haunted him, but now he would be free.

"That's enough!" Felix was pushed back as he tried to squeeze off more rounds. "We have to go!"

He gazed down at Malik, bullet holes in the middle of his forehead and a sickening grin across his face and said, "What the hell was he smiling about?" He ran behind the desk, kicked his body to the side and rummaged through the drawers. "Where are they?"

"We have to go Felix, now!"

He looked down one more time. "What's this?" A small key taped to the back of the top desk drawer caught his eye. He removed it and stuffed it into his pocket then grabbed the record-ledger folio Malik kept and rushed around the desk, but not before spitting on him. Suddenly, he felt a hand grab at his foot. He looked down and it was Juan uttering, "FFelix…don't…leave…me." The hole in his chest where the blood had leaked out rapidly spewed forth less as his heartbeat grew faint.

"Juan, I can't help you," he said.

The door flew open. "Felix, I have the car waiting down in front. Let's go, or the cops…"

"Yeah, yeah!" He looked back down at Juan, his one-time confidant. His right-hand man, his friend, and said, "I'm sorry, but these things happen." He reached for Malik's gun and aimed it toward Juan's head. "Sorry, it's just business." He squeezed, but not before Juan's eyes grew wide and he yelled at him saying, "I'll see you in hell, Fe…"

He kicked the body to the side, ran out the door and dived in the car waiting out front. The tires screeched as the old Lincoln Continental made its way down Lewis Avenue. Felix laid back breathing hard, huffing and puffing. The man from the Cartel looked over and said, "You will tell me about these papers." He reached into his inner coat pocket where he had his gun. "Right!"

Felix had to come up with something. "Yeah, I will…but, we have to find this, Mustapha." He pulled out the key from his pocket and said, "He knows where the papers are…and the money."

"Money, how much?"

Felix lied, he figured he'd get this guy to help him find Mustapha, then kill them both. "A lot…a whole lot," he stammered.

"It better be. Okay, we'll do that. Mustapha, huh?"

Felix relaxed and sighed. "What a fuckin' day." He leaned against the side door stuffing the key into his shirt pocket and peeped over at the man driving. "Hey, after all these years. What is your name, anyway?"

The man pulled down the visor trying to angle his head away from the sun's twilight on the tenement horizon and looked over at Felix. Then laughed. One of those long, sinister, mirthful type laughs, and said, "Muerte."

Felix grimaced when he heard it, then groaned. "Aw shit…"

Muerte is Spanish, for death.

CHAPTER TWELVE

Rasheed and Derek played a game of chess in the kitchen, already about an hour in, back and forth, stopping and going in between phone calls. The van was taking longer than expected. A Jamaican Cartel had a big heist upstate and it was needed there, as well as others. Devone pushed for another one, but they told them they'd have to wait and stay by the phone. So, they needed to kill time. A little downtime was what they needed anyway. Things were tense, stress was all over the place.

Rasheed's sister, Mustapha, and even Derek and his sister were spending unnecessary money. Leaving behind an expensive paper trail. Born stayed drunk most of the time and Ice was sucked into Mya's tangled web and finally, figured out why Derek couldn't shake her. The feeling was that good. Devone had spoken to him earlier about Rasheed's family getting in the way of the whole heist, but that was only after it was brought up about their bad spending habits.

Derek said he should be the one to take over the whole gang and be the leader. But the reply was simple; what gang. Derek? Leader? What kind of shit are you on? Ice knew Derek was on some bullshit and it had a lot to do with Rasheed. He knew people, there was something Derek wanted from Rasheed and he couldn't quite figure it out, yet.

'*Was it really about, Mya?*' he pondered.

Derek had Rasheed's King in check, so he moved one space over. Derek then moved his Bishop, protecting his Queen and Rasheed responded by moving his Knight as a threat. The decision now laid with Derek. He moved the Queen several spaces back-in danger of losing it, and Rasheed bought the Rook out, putting his King in check. Derek studied the Pawns, his only chance to block his escape. He scrutinized the board.

"Derek, you act like this game is that serious. A real-life situation or something," Rasheed said.

He looked up from the board for a moment and said, "It is."

"Don't know what's on your mind, but it looks like you're just going for my queen."

Ice stepped forward. "Maybe, he is, Rasheed, maybe, he is."

A scowl came across Devone's face as she turned towards them, she shot at Ice. "What are you trying to say, Ice?"

"Nothing…least not yet, Devone."

"What the hell is going on?" Rasheed asked, pushing himself away from the table.

Derek eyeballed Ice, the two of them stared each other down until Born came over and knocked the King over on the board. "Nothing, nothing's going on. The games are over for today…all of them." He stepped in between them. "We need to make a call to the Italians."

Derek stood up and said, "Yeah, you're right." He walked towards the phone, then peeped back over at Rasheed who cocked an eyebrow and said, "Derek, you got something you want to say?"

"Everything's cool, everything's cool," Devone interrupted.

She had to reel it back in before everything spiraled out of control. Ice knew something, and she'd have to find out later. But her brother wasn't making matters any better. Her plan had to work. She was borderline obsessed with having Rasheed all to herself.

Rasheed walked toward the window and stared out. "I can't tell."

Derek passed the handset to Ice after dialing the numbers. "What's up, this is Ice…about the van."

"So, uh, what's up with the ride, ready, or what?"

The thick, heavy-accented Italian paused, and Ice held the receiver close to his ear. He said, "I meant to call, but we got caught up."

"Caught up? Look, man, we trying to take care of some serious business. To hell with being caught up."

"Van needed repairs took some hits."

Ice leaned against the sink and sighed. "C'mon man, tighten up. I put money…"

"You want your money back? You don't tell me what to do or when to do it!"

"Alright…alright, calm down." Ice pulled the receiver away from his ear and whispered to Devone. "Don't look good." "Still there?" the man asked.

"So, how long is this gonna take?" Ice asked him. "'Bout another week and a half, maybe."

"Another week and a half!" Ice shook his head. "Damn, you ain't got nothing else!"

"All we had, we used."

"Alright, a week." Ice looked around the room and nodded, they all nodded back. "But if you can get it done…"

"Right, right, I'll call you. If I hear anything before then, cool?"

"Sounds cool, catch you later."

"Later."

Ice hung up the phone and said, "We looking at another week."

"Damn!" Devone spat. "Another fucking week! We ready to go now!" Ice walked over to the couch and sat down next to Born. "Look, ain't nothing we can do. We knew the van was used in another job upstate and got shot up."

"Yeah," Born butted in. "They probably got to get to rid of powder mark, look for shell casings, all that."

Ice continued, "Either that, or if we just happen to get popped with it…"

"We all go down for something we ain't even do," Born said as he looked over at Rasheed. "So, what you think?"

He slowly turned letting out a deep sigh. "Well, we waited this long. As long as we are careful."

Derek exploded, "Is this ever going to happen?"

"What's your rush?" Rasheed glanced around the apartment at the new furniture, carpet, expensive rugs and curtains. "Y'all seem to be doing alright."

"I just ain't trying to feel this poverty shit."

"Yeah, fucking ghetto superstar." Born mused. "You like that, huh?"

"Fuck you, Born, I'm just trying to be comfortable."

"In the projects."

"Look at Rasheed, he's living good. Shit, Mya just got a new shearling full length, too."

Rasheed paused; Mya had just got the coat. He knew she never wore it around the projects. "Coat?"

"Least he don't leave a paper trail behind him." "Yeah,

Devone, y'all gots to be careful," Ice added.

I'm trying to leave this shit behind me," Rasheed said.

"Leave, and go where…with who?"

"Somewhere besides New York. It's just too crazy, and it's not getting better." He looked up at her. "Like you said, look at all the hell my family's been through."

"I didn't mean it like that, Rasheed," Devone said as she walked over to him. "It's just frustrating, that's all."

"It's cool, Devone, you're right!"

"Shit happens, you know that. We gonna make it."

Rasheed got up from the couch and hugged her. "I know, I know."

"So, where the hell is, Mustapha?" she asked.

"Yeah, where the hell is, he, he alright?" Born asked.

Rasheed sat down on the edge of the chair and Devone frowned. "Rasheed, it cost too much money to be sitting on the side of that chair like that. Your momma don't even play that!" she scolded.

Rasheed had to laugh. "For real."

"So, what's up with, Mustapha?" Ice asked impatiently.

"Mustapha's in Harlem. Up there with my grandmother and Latif, chillin'. I had to get him away until we got the chance to sit down and figure this whole thing out. Then handled Felix and his boys."

Derek rubbed his chin and paced the floor. "Yeah, Felix and his boys. I heard they were after Mustapha hard! It's all in the streets."

"I heard talk about a ten gee contract on his head. Don't worry though, we'll get them."

"Hold up," Devone said. "Let's take a look at this."

"I know you're not thinking about giving up my brother to collect?" Rasheed said staring at her.

"No, hell no! But we could use him as bait."

"Bait...you crazy?"

"No, Rasheed." Born picked up on what she was saying. "I see where she's going. We could flush Felix out, right Devone?"

"Yes, flush his flunky ass out, find out where his hideout is, and everything. Mustapha, we wouldn't let nothing happen to him. I mean, we'd be right there."

Rasheed ran his fingers through his hair thinking hard about what was said. "Don't know sounds dangerous."

"Dangerous?" Born exclaimed. "That's Mustapha...danger...fuckin'...man!"

"Still, don't know have to ask him."

"Of course, of course. Well..." Devone turned and faced them. "We got a week off."

"That we do," Rasheed said as he stood up. "Least I could check out my little brother, Latif."

"Whoa, hold up, I want to go too," Born said. "I ain't seen, Latif, in a long time either."

"Sounds cool, Rasheed," Derek added. "We can all go. Make the trip to Harlem. I got the Caddy dressed up. Shit, show them, Harlem boys, this Brooklyn swag."

"Alright then." Rasheed laughed. "Make a day of it, I'll make the call, cool."

Ice kicked his legs up on the small dinner table and said, "I always wanted to ask..." Devone immediately swatted his feet off. "You know what this shit cost?"

Ice looked up at her like she was crazy, then turned his attention back to Rasheed. "I heard she was rich or something. Why y'all here in the projects, still?"

Rasheed grilled him hard, then a slight grin appeared on his face. "Good question, Ice. She's well off, but you can ask her all of that when you see her, cool." He turned and walked over to the closet and grabbed his coat. I'm going to see y'all later. I gotta pick up, Mya. I got a surprise for her. Peace!"

He left out the apartment and Ice got up. "I will," he said as he peered out the window watching the glimmer off the J-train snaking in and out across Broadway into Bed-Stuy.

Devone rushed to the closet also. "I 'll be right back." She grabbed her coat and opened the door running behind Rasheed. "Wait up!"

Rasheed turned, and asked, "What's wrong?"

"Nothing, I need to talk to you for a minute."

"Can it wait? I got someplace to be."

Devone pouted, then leaned back against the wall across from him. "Won't take long." Her long eyebrows flickered. She was nervous, which wasn't her norm, but right now, she was feeling offkey. Revealing her heart to a man she wanted wasn't her style. "Rasheed, what about me and you?"

"Me and you, what about?"

"What we talked about."

"Oh, the other day. Like I said, Devone, I got Mya."

"How do you know she's the one for you?"

"We've been down for a minute now."

"So, we have to!"

"Yeah, but it's different between us."

Devone leaned in on him, pressing her body close to his. "Is it really?"

Rasheed's body responded and so did his hands. He grabbed her around her waist and pulled her closer, then with the other cuffed her full, round ass. "Damn, Devone, you make it sound so easy."

"It is," she whispered in his ear and then kissed his lips. "I can be yours." She pulled him closer to her and looked up into his eyes. "We can do anything we want. We can make a lot of money together baby."

That statement was what snapped Rasheed out of it. He didn't want the life anymore. He wanted to be normal, have a family. To hell with robbing drug dealers. Mya wanted that life.

"Naw, I'm cool." He pushed her back. "Look, I gotta go."

Devone tried pulling him back. "No, Rasheed, don't go."

He stepped into the stairwell. "I'm sorry, Devone." He was gone.

Devone fell back against the hallway wall. Then, she ducked into the stairway, sat down, holding her hands in her hands thinking, why her? Why didn't he want her? What was wrong with her? Then, she started drying her eyes and a frown came across her face. That damn Mya. That bitch gotta go. I'll be damned if her whore ass stops me from having what I want. Yeah, she gotta go.

"What do you want, Ice? Ask her mother for her daughter's hand," Derek teased.

"Shut the fuck up, it's not like your shit don't stink."

Born snickered at the banter between them. "Y'all crazy, I'm out. Gonna find me a drink." Before he could reach the door.

Ice grabbed Derek by his throat, slamming him against the wall. It was the thump against the wall that caused Born to double back. "What the hell!"

"I'm tired of this bullshit! What the hell is up with you and Mya, Derek?"

He tried in vain to slide up from under Ice's arms as he pressed the full weight of his lean frame against him. Ice only maneuvered him around, shoving Derek back up against the wall again.

"Talk...now!"

Derek looked over at Born for some sort of aid, but he knew he didn't have no wins. Still, he hollered anyway. "Born, get him off me!"

Born paid him no mind and shot back, "You better talk"

"So, what 's up, Derek!" Ice yelled as he tightened up the grip around his throat.

"Okay...okay!" He gagged. "Just get off my neck."

Ice eased up off him as he fell folded over, trying to catch his breath, coughing. He slid down against the wall and reached into his pocket causing Ice and Born to jump back.

"It's just smokes," he said as he put his hand up.

He pulled out a cigarette and tapped the butt end against the back of his hand, then reached into his pocket for a match. After he lit up, he pulled a deep drag then tossed the matches at Ice and said, "That's the hotel where we meet up."

"Fulton Street Inn?" Ice said as he looked at them. '*So, that's where she was headed the day, he and Malik had seen her, and across from where he dropped her off afterward.*'

"I always been into her since back in the day, but she always rejected me. Said I wasn't the man for her. So, when I got into this life. I became a big man, I guess. But still not bigger than Rasheed, huh?" he snarled.

Born rushed him and said, "Still, that's no excuse to."

Ice held him back and said, "Be cool, let him talk."

"I ought to kick his ass! Rasheed's your homeboy!" He yelled as he started balling up his fist.

Derek got up and started easing back. "Look, man, it wasn't just my fault. Evidently, he ain't doing something right, cause she keeps coming back!"

"Damn, Derek, you should have at least said no," Ice said, even though he was no better.

"I feel you, but man, she's a grade-A freak! I can't stop, she like a drug!" He took a pull of the cigarette again and looked at Born. "You can kick my ass if you want, but if you tell Rasheed that'll fuck up this job we got coming up."

Born pulled back saying, "You right, but after it goes down. Then you either tell him, or I will! You hear?"

"Yeah-yeah-I hear you."

Born walked back over to the door and opened it, then said, "Now y'all see why I drink!" He slammed it shut behind him.

The echo from the door was what pulled Devone out of her trance as Born rushed past her and down the stairs.

'*Now what's up?*' she thought to herself as she got up and made her way back to the apartment.

Derek asked Ice, "What about you?"

"What?"

"What about you?" he asked again.

"Naw, I did it that one time. I really got caught up like you said. It was like a drug."

Devone was at the door, Ice, nor Derek knew how long she'd been there. She looked over at Ice and batted an eye. She'd heard what she needed to hear. "Uh, did I interrupt something?"

"Naw, just small talk." Ice stared at her. "You hear anything?" He probed.

She knew he was searching. "No, matter of fact, I just came in to, uh…Derek. I'll be back later, okay."

"Sure."

She turned and jetted back out the door. She had what she needed. Now to put it to use.

"So, what the hell were you talking about! I meant Rasheed's moms."

"I know, hell the whole project knows you're creeping." Ice hadn't realized his relationship with Waseema had been exposed, but he really didn't care much anyway. He and Waseema had already planned on disclosing the whole thing themselves. "We cool like that, but we were thinking about telling Rasheed and them anyway."

"No, hold up, fuck that. What the hell was you talking about before? When my sister came in." Derek leaned back and rubbed his chin. "Oh, hell no!" he yelled and slid deeper into the chair. "You mean to tell me, you're about to kick my ass, and you hit it, too! I can't believe this shit!" he said as he pumped his fist. "Look like the game has changed, huh"

"Naw, still the same, you need to let her go."

"Why so you can have her to yourself?"

"No, just let her go period. That's Rasheed's, old lady. Let him deal with her." Ice got up and paced the floor. "Besides, she's poison. There's something about her that ain't right. Believe me, it'll come out, and you won't want to be around when it does. So, just leave her alone," he said as he stood in front of him now. "You hear me?" He balled up his fist and mean mugged him. He knew Derek's head was hard and what he had said would go in one ear and out the other. It wasn't him he really had to be perplexed about anyway.

Derek looked up at him. He didn't have no wins, and he sure as hell didn't want to try him. "Okay," he mumbled under his breath, then looked down at the book of matches by his foot from Fulton Street Inn. "For now," he said low enough so Ice couldn't hear.

****

"Hey baby, here you go!"

Rasheed had crept up behind Mya as she watched television, or as the television watched her. Her mind was way too busy entertaining thoughts of Derek and the sex that came with him. She loved Rasheed, but he couldn't satisfy her the way Derek could. It was strange she thought. Rasheed was in far better shape than Derek could ever be. Derek was overweight and stout compared to Rasheed's healthier and much stronger body, but Derek held it on her hard and that's what she liked.

Perhaps it had something to do with the abuse. The molestation she'd suffered and been a victim to growing up. Her fine, thick body had to be abused for her to feel satisfaction, which Rasheed never did. He loved on her, rubbed her back, played with her toes, kissed her from head to toe, and even though his passion wasn't as strong, his devotion to her never wavered. He treated her like a Queen, something he picked up from his father, Khalid.

Derek, on the other hand, treated her like a piece of meat, cold, hard, and callous. He'd slam into her repeatedly until he heard moans, then he would toss her over, invade her ass, call her names like slut and whore until she yelled out and until she came. The only thing she wouldn't do was consider his wants for fellatio; sucking his dick, but he tried though, and she'd resist. Sneering, he would tell her she was going to do it one day. She was going to lick all his sticky white fluid off his dick like she does for Rasheed, and now Ice. He'd laugh, then leave her crying. He was like an addiction or a bad habit, and her loins craved for him.

Rasheed stood over her with a diamond tennis bracelet he'd picked up earlier in the week. He wanted to surprise her, knowing he hadn't been there for her lately. He knew his problems with sex made her uncomfortable as it did him also, but never in his farthest mind would he have thought she would resort to sleeping with Derek.

"Sweetheart, it's for you."

She reached out and touched the bright crystal diamonds on the dazzling gold-nugget band, at least four carats of chipped stone and smiled, knowing it was just a matter of time before he'd produce a ring even more fabulous. "Ohhh, baby, this is nice." "Little something for my lady."

She pulled him down on the couch and kissed him. Her tongue entered his mouth searching for the zone that would awaken his manhood. As she spread her legs she felt his erection rise on her thigh and she cooed, "Oh, yes, baby!"

Standing over her, his now upright penis poked against his pants, he unzipped, and it pushed through.

She moaned, "C'mon baby, come closer."

She grabbed ahold of his hard dick with both hands and wiped the precum off the tip with her tongue, then stared up at him as she guided it into her awaiting mouth. Rasheed spasmed as the hot wetness from her soft tongue engulfed him.

She rubbed her tongue around his head as he breathed, "Ahhh, damn, baby...damn."

She gulped the long pipe back into her mouth touching the back of her throat. "Mmmm," she moaned as she moved it back and forth with her lips, slobber came down the side of her mouth. She backed one hand off, then reached down and played with herself.

She pulled up off him long enough to unbutton his pants, then slowly pulled them down. Admiring his strong muscular legs only made her hotter. She reached down and nearly ripped her panties off as she turned around and raised herself up.

Rasheed eagerly grabbed her waist and slid delicately inside her. She didn't want to break her concentration, so she bit into her lip until she tasted the saltiness of blood in her mouth. He gently stroked her, and he stayed firm.

She couldn't take it anymore. "Harder...harder, baby!"

He slammed inside and she moaned louder, making him raise an eyebrow. He slammed it again, this time feeling the back of her pelvis. She convulsed again. He felt himself getting stiffer, going numb by the thrusting. Grabbing her by the hips he continued slamming into her now wet groin until she screamed out. "Oh, yes...yes!"

"This what you like?"

"Fuck me hard! Fuck me!"

He positioned himself with one leg up on the couch and braced the other on the backside. "Yeah, yeah, yeah." he cried out. He'd found his rhythm.

Mya gripped the back of the chair. Her head rocked side to side with every stroke. "*O-wee! O-wee! O-wee!*" She let out as her body contracted.

Finally, Rasheed's dick started tingling ready to cum. He tried to hold back but couldn't. "Oh, shit, I'm cumming!"

"Come on, baby, give it to me!"

He held his head back and the white, thick, silky fluid streamed out. Feeling good, it oozed all on the back of her legs as she held on to what she could as she kept it inside. "Hold it right there, baby. I'm cumming, too!" she shouted as she stroked her swollen clit until, "Ohhh, yyyeeeaaahhh!" She came, then dipped her head down as the sweat rained from her hair and said, "Oh, yes, it's so good. Oh, Der..."

"What!" Rasheed slid out of her. "What'd you say?"

'Ah fuck,' she thought! *'What the hell did I just do! He's gonna kill me!'* She whirled around as he tried to get a grip and figure out what she'd said.

"Did you just say…a name?"

She had to think fast, it couldn't go down like this. "Yes!" she said as she jumped in his arms and kissed him, "Daddy! My sweet fuckin' Daddy!" She rubbed on his legs and kissed his neck whispering in his ear, "Daddy, that's what I said."

Rasheed was still puzzled. "Daddy?" But he hugged her still. "I thought you were calling out a name or something."

"C'mon now, baby. You know there's only you." She pushed him back gently. "You think I'm messing around, silly?"

"Naw, baby just sounded like a name, that's all." He pulled her closer to him and said, "C'mere, let's uh go to the room."

As he swooped her up and carried her into the bedroom, Mya couldn't help but think, *'All this time, all he had to do was fuck me hard. I got to break this bullshit off with Derek, now!'* Looking up into her man's eyes she said, "I love you, Rasheed!"

"I love you, too, Mya! Always," he answered back.

Devone had followed Rasheed home. Tired of the bullshit, she wanted to come clean. Let him know what was going on with her brother. She bounced up the stairs and started to knock, but she heard sounds. She pressed her ear against the door, she could hear the passion and moans. She leaned against the door and breathing hard she dug her hands down her pants, stroking her clit. Moaning, she rubbed as she heard Rasheed and Mya's steamy lovemaking through the door.

At the same time Mya came, so did she. She wanted so bad to just burst through the door. Tell him what was really going on then, but instead, she pulled her hands out her pants rubbing her fingers through her cum. She cried and tears raced down her cheeks. She felt sick. Her mind screamed, "What the hell you doing?"

She eventually got herself together and started to go down the stairs on her way back home. It was over with, maybe she needed help. Mentally exhausted, she leaned back against the door and that's when she heard Rasheed telling Mya, "Baby, we'll always be together."

"We will be, baby there's no one else. I would die for you," Mya said back.

That bitch, that was the game-changer for her. Sneering, Devone uttered bitterly under her breath. "Yeah, you will do just that, too. I'll make sure of it."

Dunya: The Do Or Die

Chapter Thirteen

The rain fell light as Waseema exited the building. Looking up at the polluted Brooklyn skies she put up her umbrella. The weatherman had predicted showers then sunshine for the better part of the week, but the overcast sky mocked at the prediction; scouting at the conjecture of a forecast. A raindrop caught her lip and as she licked it off; the sweet, salty taste in her mouth was reminiscent of the tears she had at Khalid's funeral. Today, she was going to pick up her daughter Shaheeda from the hospital. A daughter she and Khalid had better plans for than being a prostitute and a junkie.

She slowly walked towards the hospital a block away, heavy in thought. Malik had promised he'd find a rehab for her upstate, at a place called Coniford Park. That had a swimming pool, tennis courts and arts, and crafts. She wondered if it was rehab or a camp? The child was hooked on drugs, not hobbies and crafts. It seemed somewhat comical to her, but she hadn't seen Malik in a while, and he hadn't called. So, Coniford Park was out of the question anyway.

As she made her way into the hospital, she glanced around at the people in the waiting area. A whole lot of pain. hopelessness and turmoil showed on their fences as the spirit of impatience fell upon them.

She listened to all the utterances like: *Nurse, it's been three hours already!"*
"Please...where's a doctor?" It made her frown.

As she pressed the elevator button she overheard. *"Ma'am just be patient. We'll be calling you soon."* While a female nurse's orderly leaned back in a padded swivel chair doing her nails talking on the phone.

Waseema shook her head as the elevator door closed thinking how sad the whole scene was. As she came out of the elevator, she scanned the desk at the nurse's station and a young, wide-eyed girl peeped up from behind her computer screen and waved at her.

Waseema gestured back and donned a smile. "Is she ready?" "Yes ma'am, she's in her room," she responded as she stood up.

She pointed down the hall. "They've been here with her all night coming and going in shifts. Your daughter must be pretty special?" Waseema only smiled as she watched the nurse admire the young Fruit of Islam posted at Shaheeda's room door. "Yes, she is."

"They, uh, gave me a number to a place they go." She pulled out a card from her pocket. "Here it is."

"Probably Mosque number seven," Waseema said as she glanced at it. "Yeah, that's it. Who knows maybe I'll see you around?"

"I'd like that!" she said as she continued to check out the young men.

Waseema left the young impressionable nurse to her whimsy, then she called out to her as she started to walk away. "Yes, something wrong?" she asked.

"Oh, yeah, I'm sorry, Asalaam Alaikum," she said as she read from the back of the card.

Waseema tilted her head sideways then looked over at the young men as they tried to avert their attention. She smiled and twisted an eyebrow. Evidently, one of them had spent a little time with her.

"Wa Alaikum Asalaam," she responded back as she approached the door.

Both men now stood at attention. Their suits were impeccably pressed, and they smelled fresh from the dry cleaners. She sniffed her approval. "Asalaam Alaikum, my brothers."

"Wa Alaikum Asalaam, sister, Waseema! We helped sister, Shaheeda pack her bags, ma'am. She's ready whenever you are," one of them eagerly responded.

"Good, but I want to talk to her for a moment before we go."

"Yes ma'am, of course. We'll be escorting you home. Orders from the Mosque."

"Orders, from the Mosque?" Her puzzled face showed the fact that she hadn't been around for a while and she wondered, why would this be an order situation? She just thought the young men were friends of Shaheeda from her days at the Temple.

'*Who would give such an order?*' she thought.

The brothers her mother had sent was only for a few days.

"Brother Captain Craig 3X, ma'am, his orders," one of them said.

She stood there thinking about the last time she'd seen him. She had heard he made a pretty upward progression in the Nation of Islam since the time when Khalid first met him. He was just a young man on the verge of drugs and prison, but she was glad he still showed respect for the family. He was a big man now.

"Okay," she replied then turned and pushed the door open to the room.

145

Dean Hamid

Shaheeda stood gazing out the window. Her frail body was wrapped in bandages, mostly around her ribs. Her face was still swollen around the jaw, but for the most part, she was still strikingly attractive. As she turned toward her mother, their eyes met. "Ma!"

Waseema hugged her and she cringed slightly in pain, her arm was hung in a sling. She pulled back, kissed both of her cheeks and asked, "You alright, baby?"

"Yes, ma, I'm alright," she answered.

Waseema held her hand and led her to the bed where they sat. "No, I mean are you alright?"

"What?"

"Are you ready to come home, Sweetheart? Remember how you got here. It's still out there. Are you sure you're ready?" Shaheeda held her head down. "Yes, I guess."

Waseema stroked her shiny brown hair and lifted her head. "Hold your head up, Child. Don't look towards the ground for no one. You hear?"

She gazed into her mother's eyes. "That's what daddy used to tell me."

"I know, baby. I would tell him the same thing." She reached into her purse and pulled out some tissue gently wiping Shaheeda's slanted doe-like eyes. "But baby, I got to know…"

"Know what?"

She held her hands tightly together and squeezed softly. "Why…why the drugs? Didn't we…I, raise you right? I mean, you were right there besides me. What happened, did I do something wrong?"

She pulled her mother close, then paused taking a deep breath before she spoke, "Yes…you did." Waseema's jaw dropped at hearing what she really didn't want to. Tears welled up in her eyes. "But it wasn't your fault, Ma."

"What do you mean? What did I do wrong?" she asked in between sobs.

"Maybe, I shouldn't have said it like that." She turned away. "Remember when you used to take us…me…Latif, to the Mosque uptown? It…it happened then…"

"What are you talking about?" she asked as she slowly rubbed her back and shifted toward her.

"When you used to leave me there for the Muslim Girls Training class. Well, Brother Craig 3X, he…used to do things to me when you were gone."

Waseema leaned back as if she was about to be hit by a truck, thinking to herself and said, "No…not that! Him?"

"He had his way with the other girls, too. So, he…you know."

146

"When!" Waseema put her hand to her mouth, visibly upset and asked, "How long?"

"When I was eight and..."

"Oh, hell no!" she said as she stood up, disgusted and angry. "I'm gonna kill that..."

"Ma, it's over." Shaheeda followed closely behind her to the window.

"Why didn't you tell us, Shaheeda? You could have said..."

"Said what!" Shaheeda shouted and pulled at her, turning her around. "You...Dad...Grandma...I would have, but it would have been an embarrassment. You know, besides, his word against mine! Those other girls weren't going to say anything! And then, he kept telling me he would marry me!"

Waseema could only drop her head as the tears ran heavy down her face uncontrollably. "I'm so sorry, baby, I'm so sorry!"

Shaheeda embraced her with the one good arm she had. "Ma," she said. "It's gonna be alright, please, believe me."

She wiped her eyes and stared into her daughter's face, somewhere beyond the pain. Somewhere deep into her soul and said softly to her, "Yes, I believe you."

Shaheeda smiled and said, "It's a new day." She walked over to the door. "Let's go." She opened it, stuck her head out and said, "Brothers, my bags are ready."

The young men jumped to their feet and replied, "Okay, sister!"

She waved her mother over as she dried her eyes and said to them, "Escort me and my mother home."

"Yes, ma'am."

Waseema stopped by her as she passed and kissed her tenderly on the forehead, without a word as she stepped through the door. Shaheeda was right on her heels as the young Fruit of Islam scurried in front of them to press the elevator button. Then, they stepped back behind them. Princes serving Queens, theirs. The nurse watched from the distance in awe and was moved.

Waseema glanced over at her as she stepped into the elevator and nodded, then said, "You're right, I will see you later. I think you're about ready." Leaning over to one of her brothers, she whispered in his ear, "Tell Brother Craig 3X, I'm coming up there to...uh, thank him personally. Okay?"

"Yes ma'am, I sure will!" The young man beamed. "He will be pleased."

Waseema peeped over at Shaheeda, who was unaware of what she'd said and turned back to him. "Good! Good."

****

Detective Giovanni sat quietly at his desk flipping through the pages of a girl order magazine out of Florida mumbling, "Hmm, Brazil." He'd been expecting a call from his friend from the FBI's office concerning the tape and it was late in the afternoon now. He figured he'd wait at least one more hour.

"Giovanni!" A voluptuously, top-heavy woman with a short, cropped haircut, spiked in the middle, stuck her face inside the doorway. "You've got mail!" He peeped up trying to conceal what he had in his hands.
"Uh...be there in a sec, Edna."

"You might want to try Russia, too. Good looking women...love Americans."

Giovanni swung his feet off the top of the desk and got up, awkwardly facing her. "It was just...uh, I found this. Yeah...by the bathroom." He tossed it face down on his desk smiling sheepishly. "Just flipping through it." Opening the door for her he dug into the mail bin she carried and said, "Sure, sure, whatever, but if you ask me. I'd go foreign."

She pulled out a padded legal envelope and handed it to him. "Trust me sweaty, I know." She winked.

He stood there for a second staring off as she trekked off into the next office. "Hmmm, trust me," he muttered.

Shaking it off, he stepped back over to his desk and plopped down. He pulled out a pencil, ripped through the top of the package and pulled out a tape cassette with a letter attached to it:

Detective Giovanni,
Detective, we pieced through what we could and it's much better now than it was. When we played the recording, we heard something quite interesting. Call me if you want to pursue it any further. Good Luck!

Agent Carter, FBI

"Hmmm." He looked up from the desk. "Hey, Scadelli! You know where I can find a cassette player?"

The fat, balding detective that sat across from him on the other side of the office put down the newspaper and in a thick Italian accent replied, "Sure, Mickey...a museum!" He busted out laughing.

"Yeah, yeah, yeah everybody's a fucking comedian," he said hearing snickers from around the office as he got up and headed for Property.

"Hey, Doug, you wouldn't happen to have one of those cassette players?"

"Sure, Mickey, hold up." The older, battle-scarred face of the officer in front of him, grinned ear-to-ear as he bent-over body disappeared into a grimy looking, caged room filled with plastic bags and tagged boxes. The officer came back out with a huge boom box, blowing dust off it. "Seized in a drug bust over on the Southside, has lots of power, too." He turned it on and the radio blast through the speakers loud enough to cause Giovanni to jump back a bit. "Oh, sorry about that."

"Damn, Doug, almost reached for my gun."

"*Gun?*" Doug's eyes narrowed as he stared around keenly like a paranoid spy. Perhaps, from his thirty-plus years on the job, but most likely from too many hours in this caged world of his and said, "Oh...gun...the radio blast, I get it now." He slid the radio over to him. "Here ya go, Mickey."

Giovanni tucked it under his arm and walked back to the office.

"Oh, yeah, Detective!" Officer Doug called out. "If you want to hold on to it overnight, you'll have to sign." He waved around a form.

He started to double back then thought out loud, "*Shouldn't take no more than a couple of minutes.*"

He placed the boom box on his desk in the office and Scadelli gawked over at him and asked sarcastically, "What the hell did you do, Giovanni? Raid a drug house over in the projects or something?"

"You know, Scadelli, you're a real dick. You might be able to do comedy ya know!"

"Huh? Yeah, right, but I did think about doing comedy."

"Good, because you're one big ass joke!" The detectives laughed, ready for Scadelli's response, but he replied dryly, "Go to hell, Giovanni."

"What's that...hell? The only reason you became a detective, much less a cop, wasn't to solve crimes, but so you'd figure out where your nuts are."

Scadelli got up from his chair and looked down at his gut. Hanging well over his belt buckle. "Hey! What? I'm losing weight."

"Sure, Scadelli, sure."

Just then, the Captain walked into the room. "You guys are all buddybuddy here, I see. You wonder why we can't seem to solve all those cases stacked up on your desks?" He handed some papers to Giovanni as the other detectives rolled their eyes talking under their breath. "Giovanni, wasn't this one of your people?"

He grabbed the papers and looked over them. "Hell yeah! Damn!"

"Just happened a couple of days ago."

"Why didn't anyone let me know?"

"Whoa…hold up." The Sergeant threw up his hands in defense and said, "They had to distinguish what it was first. Thought it might had been a robbery, and still do."

"It's still a murder regardless, it should have at least made the news."

"It did," Ravanel said as he walked through the door.

"How'd you find out?"

"I read the newspapers." He peeped over on his desk and Giovanni's eyes met his checking out the magazine he had and said, "Can't help it if you don't."

The Captain grinned at his wit as he walked to the door. "Hey, don't worry. It's too late for that now. Just get on it, Giovanni." As he walked through the door he peeped back in and said, "Hey, Scadelli? Still looking for that nut sack of yours?" His laughter echoed as he walked down the hall.

"So, what's up?" Ravanel asked as he turned facing Giovanni.

"Man, I can't believe this. City Councilman, Malik Shabazz…murdered."

Ravanel picked up the paperwork and flipped through it. "Bed-Stuy, right?"

"Yeah, his district," he said. "They found his body in his office."

"I see." He put the paperwork down, paced the floor and asked, "Why didn't the FBI pick it up?"

Giovanni stared at him for a minute, then snapped his fingers. "You're right. Why the hell did Cap come in here just to let me know?" He looked around the room. "And, no one else?" He picked up his jacket and started to dash out the door. Then stopped and turned. "Ravanel, good work. And, uh, could you sign out that boom box and put that cassette tape up for me?"

Scadelli grabbed the tape and said, "Hey, is this some of that hip hop? Man, I love that stuff." He actually made an attempt at a two-step. His girth wallowing from side to side with every move.

Ravanel shook his head and looked up at the ceiling in bewilderment. "C'mon, Scadelli, you're shaking the damn building. And no, that's evidence!" he said as he snatched it back.

He picked up the keys from the Desk Sergeant for an unmarked vehicle, signed for them, and headed to Malik's office in Bed-Stuy.

****

Giovanni pushed through the front door of the building where Malik's office was, moving cautiously he entered. He studied what he could as he crept forward. He noticed pictures in the doorway that had been either seemingly strewn about or knocked over by Police Officers, the Coroner and whoever else had made their way through since. He shook his head and cursed the Department for compromising the crime scene. Making his way toward the stairway that led to the office, he peeped around the stairs, eyeballing the six other offices behind it. All appearing to be vacant. He made a mental note to investigate them later. Squinting, he caught the light on the overhead sign marked. 'Warehouse' toward the back hallway.

His back was against the wall as he silently maneuvered up the steps, the writings on the double-windowed door ahead of him grew larger and larger as he approached: *Malik Shabazz, City Councilman, District Eighteen.* Pushing at the door, he was surprised it was open. As he made his way in, the front receptionist desk had papers scattered about. Over to his left was another entranceway with yellow Police tape across the front. That, he figured was where the body was found.

He ducked underneath the tape and mumbled how easy this whole thing seemed. Easy in, easy out. Why wasn't the place locked down? Or, maybe it was, and somebody was on their way back. He stepped in and over toward the tape line that marked the body. His mouth gagged as he saw the blood spot still wet and glistening. It had a foul smell. He heard a sound coming from downstairs. Perhaps, the killer had made it back? He'd soon find out. He eased back over to the doorway and pulled his gun. Creeping slowly to the stairway he caught the shadow of the person that had just come through the door.

'*Was it a homeless person?*' he thought. '*Or, maybe somebody trying to rob the place? Perhaps, lying in wait for the investigation to be over and steal whatever they can.*' He'd figure it out once he confronted him, but the question that dug at him most was. Why were the upstairs doors not locked anyway; after all, it was the scene of a crime? The mysterious shadow emerged back from around the steps and started to climb the stairs as Giovanni laid in wait. The doors opening gradually, and he braced himself. He pulled back the hammer on the nine-millimeter he carried.

He jumped out in front as the shadow drew nearer and leveled the gun in the face of the trespasser. "Freeze!" he said, then twisted his head and quickly lowered his weapon. "I almost shot you!"

"Glad you didn't." It was Mike from the FBI.

"What the hell are you doing here? This isn't a federal investigation or is it?" he questioned.

"It's not, I called your office and Officer...uh..."

"Ravanel...Bobby's boy. You remember, Bobby, right?"

"Yeah, sure. He told me you were here."

They walked through the door of Malik's office and stepped over a large bloody spot. "Looks like somebody did him in at close range. That's a whole lot of blood," Mike said as he kneeled down. "Too much." He pointed. "And all the blood on the walls. Hell, couldn't have been that much splatter, he was probably beaten first."

Giovanni looked around at the stained carpet and agreed with him. "Yeah, seems like." Then, he made out what seemed like a long trail leading to the desk. "Hmmm," he said as he got closer examining it. "Look at all the blood on the desk and chair."

"Damn, Mike." He looked over at the other spot. "Hell, there were two bodies! What happened to the other body?"

"You're right! Don't know, did they say they found one?" he asked.

Giovanni reached into his pocket and briefed through the report the Captain had given him earlier. "Naw."

Mike rubbed his head. "I bet this has something to do with..." "With what, Mike? You did say that Malik was tied into something. That there was some sort of investigation situation going on, right?"

"There is." He shot a look over at Giovanni and said, "The Los Andres Cartel."

"The same ones involved with that guy's death over at Central Booking?"

"But these bastards got shop set up in Mexico. A place called Michoacan, they're worse." He paced across the floor looking at the pictures hanging up. "Remember, the ones that came from Columbia and dumped drugs in Bushwick, Bed-Stuy?" He stopped in front of a photo of Malik and Khalid and stared.

"Yeah, but I thought we ran them out?"

"You kiddin' me. They just moved somewhere else, and we don't know where. They fucked up and pulled in the Mexicans, and their trail went cold. But hell, half of the activity in Brooklyn is attributed to them."
"And, you don't suppose that's how Malik got his position. He sold out, damn, this might have been a hit."

"Yep, seems that way."

Giovanni walked toward the door and said, "Look, we better go. I'ma get a car over here to watch the premises. We're going to have to go over this place with a fine-toothed comb. Find out who the hell was in here." Mike staggered behind and glanced over at the desk. "You're right, Mickey. I'll get to the office and dig up some names." He eyeballed the desk drawer that was open, leaned over and looked in, feeling his hands along the insides. Then silently closed it. He then caught up with Giovanni at the double glassed doors. "Yeah, we need to find out who knows what."

They walked out of the building and Mike took out his car keys and said, "Hey, Mickey, be careful, ya hear."

"Always, Mike, always. See you later." He walked over to a payphone and called his Precinct. "Let me speak to, Officer Ravanel." He wasn 't getting a good vibe from Mike or his story.

Ravanel sat at Giovanni's desk in the squad room shifting through papers, stacks of cases on commercial property, management, and eminent domain outlines; factories with zoning issues reaching Bedford Stuyvesant as far back into Bushwick. It was a problem. Where to put people that were about to be pushed out of neighborhoods because of inner-city sprawl. It was the beginning of gentrification. Cruising and exploring on his own time, he surveyed the areas in question. Nothing was said, so he made his way to City Hall and looked up the zoning construction bids and permits. A mall was supposedly on its way up, and after some more extensive research, he noticed the connection to Malik.

Because of the trucks coming off the Brooklyn-Queens Expressway, the district had to be re-zoned. He rode over that way and realized the reasons: degradation by cocaine, and heavy rapid poverty and infestation. All being slated for high-development, and expensive real estate properties; co-signed by one Malik Shabazz. He didn't recognize the developers. A company out of a place in Mexico he'd never heard of, Michoacan. That raised a red flag, so he dove deeper and made some calls, that's where he found it. The first records, the addresses he remembered, two warehouses, occupied and owned by The Moors Institute of Science. They were massive in size and eight blocks smack in the middle of it all.

He looked up the property and found that the owners had been compromised as a result of tax excursions. The deed and property were tied up in court litigations. Being contested by none other than the developers out of another place he'd never heard of in Mexico; Morelia, the capital of Michoacan, Mexico.

"Wow," he sighed. "All this…drugs…poverty…over a damn mall?" He leaned back. "It's got to be bigger than that." He got up and scooped up the papers, thinking to himself, *'I've got to get up with Giovanni, now!'*

His thoughts were interrupted by the squad's Lieutenant, Stephens. "Ravanel, there's someone here to see you."

"Sure, thing l-t." He waved at him and kept shuffling papers.

"Now Officer," he said coldly, then waved the person through the door.

He came over to him, stretched out his arm and said, "Mike Davis…FBI."

Ravanel tucked the papers he had under his arm and shook his head, then snatched it back from Mike's vice-grip like handshake. "Something wrong?" he asked.

"No, shouldn't be," Mike responded as he reached for the papers. "But uh, you never know." He flipped through a couple of pages and Ravanel stood with his arms crossed, noticeably nervous. The Lieutenant shooed the other cops away as they started watching the whole thing go down. "Look uh, do you have authorization for all this?"

"Well, uh, no…I."

Well, you're not privy to this then son. Let me have all you got okay, and maybe I can make this problem go away."

"Problem…what problem?" He asked as his voice quivered.

Mike sat down on the desk and said, "Well, it appears that there's a leak somewhere and we're investigating it."

Ravanel paused, then chose his words and said, "No leak here, sir. Besides, I don't know anything. Look uh, Mike, right? I really don't want no trouble."

"Well." He guided him to a seat in front. "There wouldn't have to be. If you let me know all that you know."

"I was working for, Detective Giovanni. Why don't you ask him?"

"Yeah, Giovanni. Well, we'll take care of that soon enough. But you know, Ravanel. He's got a whole lot more time on the job than you have. What'cha got two years or something?" He reached for the polished shiny tin on his chest and traced his fingers along the bottom. "Badge number, one-zero-six-eight-eight-hmmm."

"Y-y-yes, sir."

"And your dad, Bobby Ravanel. Detective killed in the line of duty. Damn, I'd hate for his own son to go down with such a uh, bad review. You agree?"

It was a wrap. Ravanel was shaken, Mike had him. "Okay, I'll give you what I got."

Mike leaned in front of him and said, "You're doing the right thing, trust me." He looked over at Lieutenant Stephens. "We 'll help you get it together, right."

"What about, Giovanni?" Stephens asked.

"Like I said, we'll take care of him." Stephens gathered up the paperwork and called over two other officers who started going through the desk. Ravanel was escorted out of the room.

Mike stood up and peered around the room at the other cops, putting the tim down, and said, "No one else knows anything, right?"

They all shook their heads and averted their eyes. Not wanting to deal with the FBI or being labeled as a snitch.

Mike grinned, now all he had to do was deal with Giovanni. As he walked out the squad room, he turned toward the Interrogation Room where Ravanel sat under scrutiny by his superiors and shook his head. He figured he'd get a good tongue lashing. Probably even get transferred to traffic duty for a while, maybe teach him to stay in line. He bought a lot of heat to the Precinct and NYPD damn sure didn't like that. But, that's far better than what happened to his old man, Bobby. He turned toward his plaque hanging on the far end of the wall. Had to teach him a lesson, too. Yeah, he snickered, much better than what happened to his old man.

Chapter Fourteen

It hadn't been much of a Summer, Fall seemed to kick in rather quickly. The colorful trees had leaves para-trooping into the grass, blown around in whirlwinds, dancing up a storm in the streets and endless gutters, leaving behind bare and naked thickets. The projects seemed to jut out to its fullest now. No longer shaded and hidden. Concrete, brick, and steel, the pageantry of urban, ghetto bliss in the midst of the progressively and at times upward city of Brooklyn in the throngs of an early Winter.

Shaheeda glanced outside her window, watched the leaves being blown around and hollered out to her mother, "Seems like Winter's about to come in like a lion. I might need a winter coat, Ma."

Waseema peeped her head out of the bathroom. "What?"

"A winter coat, I need one."

She stepped out with a towel wrapped around her head. "Yeah, it is getting pretty cold." She looked outside, too. "I need one myself."

Shaheeda took the towel from off her mother's head and after she made her way to the couch, she started drying her hair. "Just washed it, huh."

"Had to do something. See any grey hairs?" she asked.

Shaheeda smirked and said, "Now Ma, you ain't no spring chicken anymore."

"So, what you, saying?" She reached around and pulled her down on the couch and playfully tickled her. "I can remember when I was your age."

"Really?" she asked. "What was that like?"

Waseema pulled her up and leaned back into the sofa looking out, pulling up memories. "It was nice, Harlem back then...real nice."

"Really, well, when did you meet dad?" she asked, watching her mother recollect her younger years.

"Late fifties, I met your father at a rally held by, Elijah Muhammad. Your daddy was a supporter then, but he hadn't joined the movement yet."

"What was he like?"

Waseema got up from the couch and walked over to where a picture of Khalid was. "He was fine...real fine, but he was a thug. He'd been in and out of jail and was real wild."

Shaheeda laid back fluffing a pillow. "I know grandma wasn't going for that."

"You're right." She giggled. "But when he finally joined the Nation of Islam, he was a changed man!" She stood up straight imitating a soldier. "My daddy loved him and thought the world of him." She put the picture back down then stared off.

Shaheeda sensed some pain, got up, walked over and stroked her long, flowing black hair. "You think when I get myself together. I can find someone, too?"

She turned and gazed into her daughter's pretty brown eyes and said, "Baby, of course." She hugged her. "You will, I promise."

"You promise, Ma?"

"Baby, I promise. Now..." She patted her playfully on the behind and said, "Go get dressed so you can go out and find a coat."

"You coming with me?"

"No, not today. I'm supposed to be going out to eat with someone." She checked her watch. "But I haven't heard from him and it's getting pretty late. Oh, well, maybe he got caught up..."

"Ice?" Shaheeda stated. "He went up to Harlem with your knucklehead son and his friends."

"What?" She did a double take. "How did you know about..."

"C'mon Ma, please, I'd see him all the time cut through the park. But it's cool, I like him."

She leaned against the doorway. "Uh-huh, okay. Spying on your Momma. Who else knows?"

"I think Mustapha knows. I know Rasheed doesn't. If he did, he'd have said something already."

"You're right."

"But you're grown and sexy, so..."

She turned around, walked into her room and said, "But you know how protective your brothers are."

Shaheeda just smiled and said, "For real, but anyway, you're grown. Oh, yeah, they went to see, Mustapha."

"They just can't be apart, can they? That Derek just had to show off his new car. Shaheeda, you hear anything from, Mya?"

"Yeah, we talked. She's still hung up on, Rasheed. Don't really know what she wants."

"Devone either."

"I need to talk to her. Just so much has been going on, though."

"Which one, Devone or Mya?"

"Probably both."

Shaheeda walked over, gently kissed her forehead and said, "But, it's over now. At least, my situation."

"I know, Sweetheart, I know," she answered back, hoping like hell she wasn't lying to herself.

Shaheeda called a couple of her old girlfriends to see if they wanted to hang out with her. Most of them gave the excuse that they were busy. Many remembered her history and shied away from her. But she still had two faithful partners: Lisa Williams and Donna Cruz. Lisa had just recently joined the Nation of Islam. She was a single mother taking care of a son. Donna showed no interest in religion whatsoever. She had a hellafied smoking habit that didn't allow her to sit through church, much less a lecture.

After making plans she called out to her mother as she made her way out the door. "Ma! See you later, love you!"

"I love you, too!" Waseema yelled back. "Don't be out too late!"

She sat on the edge of the bed by the phone contemplating calling Malik. She hadn't heard from him in a while and didn't have a clue to what had gone on. Worried, she was tempted to go to his office but figured she'd wait it out. *'He'll be around soon enough,'* she thought to herself.

Shaheeda bounced out of the building, feeling like new money. No more shackles on her feet and her face showed it all. A new future, a new tomorrow. She showed all teeth and dimples as she spoke to the neighbors, knowing she'd been through all hell and happy to see her back-minus Randy. A lot of smiles and good lucks, and she needed them all. Cause when it rained, it poured

"Girl, you look much better! Let me look at you!"

"Thank you," Shaheeda said as she spun around. "I feel much better, too."

Donna had met her on Moore Street by the school, PS 257. As she was leaning back against the black iron fence, she spotted Sha', as she affectionately called her coming through the playground. Both went to school together since kids except for high school. Donna; being the most creative took the city-wide test for the High School of Art and Design in Manhattan and passed. After graduating, she found work at an ad agency in the city as a production assistant. She was paid good, but not enough to get out of the projects. So, she enrolled in night school at FIT University, she made the most out of her fashion consciousness and started making outfits, selling them at flea markets in SoHo.

She was single and didn't have time for a serious relationship or a boyfriend, which led others to think she was a lesbian. Though she never denied it, she continued doing her own thing. Besides, she hated Bushwick, and just wanted to get the hell out of the projects.

"What's that you're wearing, you made that?" Shaheeda asked.

"I did think about starting my own line and selling them in the Village. You like it?"

"Nice," Shaheeda said as she ran her fingers through its silk texture.

Donna hugged her and said, "You were always my biggest fan, actually my only fan." She laughed.

"That's what friends are for."

They turned up the block searching and there was, Lisa, coming from around the corner. Shaheeda grinned as she came up the sidewalk and said, "Look at you!" She wore a hijab. The female head-garb for Muslims. Waseema at one time was the only girl in the projects to wear one amidst all the stares and off-color comments.

"C'mon now." Lisa blushed. "After being around you all these years. I guess it just sort of rubbed off."

"Guess so, but uh, I heard you got your 'X,' too." She gushed.

"I'm a Vanguard, too!"

"What! No, a Vanguard…security! That's alright. Oh, sorry…Asalaam Alaikum!"

Lisa's face glowed. This was the first time she had done something positive with her life. She'd been fast, and always into something, usually trouble. She was a wild child so to speak, but now, as she stood with her eyes welled up with tears of joy. She returned the greeting with pride, "Wa Alaikum Asalaam, my sister!"

"Okay-okay," Donna interrupted. "This is getting too damn emotional for me. I mean, we're just going to get a coat, right? In all actuality, Shaheeda. I could have made one for you, you know." She reached into her purse and pulled out a pack of cigarettes. Shaheeda frowned and she caught it. "Don't even…"

"C'mon, Donna, at least try."

Lisa snatched at the pack and said, "Look at Shaheeda, and all she's been through."

Donna pulled the cigarettes back and grumbled, "You're making this hard."

"Well then…" Shaheeda pulled Lisa back and said, "The choice is yours. But remember, we're here for you."

Donna agitatedly shoved the pack of Newport's into her purse and said, "Okay-okay. We'll see how long I can go!" "Want some gum?" Lisa asked.

"Gum?" Donna smirked as she looked at the pack of Double mint in her hand. "How about a gum factory? Cause that's what it gonna take."

They were all good as they headed off toward downtown Brooklyn, but Shaheeda wanted to try the shopping areas on Graham Avenue first, just around the corner. Then, if she didn't find what she wanted they'd ride out. Maybe even go to Delancey Street in the city. They were in and out of stores, coats were put on. Outfits were modeled, and shoes by the dozen were tried. They were having fun. Something that these three truly needed. Their lives had taken tolls that had been very difficult for them. The rigorous life of being a single, young black woman in New York did them in. A hard knock life you can call it but made it to the point where they could still see some light at the end of the tunnel. There was hope it seemed and always a tomorrow.

"So, uh, Shaheeda. When you gonna get yourself a man?"

"What...a man!" Shaheeda gasped. "Where'd that come from?"

Donna stared at Lisa. "Y'all do let women in the Mosque have men, right?"

"Shaheeda's fine as hell, brothers ask about her all the time," she said.

"So then, Sha, what's up?"

Shaheeda admired a pair of shoes she'd tried on and said, "Y'all like these?" Trying to divert the conversation, unsuccessfully.

"Uh-uh, girl, don't even try to change the subject," Donna said as she crossed-snapped her fingers.

"Believe me, I'd like somebody, but I want a good strong man. Who's clean, committed and this may sound crazy, but just like my father."

Donna moved closer toward her, put her arm around her and hugged her. "Look, that's not crazy. That's real, especially after all you've been through. Am I right, Lisa?"

"Hell, you know what I'ma say. Take your time, I got one I look at every night. Take your time, Sha, he'll come." "Or she," Donna added.

"No, you didn't just go there? So, you really are..." Lisa turned toward her.

"Gay? Lesbian, well..."

"Well, what!" Lisa said as she got up in her face. "You're my best friend. All this time, you could have at least..."

"Least what!" Donna pushed past her, storming out the store.

Shaheeda was right behind her and grabbed her by the arm saying, "Whoa, hold up. It ain't that damn easy."

Donna jerked her arm away and stopped. "Yes, it is! I never said I was but believe me, I'm damn sure thinking about it." She turned around to face them. "And, I thought I could at least talk to my friends about it!"

"Damn, Donna, I'm stupid." Lisa came over to her. "I'm sorry! You know you can talk to us about anything."

"I just need to talk, got a lot of things on my mind. I can't…" her voice cracked.

"I feel you. We haven't done that in a while anyway. I need to get some stuff off, too. I never did tell…"

"No, Shaheeda, you never did. And, I'm still pretty pissed!" Lisa blurted. "Damn, girl, drugs!"

"Okay-okay, look after we finish, we can go to Sha's house. Is Mustapha there?" Donna asked.

"Hold up." Lisa's eyebrows creased up. "Girl, you ain't gay!"

Donna just laughed and said, "I never said I was…remember. Now, Mustapha, damn he's fine!"

"You're out of your mind. Trust me, you don't want anything to do with my brother!" Shaheeda laughed.

They made their way out of the store. A tall, slim man approached them and stood in front of them blocking their exit.

"Excuse me, Sir," Lisa said as they tried moving around him, but their path was blocked again. "Excuse me, Sir!" she said again.

He unbuttoned the front of his long trench coat and reached inside. "You're excused…" He pulled out a .45 automatic handgun and pointed it towards them.

One of the customers in the store spotted it and shouted out. "Oh, my God, he's got a gun!" All hell broke loose.

There were screams as people ran hysterically; ducking and diving into racks of clothes and behind shoe boxes.

Shaheeda turned to run, but he reached out grabbed her by the hair and said, "Everyone, back the hell up. Now!" He waved the gun around in the air.

Donna and Lisa stood motionless as he backed up out of the store into an awaiting car with Shaheeda in his grasp. "Now…you!" He pointed to Donna.

"Yeah? Please, don't hurt my friend. We have money…" Lisa snuck around to the side of him as Donna continued to hold his attention. "I want you to deliver a message!" he shouted at her.

"Please, Sir, just let my friend go," she pleaded.

"You tell, Mustapha, I have his sister. If he wants to see her alive again, contact Felix!" He shoved Shaheeda into the back of the car.

Lisa had finally made her way around him unnoticed. His back turned as he pushed Shaheeda into the car. Cat-like she jumped on him and grabbed him by the neck, putting him in a chokehold.

Donna rushed him too and kicked, landing a heel to the groin. "Let her go!" she shouted.

He reeled around and slammed Lisa into the side of the car. She crumbled to the ground from the force, then straightening up she swung. It was too much for him. He pulled back the chamber of his gun and aimed it directly at her head, then Donna's. "I should kill you both!" he spat as he held his stomach in pain.

Shaheeda yelled from the car, "No, don't, I'll go with you! Please, don't kill them, I'll go," she cried.

Donna pulled Lisa away from the car slowly as she looked through the window at Shaheeda. The connection in their eyes as she mouthed the words. "Don't worry, we gonna find you. Don't worry."

Shaheeda's head was violently shoved toward the floor as the tires skidded and the car sped off. Lisa tried in vain to get the tag numbers, but there wasn't any. However, she did remember a Lincoln Continental, a tall Spanish man, and a name, Felix.

Donna grabbed her from behind and said, "C'mon, we got to get the police!"

Lisa just stood still and stared up Flushing Avenue towards Marcy Projects the direction where the car had sped off. "No!" she said.

"What, no, are you crazy? We have to move fast!"

"No!" She finally looked over at her distraught friend and said, "We're going to Waseema's to find Mustapha. Trust me, this ain't got nothing to do with the police!" She straightened her clothes and brushed herself off. "They want, Mustapha, not Shaheeda!" She reached out, grabbed ahold of Donna's trembling hands and guided her toward the projects. "Let's go, we've got to move fast. So, we can get her back!"

****

New York had its fair share of potholes, but Derek's Cadillac seemed to float along them effortlessly, cruising over the Williamsburg Bridge, the big-bodied vehicle's suspension glided right over them. Derek's face glowed as the sun rays off the East River shined into the car. He'd always wanted a Cadillac. The car of the players, hustlers, and big money makers. Those who set things in motion and he considered himself the latter. It had been his idea to move in on Felix. Sticking up spots was his plan. It had since developed into something more ominous, mostly because of his sister.

Rasheed agreed to it when he was approached because he hated what Felix represented. Shaheeda was already staying out late and experimenting with drugs. Mustapha sold weed, the family started to fall apart, and Derek took full advantage. He manipulated Rasheed into being a good point man, who was fearless and precise. Devone then put together the rest of the team with him as Derek's right hand. Besides, he'd rather have him with him than against him. From out the corner of his eye, he peeped over at his childhood friend. He had that certain something he couldn't quite grasp. His swagger, collective coolness and his calm when everything else around him buckled. His looks even, he'd already been able to get a grasp on one, his woman. His mouth curled up as he deliberated.

'Just a matter of time,' he thought to himself. *'I'll have it all.'*

Rasheed had also read Derek's card and sure he'd known him for a while, but he damn sure didn't trust him. Derek had his back for sure, and he definitely wasn't no snitch. They'd pulled many heists together and they were flawless as a team. Leaving nothing behind for the cops except blood and bodies, but something about Derek wasn't right, especially lately. Like most things he reflected, it would all come out in the stretch and he damn sure was running a marathon.

"So, what's up? What you thinking about over there?" Derek asked.

Rasheed kinda gave him that look like don't ask, then cocked his head around. "About you."

Derek paused at first, that threw him, then he laughed it off. "Aw man, be serious."

"I am," Rasheed said as he stared off into the water. He figured he'd better leave it alone. "Yeah-yeah, you trippin'." He glanced into the rearview mirror catching Born's attention and asked, "Born, you like the ride?"

Born inspected his surroundings first before answering, "Leather seats, little leg room, nice pumping stereo…it's cool."

"Got it at a steal, too. Might be able to hook you up."

"Naw I'm alright, I'm a Beamer man. That's my next ride."

"I hear you, but ain't nothing like a Caddy."

"I guess if that's what you like," he said as he hoisted himself between the console. "Could you turn the music down a little?"

"Why, what's up? It's WBLS, I'll just change the station okay."

"Naw, it's cool just turn it down. I want to ask Rasheed a question, actually the both of you."

Rasheed turned toward him after the radio was turned down and asked, "What's going on, Born?"

"Check it, we've been doing this for a while, right?" He asked. "I've never questioned much, but tell me this…"

"What, Born?" Derek interjected. "I mean, we've been over the plan like a hundred times." He slowed down to make the turn onto the FDR Drive and asked matter-of-factly, "Did we actually leave something out or what?"

"Uh…yeah." Born sat back once he knew he had their attention. "How do we get access to both the money and the dope, then get to Mustapha at the same time?"

Rasheed rubbed his goatee then thought out loud, '*Damn, Derek, he's right. How?*'

"Well," he pondered the question as he gripped the steering wheel tight with both hands until they turned red. Born had indeed spotted a flaw in the plan, which wasn't always the case, and it annoyed him. "We might have to use explosives, blow shit up-the door, I guess," he answered.

"No…no, too many people would hear, and the cops would be there before the damn smoke clears. Then, we'd be shooting in the dark looking for shit."

"Then what?" He was frustrated and as was his habit, he started nibbling his lower lip.

Then Rasheed thought of something. "Malik has the keys. We have to get the keys from him, that's all."

"Sounds weak," Born said. "It's not that simple. Now, we have to let him in on shit. Why we need the keys to his warehouse and all that. Nah, he's a City Councilman, remember. Damn, near the police. When it all comes down to it, he won't take no hit for us. Nah, not him."

Rasheed leaned back against the door and said, "Only for a minute."

"For a minute, what the hell you mean?" Derek asked after he nearly collided with the side of a railing. "You want…to kill him?"

"Once he tells us where the keys are then, we out him. Look, man, we do what we do, period!" He straightened back up in his seat and said, "Maybe, we'll see first." It really didn't matter to him because he didn't like him anyway.

Born sighed and said, "Damn, he was alright, too. I could always get a drink from his ass. Oh well."

Ice rubbed the sleep from his eye as he awoke saying, "Did I miss something?"

Born nudged him. "Yeah, we'll fill you in later. But Casanova, you need to get more sleep."

"To hell with you, Born, you just jealous."

"No, not jealous." Born laughed. then glanced over at Rasheed and winked. "Just a little bit smarter than you think."

Derek switched lanes to get on the Westside Highway going to Harlem with Born's coarse laughter flooding the car.

Ice mumbled under his breath, "Fuck you, Born."

****

Latif reclined into a soft, plush leather easy chair while Mustapha kicked back in an old forties style velour love seat.

"I see you're both comfortable," Juanita said as she stepped into the spacious, cherry-wood paneled room, decorated with paintings of Picasso: Still life, Earnie Barnes: moderns and abstracts. "I call this space my quiet room, real home-like."

Mustapha watched as his grandmother gracefully settled into a chair. She snuggled, looking for that perfect fit she'd been accustomed to. "I love this old chair," she said, then once she got cozy, she glanced over and asked, "Okay, you're full now, right?"

"Oh, yeah," he answered, rubbing his bloated stomach. "Grandma, your cooking is always on point."

She smiled and said, "I can tell by your hair, it's still pretty soft, but I know Brooklyn. You ain't been eating no pork?"

"Hell no! Oops, 'cuse me."

"Just thought I'd ask."

Latif leaned forward toward her and whispered, "Chinese restaurants got him…cat."

"Oh, we got jokes now?" Mustapha shot back.

Juanita enjoyed their candor and after a chuckle, quieted them with a wave of her hand, almost majestic like. "Okay, okay, now, you wanted to know about your grandfather, right?" She leaned her still lithe body in the chair and stroked her fingers through her shiny grey hair. "It's about time I told you anyway. You remind me so much of him. You know, he wore his hair dreaded for a while, too."

"That's what's up!" He beamed.

"It was nice, but during that time, it wasn't accepted like it is now. Your grandfather was different."

"I feel different sometimes, people stare. I keep it moist, though, especially on the scalp."

"I see you both know how to take care of yourselves. That's good. Well, Jamar's family came from the islands of Jamaica. Then settled down here in the States in Charleston, South Carolina. He was strong and his skin was dark. You ever heard of the term *'blue-black'*?"

"*Blue black*? No, don't think so. Had people tell me I was as black as night before."

"That trait comes from your grandfather," she continued. "My family is Colombian, lighter and pecan. Anyway, they called him *'Blue'* sometimes."

"Sounds like they made fun of his skin color," Latif added.

"No, not really. He wasn't teased and he made light of it. Believe me, he was quite comfortable with himself. It didn't bother him at all, trust me."

"What did he do for a living?" Mustapha asked.

She crossed her legs and said, "He hustled, that, I found out later. He played no games with it either. He wasn't mean, just real serious with his business."

"Like Rasheed?" he asked.

"Yeah, like Rasheed, I guess. I never looked at it like that, but anyway. I had gone around asking some of my associates in Harlem trying to find out exactly what he did. I really didn't know if he was into dope, numbers, or what. Don't get me wrong he was good to me and bought me nice gifts. He didn't disrespect me in anyway. My parents liked him. So, I didn't question him and neither did they. Besides, coming from a family of hustlers, I just assumed he was into the business. He was, but just not like I thought."

Mustapha leaned closer, clinging to her every word.

"No one knew too much about him. Not even my own family. I figured something was up, or I was just being plain old nosy. So, one night I followed him." She snickered. "Like I was some old private investigator or something. It was strange, but everywhere I went it seemed like a car was trailing me. I got nervous, but still, it didn't stop me. I went to a club where I'd met him at and spied the door. There he was in front, talking to the owner. Harlem's biggest dope dealer at that time, Miguel Merosa," she said as she absent-mindedly played with a large carat ring on her pinky, reflecting back in time.

"I knew it I said to myself, he was a dope dealer, and didn't tell me, I was hot. My people were kinda like the competition. Thought maybe he was playing me. Then someone finally got out of the car that was trailing me. I was frightened wondering what I had gotten myself into to. I started to run, but my path was blocked. I wasn't going down without a fight!"

"Wow, Grandma! What happened next? Why didn't you..."

She held her hand up. "Okay-okay, just give me a minute!" She smiled as she reflected. "The streetlight showed on the faces of the two that got out the car. I recognized them, they were my brothers, Vito and Bobby."
"Like you young folks say, I tripped out. I was real confused then. They told me to step aside and be quiet." "Okay, what happened?" Latif asked.

"Boy, calm down, I'm getting there." She sucked her teeth and shushed him. "We watched as this player got out of a car in front of the club. His name was, Guy Reynolds. Your granddaddy stepped in front of him. Now, Jamar wasn't that tall, but he was a big man, intimidating, too." She glanced over at Mustapha. "'Bout as big as you. "I knew something was about to go down. Hell, I really didn't know what to think. Then he held out his hand and Guy just sort of smirked, arrogantly, and one of his men reached into his pocket. I watched closely it was an envelope stuffed with money. Your grandfather shook his head, then he snapped his fingers and these two big dudes came out of nowhere and surrounded Guy. Guy thought quick and smart."

She let out a robust laugh then continued, "He reached back into his jacket and pulled out this big ass bank-roll and started peeling. My future husband just backed away and was escorted safely into the club with no problems. Next thing I knew, he did the same thing to the other players that came through, Tito Johnson, PeeWee Withers, and Lonzo Jenkins...all night."

"Hold up-hold up," Mustapha said as he leaned back in his chair. "I've heard those names before. You mean to tell me, granddaddy did extortion?"

"That's what I thought, too. But my brothers explained what was going on and what he was doing."

"Uh, which was?" Latif asked. "Cause it sure sounds like extortion to me."

"Of course not! He didn't extort anybody that was illegal!" She leaned into them and whispered like they were being watched or the place was bugged, and in their curiosity, they eased forward, too. "The police couldn't stop the dope from coming in, Nor, could they stop the players from hustling. I mean, this was how money was made in Harlem, for years. So, my family and the other families suggested a tax that could be controlled. They'd be taxed for doing business, and at the same time be provided security. Folks downtown do it all the time; the Mob, the government. But instead of using their people. They wanted to use an outsider, someone that was biased. They dealt with, Jamar. My brothers wanted to just check him out and make sure he was legit. Jamar took the money, and split it evenly, then made sure his men was paid. Then they would give him donations. Those donations went to the poor, the hungry, stuff like that." "So, granddaddy was like the man?" Latif blurted out.

"No boy!" she responded angrily, then caught herself and said, "Not like the police-man! He sort of kept things in check. He was trusted." "Did anyone ever try him?" Mustapha asked.

"Oh, yeah, of course. Your grandfather was nothing to play with, though, people got missing and so did some teeth."

"But how did y'all become so rich?" Latif cautiously asked this time.

"Well, my husband was no dummy, that's for sure. He negotiated little side deals here and there. Instead of money, he bartered for the goods and deals that went down. He was the go-between for the police, too. When the busts went down, he got some of the action; liquor houses, lots. Next thing you know he had his hands in damn near all of Harlem." "His hands in?" Mustapha gasped.

"We damn near own a lot of the property and businesses in Harlem, and what we don't own, we rent." She winked.

"Momma knew all about this?" Latif asked.

"Of course."

"Then, why did she leave from up here?"

"Well, Mustapha, your mother is very independent and headstrong. She wanted to be normal, I guess. No special treatment; and believe me, she got a lot of it. Besides, Khalid had some very honorable intentions, and we backed their move one hundred percent. We loved Khalid very much and trusted him. Just so sorry..." Her voice cracked as she lowered her head to her hands. "It, it, just didn't..."

Mustapha got up, kneeled in front of her and rubbed her hands.

"Grandma, it's alright, it's alright."

Latif fidgeted around he was getting emotional. "I just wish I can find the man who did it!" He pounded his fist into his hand.

She looked up at him, wiped the tears from her eyes and glanced over at Latif. "I know, I know but revenge belongs to..."

"Me! One day…" Latif said as he got up, walked towards the window and threw back the curtains.

Mustapha started to say something, but she held out her hand and whispered to him, "He's entitled to that."

He nodded his head, he'd never seen Latif so worked up about their father before, and it worried him. He sounded like Rasheed, and they sure didn't need two of them. The silence broke as the phone rang.

"I got it, Grandma," Latif said as he picked it up.

"What's up, Latif, it's Rasheed!"

"What's up, bruh?"

Rasheed was using the payphone somewhere off 125th Street. They'd just gotten off the highway and Derek wanted to pull over and get some gas among other things, to get the car prepared to do some serious flossing. "We're up here in Harlem!"

"Oh, yeah. Where at?" Latif asked, waving Mustapha over to the phone. "You took the train?"

"Nah, Derek's with me. He brought a Caddy not too long ago. You know he wanted to floss."

"Yeah, yeah, but just you and Derek? Is his sister with him! She's still fine, right?"

"Calm down and yes, she's still fine. But it's just, Born and Ice."

"Ice, cool, haven't seen him in a while." Mustapha reached for the phone. "Here's Mustapha, I'll see you when you get here, Rasheed." Latif faced his grandmother and said, "That was, Rasheed, he's on his way here. Think he said he was on 125th Street."

"Okay." She stood up. "Haven't seen him in a good while. Did he bring his girlfriend, what's that child's name?"

"Mya, no ma'am, he's with Derek, Born, and Ice."

"Oh, hell no! Those wild ass boys from the projects?" She hastened her way to the door. "Let me go get my gun. They won't eat me out of house and home again." Latif laughed as he watched his grandmother go down the steps heading to the kitchen mumbling under her breath, "Last time those boys ate a whole cow, not today."

He laughed because that's exactly what she was literally going to prepare. She loved them like her own.

Mustapha hung up the phone and said to him. "They'll be here shortly."

Dean Hamid

"Rasheed, Derek, Born and Ice, uptown at the same time. What's up, Mustapha, everything alright?"

"Latif," he said as he walked toward him. He put his arm around his shoulders, and they headed out the door. *"The way things are going these days nothing will surprise me."*

Dunya: The Do Or Die

Chapter Fifteen

"You, stupid little whore!" Felix walked around the chair that Shaheeda was bound to. Her ankles and wrists were duct-taped together. "You don't want to tell me where your brother is?"

She kept her eyes down to the floor, not wanting to exasperate his anger any more than it was. She thought if she could just stick it out, Rasheed and Mustapha would soon be there. He smacked her, the insides of her mouth tasted salty from the blood she spit up and her lips started feeling heavy from the swelling.

"You don't want to talk, huh? I'll make your ass scream then." He unbuckled his belt and pulled it out his pants, almost falling to his knees as he did. "Aw hell." He held one hand to his now drooping pants and said, "I'll find a belt to whip your ass!"

The unidentified man who asked to be called Muerte just looked and shook his head as he watched how ridiculous Felix behaved. "You know, Felix, you should really lose some weight."

He just mean-mugged him as he struggled to put his belt back on. "Mind your business!"

Muerte got up and walked towards Shaheeda. "She is my business."

"Oh, what, you're trying to protect her?"

He stroked Shaheeda's long hair as she wriggled trying to free herself and said, "I'm not her protector. The only reason she's here is to lure her brother. The one you say has access to this money."

She looked up at him and hollered, "Money, what money! My brother ain't got none of his money!"

Felix ripped off a piece of duct tape and slapped it on her mouth. "She doesn't know what she's saying."

Muerte watched. "Well, I'll tell you this much." He walked back over to his seat and said, "If you're lying, I promise, I'll kill you myself."

"No-no, we don't want that!" He nervously backed over toward the phone. "I'll make the call to his family. Then, you'll see, alright."

"Whatever."

Shaheeda tried to understand what all of this was about. She knew for a fact, Mustapha had no access to any of Felix's money, and all this drama couldn't be about the dollars he skimmed. No, it was something else.

Something Felix was not telling. She strained with the duct-tape trying to get the attention of Muerte.

His back was turned as he waved his hand at her and said, "You'll have your time save your strength."

She also knew this had nothing to do with Randy. He was low level. Much too low for Felix to go to this much trouble for.

After Felix finished speaking on the phone he walked over and said, "Okay, I made the call, now we take her to the warehouse and wait."

Muerte got up and stretched. "No, I need to go over there and check things out first. We have to set the trap. So, call back and tell them tonight."

Felix huffed, "Call back for what? No, we'll call back when we get there…"

"No, your fat ass is going to stay here and watch her until I get back. But first I need to get some things out of the car."

'*Warehouse*,' Shaheeda thought. '*What warehouse?*'

"Yeah." Felix looked over at Shaheeda. "Do that, I'll be right here then," he said, admiring her smooth pretty, brown skin. "Take your time."

Muerte just walked off and smirked. "You're a pig, Felix."

He tipped over toward the chair Shaheeda was tied up in, bent over and stroked her hair. She tried to chew threw the duct-tape, but it was to no avail.

"It's just me and you now." He started rubbing the back of his hand across her face. "You cost me a good bit of money with, Randy." He stood behind her grinding his groin against her. "I heard you were good. Bought me a lot of business." He started unzipping his pants. "I'll see."

She cried out as much as she could with the tape still covering her mouth, it was useless. He snatched her blouse open and was immediately aroused. She shuddered with fear as her nipples got hard from the coolness in the air.

He stood in front of her, studying her body language. "Look, you do me right, and maybe, I'll let you go. I mean, we already set the trap for your brother anyway. So, do me right, huh."

She had been raped, molested, and abused too many times since she started using drugs. Her body numb to the men that would sweat and empty their poison into her womb. She hated Randy. The things he would make her do in front of others. Felix had heard about her and wanted to see for himself. She resisted, and that was the catalyst that would set things in motion for Randy's death. She was blessed to be clean and given another chance. She'd rather die first before she let another man touch her against her will and get away with it anymore.

She shook her head.

"Ah, good girl," he said as he snatched the tape from her mouth. She cried out as it was ripped off. "Okay, do me real good, then." He looked down at the chair between her legs. "Then I'll untie you, okay. And, swallow, too." He loosened her hands.

Shaheeda whimpered. "Y-y-yes."

He grabbed the back of her head and poked his erection in her face. Thrusting himself toward her mouth. She slowed down his momentum by grabbing it by the hand. She knew what she was about to do would cost her, her life, but to entertain any of his sick and perverse satisfaction, it was well worth it. She slowly and deliberately opened her mouth.

"Felix! What the hell are you doing?" He backed up surprised by Muerte.

At the same time, Shaheeda tightened her grip and lunged. Muerte managed to push him away just in time as she snapped her jaws shut. She would have bitten his now limp dick clean off.

"What, oh hell. You bitch!"

She bent over quickly and tried to undo the tape around her ankles, but Muerte ran up behind her, maneuvered her into a chokehold and she started gagging.

"Felix, you stupid ass get some more tape!" She fought wildly with Muerte, scratching, but he still hung on. Her strength started leaving her, and her mind started going black.

Felix still struggled to pull up his pants as he grabbed for the ducttape. "Here it is." He threw it to Muerte.

Shaheeda was out cold now, so he re-tied her hands and feet back to the chair, then looked over at Felix. "You're just too stupid!"

He finally got his pants up and stomped over toward her raising his hand to slap her, but Muerte stopped him. "No, you already fucked up enough!" He pushed the chair closer to him saying, "Besides, she only did what she was supposed to do."

"What was that, huh? Bite my cock off!"

"No, survive, or die."

****

The last honk was the one that finally caught his attention. Giovanni whirled his head around facing two red-faced police officers in a squad car staring straight at him. Shaking it off, he really didn't realize how long he'd been out of it.

It embarrassed him. "Uh...yeah." He didn't know what he was answering to.

The fat-faced one who now stuck his head out of the window seemed ready to explode telling him, "Giovanni, you alright? We've been honking at you for the longest!"

"Deep in thought, that's all gotta lot going on," he said as they both pulled over to the side out of traffic. He put his car in park, got out, and walked over. "So, what's up fellas. This your beat?" He glanced toward the numbers spot on Lewis Avenue off Broadway checking out the traffic spewing in and out of the one-time movie theater, now a gambling haven.

"Naw, doing a babysitting job on Sumner in front of the office where that Councilman got killed."

"Yeah, I called for you."

"Well, we're your people."

"That's cool. By the way, what number hit?"

The fat-faced officer that stuck his head out earlier started getting out of the car. "Don't know yet, Mickey, not yet," he said as he reached into his pocket and pulled out a wad of paper; shifting through, he found what he was looking for, a yellow number's slip. "Hope it's 2-2-7, played it earlier."

"Sounds good," Giovanni said as he reached for the slip.

The other officer in the car got out, walked over to where they were and snatched the paper out of Giovanni's hand. "You two should be arrested! Playing the damn numbers." His name was Lipscombe, and he turned toward his partner, Webb, and said, "Especially you! So, all that time you said you were going in casing the joint, you're really playing numbers?"

Webb started snickering under his breath, his face turning red as he answered, "Hell yeah! Where else can you get a 1-64 on a bo-leader?"

Giovanni leaned back against his car and laughed. "You got that right!"

Lipscombe had to laugh, too. He gave Webb back his slip and said, "You guys are a piece of work. Hey, Giovanni, heard about your boy?"

"Boy...what boy?"

"Ravanel." Lipscombe gawked over at Webb. "C'mon now. You don't know, do you?"

"Hell Lipscombe, it just went down," Webb butted in.

Giovanni got up off the car and asked, "What happened to him?"

"Ah damn, you see Lipscombe, you talk too much!"

"Well, I didn't know…"

"What happened!" Giovanni yelled out.

"Okay-okay," Webb responded. "The FBI came in and went through your desk. Took some papers and escorted him out, I believe in cuffs."

"You're kidding me! What happened?"

"Didn't say, it was real hush-hush. Some tall dude from the FBI. Can't remember his name, Lieutenant Stephens called him by his first name, uh…"

"Mike!"

"Yeah, that's was it!"

Giovanni stormed back to the car and said, "See you guys later!"

"Hey wait," Lipscombe ran over. "Hey look, man, you didn't hear anything from us, okay."

"Yeah, sure."

"But if you need our help. I mean, Bobby was alright."

"Sure thing," Giovanni said as he waved and took off toward the precinct.

He knew not to expect much from anyone else. To go up against the FBI was career suicide. Mike was up to something, and it had something to do with the warehouse property Ravanel looked into. Bobby was hot on the trail of something that Mike or whoever didn't want him to know about. He was pissed because he knew he was next on his list.

****

Muerte had finally put the tim down on Felix long enough for him to leave Shaheeda alone. That, and a .45 Auto. He didn't need to screw up any more than he already had. He still didn't know what Mustapha knew and Mustapha had the answers to his questions. He figured he'd find out about the money, cuff it, and then follow his other orders from the Los Andres Cartel. That was to take Felix out. He didn't have a problem with that at all, to him Felix was a waste anyway. He'd overheard some of the Don's talk about the mistakes that was made with Carlos and questioned why he even continued to live as a result.

They figured he must have hauled ass somewhere with his family because they couldn't find him but figured it would only be a matter of time before they showed up. They didn't have a clue that they were all dead. Muerte knew someone high on the food chain kept Felix's ass alive. Now he'd somehow managed to piss someone off, and it wasn't a Don. Muerte didn't care, as long as he fulfilled the obligation and finished the job, he set out to do.

His long black Lincoln pulled up across the street from Malik's office building and he got out, playing it off like he was using the phone. The Officers in the squad car that sat in front, Lipscombe and Webb's, paid him no mind. He eyeballed them and after a while they didn't seem like they were leaving any time soon. So, now he had to call Felix to have his paid flunky at the precinct get rid of them so he could go in and set up the trap in the warehouse.

****

"Rasheed," Latif called out, running over to embrace his brother. "Ah man, ain't seen you in a while!" He backed up a little and looked him up and down. "You look good."

Rasheed smiled he couldn't believe how much his one-time baby brother had grown. He was a young man now. He remembered the days when he'd have to change his diapers.

Mustapha stood off to the side taking in the moment between his brothers. Ice got out the car, eased over to him and patted him on the back. "Wow, Mustapha!" he said as he scanned the brownstone up and down. "This is nice, Grams still got it going on, I see!" "Yeah, Sugar Hill...Harlem," Derek said.

"Been a while since I've seen the both of you, too," Latif said as he stepped over to them. "Check it out," he said to them all. "Let's go up in here, get something to eat and check grandma out. Then, hey, Derek's got the ride..." He glanced over at him. "I want to see if he really knows how to pimp a Caddy?"

Derek grinned and said, "Alright lil' brother, that's a bet."

"Hmmm, I see I need to keep an eye on you, Latif," his grandmother said as she playfully swatted him on the butt. "Go upstairs and get the table ready for me." She glanced over at Born, then Ice.

"Grandma Juanita, when it comes to your cooking...we starvin." Born laughed.

She shook her head, grinning. "Come here, y'all give me some sugar."

Rasheed, Derek, and Mustapha walked quietly over to the side out of earshot so no one could hear. "Mustapha, later on we need to talk," Rasheed said as he put his arm around his shoulders.

"Everything alright?" Mustapha questioned.

Rasheed glanced over at Derek. "We got a plan if you're down. Yeah, everything will be alright."

He nodded in agreement. "Then, we'll rap later."

They all walked through the huge, stained glass doors, Derek doubled back out and said, "Damn, forgot to roll up my windows. Somebody might…"

Juanita poked her head out and said, "Derek, don't worry! Nobody's gonna touch it as long as it's in front of any house."'

Derek stopped, then looked up and down the street at the well-dressed men that read newspapers and inconspicuously eyeballed them and looked up at her.

Juanita said, "Feds…IRS…trust me, baby. They look out for me, gotta make sure they get their money."

After they ate, Derek cruised the long way up to the Polo Grounds, crossing over through 125th Street slow driving. Getting out at Wagner Projects and flossing, they were surprised at the reception Latif had gotten.

Mustapha leaned over and whispered to his brother, "Latif plays ball that well, damn near a draft pick."

Rasheed just looked over at him as he conversated with his older brother and thought, *'That's all good, but he'd rather see him in school someplace. Out of New York, but it was his choice to make. He was grown, and so far, he'd made some pretty good ones.'*

They sat on the bleachers at Rucker Park as Born made his way back from the store. "Here you go, Rasheed punch. Derek, Ice, Latif…ice-tea. And me…" He pulled out an icy-wet, forty-ounce bottle of Ballantine Ale. "This one's for me!"

"Man, you drink too much!" Derek said to him.

"I'm working on it, right now," he said as he took a swig.

Born looked over at Derek. "Give us a break."

"What?"

Born took another swig and said, "You heard me."

Derek jumped up with his fists balled. "Born, you got something you want to say…or do?"

Born looked over at Rasheed and said, "You better talk to him. Cause if I get up from here, you know what it is."

"Better get you, gun…" Derek smirked.

Born jumped up and in one swoop charged at him, knocking him to the ground. Derek was no slouch he swung him off and reversed. Mustapha rushed over and pulled them apart.

Right after, Ice looked them dead in the eyes and said, "You both need to cut this bullshit out! We've got some serious business to take care of!"

Born turned away and said, "Yeah, but after the business. We all need to talk."

"I think so, too," Ice agreed nodding his head. "This ship has run its course."

"What the fuck y'all talking about?" Mustapha stepped to him. "I mean, what y'all into anyway?"

Derek reached out his hand to Born. "You're right and uh, sorry 'bout that."

Born looked down at it and said, "Tighten up, Derek, you know what it is. Take care of it."

"I don't know what any of you are talking about." Mustapha kept saying.

"It's nothing," Rasheed said. "Right now, we need to talk to you about something."

Ice scanned the park looking for any signs of trouble. "Yeah, and this is about a good a spot as any. No one's around except us."

Derek posted in front of them and they all surrounded Mustapha. "We need to fill you in on some serious information." "Real serious," Derek added.

"Hey, uh…" Ice pointed to Latif. "We gonna talk in front of him?"

Latif picked up his drink from off the ground and said, "It's cool, I can go for a walk or something…"

"No," Rasheed said as he stepped in front of him. "It's about time you knew anyway. But you can't say anything to anyone!"

"I ain't no snitch!"

"No, hold up, wait a minute," Mustapha said as he backed away from them. "You can count me out. I got enough shit going on!" He turned and started to walk away.

Rasheed grabbed him by the arm and said, "Look, it's serious. I'm your brother, you know I'm not on…"

"Rasheed, I don't know what you're on! I ain't got a clue what you're into!" He stepped back toward them and pulled Latif off to the side. "All of y'all got some sort of secret shit going on. You don't have jobs but keep money. I know for a fact you don't sell drugs!" He pulled Latif behind him. "What are y'all into…robbing banks?" "Damn near." Derek chuckled.

Dean Hamid

"Hold up, y'all seriously not into robbing banks. Are you?"

Latif stared at Rasheed attentively waiting for a response, but instead, he beckoned them back. "I…we, want to tell you, but first, sit down and hear us out."

"Alright, I will…this time." They all sat on the bleachers off to the side of the park and he added, "Whatever y'all got to say, it better be good." After about an hour Derek finished laying out the rest of the plan. "So, that's why we need you to flush him out."

Mustapha leaned back and reflected on all he'd just heard. "So, you mean to tell me, all this time y'all was sticking up drug dealers?"

"Started out that way, but mostly Felix's people now," Rasheed said.

"Actually," Ice added. "Had you not been Rasheed's brother. You would have been robbed yourself."

Rasheed could only nod his head in agreement.

Mustapha finally got up, looked at them all, then said, "Alright. I'm down. When do we do it?"

Rasheed looked him over and answered, "Soon, real soon. We'll take you back to Brooklyn when we leave and hide you out." "Can I go?" Latif asked.

Rasheed pulled him over and walked off a little-ways telling him, "You continue doing what you doing. Go to school, do the right thing."

"Yeah…yeah, I hear you. But Rasheed, be careful," he said as he peeped over at Mustapha. "You're my family."

"We will, we will."

"Mustapha, you know how to shoot a gun?" Ice asked.

"Trust me." He sighed.

"I heard about that shoot-out at the crib," Ice said.

"Well, I hope it don't get that serious," Derek said as he stepped in between them and patted Mustapha on the back. "This is the last time anyway."

"The last time, huh?" Born said. "I guess I can retire then?"

"Oh, yeah, Rasheed," Mustapha said as he waved him over. "So, all that money you gave ma…"

"Bout a couple of grand…maybe, a hundred or so, easy."

"Then, damn, she's loaded," Mustapha replied. "I didn't have to hustle."

"I told your crazy ass that."

"You sure did, I'm sorry." "That's alright, fam, it's over." *Beep! Beep! Beep! Beep!*

"What the hell is that?" Derek asked as he turned his head toward the street.

Latif turned also and noticed the loud honking of the vehicle was his grandmother's. "That's grandma!" He rushed over to her.

"That's a nice ride," were the only words Derek got out his mouth.

Latif yelled to them, "*Come here!*"

Rasheed was out in front as they raced over to the car. "What's wrong, you alright!"

Juanita's face was flushed, and she wheezed trying to catch her breath, "Rasheed, some girl named Devone just called me! Somebody kidnapped, Shaheeda!"

"*Oh, hell no!*" Mustapha shouted.

Derek was already in his car cranking it up when he called out, "We gotta go, now!"

"Grandma," Rasheed was trying to calm her down. "We're on our way, right now."

"Rasheed, baby…" She reached out and grabbed him by the arm. "Get them! If they hurt my granddaughter, so help me!"

Latif had already jumped in the car with her saying, "Calm down, grandma, calm down."

"Take her to the house, Latif, I'll call later!" Rasheed instructed as he jumped into the Caddy after Derek backed it up for them to get in. "Grandma! Trust me we'll find her!"

"Mustapha!"

"Yeah, grandma!"

"Here." She tossed him Latif's gym bag. "You're gonna need this!" He peeped into it then glanced awkwardly back at her. "I put in an extra clip or two. Be careful!"

Derek skidded off heading toward the FDR going to Brooklyn.

Latif stared as they sped off. "I hope everything will be alright." Tears welled up in his eyes as he said a silent prayer for his family.

His grandmother reached over and rubbed his hand. "It will. Now, buckle up, I need to make a stop before we go in."

"A stop?"

"Talk to some people I know. Nobody pulls this shit on us…nobody!"

****

"Felix, you need to call your people at the police station."

"At the precinct?"

"Yeah, that's it."

"Something wrong?"

"I need to go to the office building and check out the warehouse, and there's two cops out front."

"Okay, I'll call and get them out of there. But you have to be quick!"

"Just do it!"

"What is it you're trying to do?"

"Bye," Muerte said as he slammed the receiver down hard in Felix's ear.

The two cops stopped stuffing their faces long enough to look up at him, hearing the crash from the phone. Webb leaned over and pointed toward Muerte and put his cup on the dashboard. He lowered his gaze and strolled back to his car. As he got in, he reached into the glove compartment and pulled out a loaded clip for the .45, he had positioned on his lap. He then placed it on the passenger seat and slouched down a bit waiting for the officers to make their move.

At the same time, Muerte was doing his thing, Webb pointed at him. Lipscombe was ready to get out the car. He reached over, inconspicuously pulled a round into the chamber and reached for the ignition key. He really didn't want any problems. He couldn't afford a ride to Central Booking; his fingerprints would reveal a whole lot more than patterns.

"Damn," he mumbled under his breath. "Even if I shoot these two, all the heat would be on me, not Felix, and this is his screw-up."

Officers Webb and Libscombe were now completely out of the vehicle. Webb unsnapped his holster and glanced over at him. Muerte knew right then, something was up.

A crackling sound came from inside of the car, Webb stopped and glanced back. Again, the sound, but this time he reached in and grabbed the handset. Lipscombe leaned in and after a minute of pointing in Muerte's direction, then the office building. He and Lipscombe got back in their car and pulled off, but not before they slowed down and did a quick scan into the car, and at its occupant.

Muerte averted his face as they sped up Sumner Avenue towards Fulton Street, then focused his attention towards the car that had just pulled up. Its occupant got out and walked slowly toward him. He kept his hands visibly out, intentionally.

Slow-moving, he got closer, then ducked his head to the passenger side window and said, "Felix sent me."

It was Mike from the FBI. "He said you needed some help."

Muerte sighed as he tucked the gun underneath his coat. "No, don't need you." He got out of the car. "Those officers that just left needed you." He walked past him toward the door, pulled out a key, opened it and turned around. "Well, are you coming in?"

Mike didn't know what to make of it, but he wanted to know where he was going anyway. "Yeah, sure." He followed closely behind.

Muerte smiled, that's exactly what he wanted. The door locked behind them and they walked the corridor to a door with a lighted sign above it marked: *WAREHOUSE*. Muerte pulled out a key and opened it. He stepped through and looked around. Two Mack trucks, and a dozen or so ice machines. He walked toward the machines, opened one up and peeped in, then nodded his head and grinned.

Mike was questioning his own intellect now. He noticed the machines were not plugged in, and he didn't see any signs of ice or water drainage. So, why was this guy so interested in looking inside each one. As he made his rounds toward the last one, an eerie grin appeared across his face. "So, uh, what's up with the ice machines? Why would Shabazz have ice machines stored in his warehouse? I never knew he was into vending or..."

"Never know about people these days." Muerte opened a lid to one of the machines and invited him over to see.

Mike cautiously peeped his head in, and he couldn't believe it. Blocks of cocaine stacked neatly across the bottom at least three rows deep. On the sides a darkened, sliding Plexi-glassed divider was placed, so that the ice obviously used as a front couldn't seep through, or the product be seen unawares.

'*One hell of a plan,*' Mike thought. '*Transporting cocaine throughout the city using ice machines as a facade.*' He pulled his head back out and smirked. Right in front of the bodega's, in plain view.

Muerte closed it back. "You see now?" Then he pointed to some of the beverage-vending machines lined up in rows towards the back. "Oh, there's so much more."

Mike turned toward him and gawked. He watched as he walked over and pulled out a key, opening one up. Stacks of money, to hell with the sodas. He shook his head in disbelief. There were just as many as there were ice machines.

"And we're getting in more trucks...more ice machines."

He never would have had a clue to the type of business operating here, then on top of that, in comparison, Felix paid him pennies. "That no-good muthafucka." He was feeling some sort of way.

Muerte felt the gun that was put to his head and slowly raised his hands. "What the hell are you doing?"

Mike slowly moved around in front of him. "You know what's going on, I can't let you leave."

"What the hell you mean? Hell, I'm working for the Cartel!" Muerte said as he continued to hold the .9mm in between his eyes. Muerte slowly moved back. "Okay, I see what it is. You work for, Felix?" He lowered his voice. "That's the problem."

"I do what I do!" Mike stammered.

"Actually, you work for the wrong man. I can't believe this shit. You have orders to kill me, huh?" He leveled his eyes at him.

Mike started to sweat, and his mind drifted to his son. Why the hell was he messing around with Felix in the first place? Because the bills just kept coming in too fast. His wife stayed on his ass for alimony all the time. He could have worked overtime sure, but he needed a quick come up, and Felix was the way. He'd helped him cover up a lot of crap since he started. All he ever asked for in return was the money. Perhaps too little, but hell he had to have it, and it was on the government's dime, he reasoned.

"Okay, then, go ahead," Muerte said as he leaned up against an ice machine. "Kill me."

'Okay-okay,' Mike thought to himself. '*Why is this guy a threat again?*' He needed to know what he knew. "Look, the warehouses. The others, I have the paperwork," he gambled. '*This must have something to do with the papers he took from, Ravanel. Felix wanted them real bad.*' "I also have access to this cop."

Muerte just listened, not saying a word. Analyzing the information. He was leading him on. "So, uh, what do you know about a safe?"

'*A safe...a safe?*' Mike thought hard. He couldn't remember anything about a safe. He needed to switch sides, cause, he didn't know jack. Apparently, Felix was bullshitting him, but this guy was the real deal. With him, he could retire. "I guess, I can find out," he said.

Muerte read his eyes and his mind as he watched Mike eyeball the vending machines. He knew what he wanted. "This money here belongs to the Cartel, but the real money is in the safe."

Mike began pacing the floor as he lowered his gun, then turned away from him. His hands were sweaty. The beads of sweet on his forehead dripped.

Muerte continued, "Supposedly, it's money that can't be traced, three million in cash. Money that was skimmed from the Cartel by a man named, Carlos. It was stashed away." Mike turned back around facing him. "Felix says someone stole a key from him. Some guy named, Mustapha. What do you know about that?"

Mike searched the far corners of his mind for answers. Now, Carlos, he remembered. But to fuck with him he had to put the FBI in his business. There had to be someone he's overlooking that might know. "Giovanni!"

"Who?"

"Mickey Giovanni, that's your man. He was working a case a while back. A shoot-out in the projects. Yeah, I remember now. He was also the one Ravanel was covering for. He knows!"

Muerte walked toward Mike and looked him up and down. Maybe there was still used for him after all. "Okay, my friend, you will live, but I want this, Giovanni!"

"What the hell are you talking about? Let me live, I'm the one with the gun…" Mike didn't finish his sentence before Muerte had moved in on him.

He grabbed the gun out his hand and elbowed him in the ribs, causing Mike to double over in pain as he heard the bone-breaking crunch. He was on his knees now, coughing up blood as Muerte stood over him and steadied the gun to the back of his head. "Now tell me, who is this, Giovanni!"

He was scared for his life now. He knew he'd opened a can of worms. Felix wanted him to kill this guy, but he had no idea he was as good an assassin as his files said he would be. He knew he had made a big mistake by letting him talk him into this. "He's a detective that works at the eightthree! I can get in touch with him and set him up for you!"

"How? You tried to set me up and look what it got you." He struck him upside the head with the butt end of the gun and sent him sprawling face-first to the ground.

"He knows about the girl. He'll probably come after her!"

"Who, Giovanni!"

"No, Mustapha." That's what he wanted. Kill two birds with one stone. If Mustapha came after his sister, then also this Giovanni. Find out about the money, the safe. Take them all out in one neat little package, then, kill Felix too while he had him and retire back home in Cuba.

Dean Hamid

He looked down at Mike as he wriggled around trying to catch his breath. His ribs had punctured his lung and he wheezed bad, spitting up blood. "Take me to the hospital, please," he begged.

Muerte paid him no mind. He'd gotten what he needed from him. He lifted him up and dragged him over to one of the ice machines, hoisted him up, and tossed him inside. "There you go. You wanted a lot of money, right?"

Mike was blacking out fast from the pain and lack of air and pleaded with him some more. "Don't leave me here. Help me!"

Muerte turned toward him and leveled the gun to Mike's forehead. "Like you were going to help me, huh?"

Mike's eyes widened in terror as Muerte squeezed the trigger. He tried to scream, but his cries were quickly muffled and all that was left was the sound of the closing of the lid on the ice machine over him.

Muerte picked up the shell casing, walked over to the steps and clicked the lights off behind him as he opened the door slightly. Not seeing anyone around, he quickly eased over to his car and cranked it up. Before he left, he turned around one more time to make sure all the lights were out in the building.

He'd be back later the girl would have to be brought there. This way he could grab the Cartel's money, dope, and get rid of the bodies all at one time. Even Felix's, and if the Cartel asked, he'd blame it on a botched- up robbery. He just needed to do one more thing, use the phone to call his contact in the Cartel and let them know he had access to the product. Harlem would be where he would have to take it. As he pulled off, he sighed and took a deep breath. This was definitely his last job. He was tired of it all, but most of all, tired of Felix.

Dunya: The Do Or Die

Chapter Sixteen

Giovanni pulled up behind the precinct, slowly scanning the perimeter for any suspicious activity, like any unusual cars with government FBI plates. He parked, got out and crept along the edge of the building seemingly out of sight, then he slipped into the back stairway. The third floor was where the office and squad room were located, but that wasn't where they took Ravanel. They probably wanted to question him, and as he thought more of it, the Lieutenant's office seemed a more likely place. It was secluded and out of view. He raced up the steps, peeping through the exit door, through the windows of the l-t's office. He could see Stephens, and two others dressed in black suits. They were government men no doubt, probably FBI. That sparked his curiosity. He didn't see Ravanel at all and so far, no one noticed him.

Visually sweeping the office he finally spotted Ravanel across from him far in the back sitting at a desk. He looked somewhat worried; anxiety was written all over his face as he squirmed in the chair, he sat in looking off into space. Just enough for Giovanni to wave his hand and catch his attention. He pointed Giovanni towards the restroom. Ravanel gestured a uniformed officer over and spoke to him briefly. He walked into the l-t's office and was quickly kicked out. Pissed off, he walked back over to where Ravanel sat and shook his head. Ravanel got up, strolled toward the john, then Giovanni crept in quietly behind him.

"Giovanni, good to see you! They're going crazy around here! All because of a guy named, Mike Davis…"

"Whoa-whoa, slow down." Giovanni leaned back against the sink and thought out loud. "*I knew Mike was up to something, but this?*"

"This is the deal; I had the papers set up. I was going to give them to you, but then…"

"Yeah-yeah, I heard." He walked over to the window opened the frosted pane glass a bit gulping in some air and sighed. "Damn."

"They took all my papers at least the originals." He winked. "I still managed to make copies."

"Copies!" Giovanni turned. "Good!"

"Of course, now check this out." Giovanni looked him square in the eyes giving him his full undivided attention as he continued, "I traced down the source to a place up on Twenty-fifth Street in Manhattan. A realtor for office buildings or something. Anyway, the name is on the copies, okay."

"Cool, I'll get them later. Keep on."

"Well, it seems about twenty years ago there was a robbery and some guy got killed. Your man from the tape. Would you believe it?"

"Holy."

"For real, they never found out who was involved. It went cold case, but hell you knew that, except for the two others. The guy that was killed in Central Booking. Ali, and some mob wannabe named, Frank."

"Frank Hammond."

"Yep. Check this, your guy from the tape was buddy-buddy with that Ali guy that just got killed, too and Malik Shabazz!"

Giovanni heard a sound at the door, dipped into a stall out of eyesight and whispered. "If somebody comes in…"

"I got you."

"So, what else? Most of this I already knew."

"The kicker is this, the place that was robbed owns property in Brooklyn."

"You told me that."

"I did, didn't I? Anyway, to put it in a nutshell, the only items that they reported stolen, were property titles! Then there's this whole big battle in State Court. Those same folks are fighting over replacements, evidently the one's at Records were lost also, and they're properties the City is trying to take from them. Eminent domain type of shit. Crazy!"

"Hmmm…property titles."

"The whole money a front. Hell, the titles are to warehouses that sit directly right along the edge of…"

"Brooklyn! That makes them very valuable, prime property. Yeah, I can see that, easy access to the highways. One, in particular, the Brooklyn-Queens Expressway and all the Ports!"

"And your boy, Khalid, the guy that was killed worked years ago as a security guard. He might have known about this. Maybe he might have run up on the robbery in that place by accident."

"Did you case the joint out on Twenty-fifth Street?"

"I did, but it wasn't occupied. But you wouldn't believe what I saw when I went to Malik's warehouse, though. Ice machines, about a dozen or so. What's that about? Go figure. Then, I went downtown to see who managed the properties, not the city. But once again, Malik's name came up.

Talk about a power move."

"Okay, sounds good so far, except, now he's dead."

"Yeah, something's up with that building. Warehouse properties and all that."

"I knew something was up with his building too from day one when I went in with Mike." Giovanni snatched open the stall door and looked over at Ravanel. "But what the hell am I looking for?"

"I don't have a clue."

"The bathroom door swung open. It was one of the government men from l-t's office. He walked in directly passed Ravanel and swung open the stall-door that Giovanni had ducked into and said, "Cocaine, laundered money, and we're on the trail of women, Mules, and Prostitution."

"What the…"

"I saw Ravanel duck into the John. I played the door and overheard you guys talking."

Giovanni frowned up, then stepped out the stall. "Who the hell are you?"

"Agent Carter, FBI, but you knew that. I'm the one who analyzed the tape."

"Okay," Giovanni said as he extended his hand. "So much has been going on lately. I mean, I saw you guys in the l-t's office, and all that's going on with Ravanel here. What's up with that? I mean, you came all the way from D.C., right?"

"I'm trying to get back the paperwork they took from him and release the officer here. But we have to keep things on the low-low. Too many paid-off people. That agent Mike Davie is dirty as hell and seems like he's been at it for years. The Bureau knows and they're tracking him."

"I see. But for who?"

"He's in dirty with a guy named, Felix. He's mixed up with the Los Andres Cartel. A group out of Colombia. They've been here since the sixty's doing the same shit. It all started in Harlem and worked their way into Brooklyn. Now, they're setting up shop in Mexico with the cartels there. A guy named Carlos orchestrated the whole thing, along with that guy named, Felix. We don't know where this Carlos guy is or his stash…dope…nothing. He just sort of disappeared."

"Bet, it's got something to do with those warehouses, too," Ravanel butted in.

"Probably, I wouldn't doubt it. Good spots to hide shit, and evidently, somebody wants those property's bad. The real estate, the storage…everything," Giovanni added.

Carter glanced at his watch then Ravanel and said, "Look, we've been in here long enough. We better get back before anyone gets suspicious."

"Giovanni, look under my seat in squad car numbered, eight-one-one, okay. That's where you'll find those copies."

"What about you, Carter?"

Carter looked back after peeping out the door to make sure the coast was clear and said, "He'll be alright, I'm gonna run the Federal mumbojumbo enforcement rights infringement bullshit at them. They'll be begging to leave him alone. You can trust me, Giovanni. But you definitely need to check out the warehouses. Go, get out of here!"

Suddenly. the door burst open, and they all jumped back. It was Sergeant Brown, the 2nd shift desk sergeant. "Excuse me…oh hell, Giovanni!" He looked around again and said, "Ravanel! What's going on?"

Giovanni quieted him down and directed him toward the back. "Look, Brown, there's a lot of crap going on, and I need to trust you…"

"Hell yeah, Mickey. I heard about what happened. That's a bunch of b.s. if you ask me. What'cha need?"

"For one, don't tell no one you saw me or any of us in here. I'll fill you in later."

"No problem, Mickey. But hey, I was trying to page you."

Giovanni glanced at his pager and noticed it was off. "What's up?"

"You remember the girl that got beat up pretty bad over in Bushwick?"

"Yeah, why?"

"Well, she messed around and got herself snatched up. Officer Dominic that works part-time security at the bank over on Graham Avenue saw it all. He hasn't called it in yet, and no one's reported it. I told him to hold up until I got with you. But you better get on it, don't know how long he'll let up. Thought I'd at least give you a heads-up. I know you kept ties with the family and all."

"Damn! Thanks, Brown, I need to check that out now. Hey Brown, I need the keys to a car, eight-one-one."

"You got it, Mickey. Let me take a leak first, okay?"

Ravanel and Carter left out the bathroom, Giovanni was close behind them and slipped down to the garage unnoticed where he was met by Sergeant Brown. He passed him the keys and said, "Good luck, Mickey, with whatever."

Dean Hamid

Giovanni got in and sure enough like Ravanel said, a manila envelope was hidden underneath the seat stuffed with papers. "Good looking out, Ravanel." He cranked up the car and sped down DeKalb Avenue, possibly toward all hell.

****

Waseema paced back and forth across the living room floor, nervously playing with her hands as Donna sat on the couch watching, trying to figure out just why they weren't calling the police, saying. "If we wait any longer, she could…"

Devone stood off by the window watching for Rasheed and Mustapha, she glanced over and cut her off, "Be quiet, please!"

"Be quiet? How the hell can I be quiet when someone just snatched up my friend, huh!"

Devone blurted. "We don't know if this had anything to do with her…Mustapha!"

Waseema looked over after being silent for a good while, then said, "She's right, we don't want the police in on anything, right now. They might be the ones that jeopardize her life. We'll just wait until the boys get back." She shook her head trying to figure out what to do. "I just hope they get here soon." She got up and walked towards the phone. "I really need to get in touch with, Malik, he should be at his office. He knows people." She dialed the number and let it ring, she got no answer.

Hanging up, she walked into the kitchen, started messing around with the dishes and dropped a glass. It shattered into pieces all over the floor.

Devone rushed over. "Calm down, it's gonna be alright," she said as she reached into the closet for a broom and swept.

Donna watched as Devone consoled her and figured it wouldn't do no good for her to continue ranting. "I'm just scared," she said. "That's all." "Donna, we all are." *Knock! Knock! Knock!*

"They looked over toward the door, but no one moved.

Knock! Knock! Knock!

"Okay," Devone whispered. "Did you see anyone strange come up the walkway to the building, Lisa?"

She silently tiptoed to the door and said, "No."

"Okay, Donna, go in the backroom and get my bat," Waseema said to her.

Knock! Knock! Knock!

Donna came back out and handed her the bat as she stalked closer to the door and hollered out. "Okay, coming!"

Devone posted herself right behind her with a knife she'd picked up from the kitchen sink and eyeballed her. "I'm ready."

Waseema nodded, unlocking both deadbolts, just put in place since the shoot-out. She swung open the door and jumped out from behind it raising the bat, Devone was right behind her. Hands raised above her head with the knife she wielded.

"Noooo!"

Waseema stopped as she heard the scream and caught herself. "It's you, guuurrrl."

It was Mya. "What the hell are y'all doing!" she said.

Devone put down the knife and walked off. "You were almost stabbed!"

Donna rushed over and jerked her inside, but only after looking out both ways for anyone else and said, "Close the goddamn door!"

Mya stood in the middle of the living room floor. One woman holding a bat; another with a knife, wide-eyed, peeping out the window; and two others cowering in the kitchen staring at the door.

"Hold up," she said. "I know what this is." She pointed at them. "Y'all must be on that crack shit and paranoid like hell?" She backed up toward the door. "Y'all should be ashamed of yourselves."

Waseema looked at her like she was crazy, then thought about the way they were behaving, and burst out laughing. "For real, will you look at us!"

Devone stayed by the window and smirked. "To hell with that, I'm not dropping shit."

Waseema pulled Mya over to the couch. "No, it's not like that, something's happened."

"What's going on? Is it, Rasheed...Momma...what?"

"Shaheeda's been kidnapped."

"Kidnapped...where?"

"Over on Graham Avenue. She was out shopping with Donna and Lisa when some guy with a gun snatched her."

"Damn!" She looked over at Donna, then Lisa. "Did anyone get hurt?"

"No, not really." Lisa turned toward her. "He started shooting though and held the gun to my head."

Donna walked over to her. "We tried our hardest."

"Evidently, you didn't try hard enough. Probably in some woman's ass," she said under her breath.

"What you say?" She swung at her and missed.

Mya backed up off the couch and put up her hands. "I can't stand you, lesbo!"

Devone stepped between them. "We're not doing this today!"

"Ms. Waseema, no disrespect, but I've been wanting to come over here and tell you about her ass, anyway," Donna challenged.

"I don't do anything! What are you talking about?"

Lisa sat quietly off to the side snickering. "Don't go there, Donna. I know what you're about to say, I heard about it, too."

Devone looked at them, then it hit her, her brother. Somebody must have seen them, now it was all over the place. Things might go her way with Rasheed after all, but right now wasn't the time. "Look, Ms. Waseema don't need to be hearing about no rumors."

"It ain't no rumor, my cousin saw it first-hand," Donna said. "You think I'm so-called gay. Hell, if I had a man like Rasheed, hmm…you dumb whore! It pisses me off just thinking about it." "Hold up." Mya dropped her head.

Waseema stepped between them and asked, "What's going on?"

Donna glanced over at Devone and she nodded mouthing the word, "Don't."

"It's nothing, I said too much already," Donna replied.

Mya turned to leave, but Waseema grabbed her by the arm. "What the hell is going on, Mya? Something wrong with, Rasheed and you?"

She sighed and shook her head. "I wanted to talk to you, but you were never there when I tried."

Devone came over and said to her, "It's nothing like she said. Just stupid rumors. We don't need to be concerning ourselves with that now anyway."

"Look!" Waseema blurted out. "I don't know what the hell is going on, but somebody better say something, now!"

"She's screwing, Derek!" Donna hollered out. "And you know what the crazy thing about it is? She doesn't even have the decency to at least take it somewhere else! Hell, Mya, Bed-Stuy ain't but so big!" she said as she snapped her fingers.

Mya turned toward Waseema pleading, "I'm sorry…I'm sorry! I just needed to hold on to somebody! I really don't love him!" Tears poured out of her eyes.

"Mya, either tell, Rasheed or I will!" She looked away from her, disappointed. She walked over to where Devone stood and said to her, "No disrespect to your brother, but you know how Rasheed feels about her."

"I do." Devone looked at Mya. "I would never do him like that." She hugged her. "I'll talk to my brother."

"I love, Rasheed...I do. It was just sex!" Mya cried.

Lisa crossed her legs watching her. "Love...I can't tell."

"Lisa, lay off, hell she made a mistake. A big one!" Donna stared over at her and said, "Stop crying, take care of it later. Right now, like Devone said, we got too much going on. We don't need no distractions. Hell, I never shoulda opened my mouth."

"I didn't mean to call you..." Mya tried to apologize.

"Yeah, yeah, I know."

"C'mon. Let's go get some air."

"Donna...I need to get my purse-"

"Mya! Just bring your as on! Damn! You already got me pissed off." Donna huffed heading to the door, digging in her bag for a cigarette. Devone looked out the window. "Nobody called the cops, right?"

Waseema rushed over to the window and looked out, then said, "Oh hell no. What's he doing here?" She stepped over to the door with her back against it. "We gotta get right."

"Who is it?"

"Detective Giovanni."

"Damn," Devone said as she looked around at them. "Here we go with the bullshit."

After knocking, Giovanni was let through the door and led into the kitchen by Waseema. "I came right over. What's going on with, Shaheeda?"

"How did you know? No one called."

He threw up his hands and said, "That's the buzz over at the precinct. I suggest you get ready for the barrage of cops that'll be coming this way."

"I hope there's enough time."

"Right now, it's speculation and hasn't been called in, yet. So, Shaheeda was kidnapped, what happened?"

"She went to Graham Avenue to get a coat with some of her girlfriends and..."

"Hello, Mickey," Lisa cut in. "Long time no see."

"Hey, how are you? What are you doing here?"

"I was with her."

"Okay, so what happened?"

Crossing her arms, a frown came across her face. She was upset that she didn't do enough. But she explained what she saw by specific detail. The car, the description of the tall Spanish man, and anything that stood out.

Afterward, Waseema said, "I didn't know you knew, Lisa?"

"We're cousins."

"You're from down here?"

"I grew up in Williamsburg Houses, right up Bushwick Avenue."

"Oh, okay."

"No disrespect, Ms. Waseema, but we're talking and Shaheeda's still out there. Every minute counts."

"Right, no problem."

Turning toward them all he asked, "Who took the call from, Felix's people?"

"I did?" Devone answered.

"You also need to tell me everything that was said in detail. That'll help." He turned to Waseema. "And, I believe I pretty much know why you all didn't call the police."

"Mustapha, of course."

"Right, then, we better get the story right before they get here. Hopefully before the next call. Maybe, we can get her back before then."

"You think so?" Devone asked.

"We'll see," he said as he pulled out his pen and pad and cocked his head to the side.

At that moment there was a rattling of keys at the door and he jumped up. Cautiously walking toward it, his hand pulling back his jacket as he reached for his gun. "Who is it!" he asked.

Waseema backed slowly into the hallway. Devone was right behind him.

Giovanni stood braced against the backside of the door as he reached for the doorknob. "I said who is it!"

The jingling of keys stopped, and a silence ensued. "Who is this?" Came from the other side.

Waseema strained her ear to recognize the voice then sighed when she did. "It's Rasheed," she said.

"Damn, I'm glad to see you!" Giovanni said as he quickly snatched open the door.

Rasheed moved briskly through the door along with Derek, Born, Ice and an associate of theirs from the projects by the name of Kevin.

"Everything alright?" he asked as he looked around at everyone there. "You all seem pretty shaken up. What's going on, anything new?"

Waseema ran over to him. No, baby, it's good to see you, though."

"Who called here anyway?" "Felix," Devone said.

"I can't believe he'd try something like this?"

"I heard about that guy, Felix. I got a lot of paperwork on him. I know for a fact he's the top dog in the drug trade in Bushwick Projects."

"*Bushwick Projects*!" Devone cut him off and said, "That's all y'all got?"

"For real," Ice said. "He runs damn near a third of Brooklyn." "Easy!" Born chimed in.

"So, you guys know about him?" Giovanni questioned.

Devone started to say something, but Rasheed quickly cut her off. "Yeah, we heard a little something."

"Well, I heard there was a drug war going on, or something?" Giovanni probed, looking for a bite.

"Don't know, you're the detective," Devone expressed.

Undeterred he continued, "Something about some people being found dead, too. Money missing, dope, all that. So, that's why we figured there was a war going on."

Rasheed shook his head no like he was clueless. "Don't know nothing about that."

"Okay, just thought I'd ask it might be relevant later. Uh, where's, Mustapha?"

Waseema looked around and saw that he was missing, too. "Yeah, where is, Mustapha?" She walked toward the front door. "Did he come back in?"

"He's out on the terrace with, Donna, said he'd be in soon."

"Wasn't Mya with her?"

Rasheed turned around looking for her. "Where's Mya? I didn't see her." He started walking to the door but was cut off by Derek. "I got you. You, uh, stay here with your moms, make sure she's..." He started to walk to the door.

Waseema cut in front of him and said, "That's alright, Derek, I'm okay." She turned back to Rasheed. "You can go look for her. She probably just walked to the store."

"Uh, yeah, that's cool." He cut his eyes over at Devone, she gave him the eye. He knew something was up, so he backed off.

"Be right back," Rasheed said as he slid past him. Just like Born said, he saw Donna and Mustapha on the porch. "Hey Donna, what's up, you seen, Mya?"

"She went to the store, Rasheed," she said as she looked off the terrace. "Matter of fact, there she is now on the way back."

He looked over her shoulder and spotted her coming up the walkway. He rushed to the stairway going outside.

Donna turned her attention back to Mustapha, who was pulling her closer to him, and said, "Now, what were you saying?"

"C'mon now, Mustapha. I've always checked you out. Like you don't know." She giggled.

"I didn't, shit, I heard you were gay."

"Here we go." She pushed him away. "Out of all people, why would you think I was gay?"

He hunched his shoulders. "Calm down, I didn't say I believed it. I just never had the chance to stop and ask you myself. I mean, I used to see you going to work and all."

"Why didn't you say something?"

Mustapha looked out the fence watching his brother hug Mya, then started feeling some sort of way. "Look, you're educated, pretty, independent. What kinda rap I got for you? I ain't nothing but a black ass drug dealer!"

"Maybe, but it's just might be the rap this sister needs to hear." He smiled Donna could see a spark. They were alike. Just wanted to be accepted and loved.

"After all this is over, we'll see then," Mustapha said.

Donna reached in and kissed him. "I'd like that."

Mustapha turned. "I'd better go in and speak to, Ma and find out what's up."

"Alright then," Donna said as she leaned back against the fence and dug into her purse for another cigarette. She glanced at Rasheed and Mya in front of the building.

After Rasheed hugged her for a good while he escorted her over to the bench. "Rasheed, there's something I need to tell you," Mya said.

"Everything alright?"

"Uh, yes and no. But please just promise me one thing. Promise me you'll still love me."

He braced himself for the worse, it already didn't sound good. "What is it, Mya? Tell me, I mean, it hasn't been the best day for me."

Dunya: The Do Or Die

Donna started to light up her cigarette, and turned slightly, shielding the wind off with her hand as she flicked her lighter. Peeping downstairs in front; she saw that Rasheed had his hand raised high above Mya's face. Donna dropped her lighter and said, "Now what!"

Rasheed's eyes were fixed down on her, twisted with anger, deceit, and hurt. She could see the anguish as his hand trembled, ready to strike her.

"No Rasheed!" Donna yelled. She took to the stairs, dashed out the building and ran over to where they were. "C'mon, listen to me, Rasheed!" she pleaded. He hesitated for a moment and looked over at her. "Don't hit her, don't lower yourself to that level, please."

She begged for Mya because she knew Mya's past and deep down, she understood Mya couldn't prevent the things she'd done. She was used to having things fucked up in her life. Her rational convinced her to sabotage her own happiness. Something Donna had thought about herself at times, but the difference between them was that she didn't react on it.

"Please, Rasheed, we've got other things going on," Donna pleaded again.

He finally lowered his hand, and with the other shoved Mya to the bench and said, "Yeah...you ain't worth it!"

"Forgive me, Rasheed!"

"Forgive you?" Rasheed hollered out. He sighed and looked up at the sky. "Girl...I loved you." Then shook his fist. "You just don't know how much."

"But...but, you promised!" She ran behind him and grabbed hold of his arm. He shook her off and sidestepped past her into the building.

Donna just shook her head as he walked past. "Mya," she said. "Look at what you've done to him, damn!" She rolled her eyes and walked past her as she went behind him.

Rasheed bounced up the steps two at a time, slammed open the staircase door and steeped toward his mother's apartment.

Mustapha sat by his mother talking with Giovanni, who was writing down the description of the gunman. When Rasheed charged in and b-lined straight to Derek at the dinner table.

Without hesitation, he pounced on him. "I'ma kill you!" Donna was right behind him. "She told him!"

"What the hell is up with you!" Derek yelled at him.

Rasheed held him in a headlock and beat his fist heavily into his face. "Don't act like you don't know!"

Devone stood off, debating which side to choose. Her brother, or the man she wanted for herself.

"It just happened!" Derek screamed.

She watched as Rasheed beat on her brother. No, it damn sure didn't just happen she started to think. She manipulated everything that led up to this point. Rasheed would soon be vulnerable enough to be snatched up, but still, at the end of the day, Derek was still her brother. "Rasheed, get off him!"

Ice rushed in to break it up but was held back by Born. "I knew there was something going on!" he said. "Couldn't quite put my finger on it."

Devone scrambled over. "To hell with this some other time! We've got business!" She tried pulling Rasheed off him. "Break it up!"

Derek crawled on his stomach covering up trying to avoid the beating he was getting, yelling, "Rasheed, chill, let's talk!"

"It's too late for that now!" Rasheed punished his back with his fist. "I'ma bust your ass…"

"Not here!" Mustapha gave Devone a hand and Derek finally rolled free. His shirt was ripped off him and Giovanni spotted his gun.

He recoiled and backed away slowly. "What's that!" He reached for his weapon. "Chill the fuck out." He drew it and pointed at him. "Right now, before someone gets hurt!"

Rasheed froze, Derek posted himself up with his hands high. He kept a bead on Giovanni as he moved cautiously toward him. "What the hell are you doing with a gun?"

Devone knew this would have to take place another time. She cut her eyes over toward Born, then Ice, already with their hands inside their jackets. She didn't want to kill Giovanni, he was a cop. Besides, he'd only just really walked into this whole mess trying to be helpful. But she knew she had to do something quick.

She gestured toward Ice, he was on point; moving swiftly he pulled his gun out and pointed it at his head. Born's was drawn, too.

Rasheed stepped toward him and said, "Okay, Giovanni…Detective, be cool."

Bewildered now, Giovanni's police instincts told him to fire his weapon. To act defensively, but as he looked around the room at the tensed faces, he couldn't chance it. All hell could break loose. "Alright, let's be cool, then."

He took one hand off his gun and slowly started lifting it toward the ceiling. "Rasheed, I don't want no trouble. You don't want no trouble either, right? Let's all put the guns down."

But Kevin wasn't having it. He was an ex-con a two-time loser. The only purpose for him being with them in the first place was to utilize his snitch ass and let Felix know Mustapha was back in the neighborhood so the trap could be set in motion, then he could cash in on the reward, ten grand.

He snuck up behind Giovanni and sneered. "I should kill you. You sent me to prison for five years."

Devone knew Kevin from back in the day, and she also knew his pedigree was dirt. If he went to jail, he deserved it. Besides, it was Rasheed's mother's home. No revenge cop-killing would be done today.

"Kev," she said as she moved closer to him, pointing her gun at him now. "Not today." She stepped towards Giovanni and put herself between them.

Ice finally lowered his gun. "Okay Giovanni, ours are down, let's go."

He apprehensively lowered his weapon and said, "Okay, I'm putting away the gun."

Derek straightened up his clothes, looked over at Rasheed and said, "We need to talk…"

Devone put her hands up, cutting him off. "Later, we need to handle this…now!" She turned her attention back to Giovanni and said, "We got some things we need to tell you about. But, if you choose to…" Born, Ice and Derek huddled closer to her. "Tell your police buddies, you'll be putting Rasheed's sister's life in danger."

Waseema was scared, as Donna and Lisa cowered next to her, frightened. She asked, "What's going on with all the guns?"

Mustapha pointed at her and said, "Rasheed, you've got to let, Ma know something, too."

Rasheed faced her he was right. After all, she'd been through, he owed her that. They all nodded in agreement, Kevin still mean-mugged Giovanni from across the room. That didn't matter to him, right now.

He looked around at the faces in front of him, especially Donna's and Lisa's and said, "Okay, but the same thing I told him applies to y'all, too." "Is it that serious, son?" Waseema asked. "Yes, Ma, it is."

Chapter Seventeen

Waseema sat silently reflecting on the picture painted by Rasheed about his past and imminent future. While Giovanni's face was filled with questions; some were answered, some were not, but still, there were many. His seasoned, veteran police mind could not grasp the fact that after all these years. The unsolved murders. The mysterious robberies of local drug pushers; cases that sat on his desk as well as his colleagues-that it all came down to this, or so he thought.

"That's what I…or, we do!" Rasheed explained.

Giovanni took the whole thing rather hard because he'd been covering for them. "So, all of you." He stood up trying to put it into perspective. "Together…robbed scores of drug dealers throughout Brooklyn?"

"That's the deal."

"Okay…what did you do with all the money…and dope?"

Waseema slid back in her seat at that question. She knew where most of the money, or at least Rasheed's went. An account set up at Lincoln's Bank on Graham Avenue, not too far from where Shaheeda was snatched up. For years she deposited money he would bring her, somewhere now in the thousands under different names. She never touched it, but right now she knew she'd have to move it. She didn't trust Giovanni like that. He may play the role of a friend, but he was still the police.

Her finances would be checked, searched, and if that much money was found, an investigation would surely follow. The money would be traced, and she'd be held accountable and give jail-time, easy. Her first, only, and best thought, right now was to get in touch with her mother as soon as possible and start moving it.

"But what about the killings?" Giovanni continued. "I mean, damn!"

Derek just looked at Giovanni's ass firing question after question, and he nervously ran his fingers through his hair. He might fuck around and ask the right one. Enough was enough. Born's crazy ass was responsible for the majority of those killings. Killings they told him just recently he'd have to slow down on, and still, regardless they were all in on them together. If one were to go down, it wouldn't be too long before they all did. Especially, after what they'd just told Giovanni.

"It is what it is! It's not like, the people that were killed weren't responsible for hundreds of deaths themselves!"

"But you guys are vigilantes!"

"No, we're not. But we damn sure slowed an ass of drugs from coming in," Devone rebuked. "The police didn't do, and don't do nothing! Hell, to be honest, ain't no telling how bad a shape Bushwick would be in if it weren't for us!"

"Give me a fucking break!" Giovanni shouted. "Look, I'm a cop, I have to say something." He walked over to the window kinda nonchalant and looked out, trying to spot any of the squad cars that he'd hope would be soon swarming in from the precinct at any minute. "I can't let it go."

That was it, Devone had heard what she needed to hear. He made his decision and he'd made his bed.

Feeling all eyes on him, Giovanni turned around quickly, then backed up as he saw the look in their eyes. He reached for his gun, but it was too late. "Nah...not this time." Kevin had snuck up behind him and snatched it out of his holster.

Giovanni raised both hands up high and got into a defensive stance ready for the onslaught he expected. "You guys don't want this. Maybe, we can work something out..." he said just before his mind went black.

Kevin had struck him upside the head with a pistol, then stood over him. "I should kill this mutha..."

"Tie him up!" Devone called over.

Derek rummaged through the drawers for some duct-tape and threw what he found to Ice. "We can't kill no cop! That'll bring too much heat!" Devone yelled while Ice wrapped duct-tape around his ankles.

Born said, "You're right and this ain't good."

Now that they had him bound and gagged, Devone looked over at Rasheed and asked, "Now what?"

"Take him to my mother's room for now and put him on the bed." He stepped over to Kevin. "Your people ain't get in touch with Felix yet! You already know more than you should!"

He stared at him, then the others and backed away from him slowly. He damn sure didn't want to be next, so he chose his words very carefully. "Hold up, y'all came and got me!"

Rasheed was pissed, but he was right, and his sister was still being held hostage somewhere. He didn't have time to play no games. He needed to know things, and time was of the essence. "Well, something better happen soon, if not, I'll kill..."

Riiinnnggg! Riiinnnggg! The phone rang. *Riiinnnggg! Riiinnnggg! Riiinnnggg!*

"Somebody pick that up!" Devone hollered.

Waseema came running out of the backroom down the hall. "I got it! He might not know if y'all are here yet." They stood motionless as she picked up the phone. She dared not wait for another ring and answered. "H...hello!"

"Mustapha, where is he!" Felix barked into the receiver. "He there yet!"

She held the phone away from her ear slightly and asked him, "M-mmy daughter...where is she?"

"No, first, Mustapha...where is he?"

"Look, damnit, if you hurt my daughter. I swear, I'll kill you myself!" Felix's voice paused for a second then he busted out in laughter, mocking her. "Ah, I see, kill me, huh? You really want to kill me? Then stand in fucking line bitch! Now, where is, Mustapha?"

She jerked the phone away from her ear as Mustapha eased over to her and said, "Be cool, Ma, it's gonna be alright."

"This Mustapha."

"Ah, Mustapha."

"What's going, who's this?"

"C'mon now, you don't recognize the voice of the man who pays you...and pays you well."

"Felix!"

"It me."

"If you hurt my sister, I'm gonna..."

"Gonna what, shut the fuck up! Be at Malik's office in one hour!"

"Malik's office, what?" Mustapha knew the place. Over on Sumner Avenue, but why would he want him to go there, where Malik was? What did he have to do with all this? "Let me speak to, Malik!"

"That's impossible trust me, be there in one hour."

"One hour, I hear you, but..." The phone went dead in his ear. He hung up and looked around. "He wants me to be at Malik's office in one hour. What's up with that?"

No one answered as he glanced around the room. Devone knew Malik's office building would have been the next, and hopefully the last spot they were going to hit. She'd gotten some serious info from a source of hers that, that was where a stash was kept. Whether it was Felix's or not, she hadn't got back with him to confirm it, yet. Hell, she might as well make a go for it, on blind faith, and in this business that was risky, at best.

"Fuck it!" she said under her breath. "Might as well handle the business."

"Where's Malik?" Ice asked.

"Didn't say."

"I haven't heard from him in a while myself," Waseema said. "I've been trying to call, but the phone just keeps ringing. When I did catch up with him, he said he was on his way over. That was what…a couple of days ago?"

"Guess we'll find out in about an hour."

"Damn, y'all think Malik is down with, Felix?" Rasheed inquired.

"I wouldn't doubt it," Devone answered. "My people say he's been seen with him several times, recently."

Ice thought about the day he went through there and spoke to him. He did notice there was something unusual that made him a little jumpy but figured it was the situation with Mya. "I saw him the day of the shoot-out and told him what was up over here."

"Oh, so you're the one," Waseema said. "Yeah, he told me somebody had said something to him about it."

'Damn,' he thought. 'He probably wanted to say something about the Mya thing I bet. I swear I don't need Waseema's ass to know about jack. I don't need that shit.'

"No, he didn't mention anything."

Waseema rushed over to the closet. "Okay, y'all ready? Let me put on my coat…"

Rasheed stopped her. "No, Ma, you need to stay here."

"Rasheed, that's my baby!" She gazed into his eyes they were much too reminiscent of Khalid's. She knew right then that this was more than just going after Shaheeda. It was personal. She stepped back away from the closet and sighed. "Okay."

Ice came over to her and tenderly rubbed her now wearied shoulders. "We'll be alright. We gonna get Shaheeda, trust me…and us."

"Yeah, we need somebody to keep a check on the cop anyway," Devone said to her. "Let us do what we got to do."

Donna walked over to Mustapha, threw her arms around his neck, and kissed him. "Be careful, baby. Look, y'all better go, the cops could be here soon."

They gathered on the porch contemplating the task at hand. Devone had explained to them all the information she'd gotten from her people and the type of money that was supposedly at stake. "Well over a million," she said.

Ice knew this would have to be his last job. Hopefully, he could make a life for himself and Waseema. It was painful keeping their relationship a secret from everyone, especially on her, but now it seemed like everyone knew anyway. He gazed down from the terrace, remembering the day he offered Mya the ride and what had transpired next. Mya glanced up and caught him staring. He quickly turned his head wishing none of that had ever happened. For now, he would definitely have to keep it covered up. He couldn't tell Waseema and he sure as hell couldn't say anything to Rasheed or anyone else for that matter.

Born itched for a drink, the urge was getting worse for him. D-t's had set in and thinking of rehab and getting his life together sounded good. But for what he mused and, for whom? He had no family or kids. He really didn't care if it was his last job or what. It's all he knew. He'd once laughed about going down in a hail of gunfire, but he was drunk at the time, and right now, it just wasn't funny like it was then.

Rasheed also looked down at Mya thinking, who else had she been with? At the same time Derek shot a glance his way, figuring if there ever was a chance at making a run for her, this would be it. But for sure, he'd have to get rid of Rasheed first. All of it would have to go down, but later.

"This what it is," he said as they huddled up to discuss the plan. "It's a go, it's a little sudden, but we were ready for this anyway. With all this crazy shit going on, we might as well do it now."

"He's right," Devone added. "We can't put it on hold, and it might be a good idea that after we do this everyone takes a vacation."

Rasheed took a deep breath and collected his thoughts. "Then, let's make it happen. I need a break anyway."

Derek held out his hand to him. "Truce?"

"For now, Derek, but don't get it twisted, your ass is mine."

"Born!" Devone took control. "You need to get the equipment."

He checked his watch. "I'm on it, give me…hmmm, fifteen minutes."

"Ice, can you call the Italians?"

He shook his head. "I doubt it, Devone, it's too soon." He glanced over at Kevin. "But we may still have something to work with." "What do y'all need?" Kevin asked.

"Your van," Straight to the point, Ice said. "Still runs, right?"

"It still cranks up I was going to junk it…"

"No, we'll use it, long as it runs. Then, we'll junk it later and report it stolen."

"Is this a robbery or something?"

"More dangerous," Devone answered. "But it pays more. Look, you in or what?"

"Fuck it!"

"But," Rasheed looked over at him and added. "It's do or die."

Kevin nodded, but inwardly he still had other motives. '*Cross them and get the money,*' he thought. "Cool do or die."

Ice shook his hand to seal the deal and said to Derek, "How much time we looking at?"

"I say about a half-hour, at the most."

He turned to leave and said to them, "Alright see you all by the Myrtle Avenue train station."

"Same routine," Devone said as she watched him leave.

Mustapha stepped over to her and asked, "What about me? How do I get to the office on time?"

Derek reached into his pocket and took out his car keys. "Just take care of her."

"Okay, then, let's do this. Ain't got much time." Mustapha turned to leave.

Rasheed pulled him to the side. "Hey, bro, you okay with all of this?"

Mustapha looked down at the keys in his hand. "Yeah, let's go get sis!"

They all walked out of the building into the sun setting over the 20story tall monolithic buildings that surrounded them. All focused on what had to be done. Mya sat on the benches, her mind was only focused on one thing, trying to get out of the mess she was in. She peeped her head up momentarily as Derek walked out, then turned abruptly when she saw Rasheed right behind him.

"Rasheed!" she hollered.

He waited as Derek walked down the hill to his car, then turned to Mya and said, "I need you to go upstairs to my mom's crib. I'll see you when I get back."

She moved in for the hug, but he coldly turned from her and kept it moving, and, that hurt him.

Devone spied the whole thing, and as she went by Mya she meanmugged her, then caught up to Rasheed. "Look, I'm here for you. When this is over, I'm sure you'll make the right choice." She looked up at the building at Mya.

"Where do we go first, Derek?" Mustapha asked.

He walked around to the passenger side and said, "Just a few things we need for the job."

"Thought Born went to do that."

"He did, but there's other stuff we need. Like bulletproof vests, some rope…" Mustapha opened the door for him, and Derek said, "Born handles all the firepower."

Rasheed continued to stare at Mya as she sort of lurched her way into the building. He was hard on her, but maybe she was right about some things. He wasn't there when she needed him, especially at night, and all the robberies were too much on his mind. Trying to find out about his dad's murder didn't make things any better either. All of that triggered the nightmares more than likely. But Derek of all people? He was doublecrossed, and he wasn't okay with that. A score would have to be settled.

"C'mon, Rasheed, let it go," Devone said as they got into the car. Born had made it to an old abandoned warehouse off Flushing Avenue where his stash was. He pulled back an old pile of brush he had fixed up near a hole on the side, then looking and seeing no one, he crawled in. He walked in a little until he recognized two steel drums sitting off in the corner by themselves. The sun was still up, so he had time to see what he was doing without resorting to using a flashlight, and as he thought about it, he had to move quick.

He pried open the drum lids and moved aside some old rags, there it was. An assortment of firearms: two .45 automatics, three .44 Revolvers with switched out spinners, two fully automatic Uzis, seven clips, and a pistol-grip shotgun. He opened the other drum, reached in the bottom and pulled out five boxes of .45 ammo, four boxes of hollow point .45 ammo, and six ammo belts loaded with twelve-gauge shotgun shells. He opened the large satchel he came in with and emptied everything into it.

He heard the faint sound of a horn outside the hole he came through and peeped out, it was Ice. He kicked over the drum making sure nothing was left, then scurried back toward the small breach. An old Econoline cargo van, tires half bald and windows tinted all the way around was what Ice pulled up in. The best thing about it was that it had enough space in the back to hold them all, and whatever loot they could get. At least that was the plan. Kevin opened the side door and dived in. They were on their way.

Mustapha had driven up Flushing Avenue toward Marcy Projects and pulled over by a store a little way past Throop Avenue. He honked, Derek got out and went into the building. After a couple of minutes, he came back out with a full duffel bag. He hopped back into the car, pointed Mustapha up Nostrand Avenue and had him pull over again. He opened the bag and rummaged through it. It was all there, black hoodies, black pants with big cargo pockets for ammo, black ski masks, and black leather gloves. He pulled the clothes out and distributed them to Devone and Rasheed, who put on everything in the back seat except for the ski mask and gloves, then they raced off to the train station.

Driving up Myrtle Avenue they stopped and parked the car off Broadway, then waited for Ice and them. He spotted them and waved them down. Mustapha made a U-turn and pulled up behind them. Born swung open the back door of the van and they all dived in. Then Derek opened back up the duffel bag and handed out everything needed for the night. Afterward, Mustapha slipped back into the car. He didn't need to change into anything, he was straight. He set his watch to Derek's. Rasheed nodded it was time. They figured all this would have to take no more than three hours-tops before the cops would be all over Waseema's asking questions. Giovanni would turn up missing, and she'd catch pure hell trying to explain why she had a cop held in her bedroom, duct-taped and gagged.

Ice cranked the van and slowly pulled off, heading toward Lewis Avenue. They all watched as Mustapha sped past them heading to the office. It was a go, do or die, all or nothing. For Mustapha, it was different, his only mission was Shaheeda.

****

Juanita pulled up in front of the Cotton Club underneath the el train overpass on 125th Street and motioned for Latif to get out. "C'mon, I need to talk to someone." Clueless as to where they were going. "It's about time you get a glimpse into the family business," she said as he helped her out of the car and pointed toward the alley. She led the way as they came to a side door past the kitchen area of the club. "Right there knock four times, real slow."

Latif was leery, but he stepped up to the door anyway and did what he was told. *Knock! Knock! Knock! Knock!* He could tell from the sound that it was solid steel hollowed out on the inside. According to a buddy of his who told him that his brother had done the same thing to his dope spots, and the door had steel rods running through it that prevented cops from ramming the door. This was more than likely the case here. The raps were returned.

"Okay, one more time now." *Knock!*

When he knocked once more the door opened. An older, neatlooking, attractive woman stood in front of him. She opened the door wide enough

209

for him and his grandmother to come through. Latif was close behind her. He never would have expected what he saw next. Scantily attired women, all young, different colors, shapes and sizes, smiling as they stared his way. Catching the eye of a few gave way to flirtatious stares, and he slowed his pace but was quickly jerked forward.

"C'mon!" Juanita barked.

They were guided along a long hallway and came to another entrance. This time the decor, the area directly located behind the club was slightly different. Almost as if it weren't a part of this area. It was clean, neat, and the smell of perfume lingered in the air. The dimly lit lighting gave it a peculiar aura, characteristic of the environment-it smelled like hot sex. The dozen or so room doors he noticed were all closed, sounds and murmurs came from behind them. A light came on in his head and it dawned on him.

He asked in a hushed voice, "Grandma, is this a house, uh…for women?"

Juanita smiled as the other woman that led them looked her way, then cut her eyes. "I don't know about that young man, it's a brothel," she spoke in a thick Spanish accent.

His grandmother just smirked and said, "That's another name for a whorehouse, Latif."

She sucked her teeth at the remark and rolled her large mascaraed eyes, then opened a large lavish door leading to an office that was fabulously furnished. Much like his grandmothers: it had a huge cherry deck and padded leather chairs, a leather sofa that sat off to the side next to a walled bookshelf and a collection of pictures were lined up along the walls. He strained his eyes further and spotted some black and white glossies, then got hung up on one, in particular, a pretty fair-skinned, long-haired woman holding hands with a well-dressed light-skinned man.

"Grandma?" he asked. "Is that you?" The older woman came through the door and looked over at Juanita and said, "She'll be here in just a moment. Have a seat please."

Juanita pulled Latif over to the sofa. "That was us when I was much younger."

"That's granddad, I thought you said he was darker?"

"No, that's Consuelo, he was from Columbia." A door that was situated on the side of the office opened and a small, petite woman walked through. Smiling when she saw Juanita, she asked, "Juanita, what do I owe the pleasure?" She came over to her and warmly embraced her hand.

"It's good to see you, too."

She walked over to the huge desk that seemed to swallow her up as she sat and after straightening herself up in the huge leather swivel chair, struggling to look over at her, she asked again, "So, what's going on? Is this business?" She flirtatiously gazed over in Latif's direction. "Or pleasure?"

"Business!"

She sucked in some air and sighed as she reached into the drawer, pulling out a gold case. She flipped it open and it was lined with cigarettes. Pulling one out she went through the whole routine of patting the butt end. Then reaching for the gold lighter, she lit up and said, "Too bad then. What is it?"

Tired of the questions already, Juanita eased up a ways in her seat getting good eye contact. "There's trouble in Brooklyn."

"Brooklyn?" she questioned again as she blew smoke rings into the air. "What kind of trouble and where exactly in Brooklyn?"

"In Bushwick."

"Always problem there!" she said as she reached for the ashtray on her desk and smashed the half-smoked cigarette out.

"But, this time, Maria." Juanita continued. "According to my sources and believe me, they're good. It involves your husband, Felix. He fucked around and kidnapped my granddaughter! Does that answer your goddamned questions?"

"Shaheeda, damn!" She leaned back in her seat, reached into her case and pulled out another cigarette. As she reached for her lighter, her hand quivered as she moved and dropped it on the floor. "He's always so stupid!" Pissed, she banged her small fist on the desk.

Latif got up, picked up the lighter from the floor and even flicked it for her before he sat back down. He was the gentleman, and Juanita smiled her approval as she crossed her legs and said, "Did you have anything to do with…"

"No, of course not…never!" She angrily pointed at the same picture Latif had inquired about earlier. "My father would never have gone for that!" She reached for her phone. "I'll take care of it right away!" she dialed a number, the phone on the other end rang, but no one picked up. Vexed, she slammed it down.

Juanita started getting up from her seat. "I'm sure, you will clean this mess up." She motioned for Latif to get the door.

Maria collected herself and answered, "I promise." She glanced over at Latif for a second and waited for Juanita to gesture her approval to speak.

She continued, "Did you get the package we sent to the bank this month, for rent?"

"Of course, of course, darling. You're always on time with that. That's not what I'm worried about, at all!"

She jumped from her seat with both hands pushed forward on the desk. "I don't kidnap women. You know me better than that, but my husband…" she held her head down. "…he'll be taken care of. I'll have someone go down there, right now to handle him. Believe me, I don't want any problems either."

"Sure, no problem."

The older woman came back to the door as if on cue. On the way out, Latif shot an eye back at Maria. He didn't know what part she played in this whole scenario, but she didn't seem like she was on their side. Was she his aunt, his mother's sister he never knew about? One day he'd find out more. As she returned the glance, she obliged him, also. Checking him up and down, but mainly at the hard-on that started to bulge through his pants.

Juanita yanked him through the door and scolded him, "Trust me, you ain't ready for that type of drama! She's like a spider with plenty of web and plenty of venom! You hear?"

The door slammed behind them as Maria sat wondering. *What happened to Muerte? He was supposed to kill Felix and pick up the money, easy. But, why the girl and why of all girls, Juanita's granddaughter?'* "Damn." she sighed.

She should have killed that bastard herself because based on what just went down, evidently, Muerte hadn't. She got up and brushed off, some lint from her outfit, checked her make-up and picked up her briefcase, then glanced at her Rolex. She was due back in court in about an hour to meet her lawyers for a decision. She needed the warehouses now and had paid her lawyers' good money to settle the matter out of court, quietly. She hoped everything would go according to plan. Mainly, the warehouses she needed. Sell the property back to the city and finance the mall she planned on building.

The woman came back to the door and said, "Maria, your limo is here."

"Thank you, Rachel. Please, see to it that we get the new girls that just came in, to Atlantic City as soon as possible, alright. We might be needing the extra cash."

"Yes ma'am, I will."

Maria watched as Rachel walked down the hall to the steps leading upstairs. She hoped that there wouldn't be this much trouble with the women she smuggled into the country. She damn sure didn't need any more headaches, rent had to be paid.

Juanita and Latif walked out the same way they entered, but this time he got a more focused eyeful. All that a young adolescent boy needed. They giggled when he came through, Juanita shot them the eye to keep their hands off, and they hushed.   The door slammed behind them as Rachel appeared again. Juanita whispered something to her which likely had something to do with keeping an eye out for Latif. He and his little buddies might muster up the nerve to want to come through. He was asking too many questions as it was.

"So, grandma is this the family business…Prostitution?"

"Hell no!" She frowned and said, "Of, course, not." She grabbed him by the hand. "Property, that's the family business, remember that and don't ever forget it. I only rent it out, I can't tell them what to do with it once they pay. As long as I get my money." She let him go then walked over to the passenger side. "Here." She threw him the keys. "You drive."

"Me?"

"Yeah, Latif, you can drive, can't you?" She eased into the passenger seat after he opened the door, then glanced back at the club and sighed. "This was once a good business, times have changed."

He rushed around to the driver's side and got in. "You alright grandma?" he asked.

"Just tired, that's all."

"Relax, we'll be home in a minute." Cranking up the car he pulled off into traffic saying to her, "Hopefully, we'll hear something about Shaheeda when we get there."

"Yes," she said as she watched a limo pull out from the back of the building they'd just left. "Hopefully."

****

Mustapha pulled up across the street from the darkened building. Looking over towards the entrance he spotted someone standing by the doorway. One of Felix's men, he supposed. Squinting his eyes to get a better view, he noticed a slight bulge standing out noticeably beneath his jacket, a rifle no doubt. Surveying the building he didn't see any lights except a glint coming from the warehouse window. That must be where Shaheeda was at, he figured. He thought about going through the back way, but he'd never been acquainted with the layout of the building, and he knew of no other way in except for the driveway. There was nowhere else to slip in without being seen. Trying to recall the times he'd been there with Malik, he never remembered going into the warehouse, and he wondered why. Maybe, it had too much junk, old shelves, and glass-top counters, since the building had once been a supermarket. He never asked, and it never seemed to matter, until now.

The figure disappeared into the doorway for a moment then came back out, looked his way, then waved him over.

'This is it,' he thought. He sucked in some air and took a deep breath then opened the door to the car.

He walked across the street and butterflies fluttered in his stomach. Looking down Sumner Avenue he tried to get a glimpse of the cars parked on the street, hoping Rasheed and them had already gotten there, but there was no one. Small beads of sweat came down his cheek as he hoped things had worked out well according to the plan Devone had laid out. Passing through the gate going into the small courtyard, he sighed loudly. He'd soon find out.

Stepping closer to the doorway, the man who stood post held his hand out and said, "Okay, that's close enough! You are Mustapha, right?"

Mustapha pushed up and tested him out. "Get the fuck out my way!"

He grabbed Mustapha's arm hard making sure he had a tight grip, then pulled him closer to him. "You want to be a tough guy, huh?" Coming from under his jacket, he pulled out an Uzi and stuck it into his side. "Yeah, heh, heh, tough guy." He pushed him through the door, and Mustapha put up no more resistance. At least now he knew what he was working with, so far.

A whistle came from inside toward the back of the building and someone yelled out, "Papi, what's taking you so long!"

Mustapha looked around and saw tables knocked over and something that appeared strange to him. The carpet had been cut and removed and the floor around it was wet. Like something had been washed down with a hose quickly. Maybe, Malik was probably being held there too since no one had heard from him.

He was pushed roughly from behind and out of his thoughts again. "This way!"

Mustapha jerked him and said, "Don't push me!"

"Oh yeah, tough guy." He flashed his gun again. "You're lucky, Felix, want's you alive or…"

This time Mustapha spun around and swung. He knew for sure that he wouldn't be shot, but he messed around and missed. Felix's honcho swayed to his left and ducked underneath the blow. Mustapha's force sent him sprawling against the wall on to the floor.

"Damn!" He could hear footsteps in the background running from the back.

"Papi! Papi!"

Papi stood over him now with the Uzi pointed in his face. "I should kill you..."

"No, Papi, Felix wants him alive!" The one who ran from the back reached down and pulled him off the ground. "Hey, no more games."

Mustapha knew he didn't have any wins anyway, he'd seen enough. He may have just softened him up a bit that's all. Rasheed and them, shouldn't have any problems at all, he smirked. But that was it for him. No more tests, he didn't want to do anything stupid to put his sister in any more jeopardy.

****

"Awww, shit, my head." Giovanni had finally come to. His head was still groggy and spinning from the blow and he struggled getting up. "What the..." Then he realized his wrist and ankles were tied. He tried turning over on his back to check his surroundings and mumbled. "I'm still in the apartment...somewhere." He wriggled over toward the edge of the bed and tried straightening himself out, but it was no use. Instead, he tilted headfirst to the floor.

Waseema and Lisa heard him and came running in. "You alright?" Waseema asked.

He struggled with the tape across his mouth and said, "Does it look like I'm alright? Help me!"

"Don't know about that, Detective. You know quite a bit of information and I damn sure don't want my sons to get caught up with no cops!" Waseema said.

"If you don't cut me loose, they might get killed," Giovanni warned.

"I don't know."

"Look, I promise I won't say anything! Least, let me talk to them." He didn't hear anything coming from the front room and it dawned on him that they were gone. "Where'd they go?" He struggled more now out of frustration than anything else.

Lisa whispered in Waseema's ear, "He could help get, Shaheeda."

"But you know what they said before they left." Donna had come into the room.

"You're right," she sighed. "But still, if he gets the police involved before they…"

"You have my word, Waseema!" he said as he stared up at her and pleaded.

She finally gave in, pointed to a drawer where some scissors were and told Lisa. "Cut him loose, but, I swear, if you botch this up, Giovanni. You'll wish you never crossed my path!"

Lisa cut the tape off him, he got up and said, "Waseema…" He cupped her face in his. "I promise, but you have to trust me."

She looked at Lisa, then Donna, and back at him. "Okay, you've been straight with us so far. I guess I can."

Lisa and Donna left the room, and he gave her his full attention. He asked. "Okay, where'd they go?"

"I heard them talking about an office building. Felix mentioned it, too."

"Where?"

"The one Malik's office is in, over on Sumner Avenue."

"I know the place; I was just there!" he said as he started for the door. "Where Malik was killed."

"Malik…killed!" she screamed out. "When what happened!"

That stopped him in his tracks. Evidently, she didn't know what had happened to him. "You didn't know?" She plopped down on the bed in shock, shaking her head in disbelief. "I'm sorry," he said. "I thought you knew. He was murdered about a couple of days ago." He kneeled in front of her. "I believe the same day of the shootout over here."

She lowered her head and sobbed, then said, "I'll be alright, just go get my daughter, please."

"Where's my gun?" he asked as he felt his holster.

"Damn," Donna said as she and Lisa came back into the room. "Kevin took it."

"Damn, I gotta explain that one," he said as he rubbed the stubble under his chin. "Did he go with them?"

"Matter of fact, he did," Lisa said as she handed him his coat.

"I'll get it back from him then." He turned towards the door and fumbled with the locks, then he remembered he still had his back-up in the car. "They didn't take the car, did they?"

She walked over to the window and looked out. "No, it's parked by the hydrant on Flushing Avenue. It's got two tickets on the window though."

He shook his head as he walked out the door and said, "What a day. See y'all later...with Shaheeda!"

Waseema closed the door as he left out, locked it back and turned, leaning her back against it and staring off. "I hope, Giovanni, I hope," she replied.

****

Devone checked her watch, looked over at Rasheed and nodded her head, then tapped Derek on the shoulder. "Let's go!"

He pulled off going down Myrtle Avenue past Sumner Avenue, Thompkins Avenue, Marcy Projects, then took the left going up Nostrand Avenue. Derek suggested they make the left on Gates Avenue going toward Lewis, so they could park on the blind side of the building in a parking lot set up on the backside of a five-story apartment complex right behind Malik's building. That would be their starting point.

He pulled over to the corner toward the far end and cut the lights, so the shadow from the building would keep them out of view from the windows above. Derek opened the duffel bag and pulled out the only packaged item he had, a thick, knotted rope he'd use to climb up the roof if they had to, or to climb down. Ski masks were slipped on and gloves donned. Rasheed slid the van door open and dipped out, Devone was right behind him. They looked over the railing that overlooked the small courtyard. Devone pointed to the lights radiating from the warehouse. Rasheed surveyed the building up and down. Yes, that had to be the location they were shooting for. She motioned; then tossed over the rope and tied it off along the rail.

Derek, Ice, and Born loaded their guns and tucked them securely in their waists. Born tossed Kevin some extra shells for the pistol grip shotgun he'd given him in the van. He nervously stuffed them in his cargo pockets.

Born sensed his weariness and said, "Come in from behind, just follow us. Okay?"

"Y-yeah, sure," he answered.

Ice motioned and they followed close behind Devone and Rasheed. One by one they slid down the rope. Once they hit the ground they took off in opposite directions. Ice peeped around the corner of the building and spotted the lookout. Derek had used the glimmer off his watch to catch his eye to distract him.

He looked their way, staring out toward the street. He figured it might have been the same kids from the neighborhood who were fooling around with him earlier. This time, he'd scare the piss out of them by brandishing the Uzi he had and watching them run.

He grinned. "Heh, heh, kids want to play?" He walked over and peeped around the corner looking for them. Nothing! He went a little further on mumbling to himself, "Where are they?"

Rasheed and Devone had posted up on the rain gutter's ledge directly above where he was standing. They jumped down. Devone landed on his back while Rasheed landed in front of him and delivered a blow to the jaw, rendering his scream and shouts useless. Devone put the yoke on him as Rasheed started gagging his mouth. Devone's arm clamped around his neck like a python. The more he wriggled trying to get free, the grip on his neck squeezed tighter. Rasheed kept his mouth covered and looked around. When he didn't see anyone, he motioned for Devone to finish him off. She firmed her clutch tighter and with the other hand gradually forced his head to its side continuously until she could hear the sickening, dulled popping of the bones in his neck-breaking, that was it.

Rasheed helped pull him off to the side as Papi's head hung over and his eyes bulged open. He closed them and stepped over the body signaling for Derek, Ice, and Born, to go.

Dunya: The Do Or Die

Chapter Eighteen

Mustapha was led down the dark hallway to the warehouse. The further he went, the chill in the air diminished. It was dense and damp as small beads of sweat tracked across his forehead. He could see light as he was led further, hearing faint sounds of grumbling and the occasional rant. The gunman who walked with him had his hand on his back when he made it through the doorway, he shoved him and he fell, tumbling head-first to his knees. He looked up and there was Shaheeda, tied up directly in front of him. Her mouth duct-taped, and her ankles and elbows pinned behind her back. She wanted to call out to him, but the tape over her mouth made it useless.

He looked over at her for any signs of abuse, and nothing was visible except that her blouse had been ripped open. Over to the left stood two men. One was Felix and the others he didn't recognize. Two others stood posted to the side with guns at their waist. He recognized one of them as, Diego, who had his arm in a sling from their confrontation earlier.

He walked over to him and punched him hard in the stomach. "You muthafucka, you see what you did?" He held out his bandaged arm. "I should kill you now!" He drew back and punched him again.

Felix stopped him. "No, later." He bent over and taunted him. "I should have warned you about, Diego."

His henchmen laughed as Mustapha climbed to his feet rubbing his gut and said, "Okay, Felix, what is it you want?"

He walked over to Shaheeda and stood behind her and said, "An exchange…your life for hers."

Mustapha stared at his sister as tears welled up in his eyes. If that was the choice, then it would make for an uncomplicated day. "Okay then let's go."

Muerte stepped in between them and said, "It's not that simple!" He glanced around at Felix saying, "They both know too much!"

"That was the deal!" Mustapha shouted. "She ain't got nothing to do with nothing!"

One of Felix's henchmen slapped him. Furious, Mustapha raised up and a gun was cocked, then aimed at his head.

He chilled. "What the hell y'all want!"

"Felix, you said he knew about a safe." "What safe?" Mustapha asked.

Felix stepped closer to his armed men and said, "Oh, uh, yeah, I meant to tell you about the safe."

"You lied!" Muerte shouted as he started easing back.

"Well, not exactly, but let's say I used you."

Felix had been double-crossing him. That's what Malik was trying to tell him all along. That's why Felix killed him. "You play games. The Cartel would not like…"

"Fuck the Cartel, I have enough money, dope, and connections to be my own Cartel. I don't need them anymore." He motioned to Diego who aimed his gun over at Muerte and said, "And, I really don't need you either."

He pointed Diego to a dusty, old, glass counter located to the side and told him to move it. When he did Felix came over and kneeled. A drain, small and circular no more than eight inches in circumference underneath. He rubbed the dirt away and then moved the cover. There was a keyhole exposed. He used the key he had and unlocked it. He pulled at a metal handle and the floor revealed a trap door. When he pulled it up there was a bunker underneath, Felix peeped his head in and smiled then turned toward Muerte.

"Yeah…from years of dealing with the Cartel. Money that was hidden, money that Malik helped me to stash."

Muerte thought to himself, *'I see why your people wanted you dead.'*

Mustapha tried snaking closer to his sister. He was thinking of maybe snatching her up and making a run for the door.

Felix pointed to the vending units and ice machines stacked, then started bragging. "All loaded with money and dope, ready to go! It's all mine now."

"But what does all this bullshit have to do with me being here?" Mustapha hollered at him.

"The day you killed, Randy, he was supposed to deliver something to me. You see, all the money was here. Malik was the only one with the key to the bunker. And, the only one who knew exactly where the key was, he used that as leverage. But I had already set it up for Randy to steal it from him and your sister. Yeah, your whore ass sister was the bait to pull him in. She didn't go with the fucking plan, though! She wouldn't do what she needed to do with, Malik and fuck him. So, Randy beat her ass. You can't blame

221

him for what he did. It was either him or her." He bent over and got in Shaheeda's face. His breath reeked of garlic and cheap cigars. "Now, you see how you messed up our little plan?"

Mustapha backed up a little, he realized Felix would be clear of Shaheeda and the door if he did make a move. "But why all this?" Felix

laughed. "Good question, easy to transport."

"Transport?"

"The police never ever questioned the ice machines coming in and out of here. Soda machines...ha, this place was innocent. After all, it belonged to Malik Shabazz, a big-time City Councilman. A man, the Cartel bought and paid for." He motioned to his men, they went behind one of the ice machines, dragged out a long, wrapped plastic sheet and drug it over to Mustapha. Then started unwrapping it, revealing a body. It was FBI Agent Mike Davis. His face had been bruised up from the beat down, and his eyes were still open. Eyes that told the story of a horrific brutal ending. Mustapha turned his head away. He waved at Felix's men to remove the body. He couldn't take the stench anymore.

As he watched, Felix's mind drifted back to the day Malik had explained to him that this same building had once been a supermarket. He told Mustapha the story Malik had ran by Khalid. The building was going out of business and that they should buy it and turn it into a community exchange of sorts. Malik swore up and down that the money he came up with was from donations. Now Mustapha realized the money came from the Cartel. He wondered if his father knew also.

Felix gave the order to have the body pulled back, then turned his attention back to Mustapha. "I remember he had a friend, a Muslim guy. Hell, I thought he would play by the rules like Malik did, but when he found out things. He threatened to go to the police. Of course, we couldn't let that happen. Malik convinced me to spare him. We did, we set him up with a pretty good job, out of the way to keep an eye on him."

"I gave him a better break than the fucking Cartel gave me. The Cartel was on me hard. But they trusted me, and I trusted them...then."

Muerte found a crate and sat down, listening. "Felix, you're a bastard! You told us you wanted a guy killed..."

"Yes, I did. You were supposed to kill, Malik. He was doing too fucking much!"

Mustapha's head spun all these years he'd worked for the very drug dealer that had his father killed. He'd taken money and drugs from him and gave it to his own mother. Felix didn't have a clue that Khalid was his old man, nor did he even care. Shaheeda cried as she eavesdropped, realizing too the role she'd played in this whole twisted turn of events.

"So, he was killed because he didn't want anything to do with you?" Mustapha spit.

"All we needed were the papers from the safe. The warehouse documents, the deeds. Those black bastards from that place, The Moors Institute of Science. Yeah, that was the name. They wouldn't give them to us. Regardless of how much money we shoved at them. They even told Malik to kiss their ass! Then, that cheap petty-ass crook named Frank managed to steal them from us. You screwed that up, Muerte! After all, you hired him. Hell, he tried to extort us! Muthafucka had balls, huh?" His henchmen laughed. "But eventually we had to kill his stupid ass, too."

He pointed to where Mike's body laid. "Now, that guy, he just wanted to make some quick money. He set things up for me. Hid evidence and told us where to find people, I liked him. Too bad he had to die, huh, Muerte?"

Muerte leaned up and said, "Yeah, I'm sure, you liked him enough to tell him to kill me, right, Felix? But you know it was Malik who killed the Muslim guy? He got careless, took off his ski mask and started arguing and shit with the guy. Telling him too much shit. Next thing I know he shoots him point-blank. Crazy ass, all because the guy said some Muslim stuff I couldn't understand." He stood up and faced Felix. "Now, you tell me that I let a man die just because you lied, Felix." He pulled back his jacket revealing two .45 Magnums on each hip. His fingers curled as he reached for them. "That's not good, not good at all it's bad karma."

Felix started to fall back and said, "Maybe, but that's life."

Mustapha watched as the scene unfolded before his eyes. His sister was right in the middle of it all. Somehow, he had to stall before it unraveled. A lot was said and a lot of it was explosive.

'Damn, where the hell is Rasheed?' His mind questioned as he glanced towards the door. "Like I said, what do you want with me?"

Muerte paused and looked his way. "Yeah, why him?"

Felix stood directly behind his men now. "I believe he had something to do with all the robberies of my people! I'm still getting blamed for all that shit."

"You've got the wrong man," Mustapha said as he turned toward Shaheeda. She was trying to tell him something. Her eyes blinked rapidly as she stared at the door, which was slightly ajar, he had a good idea of what it was. So, he continued stalling. "Naw that wasn't me."

"If it wasn't you, then who! Someone told me whoever was responsible was from those fucking projects. And, I know you know something. But it's like this, I'm gonna kill you anyway and tell the Cartel that it was you who killed, Carlos and his family then stole all his money.

It's my out, I mean eventually the bodies will show up at the Morgue. I'll pin everything on you. That's what I'm going to do with you."

Muerte laughed. "I can't believe it. This is all about stealing money, and people dying for nothing?"

Mustapha yelled. "Yeah, like my father!"

"Oh, shit, Malik! That was your father?" Felix questioned.

Muerte stepped back as he spotted Shaheeda's twitch. He knew something was about to go down. "Oh hell," he mumbled under his breath, then stared at Mustapha, then Shaheeda, and it dawned on him. It clicked the resemblance.

"No, Felix, their father was the guy that was murdered. The one, Malik, killed."

****

Rasheed had entered the building first, with Devone right on his heels. It was dark so Devone reached for her flashlight, but Rasheed motioned for her to hold tight because he saw light coming from the back and didn't want to give them away. So, they waited for Born, Ice, and Derek. Ice came in behind Born, but no Kevin.

"He got scared so we sent him back to the van to look out for the police," Ice whispered.

Devone nodded her head and gave Rasheed the sign to proceed. Rasheed moved on toward the light after hearing some noises coming from down the hall. He knew this had to be the right spot. He'd thought he heard Mustapha's voice. Derek crept down the side and caught a glimpse of a silhouette of the man who stood posted, they would have to be swift.

"We don't know who's in the warehouse or how many," Rasheed said.

"You're right, we have to create some sort of diversion," Devone responded.

Born tipped slightly down the hall so he could get a better look inside. Once he got near the doorway he peeped in and silently inched back, "Okay." He laid down the scenario. "There's four, not including the one at the door."

"What does it look like? How do we get in? Round the back or..." Rasheed was cut off.

224

"Naw, we go straight in, but we got to be fast with guns blazing," Devone spat.

"Where's Mustapha and Shaheeda?" Ice asked.

"Mustapha is standing off to the side in front of, Shaheeda. I think she saw me."

"Okay, then, Derek, you do you, since you're the fastest," Devone said. "Be careful check your guns." She turned and looked at Ice. "You go for, Shaheeda."

"I'll go for the one posted next to, Felix," Born added.

"Good, then I'll go for, Felix," Rasheed added. "Devone, you handle all the firepower from the side. Get a gun over to Mustapha, he can cover you." They started getting ready and Rasheed called them all back. "Remember…this is the last lick. There should be enough money in there for us to leave the city. So, be safe and keep your cool."

Devone stretched out her hand, they all grabbed it, and she said to them, "Do or die." It was on.

Rasheed busted through the door first, firing three shots quickly from the .45. Ice was right behind him he dived through and made a beeline straight for Shaheeda. She braced herself for the full brunt of Ice's weight. Devone focused on anything that moved to her left, covering Rasheed. The .44 bounced in her hand as she led out with cover fire. Rasheed ducked behind a pillar directly to his left and pulled out the Uzi. He laid the cover for Derek to advance. Born took a deep breath and hauled ass right behind Ice to the right, holding the shotgun that he took from Kevin and pumped it, then fired.

He yelled to Mustapha who ducked out of the way on the floor. "Here you go!" Devone tossed him a loaded .44 magnum.

Muerte took cover behind some counters that were set up toward the back. He pulled out his guns and aimed toward the door at Rasheed and Devone. smoke spewed from the barrels.

Felix tried to follow but he pointed his gun at him and said, "Hell no, this whole thing is your fault! You're on your own!"

Ice stayed on top of Shaheeda waiting for a lull in the gunfire. "You alright?"

"Yeah, a little sore, but I'm good."

Ice tried to ease up off her. "Sorry, but this is the only way."

"I understand! Now what?"

Ice turned his head toward the door. "Devone's gonna lay down some cover fire then we can make a run tor the door, okay."

"Sure."

Ice reached into his pocket, pulled out a knife and cut the tape off her then put his hands out to the side, signaling for Devone to be ready. Devone caught it and sprayed over at Muerte then Felix. Ice grabbed Shaheeda, with one swoop he picked her up, took off for the door and dived through. Shaheeda was out and so far, safe. Devone put up the okay sign to Rasheed then both turned their attention to Mustapha and Born who took fire from Diego and two others. One of them was the gunman who stood at the door when all hell broke loose, he dived toward them. Mustapha and Born hadn't found good cover yet so Rasheed pointed them over to one of the vending machines opposite Felix, and they took off sprinting.

Felix had a .38 he carried but right now unless he got off a good shot it was ineffective in comparison to all the firepower there. Muerte kept both guns pointed over at Rasheed and Devone, then suddenly, it got quiet and the smoke cleared.

****

"What the hell!" Kevin hollered as he jumped from behind the wheel of the van.

Giovanni came up. "I should blow your brains out!"

"I was just doing what they, uh…forced me to do." He cowered on the passenger door trying to feel his way out. Ready to rabbit at any moment.

Giovanni kept his eye on him. "Hold up!" He opened the door. "Be cool, Kevin." Slowly reaching into the van he snatched the keys out the ignition. "Look, I don't want no problems. I'm sure you don't either?"

"I was just bullshitting when I said those things at the apartment," Kevin pleaded.

Giovanni just chuckled. "I ain't trying to punk you." Then, he grabbed him by the collar. "But where's my gun?"

"It's in the glove compartment."

"You mean, that's what you were trying to reach for?"

Kevin put his hands up. He smacked Kevin upside the head. "Move out the damn way!" He reached for his gun, then took a rag out his pocket and wiped it clean. "No telling what else you did. Where are they?"

226

He pointed to the building. "They went in through the door," Kevin blurted.

"C'mon." Giovanni grabbed him by the neck. "You're coming with me." He led him across the street. As they got closer Giovanni spotted a body lying in the brush by the corner of the building. "What happened here?"

"It got crazy real fast," Kevin answered.

Giovanni searched the body for a weapon then checked for a pulse. "Don't know why I'm doing this his neck in broken in half." He glanced over at Kevin. "Rasheed and them do this?"

Shots came from inside and Kevin dived on the ground. Giovanni pulled out his gun and started toward the door. "This way!"

"Do I have to go in?"

"No, you'll mess around and get me killed. Just stay out here. Now, I see why they left you." Kevin cringed by the side of the building as Giovanni slowly inched his way approaching the door, grasping for the doorknob. The door was suddenly kicked open. Giovanni jumped in front with his gun drawn.

"Don't shoot!" Shaheeda hollered.

Ice was right behind her. "Giovanni, here's Shaheeda. I gotta go back in!"

"Whoa, hold up! What the hell is going on in there?" He asked as he peeped inside the building then turned around. "It's business, Giovanni." Ice started telling him. "We told you about it. We did our part, so leave us!" He pointed to Shaheeda. "She needs to make it home."

Giovanni said, "You're right. Kevin!" He threw him the keys. "Go crank up the van!"

Shaheeda hugged Ice and said, "Make sure my brothers are okay."

The door slammed, Ice grabbed for it and pulled frantically on the doorknob. "Giovanni! Giovanni, don't do this bullshit!" Ice banged on it. He heard Giovanni on the other side say, "Take her home, now!" "I can't leave them, we're family!" Ice said as he furiously banged. "Don't do this!"

Giovanni propped a chair to the door to hold it shut. "Ice, take her home, please, do that for me!" "Let's go!" Kevin yelled.

"Tell your mother, Shaheeda, I kept my promise!" The sounds of his footsteps lessened as he moved further away.

Ice still thumped at the door. "I can't leave them...I can't!"

227

Shaheeda moved behind him and said, "Ice, please let's go. You can't get in."

He turned toward her. "I'ma take you home, then I'm coming back!"

She looked into his eyes at the hurt and pain, the feelings of him being labeled a coward would kill him. Even though he'd never leave them intentionally. It was always about the do or die for him, she knew how her mother would feel to let him come back. It would break her heart.

Kevin pulled up in front with the van and honked. "Let's go!"

Ice led Shaheeda to the van then glanced over at the door. He knew he was coming back even if he had to get some chain and pull the door off its hinges. That's exactly what he might have to do he thought, as the van sped off. "Yeah…let's go," he said.

****

Rasheed stood by a pillar trying to survey the situation. "Okay." He peeped his head out quickly. "One right in front," he said to himself as he tried to get a bead on the distance they'd come. At least fifty feet. He looked back in front of him; another pillar and some counters stacked on top of each other by a row of ice machines. Over to his left, he spotted what looked like an old, beat-up bread van. But where exactly where they hiding? He didn't know, so he had no choice but to test the waters, "Pssst…Devone."

"What's up?"

Derek hid behind three stacked barrels. He knew he couldn't stay there much longer bullets would go right through it.

"We need to make a move quick."

"But, where? This place ain't that big."

Rasheed pointed over at Born and Mustapha. "Over by those ice machines."

"Yeah, but we still have to get past those three."

"I still got two clips left."

"I'm loaded up, too," Derek added.

Muerte had other plans. He also spotted the gap between Rasheed and them, but he also recognized the fact that in between them was the way out. After all, this really was not his fight. But Rasheed and Devone stood in his way.

"They're just going to have to die," he mumbled.

Mustapha crawled closer to Born behind the ice machine. "Yo' cuz, I think we need to make a break for it."

Born peeped around at Diego and said, "Yeah, we're just gonna have to stick and move." He looked over at Rasheed and Devone's way then said, "Hold up, I think they got something planned. Just load up I got some shotgun shells in my pocket."

Felix loaded the .38 he had six shots, that's all. He motioned to Muerte to toss him a gun, he ignored him. Felix then changed his focus to the pillar where Rasheed was. He was the only one that stood in his way of getting out.

He thought out loud to himself, "*I'll make a move whenever Muerte does. I see it in him.*" He glanced over at the ice machines. "*They don't know about the money.*" He then spotted the trap door, it was closed. "*And, the bunker, I can still come back later.*"

Diego loaded his gun and pointed towards Born and Mustapha and said to his boys. "We have to take them out now...load up!" They readied themselves.

"Rasheed!" Mustapha called out.

"What's up?"

"Felix was the one who had dad killed!" "You

serious," Rasheed sneered.

"That other, dude in here was down, too. And, you wouldn't believe who else?"

"C'mon Mustapha, just spit it out!"

"Malik...Malik was down, too!"

Rasheed leaned back against the pillar after he heard that, put his hand to his forehead and trembled, with anger blinding him. "Damn, I knew he wasn't right!"

Devone had heard everything and tried to calm him down. "Be cool, stick to the plan. We'll make sure we get him."

"Yeah, kill his ass!"

Felix recognized a voice, "You used to sell dope! I remember that voice, I know it's you."

Derek shook his head as Rasheed looked over at him. "You've got the wrong man," he said.

"Wrong man my ass, I never said if it was a man or woman, I heard. Yeah, it's you, I helped you buy a fucking Cadillac, you son of a bitch. I know it was you!"

"I just tried to get rid of the stuff," Derek spat as he looked over at Rasheed and Devone.

Devone shook her head, then looked down at the ground. "You were supposed to get rid of it."

"You're probably the ones robbing me, I'll kill you bastards!" Felix yelled out.

"Enough!" Muerte roared. "To hell with all this talk!" He held out his hand. "Now, we have a situation here." He slowly stepped out from behind the counter. "We need to resolve this. What is it we want here? That's the question."

Rasheed glanced over at Devone and nodded his head in agreement. Then against Devone's motioning for him not, too, he stepped out. "You're right." He looked at Muerte and sized him up. "I want the money," he said as he stared directly into his eyes. "Give me the money and I may spare your life."

"My life...spare?" Muerte laughed. "You've got balls!"

Mustapha and Born started to sneak around toward Diego. His boys trying to get a bead on them in the midst of all the confusion. Devone spotted them, and she also watched Felix as he stared at the doorway. Something was definitely going to happen, then Giovanni rushed through the door.

"Hold up!" he shouted. It was not what she or anyone else for that matter, expected.

Rasheed turned towards him in shock as Muerte took advantage of the situation. He took aim and fired. Devone pushed Rasheed to the side, the bullets whizzed by her. Derek pulled back to the pillar as Muerte started shooting at Giovanni who dived to the right ducking behind a couple of barrels. He drew his gun and returned the gunfire.

"This is the police!"

Muerte continued to shoot and Born hollered over at him, "They don't give a damn."

Giovanni heard him and answered back, "What the hell is going on?"

"A shoot out!" Born answered.

Rasheed pulled closer to the pillar as Devone crouched behind him. "Derek, you got anything else you hiding from me!" She pointed her gun toward Muerte and fired a round forcing her to jump back behind her cover. "Derek, I'm talking to you!"

Derek felt at the burning in his chest, while blood squirted out heavily. The hole made his breathing labored, heavy, and it was hard to speak. Blood started seeping out the corners of his mouth. Rasheed looked over at him. "Derek's been hit!"

Devone yelled out, "No, oh shit!" she yelled out, dived on the floor and rolled letting out a ring of gunfire as she made her way over to her brother. Immediately, she put her hands on the hole and searched around for some rags. "Rasheed, I need to get him to a hospital!"

Rasheed reached for his gun, he'd put down to his side to load up, but he was pushed abruptly aside by Devone who now held up the .44. She brandished it in her hand and fired. Muerte caught the shots in the stomach and wobbled back toward the door. He managed to point his gun one more time directly at him and squeezed three times. It was empty, Mustapha ran toward him and thrust his gun point-blank at Muerte's head, and it exploded like a watermelon.

Blood mixed with brains were splattered everywhere as Mustapha screamed. "To hell with you!"

Diego got up and charged them, his boys were right behind him. "Felix, we got to make a move!"

Born stood up to repel the attack and cover Mustapha, and he yelled, "Mustapha, get down!" It was too late Mustapha was shot in the back.

Rasheed got up and ran towards him. Born started shooting wildly at Diego who ducked the bullets. Then, Diego went down, and so did Born. Giovanni ran toward Born, grabbed the shotgun, dived and rolled in front of Diego's boys and they went down in their tracks. Felix tried to make a run for the door in all the chaos, but Rasheed turned and tripped him up; he tumbled down and crashed against the wall.

Giovanni ran over to where Mustapha laid and said, "Don't die on me!"

Rasheed got up slowly stumbling toward Felix. Derek struggled to hold his hand up as he beckoned him over. "Rasheed, I'm sorry for everything. I just wanted to be like you. Forgive me!"

Rasheed came toward him and tried pressing his hand on the wound. "Derek, just hold on." It was too late, Derek looked up at his friend, his comrade, his nemesis and spoke his last words, "Do…or…die." He died and Devone wept softly.

Born laid in a pool of his own blood, as Rasheed looked around and shook his head wailing. "It wasn't supposed to go down like this!" He crawled over to his brother's body. "C'mon, bro don't leave me. Be strong…" Tears streamed down his face.

Mustapha gasped for air and tried to speak, "…love you…give ma my…l…love…"

"Don't talk," Rasheed urged.

"Don't worry…" His eyes looked up, then rolled back as he said, "I'll see you again…in, Paradise."

Felix tried creeping past them, but Rasheed grabbed him and shoved him against a wall. "I'ma kill you!"

Devone watched as Felix reached under his shirt for the gun tucked in his waist. Rasheed was unaware. She jumped up and tackled him, but not before a shot was fired. Her body bucked as they both fell to the floor. She got up slowly and turned toward Rasheed. Blood was spewing out of a hole in her chest. She staggered to him and fell in his arms.

Rasheed held her snug in his arms, telling her, "C'mon now, we can get out of here and get y'all some help."

She looked into his eyes, reached, pulled his face close to hers and kissed him softly on the lips. "Always…remember…I love you." Her eyes closed with a smile on her face. She died in the arms of the man she truly loved.

Giovanni wrestled the gun from Felix, then he held it to his head. "You're going down!"

Felix pointed to an ice machine and started pleading with him, "It's all in there, take it. Just let me go."

Giovanni eased over to one of them, picked up the lid and gazed in. "Oh hell!" He pulled out bundles of money. "This whole damn thing is full of money!" He looked at the rest, then back at Felix. "All of them?"

Rasheed loaded the Uzi he picked up and shook his head. He stood Felix up and led him over to where he stood and said, "Giovanni, take it all out and fill up the bag."

"Hold up, Rasheed," Giovanni barked. "Too much has happened already. You can't go along with the plan now!"

"Yeah, listen to him…" Felix started to say.

Rasheed smacked Felix upside his head and stuffed the muzzle to his mouth. "Shut up! Look, Giovanni, they all died for this!"

Giovanni turned and looked at the money. "But still Rasheed, it's stolen money. Are there any drugs here, too?" He dug his hand into the ice machine and pushed some of the bundles aside. "Damn!" He walked over to another and looked in. "Kilos!"

Rasheed drug Felix by the neck looked around and said, "I bet all these machines are loaded!" He pointed the gun to his head. "Talk or, I'm gonna…"

"Alright…alright! Yeah, they're all filled with money. Malik had it that way, the dope, too." He pointed at the vending machines located against the back wall. "In there, too, Malik would only give me a little at a time. He dealt directly with someone in the Cartel, though. Carlos and somebody else, I don't know who. He wouldn't tell me!"

"I've been hearing a lot about this, Cartel. Who are they?"

"I can't tell you, or they'll kill me."

Rasheed slid a round into the chamber. "What makes you think I won't?"

"Okay, okay, I don't know exactly, but there's someone in Harlem who handles all their business and launders the money. I don't know anything else. I get a call…I go to Malik. But he's met the person a couple of times before. That's all I know."

"Why did Malik want my father killed? Why did he do it?"

"Malik was greedy, he wanted everything but didn't want to get his own hands dirty. I guess your father got in his way."

Rasheed shoved him to the floor. "All because my old man wanted to do the right thing?" He held up his fist. "Why!" He looked over at Mustapha's body. "Why…why!"

Giovanni shook his head it was all too much for him. He knew he didn't have the words to comfort him and he didn't try. "Rasheed, right now, we need to take him in so we can question…"

He paid him no mind. "Where's Ice?"

"Ice took, Shaheeda to the house, I made him go."

"Good." He looked over at the barrels and some gas cans over by the beat-up bread vans. "Giovanni, take the money."

Giovanni, oblivious to his plan pulled out some handcuffs and said, "We'll take him to the precinct, and they'll come clean up this mess later. We need to find out who the Cartel consists of…"

Rasheed picked up a can of gasoline, and surprisingly enough, they were half full. He turned, looked at Giovanni and said again, "Giovanni, just take the money, and go."

Giovanni stared at the can in his hand and it dawned on him. "Rasheed, you can't be serious?"

Felix's mouth dropped. "Yeah, you can't be! You're not going to burn this…"

"That's exactly what I'm going to do!" He twisted the cap off the can. "But the only thing is Felix stays here…with me."

"Now, hold up. You're talking crazy!" Giovanni eased over to him. "That's suicide!"

233

"That's justice!" Rasheed started throwing the gas on the ice machines and the floor.

Felix hollered, "We can split all the money! I'll leave Brooklyn, or at least go to the other side!"

"You see, Giovanni, he'll never change."

"You can take all the dope, too. We can make a deal!"

Giovanni watched as Felix groveled. He knew Rasheed was right. Too many people had died for this. If Felix got away, more would die, and more dope would come into Brooklyn. "You sure you want to do this?"

"Yeah, now get the money before I change my mind." Giovanni stuffed the duffel bag full until he was barely able to carry it. "Okay, we burn the place. What the…"

Rasheed took the handcuffs he had and handcuffed himself to Felix, then sprinkled gas on the both of them. "Go!"

"Go?" Giovanni dropped the bag and ran over to him. "Hell no! C'mon, Rasheed, what about your mother? Don't do this to me…no!" Felix tried to wriggle away but Rasheed put him in a yoke. "Just go!"

Giovanni stood there speechless a tear fell from the corner of his eye. "Rasheed, why are you doing this!"

Rasheed still struggled with Felix. "Don't let this crazy nigga do this!" Felix yelled.

Giovanni picked up the bag and turned away from them. He tossed it over his shoulder and silently ambled towards the door.

Rasheed called out to him, "Giovanni, tell my mother this! Inna lillahi wa inna ilah raji un!"

"C'mon, Rasheed, you know I don't…"

"To God, we belong…" He held up a lighter. "…to Him do we return."

Giovanni nodded his head and hauled ass through the door. He could still hear Rasheed as he punched Felix to keep him still. Felix's screams echoed in the hall as he raced for the door. He kicked aside the chair he'd put there earlier and struggled to keep his footing with the duffel bag and jetted out the door running straight into Ice. "What the hell are you doing, here? C'mon, we gotta go!"

Ice struggled getting around him. "No, I gotta help!"

Giovanni dropped the bag and shook him. "Ice, we gotta leave. Trust me, let's get the hell out of here before it's too late…"

"No…Rasheed, Derek, Devone…Born!"

"Rasheed wanted it this way."

A loud roar came from behind them. It wasn't the sound of an explosion, but the rush of flames somewhere in the building. Giovanni grabbed him. A huge fireball came through the door as Giovanni wrestled Ice to the ground and covered him. "Damnit, he must have fucked around and found a gas line!" He grabbed the duffel bag and hollered at Ice, "Let's get the hell out of here, it's gonna blow!" Ice stood lifeless. Giovanni pulled out his gun and pointed it at him. "Move Ice, or I'll shoot you and drag your ass to the van myself!"

Ice just stood there. "No."

Giovanni shot at the ground close to his foot. "Don't try me, or I swear!"

Ice was dazed but he wobbled toward the van as Giovanni prodded him along. The flames had subsided a little at the door, then an eerie silence filled the air. The roar of the explosion was deafening throwing Ice and Giovanni face-first into the street. Flames shot out of the top of the building like a phoenix as the ground quaked beneath them. Ice and Giovanni could do nothing but cover their heads from the debris that rained down on them.

Giovanni helped him to his feet, and they trotted towards the van. "Damn, Rasheed." Giovanni got in, cranked up the car and skidded up Sumner Avenue, with police sirens blaring in the background. He went the long way around Fulton Street and turned right.

He thought about what happened and what he was going to tell Waseema. He glanced at Ice and gave him the rundown. "Look, don't tell anything to the police. Let me handle it!"

Still in shock, but alert he nodded his head. "Sure…whatever." He looked over at the duffel bag between the seat and opened it. "What the hell is all this?" he asked.

"It's a gift from Rasheed and them."

"A gift?"

"Yeah," he said as he watched a junkie come out of an abandoned brownstone while they waited for the light. His eyes were wide open, and his lips were cracked. He wore no coat and seem to quiver from the cold, or lack of dope in his system. "Yeah, Ice, I hope…a new beginning."

Epilogue

August Mid 90s…

Waseema, along with Shaheeda eventually and finally left Bushwick Projects. They settled in Harlem with her mother who schooled her on the intricacies of the family business. Juanita shared many secrets with her, but many were lost. She died suddenly, quietly and peaceably in her sleep. Waseema buried the body alongside her father and her sons, Rasheed and Mustapha, or at least what was supposedly found of their remains.

Giovanni never told her everything about what happened that night. He rambled on and stuck to his story about them being killed in the shootout trying to get back Shaheeda. A bullet striking a gas line and an explosion. That's the way the news reported it, which for the most part was true. He tried giving her the money, and at first, she refused it. Giovanni kept pushing until she finally reconciled with the idea of building something at the remains of the site.

Shaheeda used some of the money and opened a clothing store on Broadway amidst all the new development, and regentrification of the BedStuy, Bushwick area. She also looked out for Donna and helped her start a clothing line of her own. Giovanni finally got married, then just as quick, divorced. He retired from the job and went into his own private investigations.

Waseema had just come in from her morning jog in Riverside Park when she noticed a package on the top stoop. She cautiously picked it up and looked around her then thought to herself, *'No one's here, that's strange.'* She walked into the den and kicked her weary, tired feet up on the sofa, picking up the small, wrapped package she weighed it in her hands. It was light. Noticing a folded letter attached to it she opened and read it.

Waseema,

I hope everything is fine with you in Harlem. I miss you! I have been wanting to come see you for the longest. But I've been going out of town a lot lately with work engagements. That's cool, I'm happy. Anyway, I happened to be going through some of my things from the job, searching mostly for plaques to hang up in the office and I came across this tape. I started to throw it away, but I felt you should at least hear what's on it. If you don't listen to it, I understand, throw it away. It may bring back memories that have since been forgotten for the better. I'm sorry, I didn't give it to you way back, but so much went on and you know me, I just forgot. So, give me a call if you want. I should be back in the city soon. Take care!

Michael Giovanni.

"This must be the tape he got back from the FBI…Khalid?" She quickly got up and searched around the study looking for a tape player and found nothing, then she thought about Latif's room. He used to listen to a lot of tapes, she remembered. He had to have one. She bounced up the steps to his room.

After snatching up the small boom box out of his room. She bounced back down to the den, put the tape in and pressed play.

"…Malik, not you! Why?"

"You should have left well enough alone, Khalid!"

"I couldn't let you use the building to store dope!"

"Khalid don't be stupid. It's only a freaking building. You can still do everything we said we would do. I just want the warehouse!"

"Warehouse? I don't know…"

"The cops won't be able to just go in there anyway they want. It's a front, that's all. Anyway, Khalid, they paid for it. We were supposed to go fifty-fifty, but…"

"Malik, have you lost your mind?"

"With you gone…it's…all mine!"

"Malik, what are you going to do!"

There was another voice in the background that spoke Spanish. "I've got orders, it's either him…or you!"

"Damn, Khalid, forgive me but, you just wouldn't listen."

"Malik don't do this brother! Don't listen to him don't give in. Don't live for the world…this…this…dunya!"

A barrage of gunfire soon followed, and the tape ended. Waseema fell to her knees as she heard the gunshots and cried. Knowing that those were Khalid's last words only made her realize just how good a man he was. He molded himself out of the mud he came out of and died as a result of his opposition towards all the negativity that permeated against him. The odds were already stacked against him, and Malik helped to stack them.

She stared at the tape player, reached over and turned it off. She got up to her feet popped out the tape and set it on the table in front of her. Should she pursue this anymore? Should she keep the tape as a reminder? "For what?" she pondered.

Glancing over at the pictures on her desk, she walked over, picked up Khalid's, kissed it and softly spoke, "I love you, baby." Then glanced at the others: Rasheed, Mustapha, Shaheeda, and Latif, then smiled. Taking one more look at the tape, she picked it up, tossed it in the garbage bin and walked out the room.

Latif had left to attend Morgan State University a few years earlier. He'd come home from Baltimore every so often, but since graduating and doing community outreach with Law school in preparation for the Bar, she didn't see him much. When Juanita died, he helped her make collections, then abruptly stopped, telling her he wasn't comfortable, but he still managed to keep the pick-up on 125th Street at the Cotton Club. Maria now rented four more spots located throughout Harlem, all brothels. He continued with her revenues and said it was personal. The phone rang loudly in the small office.

"Hello, Latif Muhammad, Harlem Community Outreach. May I help you?"

"Latif?"

"Yes…who is this?"

"You mean you don't recognize my voice. Shame!"

"No, I don't. Now, maybe you have the wrong number?"

"Don't get uppity on me!"

"Oh, it's you. I thought I told you to never call me here?"

"You need to make a pick-up for me…in Brooklyn."

"You know I don't do pick-ups. That's for your petty runners."

"Yeah, well, since you're on the payroll now. I guess you have to be…petty."

"Look, Maria, if anything, you're in my pocket. My grandmother kept your operation running…"

"She did! But now's she dead and believe me the Cartel appreciates all that she did. But right now, I need your black ass to pick up some things for me. Now!"

"Maybe…later…"

"Right tucking now, Cocolo! Do you understand?"

She hung up the phone in his ear and Latif stared at the receiver in his hand. "Damn." He looked around the office, there were stacks of papers on his desk he catered to, formulated into different bins, all full. Homelessness, Welfare, Substance Abuse, Pro Bono Court Cases. He glanced over at the young high school age girl he utilized as a secretary and said, "Karen, cover for me, I need to make a run to…Brooklyn."

His ambitions to be a lawyer and a scholar, along with trying to juggle the life of being a member of the Los Andres Cartel, was what made Khalid roll over in his grave.

Ice went to prison for ten years, because Kevin snitched. He pleaded out on a petty theft charge with the DA and turned State witness against Ice. Ice's head was on the chopping block. They were breathing down his neck about the warehouses. Carlos' families' bodies finally mysteriously showed up. They tried to get him on the ones in Malik's building, too, but they didn't have everything they needed. The evidence, the money, and the dope were destroyed in the fire. Rasheed and them indeed had left him a gift in the money. Waseema hired the best lawyers in the Tri-State area, and along with testimony from Giovanni, they couldn't get him. However, they had to get something. He ended up with an Arson charge. Ten years looking at five to fifteen. He agreed, just to get them off his back before they dug up more dirt.

Kevin ended up getting hooked on crack pretty bad becoming another statistic of New York's hard, cold, streets. He came up with a plan to scam dope boys out of the South but figured he'd try Jersey first. That was his big plan. Not a good one, though. Kevin hadn't been heard from since. Things went bad in Newark and he was killed. Although some people swear, they're just rumors. Some say, Waseema's people caught up with him, but that's all just rumors as well, maybe.

Ice ate good from the canteen, had extra uniforms from the commissary and all that. He lived decent, as well as he could in the joint from the money Waseema put on his books. Money from his funds from his earlier days. He sat back chilling in his cell and heard his name being called on the intercom, one of several that he used.

"Now what?" He got up and walked to the door. "Yo' C.O., what's up?"

The Officer looked up from the desk and pointed toward the Case Workers office. "He wants to see you!"

He stepped out of the room and headed toward the office. "What's up?"

The well-dressed college boy of a counselor glanced up from the paperwork that overwhelmed him on his desk and said, "You have a phone call."

Ice looked both ways and cautiously stepped into the office hoping this wasn't a set-up. He picked up the phone slowly from the desk and said,

"Hello?"

"Asalaam Alaikum, my brother!"

"Who the hell is this, I ain't no Muslim…"

"Maybe, that's the problem." The voice on the other end laughed.

"Who's this?"

"Calm down…calm down, it's me."

"Me, who?" Ice sat in a chair, more curious than perplexed. "Look…you got five seconds to tell me who…"

"Rasheed!"

Ice nearly fell back in the chair. "Rasheed, this must be a joke?" "No, joke, it's me, Ice."

"Rasheed! What the hell happened? Where are you" I thought you were dead!"

"Yeah, almost, it's a long story."

"Where you at?"

Rasheed sighed long into the phone and said, "Would you believe, Bushwick?"

"*Bushwick?*" Ice rubbed the stubble on his chin. "Why Bushwick?" Your mom's up in Harlem, she could hide you out."

"No worries, I'm good for now. I'll see her later. Right now, I got to take care of some unfinished business."

"Unfinished business…like what?"

"Hey, look, you go up for parole next month, right?"

"Yeah, looks pretty good."

"I'll be in touch around then, okay?"

"Hold up, Rasheed, suppose I don't make parole?"

Rasheed laughed on the other end. "Ice, you will trust me. I got you."

Ice walked back to his cell in a trance and laid down across his bunk thinking. This was unbelievable for him and hard to grasp. Rasheed was still alive after all these years. Where did he go? Hell, what happened inside the building with the explosion? Then, what would bring him back to Bushwick after all this time? Then, he jumped up, the thought hit him. He got up and looked out the cell window. The trees were bending from the wind blowing hard into New York from as far up as Canada. He rubbed his chin again it had become his habit.

He mumbled to himself, "No, not that, naw it can't be?"

Rasheed had to laugh a bit as he hung up the phone. It was Ice who was the one who would creep to see his mother. It irked him at first, but he knew Ice, and he couldn't think of anyone else better to take care of his mother. She loved him, he loved her. That's what mattered. He walked up

Flushing Avenue by the projects to his car and gazed over at Bushwick. The change in faces. The iron fences that replaced the chained ones. Bars on the windows now and three-foot iron railings around the buildings. The swimming pool was there but ransacked at best.

He got in his car and cruised up Flushing then turned right on Bushwick Avenue. The factories now were redone into high-cost lofts and renovated into high-priced living areas. '*Someone invested some serious money into this area*,' he thought. He got about a block away when he turned his head directly to his right. Standing in front of a bodega was a heavy set Mexican, a two-bit runner, keeping watch as the dope fiends scurried in and out to cop dope. He slowed down a bit and stared that way then nodded his head.

"Yeah, I'll be back, but this time..." He stepped on the gas catching the light before it changed. "You won't get away from me...Felix. Not this time. He gunned it up Bushwick Avenue on his way to see Mya and his daughter.

Rasheed's Redemption-Dunya 2
Coming Soon!

Check out More Hardcore Reads In My Catalogue:

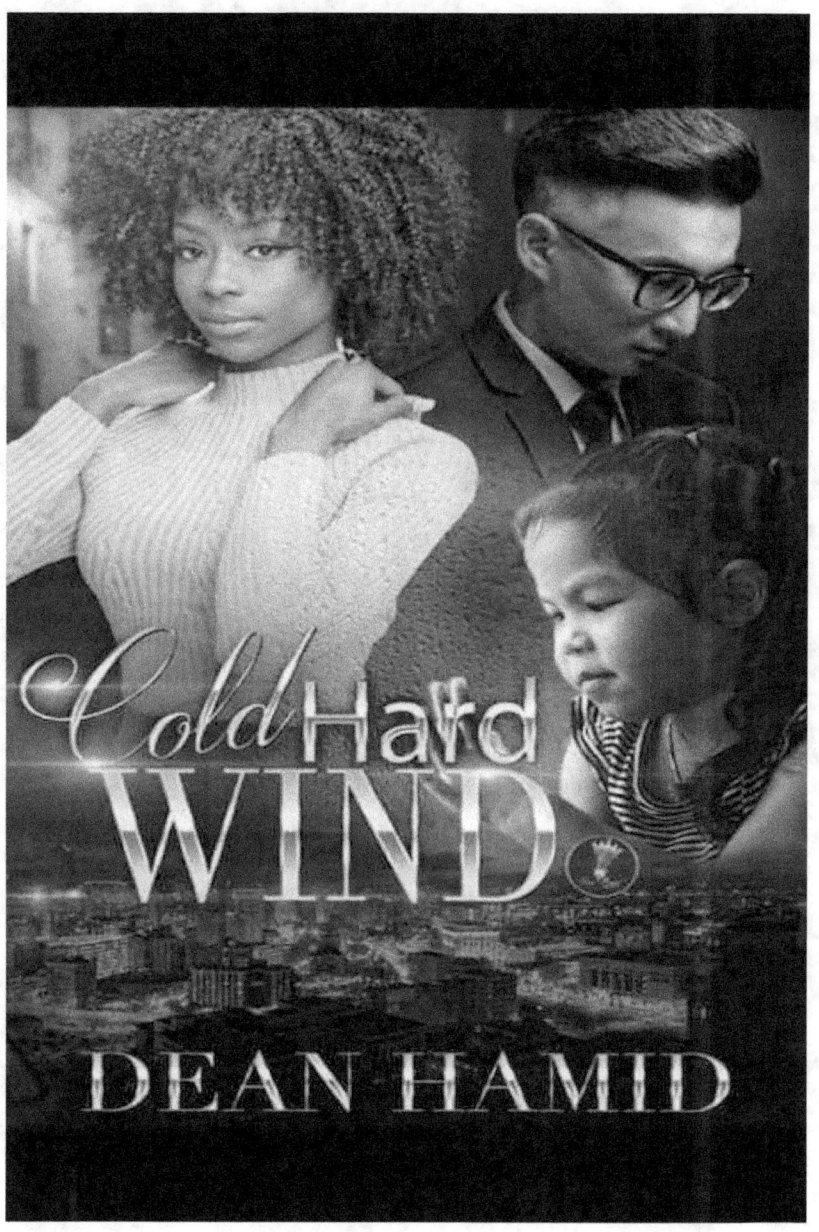